Acknowledgments

My heartfelt thanks to Dr. Jamie Teumer, not only for saving my life on a couple of occasions (and being very entertaining company while he did it), but for supplying me with information about skull fracture and oxygen consumption that allowed me to save somebody else's life as well. Thanks also to Timothy H. Willis.

CONTENTS

"... But slavery is another matter—the most vicious habit humans fall into and the hardest to break ... After a culture falls ill of it, it gets rooted in the economic system and laws, in men's habits and attitudes. You abolish it; you drive it underground—there it lurks, ready to spring up again, in the minds of people who think it is their 'natural' right to own other people. You can't reason with them; you can kill them but you can't change their minds."

—Robert A. Heinlein, *Citizen of the Galaxy*

Prologue:
The Galactic Coordinator
Yearday 162, 3027 A.D.
Augge 30, 519 Hanoverian
Primus 19, 1597 Oldskyan

A youth there was, late of Hanover,
Who courted a beauty so gay,
And all that he courted this beauty for
Was to steal her virtue away.

"Come give to me of your father's gold,
Likewise of your mother's dowry,
And the best ship that circles your father's world,
Whereabout stand twenty and three."

And all that he courted this beauty for
Was to steal her virtue away.
A youth there was, late of Hanover,
Who courted a beauty so gay.

"It's been a long time, hasn't it?" Anastasia Wheeler poured herself a drink.

"That it has, Your Worship, although it's mighty good to be seeing you again! And you, as well, Captain-Inspector darling—you know you've quite an admirer waiting in the anteroom outside. Bright, pretty—and a cunning warrior as the man said. I'd marry her myself if I were as much as three feet tall!"

Setting her drink on the desktop, she sat back comfortably in her chair, pushed a cigarette into the long holder that was her personal trademark, lit it, and gestured to the other two that they should follow her example if they wished.

It had never been the Coordinator's habit to turn to ardent spirits under stress, especially at this time of what they all agreed between them was the morning (outside, it was rather late in the afternoon, and would be for the rest of the week) especially in the presence of her right-hand troubleshooter, Captain-Inspector Nathaniel Blackburn of Coordinated Arm Intelligence, who had suffered more than his share of difficulties with the stuff over the past few years.

Naturally, the War with the Clusterian Powers had taken its toll with everybody, and certainly nobody more so than the unfortunate individual seated across the blotter from her now. (Whenever anybody asked her what it was she did in the war—everybody knew her, it was merely a setup for a very old, familiar joke—she told them that she sailed an LMD, a "large mahogany desk.") This fellow, this friend she'd known well for more than half a century, had just returned to her in a condition that would have driven any-

body to drink. He'd enthusiastically accepted her offer of
what passed for Scotch whiskey on the Moon in these trying
times, and while she was about it, it had seemed a good idea
to her (or at least a prudent one) to make and accept a similar offer to herself.

"Seventeen years old," Blackburn replied with a good-
natured scowl.

"Sixteen," the visitor corrected him, "and only just that.
But she's captained a starship across half the diameter of the
galaxy, fought your enemy to a standstill upon his home
ground, and killed more men in combat than you have."

"And that's supposed to recommend her to me?" Blackburn suddenly grinned and slapped at the holster of the force
projector hanging from the broad belt of his military kilt.
"Well, I suppose it does. However, what will I tell my wife?"

"About the joys of bigamy. Better worry what you're
gonna tell *her.*" The visitor indicated the anteroom with his
eyes. "She thinks you're still unmarried."

Anastasia took a long drink, looking a wordless apology
over the rim at Blackburn, who grinned back and shrugged.
Handsome devil, she thought, older, more seasoned, considerably soberer than when she'd first taken the risk of
employing him during his convalescence as her tactical
advisor. No more than a third her age, he'd walked with a
cane and a limp while the medical science of the Coordinated Arm regenerated the leg he'd lost in that debacle at
Osnoh B'nubo, a planet, as someone had written, of eternal
snow and hurricane-swept glaciers, punctuated by charred
machinery, mutilated bodies, and frozen pools of scarlet,
green, and gold—the blood-colors of the allied species
fighting against the Clusterian Powers. The tricolors of the
flag of the Coordinated Arm.

If the Coordinated Arm had had a flag.

Which it did not.

Despite their attempt at good-natured banter, their conversation faltered, and there was a long moment of self-
conscious silence nobody knew how to fill. Blackburn had
known her old friend, too, not as long, but nearly as well.

She could see that, for all the time he'd spent in combat, for all he'd seen in this brutal war, he was having a hard time recovering from the man's hideous appearance.

"Well," Blackburn offered at long last, "I'll try to let her down gently, then."

Anastasia stifled an impulse to get this over with quickly. Her son and daughter-in-law were bringing the kids over for a visit this afternoon, their first since she'd returned from Ganymede, and she wanted her calendar clear. If the Galactic Coordinator couldn't baby-sit her grandchildren now and again (while pretending it was an imposition), was there any point to fighting this war?

On the other hand, her unfortunate old friend had a tale to tell, of an entire civilization they'd no idea existed until now, and the apprehension of a nine-hundred-year-old enemy agent. Her friend's tale was important; it could mean a disastrous escalation of the War with the Clusterian Powers, or its sudden, welcome end. She'd heard her friend tell it once already, herself, and still couldn't make her mind up which it was. This time through it would be for Blackburn.

Anastasia cleared her throat. "Whatever our gallant Captain-Inspector has in mind for the girl—or she for him— it would be inhumane to leave her sitting in the next room for very much longer, waiting nervously to meet her idol. Old friend, you'd better tell Nate, here, the story you told me last night."

Her visitor nodded his agreement with her, reached out for his drink, and laid his other green hand on her desk. "That I will, Your Worship, that I will . . ."

Part One:
Lia Woodgate
Yearday 102, 3026 A.D.
Janne 17, 518 Hanoverian
Tertius 7, 1595 Oldskyan

They mounted up on a golden cabelle
And into the lubberlift bay,
And they sailed till they came to the open Deep,
No more than a parsec away.

"Alight, alight to the taffrail," he said,
"Alight, alight," cried he,
"Six pretty maids I've annihilated here,
And you the seventh shall be.

"Six pretty maids I've annihilated here,
And you the seventh shall be.
Alight, alight to the taffrail," he said,
"Alight, alight," cried he.

CHAPTER I:
AMAZING DISGRACE

Sedgeley Daimler-Wilkinson was the kind of man of whom it is said, "His future is all behind him."

Once upon a time, some fifteen years ago, old-style, he had been a great favorite among the loveliest, best-turned-out and fashionable ladies that the Monopolity of Hanover—a glorious entity in and of itself—had ever produced. Once upon a time, he had been a gentleman gambler, epicure, gallant, and interstellar diplomat. Once upon a time, he had arisen, hand over hand as it were, to the exalted and powerful station of Executor-General to the Ceo of the Monopolitan 'Droom.

Now, a discontented Sedgeley grunted to himself and watched a minuscule stream of silvery bubbles escape his lips, as some final corner of a lung gave up its last measure of air to the medium in which his body hung suspended. It would have been ridiculous, in all sincerity, to refer to his circumstances as "reduced," although again, in all sincerity, that was just how he felt about them.

Had it been easier, he would have sighed.

His personal apartments, as luxurious as might have been found in all of the magnificent capital city nearby, were filled, from lushly carpeted floor to highly embellished ceiling, with one of the most expensive artificial substances known to the many imperia-conglomerate that occupy the vast and star-filled Deep. Paintings and other hangings upon their walls were of the highest quality, and the sconces that illuminated them were subtle and well placed.

He squirmed to reposition himself upon a chaise lounge that felt little of his weight. This rich liquid he breathed was as clear as the very air, suffused with oxygen and vitamins and nutrients and medicines in such a manner that no man who had taken up this way of life that Sedgeley now found himself pursuing had ever died, so far, but instead had lived far beyond his natural time.

And perhaps, Sedgeley found himself thinking, beyond the time he wished to live.

Had he desired it, he might have floated upward—indeed, flown—and turned one joyous somersault or cartwheel after another in the center of the room. Instead, he sat in pensive thought, waiting for a matched pair from the latest batch of beautiful young colonial girls to fetch him a fresh dressing gown—with weighted hem—a sumptuous midday meal eaten for pleasure alone, and, as always, the unrestrained enjoyment of their smooth, tight, youth-hard flesh.

The physical reaction beneath his present attire which that particular idea provoked was a testimony, at his age, to the effectiveness of his current way of life. Out of long habit, he sought a subject upon which to contemplate that would allow him to control his rejuvenated body until such a reaction was appropriate.

The 'Droom, he reflected with some effort, sometimes referred to as the "Congress of Masques," was the penultimate locus of all governance within the mighty, dreaded, and fearsome Monopolity of Hanover. And Sedgeley, with his distinguished features concealed by a stylish and provocative *machiavelli,* or sometimes a dashing *retief,* had been the feared and powerful right-hand henchman to none other than Ceo Leupould IX, himself, absolute ruler, for his part, of the most feared and powerful imperium-conglomerate in the Known Universe.

Sedgeley squirmed again. As far as that went, the Monopolity of Hanover was still the most feared and powerful imperium-conglomerate in the Known Universe; what galled its former Executor-General was that it appeared to be accomplishing this entirely without the benefit of his particular talents and expertise.

It had all been long ago, long before Sedgeley had been

persuaded to become another humble "Initiate" of the so-called Immortal School and, like his fellow Initiates, spend as much of his time as he could contrive immersed and weightless in whole suites of oxygenated liquid fluorocarbon. And, like his fellow Initiates, Sedgeley told himself that it was a calling similar in many respects—but by no means all, it was conceded—to that of a simple monk.

The "by no means all" encompassed the finest food, the best clothing, the most comfortable quarters that their vast commingled wealth was capable of obtaining. It also included perpetual saturation of their unique liquid environment with longevity drugs and other beneficial substances. In addition, Initiates could look forward every day to an intimate and continuous attendance upon their pampered persons by hordes of attractive and compliant females, shipped in by the dozen upon a regular basis—happy to be "rescued" from the uncultured hinterlands—from the Monopolity's many starflung Drectorates.

Bother!

Unsurprised at the devious persistence of his appetites, Sedgeley once again found it necessary to redirect his thoughts. The task was less demanding than might have been supposed, for to individuals such as himself, accustomed to wielding great power, a full life consisted of far more than unremitting satiation.

A particle of self-flagellation would appear to be in order, and, for the former Executor-General, the scourge was always near at hand. The principal reason for Sedgeley's more or less luxurious state of disgrace preyed forever upon his mind: a humiliating (if not to confess, astonishing) military defeat that the Monopolity of Hanover had suffered those fifteen years ago, at the hands of a rebellious young Drector-Hereditary of a backwater colonial world, the beautiful, mountainous, everblue-wooded, moonringed—intransigent—planet Skye.

For the briefest of moments, Sedgeley was tempted to wonder why no Skyan girls, known throughout the Monopolity for their beauty and peasant vitality, seemed ever to be brought to him—then he chuckled to himself at the lethal absurdity of such an idea. Skyan girls were also known for their stiff-necked pride, proclivity to violence, and bitter hatred of all things Hanoverian. Oddly, no special effort was required upon his part this time to regain his self-control.

Arran Islay, the rebellious young Drector-Hereditary in question, had been rather better known a decade and a half ago as the infamous "boy captain" so beloved of admiring (if stultifyingly gullible) souls throughout the great galactic Deep: "Henry Martyn," interstellar brigand, starship-robber, and starport-raider. Also—and perhaps more to the point in the present context—liberator of slaves, rescuer of worlds, and redistributor of governmental wealth.

For the first time in something like nine hundred years, the Monopolity had lost territory!

In the horrifying aftermath, somebody in high places had been required to take complete responsibility for the Skyan fiasco. Sedgeley Daimler-Wilkinson had been "volunteered." Forced to resign in public disgrace, he had been banished from the Hanoverian 'Droom. His subsequent "conversion" to the Immortal School had come at the heartfelt insistence of a dear old political enemy.

Where *were* those girls?

Frantisek Demondion-Echeverria, former Ambassador Plenipotentiary to the 'Droom, was at present also in genteel disgrace—and for precisely the same cause. His commission had been to speak for the bizarre court of Ribauldequin XXIII, Ceo of the sinister Jendyne Empery-Cirot. Heretofore the Monopolity's principal rival for control of everything in the universe that was known to exist, that imperium-conglomerate had for the nonce joined forces with Hanover against the dangerous precedent this upstart Drector-Hereditary represented. It would never do to let the proletariat govern themselves, in particular if they achieved that capability by force of arms. History demonstrated with a frightful clarity that, in their blind ignorance and vindictive selfishness, the rabble could never be relied upon to take seriously such broad-minded and altruistic concerns as the continued safety and comfort of their former rulers.

Thus, as a consequence of this alliance, and no small thanks due to Henry Martyn, the utter humiliation suffered by the Jendyne Empery-Cirot at the ill-starred "Battle of Skye" had been altogether quite as complete as that borne by the Monopolity of Hanover itself. And, exactly like his counterpart Sedgeley Daimler-Wilkinson, Frantisek Demondion-Echeverria had been the highest-ranking official who could be "found" to take personal responsibility for it. He, too, had resigned in disgrace. But he had also chosen to request sanctuary upon Hanover (the requisite consent having been the onliest favor a departing Executor-General had demanded of his secretly grateful sovereign) as an alternative more desirable than facing the customary thrusting-squad at home.

But these matters of state were the merest trifles. More embarrassing—at least Sedgeley had always felt that it was so—was the fact that he had afterward become known far and wide throughout both imperia-conglomerate as the uncle and former guardian to the beautiful, brave, and clever Loreanna Islay.

Orphaned daughter to Sedgeley's late younger brother Clive and the lovely Jennivere Daimler-Wilkinson, Loreanna had been taken from him in a manner both bold and cruel at the tender and impressionable age of fourteen, and ruined—from her uncle Sedgeley's traditional Hanoverian point of view—by her captor, who else but the notorious kidnapper and rapist Henry Martyn? Of course, Henry Martyn—young Arran Islay—had himself been but fifteen years of age at the time.

Loreanna had become a prisoner and sexual plaything while in the process of being carted off (the most reluctant of starship passengers even before she had been abducted) in her uncle's stern disfavor to the coldest, most backward planetary system—what was its blasted name, again, Baffridgestar?—that he could find for her. The "crime" for which she was being punished was among the most "un-

Hanoverian" of acts imaginable: in a fit of willful temperament, the ungrateful girl had refused to wed the man her loving uncle had chosen for her!

The very thought of such behavior rankled Sedgeley, even after all these years.

Where *were* those girls?

CHAPTER II:
INFAMOUS VICTORY

Sedgeley Daimler-Wilkinson's afternoon diversion was, as he had expected, more than satisfactory, and the luncheon itself quite as magnificent as usual. Had it not been for the "discipline" of the Immortal School, he reflected—or to be more candid and precise, for the "miraculous" healing properties of its "waters," which seemed capable of compensating for even the most egregious of sybaritic excesses—Sedgeley suspected that by now he would have been quite obese.

Or quite dead.

Now, as the daylight he almost never saw began to fail outside the great doors of the Immortal School's establishment—here in what might have been called the Hanoverian suburbs, except that the municipality enveloped the entire planet of the same name—he looked forward with some enthusiasm to a weekly evening spent breathing air, playing cards, and enjoying intelligent, polite converse with a fellow Initiate of his own age and cultural sophistication. His earlier company had by no means been selected for their repartee.

There would be another sumptuous meal, a cigar (despite being saturated with oxygen, the fluorocarbon would not support combustion, since it carried away heat before any-

thing could burn), and afterward there would be letters to
write, a task that he found less onerous, somehow, without a
liquid medium surrounding him. Then, content once again,
back he would go to the comfort of his own apartments and
the warm, quivering, eager concavities of whatever well-
trained, decorative, and willing companions of the evening
the Immortal School's computer (and how well it knew his
tastes!) had seen fit to assign him.

But first, before any of that was possible, there was a
hated ordeal to endure. Sedgeley's life, like those of all other
Initiates of the Immortal School, was bounded by a pair of
gross but necessary unpleasantnesses—by a Scylla and
Charybdis, as it were—known hereabouts as the First Breath
and the Last.

The First Breath—of oxygenated fluorocarbon—demanded
some modicum of determination, although the *first* First
Breath (his recollection of it remained extremely vivid, even
after fifteen years) had been quite another matter altogether.

Everyone had his own way of coping with the Last
Breath. Some, like his friend Frantisek, favored stout lines
fastened at the ankles and a winch that wrenched one from
the liquid into a high-ceilinged anteroom constructed for the
purpose. Others preferred a carpeted incline upon which
they lay with their heads lower than their feet; female attendants artfully distracted them from the rigor of the experience, while others massaged their lungs free of the
fluorocarbon.

Neither method seemed entirely satisfactory to Sedgeley,
because each necessitated rather a deal of coughing—
unpleasant enough in itself—and involved an additional
gamble which, for his own part, he was unwilling to undertake, that of losing the wonderful meal he had enjoyed only
the hour before.

As a pleasanter alternative, he stood now, *upside down,*
upon a wire-mesh platform—having this time donned a
dressing gown with a *floating* hem—not far beneath the rip-
pling, mirrored surface of his foyer. From a tube, he
breathed air that had been treated to prevent the hated

coughing reflex, until that gas displaced every last drop of liquid from his lungs. In only a few moments, he would emerge, like an ordinary swimmer, with far greater dignity and composure than those accustomed to more heroic methods of environmental transition.

His mind, meanwhile, otherwise unoccupied by the singular but undemanding task, still focused upon his beloved but ungrateful niece who, with a degree of animation he found unseemly—and against her own obvious best interests as well as her loving uncle's most fervent wishes—had, in the end, wed the arrogant young brigand Henry Martyn by whom she had lately been abducted and despoiled.

Their wedding had followed hard upon young Islay's infamous ship-victory in the boundless Deep over the best-established military powers in the Known Universe, represented in the combined fleets of Hanover, the Jendyne Empery-Cirot, and a handful of minor, tributary imperia-conglomerate. The upstart Drector-Hereditary had humiliated the 'Droom further by having enlisted aliens—non-human beings—as his allies, among them the *seporth* and the *nacyl,* heretofore unsuspected of harboring the least spark of sapience, and commonly known everywhere for their respective body-shapes as "rollerballers" and "flatsies."

Rather than becoming disillusioned over such unsporting conduct on the part of her erstwhile paramour—as any proper Hanoverian female should have been—Loreanna had displayed the utter cheek to express her delight and pride in Henry Martyn's ill-won successes. From time to time—half in jest it was to be hoped, but to the unvarying chagrin of her much-abused uncle—she had even been known to affix the signature, "Loreanna *Martyn,*" to her correspondence.

Nor was that to be the half of it. In the fifteen years that had come and gone since Arran Islay had shattered Sedgeley's distinguished public career, his wretched niece had borne that incontinent young cockerel some indeterminate but thoroughly barbaric and disgusting number of chil-

dren—six, he thought their number was, to date—quite as
if she were some sort of agricultural breeding creature,
seething with animal passions, rather than the distant,
refined young Monopolitan aristocrat he had thought he was
bringing up.

Human memory being the wanton, guileful thing it happens to be and owing to the stubborn girl's unsolicited but
rather frequent correspondence, he was even capable, as a
matter of surprising fact, of enumerating the many children
of Arran and Loreanna Islay—strictly as an intellectual exercise.

The first, if he recalled aright, would be Robretta, a
stormy, willful maiden of fifteen, wholly Skyan in character
and attitude (again the unfortunate phrases "stiff-necked
pride, proclivity to violence, and bitter hatred of all things
Hanoverian" came to mind), named for Arran's father and
elder brother, deemed heroic by that wild world's populace.
Both had been foully murdered—Sedgeley was disposed to
concede that much—amidst atrocities upon Skye that had
led, in the end, to Arran's stunning defeat of Hanover. In a
sense, the Islays' choice of name for their firstborn was tan-
tamount to a declaration of war.

Then there was heartbreaking Phoebe, a sweet, demure
girl of eleven, called, with considerable if unintended irony,
after Henry Martyn's best friend, first officer, and lusty companion in harm's way, the formidable ship-robber Phoebus
Krumm.

Lia, he believed, was next, a brilliant scholar and wonder-
child at nine, named to perfection—and everyone's delight—
after an accomplished woman known, if for nothing else, as
her father Arran's erudite and handsome boyhood tutor.

Lorrie (Sedgeley's favorite if truth be told) was just now
a little damsel of seven, called—against the latter's modest
but flattered wishes—after Arran Islay's beautiful and
beloved wife. The thought occurred to Sedgeley that he
could never fault Arran in that regard: his devotion to Loreanna was as profound and complete as any father, surrogate
or otherwise, could wish to see it.

Glynna was but a child of five, although, according to letters that his sometimes exasperated niece sent him, already quite as difficult to handle as her eldest sister. She was named for Arran's martyred mother, Glynnaughfern Briartonson Islay, a figure of increasingly legendary stature upon the moonringed planet.

Last—at least such was to be hoped—came diminutive Arran, a son for his father at long last, Loreanna had announced with pride, some three years old.

Sedgeley felt that he could never confess to Loreanna how much he always welcomed news of this astonishing litter of rebel-spawned progeny she and her husband had created with their bodies and their love. The children's great uncle might have acted a bit differently if he could have watched them growing up. But he had been thrown off the planet without ceremony by a furious—he could never quite stretch himself to add, "much-justified"—Henry Martyn immediately after the pitched ship-battle that had set it free from Hanover. And now, although a decade and a half had passed, the once-powerful individual was still too stung and too proud—the degree to which this remained the case never failed to surprise him—to seek out his nephew-by-marriage for reconciliation.

Some understandable reasons existed for Sedgeley's tenderly solicitous—if in her view, perpetually misguided—emotions with regard to his niece. Loreanna was the only family a poor old man (he told himself) had left in a cold and cruel galaxy. Theirs was a civilization that pivoted tightly—if with some measure of hypocrisy—upon family ties. Now, all he had remaining of her were her letters, and an autothille she had given him at their final parting.

The device depicted her as she had been at the age of fourteen, here upon the capital world, dancing appealingly upon her toes to unheard music in the empty ballroom of the family mansion. She had not returned home since. Indeed, it was altogether possible that she dare not. In some quarters, she had been denounced—more as a political strategem against her once-powerful uncle, Sedgeley suspected, than for any sensible reason—as a traitor and criminal accomplice.

Nevertheless, the Known Galaxy was at all times hungry for new word of Henry Martyn and his war bride, and ever eager to emulate them in all things trivial. She and her husband, as a case in point, were known to scorn the time-honored tradition of wearing formal masques at public functions, and their example in this regard was beginning to be followed, even upon Hanover itself. And what would the celebrated "Congress of Masques" be like without the masques? Perhaps, with any luck, he would be dead by that time, and never know.

Nonetheless it pained him more than he could adequately express to have lost this final, precious linkage with his family. More than a quarter of a century ago, during what was to have been a combined business and pleasure voyage to Brunner D-421, Loreanna's parents, Jennivere and Clive (she herself, being but a baby at the time, had been left at home upon Hanover with her uncle and a nurse) had been captured in transit by slavers of the interstellar Deep.

It might have been much better if, like many another voyager, the two unfortunates had never been heard from again. Clive was taken to a location, some system somewhere, that the Ceo of many an imperium-conglomerate would have given half of his domain to know. There—once again like many another traveler—he was altered by his detestable captors, through dire secrets of chirurgy and chemenergy, into a short-lived Oplyte warrior-slave. He had died—after a long and terrible search for him—in his broken-hearted brother's arms.

Like her husband, the lovely Jennivere had been presumed vilely used and mercifully dead for the better part of—but now Sedgeley's lungs were full of air instead of liquid. He could feel the added buoyancy it gave him as a pressure upon the soles of his feet where they rested against the platform above.

He shut off the air tube he had been breathing from, locked it tidily into a wall clip beside him, "knelt," and somersaulted up and over onto the obverse side of the wire-mesh platform, just awash with fluorocarbon, into an upper, air-filled portion of the suite's foyer. There, the usual irre-sistibly beautiful attendants awaited him with warmed tow-els, fresh clothing, and a bracing beverage. As they rubbed him briskly and he sipped the steaming drink— a particular favorite of his, of his own devising, concocted of asparagus, celery, and cantaloupe juices—a liveried servant woman cleared her throat discreetly.

"Yes," he croaked, his own voice unused, as yet, to the dry air, "what is it?"

She replied in the accent that kept her and others like her in their proper station, "There be one in yon wait-chamber to see y'sair. I was t'give ye this."

"This" was a ring he recognized at once; the way the woman had pronounced "one"—she was among a few who had stayed beyond her period of indenture to the Immortal School's Initiates to become a servant of the house, rather than of its individual inmates—made him wonder whether his visitor was even human.

The ring had belonged to his brother, Clive. Seeing it for the first time in thirty years, holding it, sent chills down his spine that had far less to do with the fact that he was still naked than with uncertainty and sheer apprehension.

"Very well," he told her, "I suppose I'd better—"

"Sedgeley Daimler-Wilkinson!"

A harsh, high female voice grated, echoing off the tiled atrium walls. Sedgeley turned abruptly to a hall door whence this noise had issued. There, barely held back by another couple of girls, struggled a hunched and ancient human figure so repulsive that he could scarcely bring him-self to look upon her. Wordlessly this time, she screeched and batted at those who restrained her.

Angry that his monkish solitude could be broken in upon in this manner, and momentarily forgetting his nakedness, Sedgeley began, "What is the meaning of—!"

"What's the matter, yerself, Sedgeley my own," the crone interrupted, giving his dampened genitals an appraising leer that utterly disgusted him. She was, he realized, the very childhood image of a witch. "Too busy with your thousand teenaged whores to have a moment's chat about times past with Owld Jenn?"

CHAPTER III:
REDUCED CIRCUMSTANCES

" 'Owld Jenn', d'you say?"

The former ambassador lifted his glass—and a cultured eyebrow—at his friend and confessed wryly, "My dear fellow, I was unaware that 'owl' is a verb."

The man's companion grimaced at what he felt was an ill-timed witticism. Frantisek Demondion-Echeverria had been away from Hanover some little while, traveling throughout the numerous imperia-conglomerate as a sort of missionary upon behalf of his dearly beloved (and not altogether unprofitable) Immortal School.

It was a cause, not to mention a way of life, that he never wearied of advocating.

Upon his return to the capital planet, he had been somewhat late hearing about the unprecedented intrusion upon his old friend's fervently cherished privacy by this unpleasant and obnoxious . . . person. It was with Demondion-Echeverria that Sedgeley had planned to dine, smoke, and converse. Now they were doing all three, to be sure, but Sedgeley found that he took but little comfort from the fact. He wrinkled his nose at the cigar smoldering noxiously between his fingers and smashed it out with a grimly felt relish in a platinum tray.

Their immediate surroundings were, of course, palatial. Beneath their slipper-shod feet, the polished stone blocks with which the floor had been finished—each as ebon and

nonreflective as the Deep itself, and a full measure square—
had been obtained from a giant sunless "rogue" planet, found
entirely by accident hurtling through the night-black Deep,
with several times the surface gravity of Hanover. Their quarrying, carried out under the most unimaginably arduous of
physical circumstances—utter darkness, unremitting cold,
lack of any breathable atmosphere, and bone-crushing
weight—had cost approximately one human life per block.
Upon the other hand, the lives of the convicts who had
done the quarrying had already been forfeit, so the loss was
minimal.

Sedgeley tossed back the last of his snifter, shaking his
head at what the world—his world, anyway—was coming
to. "If only we could have her bathed!"

Exotic plants imported from a myriad of different
Monopolitan planets—some hung suspended overhead, others stood in large, elaborately decorated vases—softened the
stark effect of the hard black stone underfoot, as did the
great floor-to-ceiling windows, constructed out of many
crystalline panes beveled at their edges, that overlooked a
vast three-hundred-year-old lawn that seemed to stretch
away from the building into eternity, under the mellow out-
door radiance of hanging fabric lamps. (Ironically, Hanover,
mistress of a million worlds, possessed no moon of her own
of which to boast.) Lights of the great worldwide city twinkled in the distance. Inside, the prism-angled edges of the
windowpanes glittered, along with tableware and place settings, in the flickering light of holographic candles set in
sconces, and upon the table itself.

"Softly, my dear fellow," Demondion-Echeverria admonished, endeavoring not to appear overly amused. For three
hours, along with a late-arriving male companion, the old
woman had been held in a long-unused chamber reserved
for visitors, so that this pair of Initiates, fortified by a splendid meal, a good cigar, and the chance to confer with one
another and prepare themselves, might finally confront her
together. "When we consecrated ourselves to the Immortal
School, we renounced the popular practice of recreational

torture. I rather fear me that forced bathing may fall within that somewhat broadly written prohibition."

A tiny, multicolored birdlike reptile twittered in a cage swinging among the plants.

"Very well." Sedgeley frowned and slowly shook his head. He glanced up at a narrow-waisted, bare-breasted servitrix standing by. The sight of her smooth, unblemished skin, scrupulously cleansed, subtly oiled, and faintly scented, failed to arouse him in the slightest. Through the pocket of his silken dressing gown, he fingered the object— his brother's ring—that had been proffered by his uninvited visitor as a credential. Feeling that he had lost control of his quiet, well-planned life, he groaned to himself before he was aware of it. "Let her in, but for the Ceo's sake, bring me another drink, first!"

The girl complied with Sedgeley's wishes—it was, after all, what she had been brought to the Immortal School to do—setting the replenished glass upon the table before him, then turning to swing the chamber's double doors aside.

With the old woman this time, there had arrived a muscular, dire-looking young man, rather darkly complected, with wild, shoulder blade–length hair. He appeared to be in his early twenties. Attired, like .his elderly companion, in what amounted to rags, he affected at his waist a lengthy and massive flat black slab of machined steel, sheathed in the thick hide of some animal. In this place and time of overly developed technology, such an artifact tended to go unnoticed, the effete subjects of Hanover's automated culture having long since forgotten that primitive objects like it can be effectively employed as weapons.

By Demondion-Echeverria's wary command, a matched pair of husky girls—there being no male servants in the house—clothed in the same manner as the table servant, stood guard at either side of the young man as he leaned, arms folded, legs crossed casually, against the inner, unwindowed wall. By special dispensation rarely allowed the lower classes upon the surface of this planet, each of the girls wore a kinergic thrustible strapped upon her right forearm, spanning the distance from her elbow to the first knuckles upon the back of her hand. The slightest pressure upon the end of a curved yoke lying across her palm would generate a column of recoilless kinetic energy that could be collimated from a broad push capable of knocking a man down and shattering his sternum, to a narrow beam which could pierce through human flesh from chest to spine.

The young man eyed his attractive keepers with an unperturbed and quirky half smile.

From somewhere within her voluminous, evil-smelling rags, the old crone extracted a singular device. To Sedgeley, it resembled a miniature three-legged stool, its "seat" approximately the size of her palm. Attempting—unsuccessfully—to make it appear that it pulled both her hands along with it in elaborate, swooping circles, she pushed the object all about the smooth marble top of the dining table until her outstretched fingers pointed directly at Sedgeley.

"Your Sun ascendeth in the Trumpeter, my fine gentleman," she warned him, trying to make her shrill, whiny voice sound ominous, "and you are the Hang-ed Man!"

For her sake as much as for his own, Sedgeley felt upon his face a flush of embarrassment over the dim-witted awkwardness of the old woman's pitiable act, not to mention the belligerently stated claims that she had asserted upon first entering his presence, to possess mysterious, even alien abilities as a clairvoyant.

For all of her claimed prescience, she had appeared genuinely surprised—and considerably dismayed—at what he himself was inclined to view as his reduced circumstances. Her ignorance of events of significance that had occurred over the past dozen or more years within the Monopolitan 'Droom and off the capital planet of Hanover had likewise appeared genuine. For example, she still believed that the old Ceo Leupould was in power. Sedgeley had been informed that she had even spent several days waiting to see him outside the Daimler-Wilkinson family residence in the city, before finally seeking him here.

He and his colleague Frantisek had observed immediately that she employed nothing more than an impoverished
handful of simple, amateurish parlor tricks and a jargon
transparently derived from astrology, the Tarot, and the
Ouija board.

She glared at Demondion-Echeverria. "And you, sir, are
entering upon a cusp!"

Salon chicanery of this sort had enjoyed a vogue within
the Monopolity for uncounted generations. Exactly like gar-
rison troops, married females of the Hanoverian aristocracy
were given to all of the devices—and vices—of boredom.
Some upper-class spouses entertained one clandestine affair
after another. Others became addicted to various chemical or
electronic intoxicants available to the Monopolity's rich and
powerful. Those among the elevated but essentially powerless ranks who chose neither self-destructive course often hit
instead upon self-deceptive mysticism to fill their otherwise
unproductive lives.

As if to bear out his judgment, her caustic, lower-class
accent sounded falsely to his well-trained ear. Underneath it,
somewhere, he fancied that he could detect the cultivated,
broader, and more crisply enunciated tones of the upper
class.

Sedgeley had always found the whole thing rather
pathetic and disgusting. Yet to credit the malodorous creature who imposed herself upon his hospitality, it was the
way in which she had eked out her existence for some considerable number of years. She earned her clothing, such as
it was, her food, lodging—and in the more recent past, her
transportation across the great Deep—by telling fortunes,
she had informed him, at the same time claiming to possess
paranormal faculties which protected her, she maintained,
from every manner of harm.

"And perhaps they have," Sedgeley's friend observed
offhandedly, as if the old woman were not present. While the
two friends conversed, she muttered what may have been
intended as incantations. Across the room, her companion
watched, unmoving. "In some forlorn corner of the uni-

verse," continued Demondion-Echeverria, "where populations remain backward enough to believe in them."

Sedgeley nodded agreement.

"That being so," Owld Jenn looked up at them slyly, "have him explain how I come to know of the serried scar upon the roof of his mouth, which he received in a boyhood misadventure—a long fall from a slerrab tree, I think me!"

Sedgeley started violently before he could control himself. Despite the wretched childishness of her act, the ridiculous old crone had clearly made an impression—even upon the unsurprisable Demondion-Echeverria—and she knew it.

"Or ask him after his great aunt Eulalie Husqvarna-Puch," she tittered, "who abandoned her husband and children to run off with a Frenkelian portrait programmer!"

Sedgeley leaned forward, convulsed with amazement and shame. "This is monstrous! Infamous! How in the name of—!" The family scandal to which she referred had been successfully suppressed for more than seven decades. How many other embarrassing personal details and long-buried secrets would the woman prove able to reveal, concerning himself, his long-departed relatives, and their forebears? And if to Sedgeley and his friend, then to what others, besides?

"None but a genuine seer," she asserted with the most evil leer he had ever seen, defying him to prove her wrong, "could know these things, could they?"

"Or perhaps another Daimler-Wilkinson," Demondion-Echeverria blurted, uncharacteristically, before he realized what he had implied. He winced, and Sedgeley could almost see the man observing with chagrin that his much-vaunted diplomatic capabilities had suffered from their long disuse. It was, however, clear from Owld Jenn's reaction that his friend had hit upon a truth of some kind, for she was quite as taken aback as he had been by revelations she had made.

A stark and terrifying realization began slowly to dawn upon Sedgeley. He clutched at the ring, with its family crest, lying in his pocket. This wizened, ugly, babbling figure before him could be none other than his once-beautiful and clever sister-in-law, now half-mad, apparently, and aged beyond her years.

"You two!" Sedgeley commanded, suddenly himself again. He indicated the pair of females flanking the young man Owld Jenn had brought with her. "Turn and point your weapons at this fellow; see that he moves not more than a siemme."

To the table servant: "Summon the medical attendant; tell her to bring what she needs to confirm identity." The woman nodded and vanished from the room.

He turned to Demondion-Echeverria. "If I may prevail upon you, as well, would you be so kind as to dust off the house lasercom, establish a connection with the Monopolitan Bureau of Identity, and then bring me the portable terminal?"

"Consider it accomplished, my dear fellow."

The old woman had been gawking at him, openmouthed.

"You are my sister-in-law, are you not?" He took the ring from his pocket and held it up in the synthetic candlelight. "Are you not Jennivere Daimler-Wilkinson?"

Although she jumped a trifle at the name and regarded the ring with a wild, rolling eye, she remained silent, as if she, too, were stunned by this information.

"You are confusing her!"

The voice was male and had come to him from across the room. Sedgeley looked up just in time to see the two guardswomen tense and press the lenses of their thrustibles against the young man's ribs. "She is, indeed, the very woman you accuse her of being. She came here, at an unspeakable cost, to tell you that. But she is very old, injured, and nebulous of mind, and you are not helping."

"Injured?" Sedgeley repeated, sensing that he was losing control once again.

"By life—and upon your life, sir, have a care, for she is also my mother!"

The old woman lifted her head, tilting her ravaged face in

an attitude of proud defiance. "This is Woulf," she told her stricken brother-in-law, "my son."

Woulf grinned at Sedgeley. "Which I believe makes me *your* nephew, Uncle."

CHAPTER IV:
DAMAGED GOODS

"It is as I thought."

The Immortal School's medician collected her equipment and prepared to leave the room. She had drawn blood from the old woman, analyzed it in a small *ulsic* device meant for the purpose, and sent the resulting information to the Monopolitan office in question, which had identified the donor after only a moment's wait. Sedgeley watched the attendant take her leave without truly seeing her. Instead, he addressed his newly found sister-in-law and her son.

"There are a great many questions to ask and to have answered, upon both our parts, my dear sister-in-law, but I believe it would be appropriate first to enthille a message to your daughter. As Frantisek, here, can well attest, having only this afternoon descended from where he left her standing in orbit about Hanover, the Immortal School maintains the swiftest of courier sloops to carry it for us. But even so, I fear me that it will be some several weeks before—"

"Daughter?" Jennivere Daimler-Wilkinson blinked and cast about herself in momentary confusion. For the briefest of instants, blood analysis or not, Sedgeley entertained a residual doubt with regard to her identity. Then: "I have a— Lor . . . Loreanna! I have a daughter Loreanna! Woulf, you have a sister—"

The young man lifted a hand, answering her patiently.

"Yes, Mother, I know." Apparently it was not the first time that something like this had happened.

Owld Jenn shook her head, as if attempting to make herself understood to one who could not quite hear or comprehend her. "She is only a baby, you know—"

"She is twenty-nine years old, I'm afraid," Sedgeley told her, wondering whether it was the right thing to do, "and lives far away from Hanover, upon Skye. She is the mother of six children of her own, believe it as you will, which makes you—"

"Six . . . *children* . . . d'you say?" Jennivere's puckered mouth dropped open to reveal uneven rows of gray, broken teeth. Sedgeley had to struggle not to avert his eyes rudely. Such a number of children had been even more outrageous in her own day than it remained in this. "Is . . . tell me, she *is* wedded?"

Before Sedgeley answered, his companion spoke, "Would it were otherwise, madam, for she has wed none other than that most notorious ship-robber Henry Martyn—"

"Ship-robber!" the woman shrieked. "My baby's wed a ship-robber!" She screamed and rolled sideways from her chair, hitting the stone floor with a dead sound that gave Sedgeley a brief, sympathetic pain. Upon the floor, she babbled, throwing herself this way and that, striking a table leg, and then a chair.

"She must not be allowed to swallow her tongue!" Woulf shouted, leaping to her side, kneeling to restrain her shoulders. Demondion-Echeverria stood well out of the way. Sedgeley, kneeling upon her other side, seized a utensil from the table, but Woulf waved him away. "She will recover, now the moment's over."

Nevertheless, Sedgeley, a pair of servants, and even Demondion-Echeverria were required, in the end, to lend the woman's sinister companion their aid before she had been calmed and returned to as great a semblance of rationality as she had demonstrated heretofore. Together they lifted her onto a chair and ministered to her, with an olfactory irritant and ardent spirits, until she proved willing and able to continue the conversation which her collapse had interrupted.

"My niece was but an infant," Sedgeley informed Woulf as they waited for Owld Jenn to recompose herself, "when Jennivere and her husband—my late brother Clive—were taken as they sailed from one frontier stellar system to another. Your mother must have dwelt upon her daughter often over the many ensuing years. Little wonder, then, having of a sudden learned that the girl has grown up and wed a Deep-rover of the sort who ruined all their lives, that she . . ."

"I can still hear perfectly well, you know, Sedgeley," his sister-in-law abruptly told him in an accent elevated several social levels higher than that which she had employed upon her arrival at the Immortal School. "There is scarcely any need at all to speak of me in the third person, as if I were a servant or an article of furniture." She sniffed haughtily. "And before it occurs to you to ask," she declared with an open expression of defiance, her chin lifted and her shoulders suddenly straight, "I am not altogether certain by *whom* I have borne this son you see before you, my own little Woulf. Nor would any of the candidates for the honor likely be prepared to acknowledge it."

For a moment, she seemed to be something more than just a haggard crone. For a moment, despite all that she had been through, she appeared undefeated by life. For a moment, she was the aristocratic Jennivere Daimler-Wilkinson once again, sprung of the same admirable stock—if only by marriage—that had once, in the Ceo's name, held and ruled the 'Droom of the Monopolity of Hanover.

"My dear Jennivere, I had not thought to ask—"

"Perhaps not, my dear brother-in-law, but sooner or later, you would have done." With these words she seemed to shrink in upon herself again and fell silent.

"You are undoubtedly correct," he answered her frankly, but in a gentle tone, "undoubtedly correct." And yet it was the indomitable spirit that he had perceived flaring up within the woman for however brief a time—more than anything else in particular that she had managed to convey to him thus far—which had at last convinced Sedgeley to lend her his full sympathy and credence.

He had other excellent reasons, as well, although to voice them openly, even from the state of virtual exile he endured, would have been an act of the sheerest madness. In many ways, he knew, theirs was the cruelest of history's civilizations, particularly where the lives and dreams of women happened to be involved. All of the imperia-conglomerate, Sedgeley reflected, had—for as long as anybody could recall—regarded the traits of feminine innocence and beauty as no more than mere proprietary commodities, rather than a basis for a woman's personal pride or self-proprietorship. Invariably were they proffered and purchased instead, by the powerful men—fathers, brothers, guardians, husbands, and yes, even uncles—who laid claim to them upon one pretext or another.

Any notion that this broader, more humane opinion happened to contradict his earlier embittered thoughts about his niece never occurred to Sedgeley Daimler-Wilkinson.

Few, men or women, gave much thought to any possible injustice that such a custom happened to engender or perpetuate. The arrangement was observed and approved by virtually everybody, everywhere, with what amounted to a rare universality. This was true, in particular, of women themselves, who always had one eye—if not for their own sake, then for that of their daughters—upon the 'Droom of Hanover and upon equivalent concentrations of political and monetary power elsewhere. It was they who ensured that the "wisdom" of the custom—or at least its inexorability—was passed from one generation to another.

Observing his friend lost deep in thought, and fearing for the niceties of the occasion, Demondion-Echeverria ordered all the servants from the room except for the armed guards who, should they overhear more of their betters' personal and private lives than was desirable, would simply be disposed of. His own culture, that of the Jendyne Empery-Cirot, was not given to queasiness in such matters, and he would attend to it himself if need be. Having seen everyone—except the guards—comfortably seated once again, he provided each of them with a hot stimulant beverage and more ardent spirits.

And waited.

In this culture, he knew, exactly as in his own, the merest hint of her unchastity abrogated a woman's primary value to others, as well as to herself. It was an admission to having become "damaged—and therefore unsalable—goods." An open confession such as Sedgeley's sister-in-law had just made to having borne an illegitimate son or daughter—even against her will, through rape—was the social equivalent of suicide, and often, perhaps even *most* often, led straightaway to the real thing. Which, he felt, was as it should be.

Owld Jenn, however, having long since journeyed far beyond such purely social considerations, now stirred herself once again under the impetus of the refreshments Demondion-Echeverria had provided her (and perhaps even the heavy and accusatory silence all round her) to inform Sedgeley that—certainly no less than the many friends and relatives she had left behind upon Hanover—she had regarded herself, almost from the beginning of her travail, as already deceased.

"It is true," she seemed to speak the words into her lap, "as difficult to credit as you may feel it is, dear brother-in-law, that I no longer care for any reputation I may have once enjoyed in what amounts to another lifetime in another universe. Having suffered the same bitter fate experienced by many another captive female quickly relieves one of such petty and delusionary concerns."

"My dear, you needn't speak about it if you—"

"Ah, but in this you are singularly mistaken, Sedgeley, for I *do* wish to speak of it, and I believe I must. To an overly pampered subject of the Monopolity like yourself, it will be an education. Moreover, I will not be deprived of the satisfaction. I have dwelt upon this very moment, rehearsed it over and over in my mind, and looked forward to it for more years than it seems physically possible can have passed since that evil instant—only days ago, it often seems—

when, forcibly separated from him immediately following a violent and terrifying capture, I was never to see my beloved husband Clive again."

Sedgeley opened his mouth to speak, but now Jennivere would brook no interruption.

"I was used once or twice by the captain of the raiders, himself. Pray do not flinch, my dear Sedgeley, for that is the appropriate verb, 'used,' and believe me, it is only the very least of what I have to reveal to you tonight, so do stand fast, will you? When I proved too intractable for recreational purposes, I was sold as quickly afterward as he could contrive. And it was at that point that I somehow discovered within myself the courage required to deliberately disfigure my own face, in order to quench the ardor of my . . . er, suitors."

She swept her long, gray, matted hair back to reveal what she obviously imagined were scars too terrible to look upon. And perhaps they had been at one time, Sedgeley thought, but they were invisible now. They had long since been lost among the runnels and furrows that time and fate had etched into her countenance.

"Is it not an act entirely appropriate to a Monopolitan aristocrat," she asked him, letting her malodorous hair fall once again, "to make of one's own face a hideous masque—perhaps a *pattieschroeder* or a *janetreno*—to hide herself behind? In this way I had hoped to destroy any further utility I might possess as a sexual plaything. If only I had comprehended the economics of the situation with a trifle more clarity. But then what woman of Hanover is ever educated in economics? Unfortunately for me, my strategy of despair produced quite the opposite of the effect intended, with the most tragic of results."

Sedgeley could not help himself. "How is this so?" he asked.

"You see, I might otherwise have found myself some single owner who would come to value me and care for me humanely, and perhaps, someday, even wed me. This sort of thing has been known to happen, even to the basest, most abject of slaves. I was not unattractive in my youth, to that much I am certain you will attest, will you not, dear Sedgeley? Instead, all that I accomplished was to lower my value—and the political and economic status of those who continued to find a use for me. Instead of being a plaything for officers and gentlemen, I became a plaything for the commonest hands belowdecks, not all of whom were male, by the way, nor even, as I soon found to my disgust, always human."

Sedgeley was compelled to suppress a wave of nausea at this appalling—and, he believed, gratuitous—revelation. He could see from the man's face that his friend Demondion-Echeverria suddenly felt ill, as well.

"Well, to make a long story shorter . . ."

Jennivere, now apparently in full possession of her faculties, picked up the tumbler of spirits Demondion-Echeverria had earlier placed before her, peered through its amber depths, took a deep, unfeminine draft of the liquid, and, bestowing upon both men a knowing grin at their obvious discomfiture, belched.

". . . I found myself handed from one owner to the next too often to keep track of. Never a good slave, I was traded from one Deep-sailing vessel whose name I never had occasion to learn to another. I was transported many times, planet to planet, system to system. Much of that time I passed in a delirium from repeated beatings and other maltreatment, so that I can no longer attest to which regions of the Deep, or even to what imperia-conglomerate, I traveled through.

"I shall never forget, however, the place we were first taken to, where they transform men into monsters, and the captain was paid for bringing them my husband. You see, can you not, Sedgeley, why I have no idea which of my countless tormentors may have been Woulf's father? I scarcely remember being pregnant, let alone giving birth, or caring for him afterward. It only seems that, growing taller all the time, and handsomer, he has always been at my side."

From the chair next to hers, young Woulf leaned forward to take both of his mother's withered hands in his own. She looked down at them, enveloping hers, pressed a care-ravaged cheek against them, and sighed deeply. Sedgeley was torn between all of the emotions that any decent Hanoverian might feel in circumstances such as these, nausea, pity, and . . . and something else, perhaps embarrassment.

"You are at home now, my dear Jennivere," he told her, reaching out to pat her gently upon one shoulder. It was all the physical demonstration the man was capable of, and almost immediately—when he was reminded of what the old woman smelled like—he regretted it. "You are with your family now and will be taken care of no matter what else happens. But you haven't yet told us how you managed . . . how you came here. Pray ask me for whatever it is you desire."

She looked up at him. "What I desire, brother-in-law, all I desire—is *revenge!*"

It would remain unclear to Sedgeley for some time precisely upon whom she wanted it, and what it might consist of.

CHAPTER V:
AN UNWANTED TIME OF TRIAL

Brother Leo did not know what to say.

Nor would it have made much difference if he had.

When his old friends Sedgeley and Frantisek burst in upon him—or as close to that as possible given the liquid nature of the environment in which they had chosen to spend their lives, each of them was brimming with that dire excitement that only politics seems capable of inspiring in human beings. It was some time before he could begin to sort out one word from another, or to be certain which of the pair was speaking, at any particular moment, or of what.

Brother Leo raised both of his broad, powerful hands, palms outward, in what proved a vain attempt to bring chaos to a halt. Surely they both remembered that this was the very sort of lunacy that had driven them all into the refuge and surcease of the Immortal School. Surely they both remembered that he could not reply because he had, more than a decade ago—or had it been a decade and a half, already?—taken a solemn and perpetual vow of silence.

The merest sight of the man should have dampened their enthusiasm, were they not long accustomed to it. Brother Leo "sat" in the very center of the room, a full measure from the floor below and the ceiling above, conspicuously naked, cross-legged in a posture that he referred to in his speechless manner as the "lotus" position, his muscular legs entwined in a form any starship's crewbeing would have recognized at once as an overhand knot—a rare feat for one who had attained no less than twice the mass of the average individual. From the rear, he gave the appearance of an animal, so covered was he—back, shoulders, arms, legs, even the backs of his great hands—with black, curly hair.

The one female a day he allowed himself had already staggered from him, if that, too, were possible here, shattered and exhausted as they always were when departing his presence. At this point in his routine, he would have shut his eyes and tried losing himself in the contemplation he had sought for so long.

"My dear Leo," Sedgeley begged, "forgive an old man who's just seen a ghost!"

Brother Leo raised his thick black eyebrows, articulate with curiosity, looking to Demondion-Echeverria for explanation. Having overly exerted himself in this medium, Sedgeley would lack the "breath" to converse for some time.

The former ambassador shrugged, the gesture momentarily lifting his feet from the floor. "It is precisely as he tells you, my dear fellow. Sedgeley's sister-in-law, missing for some thirty years and presumed dead, has just turned up alive, if not exactly well. Here, of all places, at the Immortal School. It is a most harrowing tale with which she has regaled us, of ship-battles, pillage, rapine, and bitter captivity. Yet this is not what brings us to you now."

"He's right!" Still breathless, his lungs working with great difficulty against what served them at the present for an atmosphere, Sedgeley tried to nod and shake his head at the same time, gave it up, and then threw himself impatiently into a nearby chair. That gesture lost much of its theatrical effect when performed against liquid resistance. "Oh, do come down from there, will you, Leo? It's perfectly distracting watching you levitate like that!"

Brother Leo grinned down at Sedgeley and unbent his legs, waving his arms until his broad feet lay flat upon the floor. He picked up a brilliant swath of yellow silken fabric lying upon a sofa, wrapped it about himself, and tied an interminable belt about his middle. Draping himself across the sofa in the place of the robe, he rang a tiny silver bell which he had taken from an end table.

A pretty maidservant stuck her freckled, upturned nose through a doorway across the room from where the two men had entered. Brother Leo indicated his guests.

Sedgeley glanced up. "Sullestule, I believe." The astringent beverage was popularly believed to sharpen and accelerate the processes of mentation. Scarcely, Brother Leo thought to himself approvingly, the preferred drink of a sybarite.

"Vairy gewd, ahnd fair yew, sair?" Her colonist's accent was heavy but lilting.

"For me, as well, I greatly fear me," Demondion-Echeverria sighed at what he conceived to be a deprivation. "Some events demand to be confronted with a clear head." Seated in another chair, he slumped. "This is certainly one of them."

"Yeer usewel, Brether Layo, sair?" The girl's violet eyes sparkled, even through the liquid. He kept her about because she was one of the few who did not fear him. Nodding absently, he turned all of his attention—he was good at that—to his two friends, who, for all their earlier agitation, appeared reluctant to begin. By strict interpretation, he was forbidden even to clear his throat to get them started. For once, the self-imposed restriction galled him.

"Even at this stage of my life," Sedgeley spoke abruptly and, in Leo's view, incongruously, "I believe that I am well remembered. Would you agree, Frantisek?"

"Yes, I would hazard a guess, my dear Sedgeley, that you are not entirely without partisans here in the capital city, or even elsewhere, throughout the Monopolity. Nor did the regrettable train of events which, er . . . indisposed you leave your detractors in the 'Droom completely unscathed." He cast a wily eye toward Brother Leo. "I have even heard it rumored about in some quarters that the old Ceo was compelled to abdicate, as the cost of forcing you into exile."

Sedgeley nodded in a particular way and Brother Leo knew from his long experience with the man that he had just accepted—as a metaphorical first brick—a presumption that he would add to, one brick at a time, until those who listened to his thoughts found themselves surrounded by a high and sturdy wall.

"Through whatever modest skills I may possess at the gambling tables and the investment console, would you likewise agree that I am a rather wealthy individual?"

Brother Leo wished to seize the lapels of his friend's dressing gown and demand, "What in the Ceo's blasted name is all this in aid of?" but he knew better; this process must be endured. Demondion-Echeverria observed Leo's discomfiture and refused to show how much it amused him. He regarded Sedgeley from beneath half-closed eyelids and replied, "Except for your use of the word 'modest.' "

Sedgeley steadfastly ignored the gibe. "Also, that I was legally named some fifteen years ago, following upon my niece's unfortunate and regrettable defection, the sole executor and heir to a very ancient and considerable fortune?"

"Hanoverians," drawled Demondion-Echeverria, "offering aid and comfort to an enemy are stripped of their wealth as a matter of course. Marrying one and bearing him a dozen children would seem to fit the category, would it not, Leo?"

"Half a dozen only!" Sedgeley protested vehemently

before he caught the twinkle of mischief in his companion's eye. A glance at Brother Leo revealed a mostly unsuccessful attempt to conceal his own amusement at his old friend's expense.

Demondion-Echeverria continued, but in a more seriously expository tone. "Oftenest, their wealth is expropriated for the imperium-conglomerate, but exceptions are sometimes made upon behalf of next of kin with sufficient influence."

Sedgeley glared, "Then it is granted that I am not without considerable resources."

Their refreshments arrived at last, flexible tubes with valved orifices, served by the freckled peasant girl. All about the tubes, the fluorocarbon shimmered from the heat. Demondion-Echeverria eyed Leo, spread his hands, and let the gesture broaden into a shrug. "Have I suggested differently, my dear fellow?"

"Then we must act for the sake of civilization itself." Sedgeley reached the table where the little bell was kept. In the liquid, it was unnaturally loud.

"Sair?" The pretty colonial girl peeked into the room again.

"Pray look for the house lasercom, and bring it to me as quickly as you can."

For the first time, she displayed a fearful countenance. "But sair, I regret t'tell ye we've nor boot ahn ald-fashioned comset t'ploog inta yon wall."

"Then bring it as quickly as may be, my girl," he replied as mildly as he could manage. He glanced significantly at his companions. "We'll make do somehow."

"This button, I believe!"

So obsolescent had the device proved (Initiates generally avoided contact with the outside world) that its base mechanism in the kitchen was connected by physical conductiles, rather than by beams and beamguides, to an exchange several klommes away that remained in operation merely to serve this single instrument.

"Are you absolutely certain, Sedgeley? That one seems far likelier, eh, Leo?"

For the most part, Sedgeley found the company of his old friend and former enemy welcome in this unwanted time of trial. This moment was an exception.

Brother Leo's end table had been moved so that Sedgeley could place the communicator upon it. Not meant for immersion, it had been fastened down with wrapping tape to prevent it floating away. The liquid they breathed, being as near inert as technically feasible, did not otherwise affect its operation.

Their bemused host offered them a shrug.

Finding the device was used in a manner little different from those with which he was more familiar, Sedgeley achieved connection with the palatial Daimler-Wilkinson mansion, set, as had befitted the residence of the Ceo's right-hand man, in the heart of the capital city, along its most stylish boulevard. Following his disgrace and subsequent retreat from the world, it had been closed for many years. He had not set foot within its doors for a decade.

"I say, Brougham—ahoy, Brougham! Can you see me and hear me plainly, Brougham?"

"It is most gratifying to speak with you, sir." Brougham was a trusted family servant and caretaker, a being of the peculiar *yensid* species. With a small staff of other non-humans, he maintained the place during his master's long, possibly permanent, absence. "Forgive me, sir, I see you and hear you plainly."

"Capital!" Both delighted to see one another, each betrayed it in his own way. "Now, Brougham, you are about to receive guests—houseguests, I mean—there at the, er, house. I want you to look after them as you would after me. They are to stay there for as long as they wish. Do I make myself understood?"

As the *yensid* had evolved in twenty times the gravity of Hanover, the important parts of their anatomy were protected by a thick clutch of tendrils upon which they walked and which was presently below the image Sedgeley spoke to. From this arose, thicker than his thumb, a wandlike extremity a measure and a half high, where the organ of sight, hearing, and other sensibilities was located. More than anything, it resembled a round-ended wooden dowel, adorned with a pair of stringy but robust arms, ending in surprisingly human-looking hands.

"How am I to know them, sir, when they arrive?"

"A polite way of asking who the devil they are. You will find it hard to credit, old stick, but they are none other than your mistress, Jennivere, Master Clive's widow, and her son, who goes by the unlikely appellation of 'Woulf.' Tell me, my good fellow, how quickly can you prepare to receive them?"

"Immediately, of course, sir." He was incapable of expression, nor was there inflection in his voice, yet he managed to convey his feelings. "And may I take the liberty of saying it will be gratifying, for however brief a time, to feel the light and warmth of human occupation in this house once again, sir?"

His master grinned although, given the character of Owld Jenn and her son, it was improbable it would ever ring again with anything resembling human laughter. "You may indeed, Brougham, and many thanks. We shall speak again soon."

Switching the device off, he dismissed it from his mind and addressed his host. "I beg your pardon abjectly, Leo, for this unseemly disturbance of the tranquility to which we have become accustomed in recent years. Frantisek and I judged it imperative to seek the counsel of that Initiate whose wisdom, kindliness, and comradeship we hold in highest esteem. We are long used to considering matters of importance in the congenial, if silent, company of our bearlike and jovial Brother Leo, and this scarcely seems a time to alter that habit."

Out of wisdom, kindliness, comradeship (not to mention congeniality and joviality), Brother Leo forebore to wring Sedgeley's neck for not coming to the point.

"Together, the two of us have agreed—and with considerable reluctance, I might add—upon what seems, even to us, a desperate but necessary course. As painful as it will doubtless prove to all three of us, we must presently relinquish the comfort and solace of the Immortal School and all of its, er, facilities."

The alarmed look upon Leo's face was something Demondion-Echeverria would have given a great sum to have recorded. The man was strong, but there were limits.

"I regret deeply that I must agree with Sedgeley," he told his friend. "Once again, we must strap stylish but deadly thrustibles about our arms and return to the 'Droom, to the 'real' world of masques and masquerades. There we must gather and utilize every morsel of political influence remaining to us. We must request—indeed, we must demand—a private audience for the former Executor-General with the duly designated Ceo of the Monopolity of Hanover!"

Sedgeley nodded energetically. "This we must accomplish as soon as we can manage, and at whatever cost. We must act despite my crippled political reputation—"

"And, in part," Demondion-Echeverria interrupted, "in hope of redeeming it."

Consumed with frustration, Leo seized the wrist of the girl who had come back to clear off what served as dishes in this environment. She squeaked as he thrust a huge hand into the pocket of the abbreviated apron that was all she wore and extracted a tube of lip color. Whirling her like a toy, he laid her across his lap as if she were a child about to be spanked and used the lip color to write upon her naked back, in letters a hand's width high, a single word:

WHY?

Sedgeley swallowed. "Because of a single, jarring item among the countless, endless hours of Owld Jenn's rambling, vitriolic narrative."

"Sedgeley was perspicacious enough," Demondion-Echeverria volunteered, "to enthille everything the woman had to tell him. This single item received his fullest and

undivided professional—which is to say, political—attention."

As anger began to color his host's face again, Sedgeley
continued. "It appears the woman is intimate with the
galaxy's most guarded information. She knows many of the
innermost workings of the secretive interstellar Oplyte
Trade."

Had they been in some environment other than liquid fluorocarbon, the girl, still lying across Leo's lap, would have
fallen to the floor with a thump.

CHAPTER VI:
THE BRAND OF BASTARDY

It had been her predecessor's favorite retreat.

And now it was hers.

Here, she permitted no real-time telecommunications of
any variety, very nearly no guests (not more than three or
four in the past decade), no hint of butlering or valeting, and
any urgent news that the other servants brought her here had
damned well better be world-shattering in character. She did
allow one small, striped, butter-hued predator, presently
sleeping about a measure away.

The entire room, from the floor beneath her slender,
sandal-shod feet to the ceiling somewhere above her head,
was carpeted in a night-black velvety material which
reflected no light, approximately the same amount of sound,
but showed plainly where her little yellow favorite had
climbed and shed upon it. Thank goodness, she thought, the
animal was thoroughly housebroken, for one's nose would
have discovered a mistake upon its part—an indelible mistake, in her long, affectionate experience of pets—long
before one's eye could have done.

It was impossible even to tell what shape the chamber was: she surmised that it was cylindrical—its floor plan was certainly circular—with a low, domed ceiling and not a right angle anywhere to be seen. She had never discovered precisely how high the ceiling was nor, for that matter, even where it began: upon more than one occasion she had been tempted to appropriate a broom or ladder from the household staff in order to see if she could reach it.

All in all, the room had the oddly contradictory effect of relaxing her, while reminding her at the same time of the awesome responsibilities she had accepted—indeed, that had been all but forced upon her—a dozen or more years ago. All about a circumference of some thirty-odd measures, even where the disappearing door stood, there sprang a narrow waist-high shelf. A few siemmes above it hovered sixty globes—lit from within and the only color in the room—of some of the millions of worlds controlled by Hanover. She had programmed them to display a different assortment of planets every time she entered the room, but she knew that she could never see them all. Fifteen quintillion sapients—human and otherwise—lived upon the worlds they represented.

It was bad enough not to be able to deal with individuals, as such, she reflected for perhaps the ten thousandth time since assuming this position, but not to be able to deal with whole worlds, one at a time, seemed absolutely unbearable.

Two short, low-backed couches occupied the room's center, left over by a predecessor more inclined than the present occupant to entertain and interview within this room, along with a more than ample recliner, where she sat at the moment.

These articles of furniture, upholstered with the same fabric as the room itself, centered upon a round transparent table over which stood another globe glowing like the others with its own internal light. The planetary surface it had unceasingly displayed, from the first day she had laid claim to this place, was not that of the megalopolitan capital, as any stranger might have expected, but of a cloud-wrapped, blue-green, mountainous orb of small, cold oceans, vast expanses of gloomy, trackless forest, and sunlit, grassy steppes.

She glanced at the creature on a nearby couch. She'd missed not having a companion there. It was one of the few worlds where—due to an allergic reaction to the spores of fungoids the planet was famous for—they failed to prosper. The locals often kept a peculiar three-legged animal they called a "triskel."

Primitive: it was an unruled and unruly planet upon which her life had been forever changed by turns, for better and for worse, and this, too, served her as a reminder: of love, of happiness, of despair, of outrage, of death, and of revenge. By rights she ought to have loathed the very sight of it. For one thing, it no longer permitted itself to be numbered among the millions of worlds governed by the Monopolity of Hanover. What she felt, instead, was warm affection, and a degree of yearning she believed she must never admit to anyone.

But all this reminiscing was getting her nowhere, she realized, and the appointments she had put off this morning were a burden she could feel lying heavily across her deceptively frail-looking shoulders. Beside the floating globe and a cup of hot infusion she had brought with her, the one other object upon the table was a self-playing thille she had just received, bearing the electronic signature of a famous man. She should be reviewing the historical facts pertinent to the startling information it contained, information which had driven her, at such an unusual hour, to this place of contemplation and refuge.

The animal yawned in its sleep, exposing a mouthful of tiny, needle-sharp fangs, rolled onto its back without opening its eyes, stretched until its limbs trembled with tension, then rolled back into a ball of unconscious fur.

Very well: the infamous trade in Oplyte slaves, she told herself—as if this were twenty years ago and she were addressing a classroom of bored, overly privileged, and reluctant young students—was a source of unspeakable power and untold wealth. This had been true for as long as anyone in this region of the galaxy could remember, or as long as history itself had been enthilled.

Many imperia-conglomerate—not to mention other polities too small or powerless to warrant the name—flourished throughout the length, breadth, and depth of the Explored Deep. In manners both direct and indirect, what was often melodramatically deplored in the mass media as "the Vile Commerce"—usually by commentators with personal investments in the Trade—enhanced and enriched the rulers and the ruling classes of each and every one of them. No individual, despite the most sincere and vociferous of his protests to the contrary, failed to be touched somehow—or to be tainted—by the Oplyte Trade.

However, to those participating in and profiting by it, the Trade had also been a continuous source of annoyance for the same considerable length of time.

She picked up the delicate cup and saucer, took a sip of sweet, steaming liquid, then placed them in her lap among voluminous folds of heavy velvet (these days a trifle out-of-date and usually covered with fine, yellow animal hair by this time of the morning) and settled back into her recliner. A brief digression—or, at the least, an appropriate analogy—now seemed to be in order.

Throughout the Known Deep, although such technology was presently deemed hopelessly passe, thermonuclear weapons of mass destruction had once been very familiar to a long-bygone, but not entirely forgotten era of human experience. In this respect they were not unlike the ancient chemenergic "firearms"—now largely relegated to the status of heirlooms and quaint artifacts depicted upon family coats of arms—which had been outmoded and replaced by personal thrustibles and ships' projectiles, due less to any moral evolution among men than to the development of §-fields which had rendered thermonuclear weapons ineffective.

To a degree, Oplyte warrior-slaves were the thirty-first-century equivalent of nuclear weapons: no ruler wished to use them if it meant they might be used upon him; yet no ruler would hesitate if he believed he could get away with it.

To another degree, Oplytes were comparable to a homelier, more natural scourge. Legendarily destructive swarms of insects had been described in folk tales of many worlds and figured in human mythology from the half-remembered times of the Hebrews and the Mormons. Like those overwhelming insect armies—"locusts," she now recalled, was the traditional term—vast swarms of the dreaded, infamous, nearly mindless, and all-but-invincible warrior-slaves had been known to sweep across whole planetary systems, killing, raping, eating, and burning everything in their path. Another traditional expression came to mind: Oplytes were expected to "provide for their own requirements in the field."

Enough of that, and in a while, the mere threat of using Oplytes against an enemy not similarly provided was often enough to cause worlds to change hands.

In the process of carrying out such incredibly inhuman atrocities upon such an incredibly inhuman scale—her little predator toyed with its prey, to be sure (just as she was wont to do, herself, at the card table), but it was kindly by comparison—Oplytes had carved out for their owners immense additions to already prodigious empires. Thus it came to pass that for centuries untold, they had played a significant part in shaping the history of the Known Deep.

Taking another sip, she discovered with surprise that her beverage had grown quite cold while she was lost in thought. This had happened before, and she was undismayed. Few individuals that she was aware of appeared capable of this degree of concentration, and she considered it almost her only advantage in the dangerous and exhausting game that was interstellar politics. Setting the cup and saucer back upon the virtually invisible table before her, she folded her hands in her lap, intellectually composed herself, and resumed her contemplation.

The principal trouble with the Oplyte Trade was that the various Ceos of the various imperia-conglomerate who benefited most from its existence, did not control its production or distribution, and could only guess at its broad outlines, knowing precious little of the details. Century after century had they wasted prying at its edges, often employing the best intelligence "assets" at hand. Most of the time those "assets" had failed to report back, let alone to return home to their masters with useful information. So it was that even after all this trouble and expense, the Ceos still knew next to nothing of the Trade.

And yet now she had been offered this singular opportunity—ironically manifesting itself as a quaint, old-fashioned two-dimensional image apparently enthilled employing lasercom equipment at least two centuries obsolete—to learn more in one astonishing afternoon than had ever before been known about the Trade, within or without the far-flung borders of the Monopolity of Hanover.

And so it was that she momentarily turned her thoughts from the message to the messenger, to this single individual among fifteen quintillion whom she had briefly known so long ago in the service of her predecessor. Even before his recent stroke of fortune (time alone would reveal whether it was good or bad) in finding his lost sister-in-law (or in having been found by her), the former Executor-General had been considered by everyone within the 'Droom to be the imperium-conglomerate's greatest living authority with regard to the Trade.

Although he had been visibly gratified to receive a welcoming word from her—she had immediately and personally returned his message; it had most likely cost him a lifetime of accumulated favors simply to get through to her—Sedgeley Daimler-Wilkinson had not been surprised that the young Ceo had proven interested in what he had to tell her. Her curiosity on the subject was, in fact, most fervent. Before making the grave decisions that lay before her in connection with it, she must hear more, too, of what Owld Jenn had to say.

She glanced, distracted for an instant, at a small movement above the tabletop. A thunderstorm had broken out over the north temperate zone of the planet depicted by the globe. She shivered, irrationally hoping it was not an omen of some kind, for this primitive, unimportant world—or rather certain of its more notable inhabitants—were also pivotal to the decisions she must make.

For his part, at the finish of their conversation, Sedgeley had assured her that he looked forward greatly to meeting his Ceo—once again. For her own, she wondered whether he had meant more by that than the words themselves had conveyed. Was it a subtle reminder, she mused, of the distance which had existed then—and which might yet still exist in his mind—between their stations?

As his hyphenated surname implied, he was an old-line aristocrat of the Monopolity. His family claimed uncluttered and unquestionable descent from those who had settled this entire section of the galaxy. One of his names was that of a transportation dynasty native to the mythenshrouded birth world of humanity. And, according to legend, the other was that of a maker of fabulous weapons.

Her own exacting scholarship threw considerable doubt upon assertions of this sort (and, as an educated man, he must have been as aware as she of the facts).

Yet ironically, their very nature reemphasized the ancient lineage of his family and those like it which, following a practice in vogue at the time, had assumed these highly distinguished names well after their historic milieu and therefore, by her estimate, could be no younger than nine hundred standard years. After such a yawning interval, it hardly mattered whether a Lord Chrysler or a Lady Jello were actually related to those who had first borne those names or not.

Her own surname (unfortunately, it was that of her mother) betrayed a background but a single step removed from rural peasantry. Her father's was little used, and, despite the supremely exalted position he had eventually come to occupy, was of precisely the same nature. Both had attended the same institution where she herself had been educated. It was where they had met and loved each other for a time. It was where she herself had been conceived, according to her mother, upon an evening supposedly devoted to preparing for examinations.

Although Sedgeley appeared to be too polite to mention it—producing a silence vastly louder than any remark he might have made upon the subject—he knew (and knew perfectly well that she knew) that even the most rigid of social rules are invariably applied differently to different genders. More to the point, they are also applied differently at different levels of power.

Thus to one individual, especially to one of the aristocracy, the brand of bastardy is likeliest to become a life-destroying curse, while to another, less fortunate by right of birth, it may become the key to unlimited wealth and power. And even if Sedgeley were not personally motivated by a genteel resentment toward her and the course her life had taken, many among his social class were, and they concealed it in the 'Droom with a deliberate lack of competence.

For perhaps the hundred thousandth time since she had—all unwillingly—assumed this position, she sadly shook her head, wishing there were someone whom she could trust, someone she could call a loyal friend, within the sound of her voice, or even a parsec of the capital planet. It was inevitable, the young Ceo supposed, that the illegitimate but (in recent years) acknowledged daughter to her immediate predecessor, Ceo Leupould IX, should often feel this way.

It was inevitable, she corrected herself, that *anyone* with great power should do so.

But she found that it was increasingly intolerable to the former Mistress Lia Woodgate. Her furry, striped, and butter-hued pet awakened all at once, raised delicate antennae, and jumped to the floor, landing simultaneously on all six feet. It looked up at her expectantly and made a friendly chirruping noise.

She picked up her cup and saucer and arose.

"You're right," she momentarily dismissed her cares. "It's time for lunch!"

CHAPTER VII:
BIG, SILLY BIRDS

It was at times such as these that Lia hated her once-illustrious father most.

The vast floor of the Monopolitan 'Droom was said to be a million square measures in extent, exactly one square klomme, precisely the same area—to a ten thousandth of a millimeasure—as each of the four walls standing above it. Unlike those walls, fifty measures thick and fashioned from the purest, most optically perfect glass known at the time of their making (or at any time since), the floor was of age-blued and traffic-polished nickel steel, a massive block cut from the heart of an asteroid and lowered from synchronous orbit to the surface of Hanover, it was said, over the course of an entire year.

It was also said this floor was the foundation for the stablest (if not verifiably the largest) edifice in the Known Deep, extending hundreds of measures below ground level. A similar time, "not one of your short, 365-day standard years, but a full 708-day Hanoverian year," had been required to raise its temperature from that of the night-black Deep whence it had come, to that of the surrounding countryside, employing heat exchangers of more than ninety dozen municipal annihilators which provided the planetwide city with light and power. Even now, were not such heroic efforts still in effect, the temperature within the "Greatest Hall of All" would have been bone-chilling, with so much naked metal in such intimate contact with the bedrock for so many centuries.

Legend held that all this had come to pass eleven hundred—standard—years ago, and that the building, meant as a kind of temple to unfettered mercantilism, predated the Monopolity which had confiscated it. That individual sometimes referred to as the "Proprietress of Hanover" entertained scholarly doubts as to the date—her research indicated that the 'Droom was certainly no less than two centuries younger than what was claimed—but not the order of the events. Sometimes—and this was surely one of those occasions—Lia thought she could feel the added gravity created by such a mass of dense material beneath her feet.

A thousand measures overhead, the ceiling—which also had been glass until an orbital attack by unknown terrorists had brought it crashing to the steel floor—was composed of the glowing metalloid mesh from which starship sails were fashioned. In her opinion this was the only cheerful feature to be found in a prime example of the variety of architecture intended to intimidate the intellect and shrink the spirit of anyone unlucky enough to have to occupy it.

Yet none of this took a significant part in the reasons she resented her predecessor just now. Those had more to do with the fact that each of the million square measures of floorspace before her seemed to be occupied by some individual—only a bare majority appeared human lately—demanding her attention.

"*Revlan hatu,* Ceo Lia!"

The mixture of alien and familiar words came to her as if released from the tightly stretched orifice of a child's balloon. The odd creature who had spoken them stood before her, three full measures tall, on a pair of legs no thicker than her own wrist. It waved four equally spindly arms at her in a way its species considered friendly, doing its best to smile—an expression that did not come naturally to it—with the tiny features on its fist-sized head.

"*Revlan hatu,* yourself, Adaven Sagevsal!"

Among the more numerous of the non-humans to be seen

upon any given day at the 'Droom were the "stiquemen," a Deep-traveling race who had "discovered" the Monopolity at about the time Lia was born. Their interstellar territories—it was still unclear precisely how they organized and governed themselves—lay just beyond those which had been explored so far by her own species.

At least the stiquemen had the decency to go naked, she thought, the very idea of clothing being a hilarious novelty to them. How much better that was than all of this counterfeit buccaneer finery she saw about her at the moment, a fashion trend that she found—with excellent reason—particularly repulsive.

Today, as upon all previous occasions when they had come to the 'Droom, the stiquemen wished to discuss trade. Lia believed that sooner or later—provided she succeeded at revitalizing the human exploratory urge—there was bound to be some kind of border disagreement with these beings. Then the talk might turn to other forms of "communication." She wished to understand them when that day arrived, which was why she had granted an extended audience to this individual, who seemed to be acting as ambassadorial spokesman for them all.

Any real negotiations would take place later—were taking place already—between this fellow and various legatees whom she had assigned to what she called "Stiquemannish Affairs." However, from time to time, it was politically necessary to exchange a vital word or two with him in public, sending signals to all who had something to win or lose by her diplomatic relations with the creatures. A few empty pleasantries, and the forms were satisfied; the stiqueman moved on to his real business. Yet he was just the first of many, stretching away in a long, broad line, whom she must greet today, their number augmented horribly by those she had put off this morning in order to steal some time to think.

Meanwhile, servants by the hundreds, *yensid* mostly, scurried about the room upon the orders of their principals—or hired place-holders—waiting in line, fetching food or drink or drugs to make the waiting less unpleasant. Nothing could ease the hardship of the unforgiving steel floor, however, and—following the wise example of her predecessors—except for the wheeled chairs or powered litters of her low-gravity subjects, Lia would neither allow furniture of any kind nor carpets upon the floor to render the waiting easier. If she had, the line before her would have been ten times as long as it was now.

Briefly, she considered also banning eye patches, artificial facial scars and crude prosthetic limbs—metal hooks and wooden legs—voluminous white blouses with puffy sleeves, factory-soiled velvet knee breeches, and slippers sporting silver buckles. If she had to look upon or hear another artificial bird, she might very well thrust it off the shoulder of its cretinous owner herself.

The women were even worse, of course, with their artfully tattered gowns, and fetters fashioned out of precious metals and bedecked with jewels. Like many another of history's rulers, Lia had herself worn chains upon one overly protracted occasion, and had found nothing romantic or even prurient about them.

And yet, somehow, the 'Droom would outlast this foolishness, just as it had outlasted every other foolishness its occupants had thought to practice over nearly a millennium. Smells of food, perfume, and body odor—human and otherwise—blended in a miasma almost legendary in itself, despite elaborate measures employed to dispel it. The noise (talk, music, the clamorous demands of media "personalities") would have been equally appalling had it not been for the abatement devices deployed at intervals throughout the room, replaying each and every sound precisely out of phase so it was—almost—canceled out.

Something with a blunt, sticky tongue the width of her shoulders licked her outstretched hand. She had been told it was a religious leader of a world only recently found to harbor sapient life. Although it lay many parsecs deep within the boundaries of the Monopolity, it had apparently been overlooked time and again by explorers. As soon as she had greeted it, been greeted in return, and dismissed it, she made surreptitious use of the small box of moist wipes she had brought with her this afternoon in anticipation of just this moment.

Given a brief respite, she took a breath and glanced about. From the measure-high dais (a raised area "merely" a thousand measures square, cut from the same giant asteroidal block as the rest of the building's underpinning) upon which she and her retinue sat or stood, along the length of yet another elevation known as the "Ceo's Table," down to the floor of the 'Droom itself, the queue extended to great doors, half a klomme tall, that had permitted entry in the first place. Briefly, she enjoyed a fantasy of ordering the doors welded shut.

Her greatest regret was that there had to be guards everywhere, standing about her in a living picket fence, forming a perimeter upon the lower tier of the Ceo's Table, circulating throughout the 'Droom itself (no few in civilian attire), hovering upon §-field harnesses above the crowd. Although she had inherited this situation, she could not help but believe that any leader who required guarding like this was a *bad* leader, who probably deserved whatever fate his guards strove to protect him from. At least she had replaced the mindless Oplytes, who had performed this hateful task, with sapients, mostly humans.

Any deficit of security this created she made up by carrying a personal thrustible upon her forearm beneath one highly embellished sleeve. As far as she knew, she was the first Ceo to take such a precaution. Or accept such a responsibility.

On and on her endless duties went. Eight hundred individuals with evil intentions and excellent tailors spoke her name in a variety of accents as she spoke theirs, prompted by a tiny whispering device she wore behind one ear, concealed by her wavy hair. She glanced backward for the briefest instant at the whisperer, standing a few measures behind her, speaking as discreetly as he could into a microphone, then, before she turned back to the next person she must greet, transformed her glance into a grateful smile which caught him by surprise.

One advantage to this enormously public routine, she had found, was that, once a rhythm had been established, she could go on with the reasoning process she had begun earlier today. And a good thing that was, for there was much to contemplate and plan before she could make the final, fateful decision lying ahead.

Despite the many rumors always circulating among the masqued habitués of the 'Droom, even the Ceo Lia was uncertain why her father had abdicated his august position in such a sudden manner, without giving any warning. Nor, she had determined, during the brief time left to him afterward, had he bothered trying to explain it to anyone else, not even his most trusted confidants. It certainly had not been over these weekly public audiences she dreaded so well. He'd loved them more than any other single aspect of ruling the Monopolity of Hanover.

She shuddered at the memory of his enthusiasm.

To every appearance, as absolute rulers go, Leupould IX had been a decent and conscientious one. Virtually everything he had tried to accomplish had been directed toward genuinely enhancing the lives of his fifteen quintillion subjects. For the most part—this was a quality which had made him unique among rulers—that had amounted to leaving them alone to enhance their own lives.

As an historian, Lia knew well that, despite millennia of propaganda to the contrary, great power seldom attracts great minds. No matter what form a government might take, the most important proficiencies of leadership are those of ingratiation and intimidation, not creative or contemplative intelligence. The only difference among forms is upon whom those proficiencies are practiced (more than sufficient reason for political power to be stringently curtailed). Who had said, at the dawn of antiquity, that great men are nearly always bad men?

Yet nearly every authority agreed that Leupould had been extraordinarily intelligent for an individual in his position. Some there were, in fact, with much experience in the

'Droom, who might even have insisted upon calling him wise.

"Plain Leupould Wheeler" (as he had often styled himself) had lectured and written for many years as a university professor—another line of work which seldom attracts great minds. Nevertheless, he had ascended to head the imperium-conglomerate as a leader most unusual in the extent of his education. Since his abdication, academic scholars and media reporters alike had expended thousands of hours vainly scouring his earliest writings word by word for any clue to his later behavior. Lia had spent almost as much time searching the Ceo's several official Residences herself, for the same kind of clue. Even after more than a decade, new theories, each more absurd than its predecessor, still flapped through the agitated Monopolitan atmosphere like big, silly birds.

Nor did anyone know why, of all people, he had selected his illegitimate daughter Lia Woodgate to succeed him. Even she believed that Leupould must have been aware of many wiser, more illustrious, more accomplished individuals who might have replaced him better than she had—not to mention, in a milieu dominated top to bottom by men, his countless male children, illegitimate and otherwise. She was not the youngest individual to hold the Hanoverian reins of power, nor was she the first female ever to occupy the Monopolity's most powerful position. She was, however, the *second* youngest, and the second *woman,* to be thus designated. The last female Ceo of Hanover, a legendary figure all but lost in the mists of antiquity, had been its first. Lia hoped that she would not turn out, completing the symmetry, to be the Monopolity's last.

Those, like the former Executor-General, who had been privy to every confidence Leupould could bestow, nevertheless had been left by their departed leader as completely in the dark as everybody else. They assumed, although it was nothing but a wild surmise, that his choice of Lia must have had something to do with the covert intelligence work she had performed for him for many years.

This, of course, had been long before either of them had acknowledged in public, or even to each other, what each of them had known in private for so long: that she was, indeed, his daughter. One need not conceal one's facial features, she thought now (although not for the first time) in order to wear a masque. It was believed by nearly everyone that her mother had been another academic, although neither of them had ever named her or ever would. In the pursuit of this information, the same useless scholars and reporters had spent thousands of hours poring over Hanover University faculty likenesses, but to no avail. Lia changed the mental subject: beyond this point lay nothing but pain.

But she had digressed to a degree that was uncharacteristic of her. It was fascinating, in light of current events, how much her intelligence work had thrown her into contact with elements of the Oplyte Trade—not that it had done her any more good than a million others before her. To her, the most astonishing fact of all was that no one even knew whether the slavers were human! Hundreds of sapient aliens—stiquemen, flatsies, rollerballers—could be seen upon the capital world every day, in ever-increasing numbers. They served in many stations and capacities, from interstellar ambassadors to common dockhands and crewbeings. It was far from impossible that one variety of them alone was responsible for creating and trading in Oplyte warrior-slaves.

In any event—whoever these mysterious, unknown entities turned out to be—one thing was undeniable: for generations uncounted, unlike an equally uncounted number of jealous Ceos, they had *controlled* galaxywide production and distribution of Oplytes. This was, in the Ceo Lia's much-exalted opinion, an obscene political and moral circumstance, one, in her view, no longer to be borne!

But what was this?

Before her stood three forms—she believed them to be human—shrouded in loose gray hooded robes indicating clerics of some kind. As they stepped closer, side by side, under the watchful glare of her personal guard, one of them raised his hands a fraction of a second before the others, pushed his hood back to reveal a heavily bearded face beneath a thick mop of curly black hair, and winked a highly insubordinate but startlingly blue eye at her. In an instant, all her boredom and resentment melted away, replaced by helpless affection.

"Hello, Father," she told Brother Leo. "I had hoped that you would come with Sedgeley."

CHAPTER VIII:
TOO TERRIBLE TO TOLERATE

"My dear Ceo, surely you are *joking!*"

"On the contrary, 'Uncle' Sedgeley, I am completely in earnest." This time, Lia insisted that he take the long-handled mallet with the brightly colored bands she had offered him. "I trust that you find yellow acceptably cheerful."

Sedgeley examined the mallet. "Since you ask, the truth is, I prefer red."

Lia clucked at him and shook her head. "Now, now, I have claimed that color for myself. Permit me to be childish in this regard. Father, I am well aware of your own partiality to blue. Tell me, what color would you prefer, Frantisek?"

Demondion-Echeverria showed excellent, evenly spaced teeth, "As your guest, Ceo, and your subject, it would be ungenteel to tell you of *my* preference with regard to this game."

Lia laughed.

Demondion-Echeverria had gratefully abandoned his gray monk's habit for what he had on underneath: a stylish shirt of white satin, ruffled at the neck and wrists, a patterned velvet waistcoat with many gold buttons, a tailored surcoat of the same material with enormous pockets and long skirts, matching knee-length trousers that fit tightly across the buttocks, and tall leather boots turned over at the top into a sort of cuff no less than twenty siemmes deep.

With his dark complexion, that gigantic hook of a nose, and his amiably villainous bearing, Lia thought, the former Jendyne ambassador may have been the one man upon Hanover whom the latest fashion truly suited. At least, she observed, he had rejected the false disfigurement which often went with it, as well as the sartorial burns and tatters that served as "decoration." The day Frantisek Demondion-Echeverria wore scorched rags in public might well be the day that all of the imperia-conglomerate collapsed, simultaneously. He did affect a brightly colored kerchief over his head, tied somehow at the corners. Although intended to be rakish, she thought it made him look just like one of the Residence's cleaning ladies, right down to the small mustache he always wore.

His companion, on the other hand, who had not departed the grounds of the Immortal School more than three times over the past fifteen years, had selected clothing half a generation out of date, although it was of the highest quality and as elegantly carried as anything Demondion-Echeverria essayed. Lia often had to stop and remind herself that this elderly, increasingly grandfatherly fellow she fenced with verbally today had once been a famous (and infamous) duelist in the literal sense, an interstellar adventurer, and an acclaimed diplomat.

Moreover, the man's legendary feats of daring and personal generosity as a gambler, his discriminatory powers as a gourmet (and respected chef in his own right), the stories—told behind the winsome masques and fluttering fans of Hanoverian ladies of the previous generation—of his accomplishments (if that were the proper word for them) of heroic gallantry in the boudoir, all contributed to a reputation of mythological proportions. The man was no mere empty celebrity of the passing moment. And were it not for his powerful and subtle intelligence—not to mention his long experience at the very highest level of galactic politics—she would not have asked him here in the first place.

Her father, the former Ceo Leupould IX, had elected to retain his monkish garb, and had accepted the blue mallet and ball with an expression of shared mischief and amusement she seemed always to remember him by, no matter how grave the circumstances. What he would contribute to this consultation—especially given his solemnly observed vow of silence—remained to be seen. Clearly Sedgeley and Demondion-Echeverria placed the highest value merely upon his presence, and Lia herself had always found it heartening, as well. In any case, Leupould could easily denounce or endorse any idea or proposal with the slightest elevation or lowering of his articulate, bushy eyebrows. And his indomitably positive demeanor was infectious. She was glad he had decided to come.

For her own part, although Sedgeley (addressing him as "Uncle" had been a rare, deliberate probe) and Demondion-Echeverria undisguisedly felt it foolish or demeaning, she had chosen the present setting and the prehistoric game of *krokay* for their very air of detachment from the problem at hand. In this, she had learned, she was rather like her father. Permit the body to distract itself with some wholly inconsequential task, she had discovered, and the mind will thus be liberated from it to operate at its most efficient and productive capacity.

Which was exactly what they needed now. And from his expression, it was clear that her father agreed. At least as far as history was concerned, even the motives of the unknowns behind the Oplyte Trade remained mysterious and, not for the first time, it struck Lia that the business seemed, intentionally or otherwise, to be another one of masques—worn over masques, worn over masques.

Demondion-Echeverria interrupted her train of thought. "Pray pardon me for asking, Ceo, I am unfamiliar with the rules by which this game is played." He indicated the mallet he had been given, the ball striped with the same colors, and the colored pegs and wire wickets which had been driven into the lawn.

Although it was a familiar green in color, the growth beneath their feet was nothing any human of a thousand years ago would have recognized. More than anything, it resembled the tightly curled fur of some woolly mammal. For almost that same length of time, it had been cultivated throughout the grounds of the Ceo's Residence, seeded, weeded, fed, watered, and rolled by countless generations of patient servants, until it lay as flat and uniform as a gaming table.

Hanover, for the most part, was a bone-chillingly cold, gray world, whose deep, wet winter snows never transformed themselves further, with an annual precession of seasons that took almost twice as long as upon the birth world of humanity, than into endless summer drizzles. That, and a significantly more oppressive gravity than human beings were thought to have evolved in, made it not the pleasantest of planets upon which to dwell. It was often said that Hanover had chosen mankind, rather than the other way around, its earliest settlement having resulted from an unintentional crash landing a millennium ago.

These unlovely qualities were offset—at least in the Ceo's Residential park—by §-fields overhead, not unlike those that formed the roof above the 'Droom, although their principal purpose here (aside from providing a certain measure of physical security from various methods of attack) was to abate the drizzle, and to tint the Hanoverian sky (whatever shade of gray it happened to be at present) a dazzling and cheerful blue, with hints of the yellow sunshine that humanity, far from home even after a thousand years, found most pleasing to the eye.

The best part of returning to this place at this time, especially after her long half day in the 'Droom, she thought, was that, aside from the welcome temporary presence of her father and his colleagues, not a single other being was in sight. She knew the truth, of course, that her household guard lurked everywhere, remaining inconspicuous not only for the sake of her privacy, but for that of any potential assassin or interloper who might thereby be taken by surprise. But, exactly like a mirror placed strategically so as to give the impression that a room is larger, what she knew seemed not to spoil what she saw.

"Perhaps it would be best, sir, to watch me and follow my example." Lia leaned over, held her red-striped mallet in the approved manner (not an easy thing to do against the heavy and voluminous skirts of her dress), and struck the ball smartly. As it rolled toward the first wicket, she turned to her companions.

"So far," she observed casually, "those who ply the Oplyte Trade have never attempted to capitalize upon the many political and military advantages they are perceived by their clientele to possess. Just to observe a single frightening example, they might many times have denied their warrior-slaves to the Monopolity of Hanover—at some strategic moment when our survival depended upon having them."

Demondion-Echeverria made no pretense whatever to proper form, but simply reached down and rapped his ball one-handed, uncaring about its destination. "For that matter, my Ceo, they might easily have deprived *any* of the many imperia-conglomerate—to the consequent advantage of any other—in some interstellar dispute where they had possessed a hidden interest of their own to nurture."

"However, all they seem to care about," Sedgeley offered, always, and by reflex, a competitor at heart and striving hard to imitate the manner in which Lia had skillfully opened the game, "is whatever passes for currency among the imperia-conglomerate from one epoch to the next. Money is all that they seem ever to have cared about, for countless millennia, as far as anybody knows." Unfortunately, his ball was not nearly as well struck, and rolled off to one side.

Brother Leo's blue-striped ball stopped rolling only a few siemmes from that of his daughter. He grinned as if to say that he had let her off easily, but offered no indication as to his opinion in the matter they were discussing as they played, which the others took to mean that he agreed with what was being said.

"Personally," the cynical Demondion-Echeverria replied, "I consider this ample evidence that they are not human at all, but aliens, known or unknown, with motivations totally incomprehensible to us. Members of our own species, in my sad experience, are willing to sacrifice virtually any sound material consideration for the benefit of petty enmities and microscopic amounts of power."

Sedgeley, having observed Lia and his friends take their second strokes, and struggling to bring his own ball back into play, chuckled politely over the former ambassador's witticism, although it was unclear to Lia whether he shared the bleak opinion of their species that it had advanced. "Well said, my dear Frantisek, but the mere notion they *might* someday take such an advantage represents a constant threat to the peace and order of the Known Galaxy."

"Indeed," Demondion-Echeverria replied. No inept participant himself in the many fields in which Sedgeley excelled, he had begun to get a feel for the game and was more delighted with himself than he would freely have admitted. "Such a threat is much too terrible for any intelligent ruler to tolerate if he—"

"Or she," Sedgeley corrected diplomatically.

"Or *she* is not obliged to."

"Oh dear, what was that?" For a moment they were distracted by a bright flash in the sky as a bird flew into inadvertent contact with the §-field a hundred measures overhead and was annihilated. It was this effect that kept a Ceo safe from an assassin's bomb or trajectile. The same process, applied to droplets of mist filling the atmosphere, was the source of the brilliant light which made it feel to them, within the field's confines, as if it were a sunny day.

Lia let the men talk—it was the very reason she had brought them here—while she considered what they said. Information of the character that Owld Jenn had brought back to the Monopolity was unspeakably rare. The deadly and dangerous efforts of hundreds of polities and thousands of intelligence missions over a great many centuries had failed utterly to produce anything to match its quantity and quality. The Ceo knew this at first hand, for she had undertaken many such deadly and dangerous missions herself, vainly attempting to ferret out the Oplyte Traders' secrets for her father. Now, given this potentially strategic windfall, she meant to make the fullest possible use of it.

But she had been anticipated.

"I would wager," the former Executor-General suggested correctly, "that our Ceo has an eye to ending the risky and repulsive Oplyte traffic forever. In this respect, she differs to a highly significant degree from every other leader presently known to humanity. She is, of course, an extremely moral individual—"

Demondion-Echeverria nodded. "And equally an idealist."

"It is regrettable," Sedgeley continued, "that even her own underlings who populate the 'Droom would more than likely disapprove of what she now contemplates."

"While others would do rather a deal more than simply sneer at such a high-minded undertaking. Fearing for their economic and political well-being, they would actively obstruct her, even take physical steps against her, if they knew of what she purposes, struggling at all costs to maintain the status quo."

"You make a most telling series of points, my dear Frantisek," Sedgeley responded. By now he had abandoned all pretense at playing *krokay* and tried to lean upon his mallet, which proved too short for the purpose. "Even more sadly, in my experience, there are others—likely more numerous than those with such selfish interests—who might not care for current circumstances, but are long and well accustomed to them. At least they know how to comport themselves, as they might not in a universe devoid of the Oplytes and their creators."

"And if, to redress the balance, the more progressive among their number felt 'compelled' to replace the Monopolity," the former Jendyne ambassador added, "as the largest and most powerful imperium-conglomerate, so much the better.

Lia spoke at last; her tone ironic but not unkindly. "I sincerely thank you, Frantisek—if I may—for offering us the benefit of your experience as one of those who once aspired to replace us. As a student—and onetime teacher—of history, myself, I understand this type of conservatism all too well. I also know that state secrets of the kind we now possess, thanks to Sedgeley's perspicacity, are short-lived at the best. I appreciate the fact that our actions must be swift if we are to remain unhindered and achieve success."

Demondion-Echeverria actually bowed. Costumed as he was, Lia found the gallant gesture appealing in the extreme. How sad, she thought, that it arose as part and parcel of a barbarism too terrible even for the former Jendyne to tolerate. "And I, in my turn, thank you for your extreme kindliness, my lady Ceo."

Of a sudden, for some unknown reason, Leupould seemed to be watching her closely.

"Pray think nothing of it." She waved it away. "Furthermore, I have an excellent idea upon whom I can rely to help me in what you now know I regard as the noblest of campaigns. I have had, since Sedgeley first contacted me in this connection. And now you have made my mind up. Uncertain allies they may be at other times, concerning other issues; I know I can count upon them in this."

These enigmatic words evoked a puzzled expression from each of her three companions, which she ignored. "Therefore, my first decision in the matter before us will be to reappoint Sedgeley—now, now, hear me out!—to his once-exalted function as Executor-General. You must understand, Sedgeley—I *will* have you understand, sir— that this is strictly upon a probationary basis." Sedgeley gulped and nodded. Knowing him, she wondered whether he was sincere.

"My second decision—and with all due respect to you, Sedgeley, more important and farther-reaching—is to send word to the Monopolity's nominal worst enemy. By liveried messenger, entrusted with an entreaty I myself shall have enthilled, I purpose to summon the infamous rebel and plunderer, Henry Martyn!"

All three men, including her father, opened their mouths to react. She forestalled their emotional objections—and Leupould's violation of his vows—with an outturned palm. "By separate messenger, I intend also to summon his no-less-infamous henchman and former first officer, the formidable Phoebus Krumm."

She found that she enjoyed observing their reactions. Each of them had his own reason to be astonished at the boldness of her plan. Henry Martyn she had known well— since his boyhood, in fact—as Arran Islay, now Autonomous Drector-Hereditary of the moonringed planet Skye. It was upon that world that a rather younger Mistress Lia Woodgate, now Ceo of the Monopolity of Hanover, had once been no more than a humble governess and tutor to the family Islay. And, of course, an occasional spy for her august and terrible father, Leupould IX.

As they gaped at what she had purposed, she lifted the mallet and drove her *krokay* ball straight through the hoops, striking the peg and winning the game.

"NOW TURN YOUR FACE TO THE §-FIELD,
AND YOUR BACK TO THE TALL MAST-TREE;
AND BEFORE YOUR HEART BEATS AGAIN IN YOUR BREAST,
I SHALL ANNIHILATE THEE.

"BUT FIRST TAKE OFF YOUR KEFFLAR SO FINE,
AND YOUR GOLDEN STAYS," SAID HE.
"FOR THOUGH I'M GOING TO ANNIHILATE YOU HERE,
I HAVE USE FOR YOUR FINERY."

"YES, I'LL TAKE OFF MY KEFFLAR SO FINE,
LIKEWISE MY STAYS," ANSWERED SHE.
"BUT BEFORE THAT I DO, YOU FALSE YOUNG MAN,
YOU MUST TURN YOUR BACK ON ME."

CHAPTER IX:
A MESSAGE FROM HANOVER

"Damn!"

Arran Islay, sitting up, had struck his forehead against the underside of the draywherry he was repairing. Sliding more prudently from beneath the vehicle this time before attempting to arise, he dropped wrench and neutrino scanner into a nearby tool chest and wiped his greasy hands upon his peasant trousers.

Five-year-old Glynna laughed, deepening the lines in her father's scowl. Audibly breathing his annoyance at having been diverted from an unpleasant and demanding task it had taken him some time and no small exercise of character to confront, Arran set one hand upon a hip and rubbed his forehead. "Now tell me once again," he demanded of the overdressed stranger responsible for this miniature calamity, "who the devil are you, and what, precisely, is all this nonsense?"

The remainder of the fabled Islay family (save for their eldest daughter) crowded round the masqued and perfumed interloper. The eldest child here, the stranger had been given to understand, was eleven-year-old Phoebe. Next were nine-year-old Lia and seven-year-old Lorrie. Last, after five-year-old Glynna, was three-year-old Arran, squirming in the arms of his mother, Loreanna. It was she who had brought the visitor from the great Holdings Hall which had been the initial destination of his tiny, §-levitated capsule, no different in its operating principles from the machine Arran labored upon now. The older girls were aquiver with curiosity at this unprecedented manifestation from what they held (despite the preferences of their father) to be the center of the Known Universe.

The lace-and-velvet-clad messenger felt out of place in this excessively rustic setting. They all stood with actual *mud* oozing about their shoe soles—those of the children who condescended to wear them—in a workyard behind the Holdings formed by a surrounding number of lesser out-buildings. One was a hangar of sorts, in which the dray-wherry, metalloid mesh-constructed like the hull of a starship, was ordinarily housed. The harsh odors of alien livestock animals and agricultural products filled the air. How ever, he wondered, could people—ostensibly of good quality—lower themselves to lead such a vulgar existence?

The figure he found himself confronting now, and for whom he bore his message, was hardly overbearing in his physical stature, but he appeared to radiate a compelling power of personality that the messenger had only before experienced in the daunting presence of the individual (only an hour ago he would have made it, "the *unique* individual") who had sent him here to begin with.

Arran Islay was of a trifle less than average Hanoverian height. His blond hair was worn at medium length, conceal-ing his ears, but lying not upon his collar. He affected a respectable mustache about the same color as his hair and drooping at the ends; he was otherwise clean-shaven. His eyes were of the startling hue to be seen—or so he had dis-covered in his many travels—upon a sunny day within the heart of an iceberg. They were the eyes, the messenger reminded himself, of a man who commanded all the forces of pillage and slaughter, who had rebelled against duly established authority and killed hundreds, if not thousands, of his fellow human beings. And yet they were surrounded by fine lines which revealed that their owner laughed often and heartily.

Abruptly, as if to confirm this inference, the man grinned, threatening his several daughters with a hand that, despite his perfunctory efforts at cleaning it, remained oil-blackened and grimy. They squealed in mock terror and rushed him, seizing his legs as he stood helpless, unable even to pat them upon the head, under the fastidious gaze of their mother. Of

a sudden, they were all tripped up and bowled over by a
hurtling ball of fur, as the girls shouted, screamed, and
clapped their hands. Their father laughed, as well. One of
them—Lia—caught the thing and held it to her as it
squirmed like young Arran had (it was just the boy's size, as
well) in his mother's arms.

All of the higher life-forms native to the moonringed
world Skye displayed a trilaterally symmetrical morphol-
ogy, according to the preparatory briefing given him by the
Monopolitan Courier Service. This was an excellent example: a triskel, if he remembered correctly, an intelligent little
predatory beast domesticated virtually from the instant
humanity had placed a foot upon this planet. The Islay girls
were taking turns stroking it, murmuring a name over and
over which, to an ear unpracticed in the Skyan accent,
sounded rather like "Wednesday."

"I beg you to forgive them, sir," Loreanna asked with a
winning smile and a formulaic politeness to which the messenger was aware he was not technically entitled, "for the
girls have not seen their father since breakfast time. And
pray convey to him as you have to me this message you have
brought to us from Hanover."

The messenger nodded to her and cleared his throat: "To
Arran 'the' Ithlay, Autonomouth Drector-Hereditary of
Thkye, thometimeth and variouthly known—"

"Mummy—why is his face so red? It clashes with the
purple ruffles at his throat!"

"Hush, Glynna," Loreanna stage-whispered. "At the least,
pray allow the fellow to finish with his recitation before asking him embarrassing personal questions."

But he could not finish it. Required by its sender to
deliver it in one piece, he was obliged to begin again: "To
Arran 'the' Ithlay, Autonomouth Drector-Hereditary of
Thkye, thometimeth and variouthly known ath 'Henry Martyn,' we thend Our thintherely fondetht Greetingth. Know
you by thethe prethenth—"

"Presents?" This time, it was Lorrie who interrupted,
amidst delighted giggles from the other children. Little

Arran, too, had perked up at the reiteration of this word, being one that is highly significant to children of his age.

" 'Tis only a manner of speaking, Lorrie," her sister Phoebe said with an embarrassed tone, as if recalling her own seven-year-old foolishness. "He only means that we are to understand something by this message he presents us with."

"But what?" Lorrie asked, disappointment written plainly upon her pretty face.

"We do not know yet, silly triskel, because you have interrupted him again!"

"Oh." She looked up at the messenger with enormous, tear-brimming eyes. "Sorry."

Her father was consumed with the effort of suppressing laughter. "Pray continue."

"Ahem . . ." The messenger, tugging at the pleated skirts of his maroon velvet livery doublet, recited rapidly. "To Arran 'the' Ithlay, Autonomouth Drector-Hereditary of Thkye, thometimeth and variouthly known ath 'Henry Martyn,' we thend Our thintherely fondetht Greetingth. Know you by thethe prethenth—"

He paused for an instant to glare about at the children, who giggled at him.

"—that you and yourth are hereby requethted and required to attend upon Our pleathure in the 'Droom of the Monopolity, following an interval no longer than that in which the thwiftetht vethel can deliver you, there to conthider with Uth thertain thubjecth of mutual and motht urgent interetht. To which we thith day thet Our hand, Lia Woodgate Wheeler, Theo of the Monopolity of Hanover."

For a moment, no one spoke. Then: "Is there no more?" Loreanna failed to disguise her disappointment. "Is this what you traveled all those parsecs to say?"

The messenger blinked, as if confused. "Yath, mum—I mean, no, mum—I mean, I had not known, mum, before you athked me. But I bear thith object, to be hand-delivered to you." He lifted a jacket-skirt to reach a pocket from which he extracted an autothille, which he laid in Loreanna's out-stretched palm.

Arran frowned again. "Posthypnotic. I had not known Lia, in the past, to use her servants in so inconsiderate a manner. I do not care for what it may portend." He turned to the Ceo's messenger. "And you may tell her I said so."

"Oh, no, thir! She requetheted my permithion before she did it, thir! I recall clearly, now. She offered theveral oppor-tunitieth to decline, I athure you!"

"Pray excuse me, sir." This time it was gentle Phoebe who interrupted, "but I had been given the distinct impres-sion that the lisp Castillian had by this time fallen out of fashion within the Monopolity of Hanover. Is that not cor-rect?"

The messenger was no more taken aback than if the triskel had asked him such a question. Then he recalled the stories he had been told about these children and their par-ents, smiled down at the erudite eleven-year-old, took her hand, and kissed it before releasing it. She caught a glimpse of the deadly, brightly plated, highly engraved thrustible he carried beneath his ruffled sleeve. "Oh, but it ith, my dear. My lithp ith a natural one which before now wath an athet. Now it hath become a liability; yet the Theo, in her great kindneth, hath retained my thervitheth until my retirement, thome two yearth henth."

Arran laughed and clapped just like his daughters. *"That* sounds more like the Lia I know! Phoebe, take this gentle-being back to the house and find him something to eat and a place to rest. Perhaps he'd care to change into more com-fortable clothing. Then find your elder sister, for I have news for her."

To the messenger: "Kindly accept our humble hospitality while we view this autothille, give it the consideration it deserves, and compose a suitable reply."

The messenger bowed deeply. "I would be motht extheedingly honored to do tho, Drector-Hereditary." *And then,* he thought to himself, *get out of this smelly, barbaric pesthole immediately, and back aboard a starship bound for home!*

"How long has it been, Loreanna-my-love?" Arran Islay asked of his wife rhetorically. As they ambled along, he placed a caressing hand at the nape of her neck, exposed by the manner in which she had arranged her long auburn hair this afternoon. Only a trifle over a measure and a half tall, at the age of twenty-nine, brown-eyed and freckled Loreanna was frequently mistaken for one of her daughters.

They were at the front of the Holdings Hall now, having crossed a neatly graveled track and entered a sunny meadow perhaps three klommes wide, half of that distance deep, and dotted with colorful wildflowers. It lay bounded upon two sides by thick everblue forest and upon the third by a shroom bog. Both wore clothing that failed to distinguish them from the peasants hereabout who owed them fealty. In one hand she carried a bundled kerchief containing their luncheon.

The Islay children were all gathered—save for the eldest, who had not turned up as yet—in the Holdings' great kitchen at the moment, having their own midday meal with the house servants they had grown up among and the Ceo's official courier, mercilessly plying the latter with questions of Monopolitan affairs and of the capital world, freeing Arran and Loreanna to have their picnic.

Loreanna grinned without turning her head, regarding him from the corner of her eye. "Do you mean since we've been alone together? How old is your son?"

He laughed, shaking his head as parents will upon such an occasion, but his expression soon grew serious again, and she gave him the real answer he had sought.

"Fifteen years this coming Primus. Fifteen years since Henry Martyn's notorious and celebrated victory upon the bosom of the Great Deep, and his defeat—"

"With a little friendly alien help," he interjected, as had become their custom. Somewhere, something another world might have called a meadowlark (in plain fact, it was a

scaled, flightless creature rather like a lizard) warbled cheerfully, and large yellow flies buzzed in a manner that was not
unpleasant. For a brief while, during the regime of the Black
Usurper, there had been a vice-polluted shantytown upon
this meadow, but it had been burned down during the final
struggle, and since then, every trace of it had been painstakingly eradicated.

"Just so," she acknowledged, paraphrasing what the
Hanoverian media had said afterward of that day, "his ignominious defeat—with a little friendly alien help upon that
most historic of occasions—of the superior combined forces
of the Monopolity of Hanover and of the Jendyne Empery-
Cirot, along with an as yet to be determined number of their
lesser and subsidiary imperia-conglomerate."

They both laughed. In truth, however, such reminiscences
were rare with them. Like many another modest man with a
fighting past, the former Henry Martyn, starship-raider and
liberator-of-worlds, preferred to be known merely as Arran
"the" Islay. Had he thought much in historic terms, which he
did not, he saw himself as no more than something less than
a duke and something more than a country squire. As his
father and eldest brother before him, he told himself, he was
a simple man, the Autonomous Drector-Hereditary of the
moonringed frontier planet Skye. It had been for nothing
more grandiose than that all-important word "autonomous"
that he had fought so savagely, so long ago.

He sighed. "You could be quite as distinguished an historian as the Ceo Lia, dearest. Why is it that you let me hold
you back professionally in this manner?"

She stopped, ankle-deep in blossoms almost too colorful
and fragrant to be real, and turned to him, standing upon tiptoe and throwing her arms about his neck. "Because of this,"
she replied, kissing him as passionately as if for the first
time. He encircled her tiny waist and returned her kiss with
the same fervor until at last they were compelled to break
off, gasping, and she finished her sentence breathlessly. "As
you know perfectly well, Arran Islay!"

He held her tightly. The Ceo's personal message still lay

unread in the pocket of Loreanna's dress. Both of them sensed that in some way their lives were about to be altered by it, perhaps irrevocably. Neither of them wished to discuss it yet, nor even to consider it. "Then tell me, my darling, why it is that we have only six children, when, upon such overwhelmingly convincing testimony, we ought to have made at least nine by this time, or maybe an even dozen!"

"If we had more time," she giggled, "or you were more conventional of taste . . ."

"Enough, woman! Precisely *whose* tastes are unconventional round here, my little mermaid? And what, since you have reminded me, have we brought for luncheon?"

They had found their favorite spot now, a little hollow in the meadow in which they fondly imagined they could lie unseen from the house. It had never occurred to either of them to test this optimistic hypothesis. Lie down they did, with Loreanna's kerchief spread between them as a table-cloth, until their modest meal was eaten. Although they knew it not, no fewer than two of their daughters had learned much of life, watching this place from a certain tower window.

Reluctantly, Loreanna had revived the subject of the Ceo's recent demands.

"We have discussed this," Arran told her, tipping back the last of his Skyan beer. "Thanks to our historic victory, I could claim to be a Ceo myself, albeit upon a small scale. We Islays could gather leaders of a hundred worlds who would pledge their fealty. And yet never have we done so, despite the independence we have won—not to mention the gratitude we could command if we but wished it, of the worlds we freed from many an imperium-conglomerate. I consider myself a loyalist even now—in my own way—to the Monopolity of Hanover."

Loreanna laughed. "A loyalist, that is, at an interstellar arm's length—and within limits that any vassal of England's King John I would certainly admire!"

"There you go again, dear, with your history," he pretended to complain. "And yet despite that, she addresses me as if I were a rebellious underling who had *lost* the Battle of moonringed Skye! Whether to be angered or amused by this message of Lia's, I do not know. Which would you be, finding yourself in receipt of such a boldly peremptory summons: a personal audience with the mightiest ruler in the Known Galaxy—a ruler whose predecessor you trounced thoroughly?"

"You know, in matters like this, that I *am* you, my darling, that we are inextricably melded, interwoven, fused, now and forever, into one and the same being, of the same breath and heartbeat. Oh dear, why have I always found the talk of politics so stimulating? And there was Loreanna, less than an hour ago, with the temerity to criticize what might be considered her *husband's* perversities!"

She laughed, reaching for the kerchief that was all that separated them, tossing it to one side with considerable enthusiasm. " 'Trounced thoroughly,' " she repeated, as if considering his words carefully. "Now, there's a likely turn of phrase. Would you mind terribly showing me exactly what you mean by it?"

He began unbuttoning her peasant dress from the hem up, exposing fine, smooth legs that seemed unusually long for one of her slight stature. Above her waist lay other assets unusual in one of so small a size. Seizing one such and giving it a long, languorous kiss, he spread her legs and lay atop her.

"And now," she gasped once he had penetrated her, but before he could stop her mouth with another kiss, "with regard to that even dozen children you mentioned . . ."

CHAPTER X:
THE USAGES OF POWER

In the high tower office that had been his boyhood bedroom not too many years ago, the Autonomous Drector-Hereditary pondered far into the ring-lit night.

Some hundreds of years previously, this small but lofty room, with its circular floor plan and massive rafters overhead, supporting a conical roof, had been the personal domain of one of his predecessors among the ill-starred "First Wave" of Hanoverian conquerors to dominate Skye for a time. A seven-year-old Arran had discovered this splendid chamber abandoned, disposed of the insectoids, web-spinners, and three-winged eaves-dwelling night flyers, cleaned it out, and restored it to usefulness, with only a little help from the servants.

Whoever had occupied this room once upon a long-forgotten time—Arran had never been able to discover the person's name, nor any sort of writing at all—he had chosen as his personal talisman the image of an animal, now long extinct upon Skye, which humans had brought with them to this planet, to all appearances for riding upon. The animals had not prospered here, the last being dead long centuries before the Islays took up residence at the Holdings. Despite this, it was familiar, the same beast to be found between the Minister and the Starship on a chessboard. He didn't think it was called a Knight—that was the human being who had ridden it—but something else he couldn't remember.

In any case, many of the personal items he'd found here (or stored in one particular spot in the cellars)—or their remnants—were adorned with the animal's likeness, including the self-heating lidded cup from which he drank the steaming orange-grass and blackherb tea he'd brought with him here this evening.

Blackherb was known upon Skye as "chocleaf." He sipped the bittersweet concoction.

Outside one of the room's several arch-topped windows, ordinarily sealed with many-paned beveled glass, but propped wide open upon this unusually warm summer evening, a falling object illuminated the nighttime sky. This was far from an unusual sight upon a world whose single moon—within historic times, as the old story had it—had been shattered and transformed into a brilliant ring about the planet. Legend held that it had been an accidental act of war, during Skye's initial Hanoverian conquest. Whatever the truth of that might be, fragments of the broken satellite still plummeted many times a minute into the dense atmosphere of Skye. Had it not been covered with seas and trackless forest, no doubt many craters would have been visible from long centuries of bombardment.

He took another sip of his drink. For once, Arran was more than simply postponing sleep for as long as he could, with an eye toward avoiding the guilty, terrifying nightmares of events long past that sleeping brought to him all too often. That was merely a ritual that he had become accustomed to performing over the span of fifteen otherwise productive and satisfying years. Tonight, he thought, his habitual sleeplessness may yet prove to have served a more useful purpose.

He suspected that his beloved Loreanna lay as sleeplessly as he did, just now, in their bedchamber far below. For her, with her unblemished conscience and eternally cheerful disposition, this would be extremely uncharacteristic. Nevertheless, he thought, it was more than justified upon this extraordinary occasion. For a fleeting moment, he wished that he could go to Loreanna, or to call her here to his side. But, even within the warm embrace of his own family, he was a man, in many ways, of solitary habits—perhaps it was the very warmth of that embrace that made such habits tolerable—and he felt a need, at the moment, to be alone with his misgivings, for at least a while longer.

Another meteor streaked after the first and vanished, having consumed itself. He took another deep draft of his tea and struggled to organize his thoughts.

Both he and Loreanna had experienced considerable difficulty crediting everything that they had heard this afternoon. This, in spite of the liveried Hanoverian courier, his memorized summons, the posthypnotic conditioning, the officially sealed autothille from their old friend Lia, and, upon her behalf, the many nervous, *unofficial* assurances they had been offered in addition, once the appropriate cue words had breached the message-carrier's artificial forgetfulness.

Even if, in the end, Arran decided to comply with Lia's sudden "request," it would be some time before he could make good his arrival upon the capital world, so many parsecs away. At this particular juncture in galactic history (he could still remember his erstwhile tutor, Mistress Lia Woodgate herself, acquainting him with these facts), the speediest method of communication known to any of the imperia-conglomerate also happened to be the speediest method known of physical transportation. This method—so romantically beloved of nearly everyone, despite its many admitted faults—was the tachyon-sailed starship.

Indeed it was this basic scientific fact—a phenomenon sometimes known as "Anderson's Law" after the ancient philosopher who had first identified it somewhere in the nearly forgotten mists of history—which made shipborne brigandage, and everything that went with it, possible upon the face of the Deep.

Arran himself was well aware of certain alien civilizations in possession of vastly swifter methods of communication, his old allies the *nacyl* being a particularly unforgettable example. Had it not been for these methods, he and his old friend and first mate Phoebus Krumm would almost certainly have met a most unpleasant and untimely fate, in what they afterward referred to as their "Adventure of the Elementary Huatzin." And yet since Anderson's Law preserved his political independence, as well as the safety of the planet Skye, he had avoided telling anyone about them, save his own family. There were additional reasons that this was not a series of associations he wished to reevoke—although it was scarcely the fault of the *nacyl* (or the "flatsies," as they were often called elsewhere) that he could no longer even bear the sight of them.

He sipped his tea and shuddered.

Beyond the arched window, his gaze and attention were momentarily caught by a spectacular flurry of a dozen or more shooting stars, diverging slightly from one another as they fell toward a surface they would likely never reach. Within scant seconds, their brief passage could be heard as a kind of faraway thunder.

In any case, and for whatever reason, technological or political, within all known human cultures, the most urgent word—even from the august Ceo of the Monopolity of Hanover—took its own sweet time reaching out as far as moonringed Skye. And, whatever advanced medium it may have been recorded in to begin with, it mustneeds be delivered as in days of old, by voice or by hand.

Upon this occasion, the delivering voice and hand belonged to an official messenger from the most powerful individual in the Known Galaxy—lately a pampered passenger aboard the swiftest Monopolitan vessel available, orbiting at present between the Skyan moonring and the planet of that name which it encircled, half a world away from Arran's own personal starship. The advanced medium happened to be an autothille, a slender cylinder some eight siemmes in length and a third of a siemme in diameter. Technical progress within the Monopolity was slow, even in these times of exploration and initial contact, but, unlike earlier thilles requiring a separate playing mechanism, this new variety was capable of playing itself to whatever individual it was intended for.

Having finally delivered himself of the Ceo's memorized official message, the messenger had been authorized and instructed to beg Arran—"entirely off the record," it was to be understood—not to accept the peremptory language of her summons as anything other than the merest of formalities. An immediate outpouring of uproarious (and, Arran suspected when he gave the matter careful consideration afterward, rather intimidating) frontier laughter had prevented the poor citified fellow, once again, from finishing what he'd started out to say.

Arran sighed, taking yet another drink of tea and, quite unlike himself, wishing for a fleeting moment that it were something of a different, analgesic character. What barbaric ruffians he and all his family must have appeared to a stylish individual obviously never much beyond arm's reach of his perfume atomizer. Outside, he watched an unusually flat-traveling meteor parallel the ground. He could even see it from the next window before it vanished over the horizon.

When he was able to speak once again, the Ceo's nervous minion had unbent himself sufficiently to offer Arran even further assurances: somewhere along the way, the young Drector-Hereditary was grandly informed, they would be joined, provided they took a quick enough ship quickly enough, by Arran's old friend and onetime first officer, Captain Phoebus Krumm, who also had been ordered by the Ceo to present himself at the Monopolitan 'Droom. Otherwise, Krumm might have arrived at Hanover already, by the time Arran and his traveling party got there.

"Of course that's always assuming . . ." For the moment, Arran decided to ignore the ridiculous implication that he and his family would be expected to travel aboard the small, cramped courier ship—captained by some stranger—that this absurd fop had just arrived upon. Nor would Arran consider taking the fellow back to Hanover aboard his own ship, certainly not at such close quarters for that long a voyage. Instead, Arran went on teasing the terrified messenger: ". . . that the estimable Krumm has not already *cooked and eaten* his own message-deliverer first! Scarcely for nothing is he called 'Krumm the Baker'!"

The man had briefly looked to Loreanna for reassurance, and received none.

Now, Arran chuckled at the memory, wondering what ill

fate had befallen the highly touted dry sense of Hanoverian humor. (In this, he suspected, Lia had not been particularly beneficial in her influence upon her domain, for she had never displayed much of a taste for jesting.) Upon the other hand, as he appreciated all too well himself, there were limitations even to the charms of jocularity.

By now, he and Loreanna had "read" the autothille from Lia several times through.

"My dearest sister," it had begun, as messages from Lia often had in the past, *"you will wish from the beginning to share what I have to say with your husband, as it will concern him rather more than it likely does either of us."*

Well, that was a lie, Arran thought upon first hearing these words. There was *nothing* that did not concern the Ceo of the Monopolity of Hanover, and very close to nothing with which she was not known to concern herself, upon a personal basis, besides. Straightaway, Loreanna had recognized the chamber in which the message had been enthilled; she had briefly visited Ceo's Leupould's innermost sanctum, the velvet-lined chamber with all the globes—in a loving and heroic attempt to obtain clemency for that ship-robbing villain, Henry Martyn, who had kidnapped and ravished her—when Lia's father had ruled the Monopolity.

"It would appear," Lia's message had continued, *"that substantive and reliable information has at long last reached us, here within the Monopolity—precious information—of the nefarious Oplyte warrior-slave trade which, throughout recorded history, has by turns enriched and threatened so many of the imperia-conglomerate. And even more fantastic, my dear Loreanna, these unprecedented data have made themselves manifest here upon the capital world in the person of none other than your natural mother, Jennivere Daimler-Wilkinson."*

Far away, Arran felt rather than heard the dull booming of a celestial body that actually reached the surface of the planet. In another, somewhat drier season, a similar strike might readily have started a forest fire; such fires occurred upon moonringed Skye rather more often than those initiated by lightning storms. And yet Skye's original human inhabitants had prized such "starfalls" as sources of good metal, a commodity otherwise rare upon this world.

Arran pondered.

The once-beautiful and long-missing Jennivere Daimler-Wilkinson had been believed dead for decades by everyone within the Monopolity who had ever known or loved her. Death, in fact, was much to be preferred to many another fate her grieving friends and relatives might otherwise have envisioned for her. This, in a generation past that naturally seemed quite remote to the daughter who never knew her, although no doubt it felt like yesterday to Jennivere's contemporaries, such as her brother-in-law Sedgeley. But according to Lia—Arran had never known his former tutor to soften the blow unduly—Jennivere had returned to Hanover as a weird, ancient, unlovable hag. What was more, incredible as it appeared, the old woman had brought with her a grown bastard son.

"I am told he calls himself 'Woulf.' But this was not intended as the principal burden of this message. Upon the contrary, it is an attempt to convey to Arran, in the most personal of terms, how anxious I am to confer with him and with his colleague of old, Phoebus Krumm, face-to-face. You will appreciate, I am certain, that I welcome this opportunity to see you, too, once again, while in many ways regretting the circumstances that have made it necessary."

In this, despite the exigencies of interstellar politics, Arran believed his former tutor, for no one knew better than himself how well and for how long she had loved the family Islay, of which she rightly and deservedly considered herself a member in good standing: not a whit less than all of them loved her.

"Arran, you and Captain Krumm will know more," she had attested with all the appeal she could bring to bear upon the subject, *"of the vile and dreaded Oplyte slave trade, than anyone else I am aware of within the Monopolity of Hanover."*

Arran laughed to himself: with this casual, innocent-sounding phrase of hers, "within the Monopolity of Hanover," Lia was once again reasserting the imperium-conglomerate's claim to moonringed Skye. He knew her better than to believe she misunderstood what she was saying. It was (for the most part) a humorous gambit in an innocent (for the most part) game they had played for years.

Lia's message played through for the hundredth time and began to repeat itself for the hundred first. He twisted the knurled end of the device to silence it, then arose for a moment to peer out the window. Was that a glow he saw upon the horizon? Had that latest meteor strike started a fire, after all?

"An innocent game," he repeated the thought to himself, aloud. Yet he, too, understood how the usages of power may affect the best of friends and the best of friendships. Someday, under different circumstances, it could all, of a sudden, cease to be a joke. This was but one of many reasons he refused any title grander than Autonomous Drector-Hereditary. Presently he would manage, somewhere within his casual reply to Lia, to reassert Skyan sovereignty on the theory that rights left unasserted are inclined to atrophy much like unused muscles.

"An innocent game."

Moreover, it had occurred to him long ago, a duly vigorous reassertion of his rights might well preclude a future need to defend them by force. Perhaps this was all that his former teacher had in mind—although he rather doubted it. Not even his eldest brother, who had married her, more or less, had quite appreciated the subtle complexities of her intelligence in the same way Arran had come to do: she seldom had only one thing in mind. Poor Robret had been deprived of an opportunity to appreciate her fully by his untimely, wrongful death—for which more than just the guilty had been eventually compelled to pay.

Meanwhile, the Ceo was correct in at least one of several observations. Arran "the" Islay and Phoebus Krumm were, of an unquestionable certainty, capable of finding out more about the Oplyte Trade than anybody else, *"by methods best known,"* Lia had enunciated carefully, *"to the infamous Henry Martyn."*

Arran laughed all over again, wondering what his old friend Phoebus must be thinking of at this particular moment. Better than anybody, Phoebus knew—or so Arran believed—the unglamorous, unromanticized truth about Henry Martyn. Better than anybody, Phoebus was aware— or so Arran believed—how fifteen years ago, Arran had been nothing more than a small, frightened boy without options, who had only done what he had been compelled by circumstances to do. Better than anybody, Phoebus understood—or so Arran believed—how he had merely been pushed along by historic events larger and more powerful than he was.

By now, the glow upon the faraway horizon had faded and disappeared with the rising of Eigg, a brilliant sphere of granite that was one of the system's several uninhabited planets. It was this familiar light which Arran had taken for a distant fire. For a moment, he felt ashamed of himself, in the manner of someone who cannot recall a good friend's name. Then he shrugged and chuckled.

That any number of well-informed individuals—including Phoebus himself—would have differed violently with the younger man's unheroic assessment of the personalities and events of fifteen years ago was something he never allowed himself to consider. In his view (and in this, he was correct), Krumm knew too well the awful price that had been paid for Henry Martyn's renown. That there was more to the story was another thing that Arran never contemplated. For him, it went beyond mere belief: his victims' faces haunted his dreams every night.

The usages of power were invariable, in his own bitter experience, and invariably ran roughshod over the lives of "mere" individuals. And this was the best reason of all why Arran always refused to take up the reins of real power.

Still, the principal question concerned itself with Jennivere—rather, with the information she had brought with her. Would this recent unexpected "starfall" prove a lucky find of metal, or result in a tragic, all-consuming blaze?

CHAPTER XI:
MEMORIES OF WAR

A shadow crossed her face.

"Darling, 'tis quite true, and you cannot deny it."

Entirely unperturbed, as a curious three-winged predatory flyer hovered scant siemmes from her eyes—its flight-
feathers spread to catch a morning thermal, its long, curved,
cruel talons distinctly visible—Loreanna poured them each
a second cup of breakfast stimulant, adding shrub-milk and
lemon herb.

"For the task Lia requests you to undertake, your qualifi-
cations are manifestly greater than those of any other man.
This is true of Phoebus, as well."

"It would more appropriate, I fear me," he raised his eyebrows, watching the graceful movements of his wife's clever
hands and slender wrists with the unconscious appreciation
of a long and happily married man, "to call it a *quest.*"

The extraordinary room they occupied at present had
once been a skylight window, set in a lofty and steeply
pitched roof of the Holdings. Even now, Loreanna's features, fair and flawless unless one were to quarrel over the
many freckles which scattered themselves charmingly
across her cheeks and upturned nose, were protected from
the raptoroid's claws, as were her large and long-lashed
golden-flecked eyes, by a great sheet of the same transparent substance from which the viewing ports of starship lub-
berlifts were ordinarily fashioned.

"Call it whatever you desire, my dear," Loreanna replied
to her husband, observing him with a certain wifely appreciation of her own of which—like most happily married
women—she was more consciously aware. "Both of you are

extremely decent individuals, to that I am well able to attest personally. As your wartime deeds and subsequent actions clearly demonstrate, both of you are highly skilled and well practiced at all feats of arms and ship-handling. Both of you are combat-hardened, yet you are uncommonly kindly and remain of an adventurous turn of personality. Both of you are most intelligent and have somehow managed to remain as curious as youths about the universe all round you."

"I thank you more than I can say, my dear." Arran accepted his cup along with the compliment, deriving satisfaction, as he always did, that everything within it— shrub-milk, lemon herb, even to the stimulant leaves themselves —had been harvested here at the Islay family Holdings. He was by no means the farmer his eldest brother had been, nor would he ever be, yet the two had certain attributes in common, one of them being a prudent desire for self-sufficiency. "Of course you possess no personal prejudices in the matter, at all."

Arran's loving indulgence of one of Loreanna's rare whimsical wishes had transformed the simple opening in the Holdings' roof into something altogether remarkable: a room half-embedded in the broad, slate-tiled expanse, lending it the second highest point of view in the whole monumental edifice. In shape it was no more than a pair of cubes four measures in extent, fused side by side: a sunny chamber fashioned wholly out of transparent surfaces, excluding not even the floor upon which they now stood—rather, upon which stood the elaborately embellished, whitewashed wrought-iron chairs in which they were seated at their elaborately embellished, whitewashed wrought-iron breakfast table.

Loreanna affected an expression of tolerant exasperation which he knew to be counterfeit. "If I had any personal prejudices in the matter, my dearest, t'would be to disqualify you, rather than see you triskelling off again into danger."

" 'Triskelling off, is it?" He weighed the turn of phrase. Despite her falsely sour expression, the tone of her voice was light and bantering. Nevertheless, having lived some fif-

teen years with the woman, having sired six children upon
her, he knew better than to accept anything she had to say
upon this topic at its immediate surface value. Loreanna
meant what she had said.

Watching her lovely mouth, her moist, full lips, her even
white teeth and clever tongue move, as he often did with so
much interest, he remembered: it had never occurred to
Loreanna—not until the first time she had climbed the elaborately embellished, whitewashed wrought-iron spiral staircase which led to this special, sunlit breakfast room of
hers—that it was not the sort of environment in which to
affect what she understood to be the current feminine attire
within the Monopolity. She had discovered this fact, somewhat to her chagrin, when Arran had remarked—albeit in an
entirely approving manner—upon the color of her under-
most petticoat. Since she would not give up the novelty of
her transparent floor, what she had originally intended as a
formal morning chamber therefore became the location for
considerably more intimate and informal meals, during
which somewhat less revealing clothing was to be worn.

This morning it was a most fetching pair of kefflar
trousers of the style customarily issued to common hands
aboard the warships of the various imperia-conglomerate.
Loreanna's chagrin had been mollified by her taste for wearing men's clothing—which she liked chiefly for the freedom
of movement it engendered, and which, like many another
woman of strong character, she seized upon every possible
excuse to indulge. He smiled inwardly, reflecting upon their
experiences together over the past decade and a half. For
some reason, what Loreanna had decided to call "The
Adventure of the Komanian Monorail" came to mind this
morning, perhaps because of what had transpired afterward.
If he recalled correctly, that was when their second eldest
child had been conceived.

Even now, he could contemplate the moment with considerable satisfaction. Still, a part of him had been listening
to her all along—a skill particular to married men—and following her line of thought perfectly. "I do believe that I know

you better than that, my dear, speaking of 'an adventurous turn of personality' and 'as curious as a youth.' I think me that the gravest danger would lie in attempting to keep you out of it, were I foolish enough to essay it."

They laughed, Arran's laughter being shut off a trifle prematurely by a yawn. Although it was not the first such sleepless episode in his life, his present view was jaundiced to a slight degree by the seemingly endless night he had spent alone in the ring-lit tower room. Moment by moment, he had to struggle a bit to keep from being cross with her for no reason she was guilty of.

"Triskelling off." Arran shrugged now, and shook his head. "Be that as it may, what it actually amounts to, I'm afraid—this laundry list of highly dubious qualities which you impute to me and Phoebus—is next to nothing." He sipped at his cup and smiled pleasantly as a young servant girl appeared at the head of the spiral staircase, bearing the main portion of their breakfast upon a polished steel tray. Arran remembered clearly when her father had been that young, a fieldhand who had stepped upon the sharp and poisonous tail of a glass lizard and still limped upon that foot to this very day, lucky to be alive.

"Thank you, Evvie; that will be all, I think," Loreanna told the girl, who curtsied and returned downstairs. Loreanna turned to her husband. "How so?"

Choosing the cup-mounted, soft-boiled egg of a common domesticated Skyan waterfowl—the heart-shaped delicacy was the size of both his fists clenched together—along with several slices of shrub-buttered toast, Arran glanced up at his wife, who was busying herself replenishing his cup. "Well, to begin with, my dear, let us consider the case of our good friend and trusted comrade Phoebus Krumm, who at the time of his boyhood—according to the man's own telling of the affair—was nothing more than a humble and ignorant baker's apprentice."

" 'Nothing more'?" Loreanna had taken an egg and toast of her own off the tray and was pouring herself another cup of stimulant. "That scarcely sounds like Phoebus—or you, my dear, for that matter. Does the galaxy not require bakers' apprentices just as badly as it requires ships' captains and Drectors-Hereditary?"

Arran was about to deliver a retort, when he noticed the mischief in her eye.

She paused, grinning. "I know the story well."

"So you do." Arran laughed.

For years the mighty Krumm, along with his plump wives Tula and Tillie, had been a frequent and very welcome guest at the Holdings-upon-Skye. Arran's old first officer had never been averse to recounting his manifold and varied experiences of life to the invariable delight of the Islay children, who by now knew each of his stories by heart, and could recite them with him, word for word.

"So do we all, my dear, right down to your three-year-old namesake. So there he was, me hearties, our young worthy Krumm, commendably at work already in the cool, quiet twilight hours before dawn, innocently mixing and kneading and baking away—when along came that rare planetary 'recruiting' raid which the Oplyte slavers were carrying out upon the densely settled surface of his homeworld.

"And a very foolish raid it proved to be," Loreanna nodded solemnly and tried her best to imitate their friend's distinctive voice, "in which Phoebus narrowly escaped becoming a mindless warrior-slave himself, by the grace alone of an enormous, razor-sharp oven implement referred to as a 'peel,' with which he beheaded no fewer than thirteen—a literal 'baker's dozen'—of their evil number."

Arran guffawed. "You tell the story remarkably well, my dear—and so much more succinctly than Phoebus has ever managed to do. Nonetheless, he was only my first example. Let us move on to consider the case of my own late father—"

"The celebrated war hero, Robret Islay."

Arran understood his wife and knew that she meant this literally, without the slightest hint of sarcasm or disrespect. She had never known the man, but was closely acquainted with hundreds upon Skye who had. To the common people of the planet, who could be somewhat naive with regard to the intricacies of interstellar cartography and politics, Robret had begun as nothing more than another of a long series of Hanoverian conquerors. That the man had somehow won the heart of the rebel woodsrunners' most famous beauty nevertheless, had been sufficient to make him a legend in his own time. That he had, in the end, willingly sacrificed his own life for the sake of a light-handed and intelligent governance of this world had transformed him into its most beloved hero.

"The same," Arran answered, "whose alacrity and valor during an otherwise obscure war earned for him—and his family—the hereditary Drectorship of our beloved moonringed planet Skye. No more than a humble, noncommissioned conscript, with aristocratic officers dead and dying all round him, he seized the battlefield command of an entire regiment of Oplyte warriors and won the day."

Loreanna nodded, understanding. One of the aristocratic officers Robret had saved that day had become, by turns, his best friend, then, as the Black Usurper, the betrayer of his life. This story, too, was one that she knew well.

Arran continued. "And yet, alas, entirely unlike the title he bequeathed to me, whatever my father's knowledge was, of the bizarre creatures we know as Oplytes, it was by no means hereditary. Alas, too, like a great many 'citizen soldiers' of his day, he had not been much enamored of fighting when he was in the thick of it—in fact, he had despised it as thoroughly as it is possible to do, wishing only that it would end—and cared even less to speak of his wartime experience after he had survived it. Also, I believe that he greatly feared recounting it might encourage his three sons to follow the drums of war themselves, or, at the very least, be perceived as unseemly boasting upon his part."

Loreanna observed her husband closely as, with an apparent frown lowering his brow, he peeled the shell from his egg and began to eat it with the toast. "Your father, my darling, was a man of peace. You speak, somehow, as if you disapprove."

A rueful Arran reflected upon her words: "Not at all. For

one thing, he could acquit himself remarkably well in combat, if he saw the need for it, as he proved upon more than one occasion. 'Each to his own' is the proper order of things. My father simply happened to have been endowed with a different range of interests and aptitudes than I. For one thing, he actually *liked* farming."

Loreanna grinned. She knew her husband. Arran liked to watch *others* farming.

He went on. "It was, apparently, by the merest of chances that I happen to be well suited to combat and excel at it. I began with no greater choice in the matter than my father had. But for the most part—and upon the most honest of self-examination—I confess that I rather enjoy it. As you know, I have trained each of my children to fight in turn, and I am by no means ever reluctant to discourse upon the subject at length and detail with the proper individual."

She nodded. "You taught me to fight."

"Upon the contrary, Loreanna my love, I only taught you the way to fight more *efficiently*. When I first laid eyes upon you, you already possessed the rarest and most requisite quality of fighting, a game willingness. For my own part, I think me that I have *missed* a good fight in a righteous cause and might well benefit from a return to the rigors and discipline of shipboard life."

"What?" In truth, it came as no surprise to her. She had been expecting something like this for several weeks. She turned now, so as to display her figure—in flattering profile. "And leave all the comforts of home behind?"

With a dramatically lecherous flamboyance, he laid a hand upon her thigh. "Upon the contrary, medear. Like many another intelligent ship's master, I should contrive to take all the comforts of home with me!" His expression suddenly grew serious. "And yet now we must force ourselves, no matter how delightful our present ruminations, to return to the original subject of our conversation."

"Which was what? I quite forgot, the moment you placed your hand upon my thigh."

He cleared his throat, not daring to reply to her remark,

out of fear of further digression. "Which was that, if anything, what old Phoebus managed to achieve was to *avoid*
learning as much as he might have about Oplytes. And while
it is true that Oplyte warrior-slaves were once used in mod-
erate numbers here upon Skye, with one notable exception—when I killed an Oplyte myself by thrusting it in its
eye with that ancient cartridge pistol of yours—mostly what
I managed to be was *elsewhere* during that unfortunate
period of time."

This had been during the short-lived but terrible occupation of Skye by the old Ceo's vile surrogate, Tarbert Morven.
Even after all these years, Arran shuddered as he thought
about the man—who had once been his father's best
friend—remembered afterward in Skyan song and story as
the Black Usurper.

"A wise choice it was." Loreanna had seen the cloud passing momentarily across her husband's visage. She had not
corrected him when he had claimed never to be reluctant to
discuss his war experiences. No one knew better than she of
the menacing void his storytelling to the children left
unbridged. He was coming uncommonly close to speaking
with satisfaction of achievements that his memory of the
deaths of four hundred innocent individuals tarnished so
badly. This couldn't last, she knew, although she hoped it
would. "Besides, you were busy at the time, as I remember,
raiding planets, robbing ships, kidnaping and ravishing me,
and generally becoming known to the galaxy as the infamous Henry Martyn."

He blushed. "Girl, you are the absolute death of any dignity to which I aspire."

"Pray, Arran Islay, when did you begin aspiring to anything resembling dignity?"

"Ah, madame, again ye've sighted in upon the only
imperfection in me argument."

For a while they sat steeped in a warm, comfortable
silence, enjoying the uncharacteristically brilliant Skyan
morning and each other's welcome and familiar presence.
For her part, she was happy to have diverted their morning

conversation from a topic that might have spoiled it, and the morning with it. Meanwhile, Arran never ceased to be astonished at how much he loved the woman sitting across from him, or at the astonishing fact that she loved him, as well.

Some individuals in a state of acceptable mental and spiritual health (he often told himself with what he hoped was an objective comprehension) actually enjoyed combat. And yet, for the sake of civilization itself, he understood that it was vital to avoid one temptation almost invariably associated with war. As a ship's captain, this truth was underlined for him by the fact that even the most technologized warfare usually turns out to be a labor-intensive undertaking.

Such "individuals in a state of acceptable mental and spiritual health" must at all costs be prevented from involving *involuntary* others in their struggles. He himself would never conscript or press-gang another person as long as he lived—and he would willingly kill to prevent anybody else from doing it.

"At any rate," he told Loreanna, returning to the original topic, "in the end, the notorious villain who blighted our lovely world with the presence of Oplytes (not to mention his own) died at the bloody hands of his own warriors, along with his evil, incestuous, and inhumanly beautiful daughter, Alysabeth." Like his own middle brother Donol, Arran had long suspected, that traitorous wretch of vile reputation. He had a long-standing wager with himself that this was due— and well justified—to the many unspeakable mortal outrages Donol had inflicted upon Mistress Lia Woodgate during her captivity here, although she always declined to discuss the matter with him, as who would not in her place?

"Your point, sir?"

"Merely a question: how familiar does one have to be with Oplytes to understand them? Certainly more familiar than either Phoebus or I can claim to be. And whatever understanding Morven had did him but little good in the end."

He shook his head as if to clear it, recognizing by the gesture that he would require a nap later that day. Momentarily forgetting his sleepless night, the idea of requiring an afternoon nap suddenly made him feel rather old.

"But I am remiss, my dear. Lia had another reason for having sent this urgent message of hers from the 'Droom to Skye, and we have scarcely discussed it."

CHAPTER XII:
RUMINATIONS UNDER GLASS

Their breakfast dishes had long since been cleared and a final cup of stimulant infusion consumed, but the Islay family conference was far from concluded.

Spread before him upon the transparent top of the table at which they sat lay Arran's favorite pair of thrustibles—rather the parts of which they had been constructed. Unlike the highly antiquated internal-combustion device—a love-gift from her husband—upon which Loreanna was accustomed to relying for self-protection, Arran's weapons, almost a millennium more recent in their design and manufacture, contained not one moving part, depending, as they did, upon the subtle interplay of the principles of §-physics. Nevertheless, they did acquire dust and grease from their environment which could severely impair their deadly function, and it was this that their owner was in the midst of removing.

He had offered to clean her pistol, as well, the ancient *walther modell pp twentytwo* he had restored as a boyhood project and intended as a present, ironically enough, for Lia, upon her wedding to his brother, Robret. However, history, as it will, had had its own way with his intentions. The wedding had been interrupted by the Black Usurpation and Arran had taken the little pistol with him—having killed with it an Oplyte who had seized him—when he and his two brothers had made good their escape. In the end, he had given it to Loreanna; with it, she had saved their lives and liberty upon more than one occasion.

Loreanna sniffed at what she maintained was a double insult: that her weapon was not preserved at all times in an immaculately perfect state; and that she was incapable of preserving it in that state, by herself. The truth, she knew perfectly well, was that Arran's weapons were always well maintained as well. It was just that their moment for talking was all but over, and the time for forward motion of some kind was nearly upon them. This last-minute tidiness was simply his way of conveying those truths to her, as well as to himself.

Arran, upon his part, was thinking that if there happened to be a limit to how many times an autothille could be used, they would discover it within the next few times this particular specimen was replayed. His thoughts, he believed, should be upon the ordinary business of the Holdings this morning, especially if he were to be called away upon the Ceo's service. Yet he stayed beside his wife, comforting her, and attempting to decide what was best to be done.

"The Ceo Lia's dear friend Loreanna Islay," the official portion of the autoenthilled message continued as they watched it once again together, *"will certainly wish to be advised and informed that her long-lost mother, the Lady Jennivere Daimler-Wilkinson, has recently come forth and identified herself. It is likewise presumed that Loreanna will also be interested to learn that she has an unexpected, fully grown half brother, known only by the name of 'Woulf.' "*

The grip that Loreanna took upon her husband's hand—interrupting his unnecessary busywork—was not a whit less forceful than the first time they had let this autothille play its message. Arran knew well that the loss of his wife's mother at an early age had indelibly marked her life, although she had gracefully risen above whatever spiritual damage it might have done to any individual who customarily exhibited less moral character than she.

"I appreciate the compliment you pay me, darling," Loreanna replied once her husband had spoken this thought, "And yet, even if it is true—however commendable it may be—it does not help me feel the loss any less, I greatly fear."

He nodded his understanding, having lost his own mother at an early age and suffered accordingly. "And to be precipitously informed of a sibling, when one has grown up as an only child, must surely be one of life's greater surprises."

"In truth, it scarcely feels real to me. Why should it? I know nothing more at the moment than the naked fact of it and—speak of surprises—have not quite absorbed the news that my mother lives." She turned to embrace her husband, sighing (not in an unhappy way) into his shoulder. "Yet life itself—as anyone with more than half of an occasion to associate with the Islay family quickly discovers—seems often to consist of nothing *but* surprises! I say, does not that interociter coil, there, belong in your other thrustible, dearest?"

Arran laughed. "My darling, you are far from the first to stumble upon this singular phenomenon—I mean with regard to those who associate with my family. You know that, as a younger woman, originally hired merely as the family tutor, Mistress Lia Woodgate was at one time happily affianced to my eldest brother, Robret *fils*. This, of course, was long before she was unexpectedly named by her father, Leupould IX of notorious memory, to succeed him—"

Loreanna nodded. "His still-mysterious abdication having been equally unexpected . . ."

"—as the mightiest ruler in the Known Universe, Ceo of the Monopolity of Hanover. From the outset, the relationship between Lia and Robret appeared to everyone to be serious, and passionate into the bargain, at least upon her part."

It was still not known, and never could be now, whether Lia had actually been selected with an eye, at least in part, to her suitability as a wife for Robret, one of the individuals who might have contrived to such an arrangement being dead these fifteen years, and the other having undertaken a vow of perpetual silence.

"True, Robret always seemed a trifle more reserved than she with regard to their relationship, but this was attributed not to any manner of disregard for Lia—at least so I always believed—but to my brother's fundamentally conservative personality, and to the careful and deliberate manner in which he had been brought up, presumably someday to assume his own father's solemn obligations."

Arran had no need to tell his wife that, for his own part—that of an eight-year-old child who had virtually worshiped her—Lia had embodied the very definition of feminine pulchritude and exotic glamor. The boy had never really known his mother; Loreanna understood, wisely, and without resentment, that it was by no accident that she herself bore something of a resemblance—perhaps more in manner than in appearance—to Lia. She also knew that even now he was compelled to struggle not to be overwhelmed by life-long feelings of unconditional filial adoration for his erstwhile tutor—now in some ways his competitor—feelings that could undermine the hard-won autonomy of his Drectorship.

"In any case," he went on telling Loreanna now, "the growing emotional and intellectual understanding between Lia and my brother inevitably ripened into romantic love and eventually got as far as the most spectacular wedding that the Great Holdings Hall upon Skye-under-the-Moonrings had ever witnessed. I had been rather seriously ill, and had missed my father's remarriage to his best friend's daughter, Alysabeth Morven. (How ill considered *that* turned out to be!) For me, this would be the occasion to make up for my previous absence.

"It was, furthermore, a wedding to which hundreds of native Skyans had been asked, along with dozens of decidedly more aristocratic, but no more warmly welcomed, interstellar guests, principally of Hanover and Shandish. It was a wedding that, in the end, was to be violently interrupted in a dramatic and premeditated—many termed it, afterward, 'theatrical'—manner, by the first blow of a coup d'état engineered by that Shandeen traitor, Tarbert Morven."

"Father," Loreanna had heard the story often, "of your father's bride, Alyşabeth."

"None other. Oplyte warriors who had been brought, ostensibly to salute the newlywed couple, were used instead in an only partly successful attempt to arrest the members of my family and our household. My dear old friend and retainer Henry Martyn perished, protecting me from the Oplytes, which is why I assumed his name in order to exact revenge for all of us. With his brothers Donol and me, Robret accomplished the unforeseen, escaping into years of bitter exile as a woodsrunner, where, hopelessly separated from Lia, who was afterward held hostage at the Holdings, he eventually took a mistress—the beautiful and spirited Fionaleigh Savage—and perished fighting the Morvens' tyranny."

"For his own part," Loreanna smiled, taking her husband's other hand, as well, "Arran stowed away aboard a starship, hoping to reach Hanover to appeal for assistance from his father's political friends. At that time, of course, he had had no way of knowing that his father no longer *had* political friends upon the capital world, or that he himself would never reach Hanover. Instead, after many a hair-raising adventure aboard any number of different vessels, he would go on to secure everlasting glory as the beloved world-liberator Henry Martyn."

"And eventually to discover Loreanna, the one love of his life." They kissed, and in that moment understood that, however long they sat conversing here, they would not be attending to their various domestic chores upon this morning. The only consideration that kept their hands from one another's clothing now was that they still occupied a room with transparent walls and floor.

He sat back and cleared his throat, flushed and sweating, conspicuously keeping his eyes from the open throat of Loreanna's blouse as she attempted to regain her own composure. To occupy his shaking hands, he began to reassemble his pair of thrustibles once again as he continued speaking of his family's history.

"Meanwhile," he said, "by what was understood by us, his brothers, merely to be a strategic arrangement, Donol formally surrendered himself to Morven, who was becoming known across the breadth of an unwilling world as 'The Black Usurper.'

"This docile compliance upon Donol's part was supposed to have been in response to the Shandeen villain's broadcast promises of amnesty and perhaps even a share of power under the Skyan moonrings. My poor father having been murdered, Donol was led to understand that he might someday possess Morven's daughter Alysabeth and, in the throes of his abject moral collapse, he even accepted this incestuous offer. Instead, it was Lia who was given to him, ostensibly as an initial token of good faith, but in fact as a mere diversion—we never knew how much he had always secretly envied and resented Robret—to serve as his sexual plaything, as an initial reward for his treacherous collaboration.

"All the while, his visible approval of Morven was used to legitimize the Usurpation."

In the time he had with her, an increasingly dissolute Donol had made the most energetic use conceivable of his ill-won prize. Arran and Loreanna knew that Lia still bore profound physical and emotional scars from her endlessly humiliating captivity and brutal maltreatment. Ironically, or so she had once confessed to Loreanna, there was but little which the depraved middle brother had inflicted upon her that she might not willingly have endured at the hand of the eldest, the issue being what it always is in such cases, one of loving consent.

The Islays had always assumed that these soul-shattering experiences, the tragic murder of her intended and her hideous abuse by his younger brother, were the reason that Lia—often misrepresented by mass media as the "Virgin Ceo"—had never married or shown even the slightest inclination to do so. And yet, Arran knew (although it had taken him a long time, tremendous effort, and no small amount of money to discover the truth) she carried within her the grisly satisfaction of having castrated Donol with a makeshift knife she had fashioned for herself, and dangled the results of this long-planned vengeance before his horrified and all but unbelieving eyes. Then, possessing secret means of commanding them, she had given him over, still living, to the first squad of Oplyte slave-warriors she had happened upon, to be raped, killed, and eaten.

Not necessarily in that order.

Lia had disappeared for three years, immediately following the Battle of Skye. It was even now a period in her life of which, save for one rare moment of openness with Loreanna, she refused to speak with anyone. She had come forth again, only with the greatest of reluctance, when public announcements had been carried from world to world and broadcast far and wide to the effect that her father, Ceo Leupould IX, prayed urgently to see her. Accompanying the proclamation was a deceitful implication that the poor fellow lay upon his deathbed. When he had greeted her in a condition of perfect—and libidinous—good health, she had angrily remonstrated with him, and he had laughed uproariously.

Later, and in secure privacy, she had laughed at her father's joke, herself.

Thus it had come to pass that a certain Lia Woodgate Wheeler, lately Ceo of the Monopolity of Hanover, and an Autonomous Drector's Lady, one Loreanna Daimler-Wilkinson Islay, late of the Hanoverian capital planet herself, having first been swept together by an implacable and undeniable current of titanic historical events, violent tragedies and triumphs, and most of all by the love of strong-willed and heroic men larger than life itself, had—for those and many another reason—chosen to keep up a voluminous and lively personal correspondence between the Monopolitan 'Droom and moonringed Skye all these years.

The encrypted section of Lia's message was less restrained. She lounged beside a pool, not in swimming costume—that would have been too much—but in comfortable working trousers not unlike those that Loreanna affected, and a blouse printed in a cheerful floral pattern, tied at the midriff. Either it had been an unusually beautiful day upon Hanover or—as Loreanna believed more likely—the area where the Ceo relaxed was covered with a dome or §-field, simulating weather which almost never occurred upon the gloomy capital world.

"I am extremely happy for you, dear Loreanna," the most powerful ruler in the Known Universe told the device focused upon her. She clasped her hands before her as if to show the sheer joy she was feeling. *"I wish to greet you here as soon as can be contrived. The fact that I may have been an agent, in some small way, of this unlooked-for reunion with your family, fills me with satisfaction."*

Lia went on to speak of other matters, including accommodations she might arrange for them upon their arrival. The woman was almost chattering, which was uncharacteristic of her. It was not the best performance she had ever given, Arran thought—and told his wife as much—which probably meant that it was genuine.

"Once again, however, I must force myself to ignore the obvious with Lia and to read between the lines. In all things, whether she relishes it or not—indeed whether she chooses to acknowledge it to herself or not—she must remain her father's daughter. And no one with that much power can be trusted wholeheartedly."

Loreanna nodded, for she had long since come to similar conclusions. All that to one side, it seemed easier to remain friends with Lia at this distance than to contemplate, as Lia now seemed to desire, becoming a houseguest in Lia's home, in Lia's city, upon Lia's planet, within the boundaries of Lia's empire.

"In this connection," Arran calculated, "she enjoys a singular advantage of having been my tutor as well as my brother's 'unwed wife' of Skyan song and legend. And it would be altogether unlike her not to avail herself fully of it. Except for you, my dearest, she appreciates better than anyone how deeply I loathe the Oplyte Trade, and that I would be willing—belay that, eager—to aid her in destroying it, root and branch. After all, was it not she who gave nurture to this strong natural inclination upon my part to detest all slavery?"

He sighed with amused resignation. "I fear that my instructress knows me all too well—and knows that I know it, and enjoys the fact extravagantly! And she knows that I know *that,* as well! Ceo blind me, where will it all end?"

Loreanna opened her mouth, but had no chance to reply.

"In the end—precisely *despite* all her assurances and the personal cajolery to which we have been subjected—she knew I would decide to go to Hanover!"

Loreanna dimpled. "And you knew that she knew that you knew that she knew?"

He threw up his hands in a gesture of helplessness. "Well, if nothing else, it has been far too long since my old friend Phoebus and I shared an adventure!"

Loreanna laughed, seizing his hand again. Adventure with Phoebus it was to be. But there was their strong-willed, high-spirited eldest, fifteen-year-old Robretta, to consider, as well, and although Arran himself was unaware of it, Loreanna understood that the girl would soon be uppermost in his mind. He had long believed her quite as sorely in need of an adventure as himself. However, at this juncture, he preferred to choose it for her—and in this his wife agreed—before she ventured out and found it for herself. Loreanna judged her husband an excellent and observant father—although this was something else he was unaware of, believing all men to possess virtues which in truth are rare. Arran knew his daughter better than she would understand until she had children of her own, "in thirty or forty years," he often said, only half-jokingly.

Robretta had been named to honor her grandfather and uncle (her father's elder brother) neither of whom she had had a chance to know. Both had fought and died horribly in the struggle which had brought her into being. She had, since the moment of her birth, been known to her adoring father simply as "Bretta."

Having been that young himself (for what had seemed no

less than ten thousand years) Arran appreciated tolerantly
that, at this particular time in her life, Bretta preferred not to
think of herself as the eldest—and presumably, most responsible—child of Arran and Loreanna Islay. It was not that she
failed to love them both—upon the contrary—it was simply
that they were too excruciatingly boring for words. For after
all, had he not had a moment or two exactly like this—
perhaps even several million of them—in his own youth?

As he snapped the two remaining parts together, Loreanna knew that he had come to a decision. He would bring
his family with him to Hanover as Lia had implicitly
demanded. And, although the Ceo would doubtless disapprove (Loreanna believed that Arran suspected that Lia
wished to acquire hostages to guarantee his tractability), to
wherever else this desperate business took him.

Bretta would be given opportunity to see what her boring
old dad was made of.

And maybe her mother.

And she herself, perhaps, as well.

CHAPTER XIII:
OF PARENTS AND CHILDREN

THWACK!

In the comparative silence of the great forest all about her,
the report—her quarrel had struck hardwood no more than a
finger's width from where she had aligned her sights—came
echoing back in a way she found more than satisfying.

Far away, deeper in the forest, a feathered insectivore
heard the noise as a challenge and, answering the affront,
dashed his beak against another tree.

Robretta Islay lowered the front end of the crossbow she
had fashioned two years previously with her own two hands,

to the moss-covered ground before her. She placed a small, well-formed foot through its stirrup, leaned over, and seizing the stranded steel string in both fists, drew it back until it locked into the nut.

The task required all of her strength. Even now, she might have used a compound lever or a crank to do the job, but in her view, that would just have added one more component to go wrong. And although it might have come as a surprise to many who falsely believed they knew her well, Bretta valued rugged simplicity and reliability above all other qualities in weapons—as in other things.

Without setting her cocked weapon aside, she swirled the pointed end of the next projectile in a small gray crock she'd brought with her—everything required for this task having been laid out neatly upon a kind of soft yellow leather kerchief her father called a "shammy," which she had spread upon the ground before her—before setting the quarrel carefully within the grooved barrel of the crossbow and sliding it back to the nut, into contact with the string.

Again taking careful, well-practiced aim through the tiny aperture of the rear sight, past the simple post at the front end of the weapon, she squeezed the long trigger with all four fingers where it lay against the underside of the stock, until—*snap!*—it released the nut, releasing the string, permitting the stiff alloy limbs of the prod, or bow, to drag the unfletched quarrel and its precious microscopic load forward at a higher and higher velocity.

THWACK!

Once again the quarrel hit its target, a different tree this time. Once again, after nodding satisfaction to herself, she stooped over to recock her crossbow. At this rate, she thought, by the end of summer, there would be no one in this hemisphere of Skye to match her marksmanship. But, no matter how the work she did improved her aim, the strength of her back and arms, or the fine coordination between her eye and trigger hand, it was far more than idle target practice which had brought her to the rounded crest of a low hill this afternoon.

It was, although she did not know the expression, no less than *noblesse oblige.*

THWACK!

The physical strength that Bretta had to call upon was considerable for one of her age and gender. She was already taller than her mother, with long, smooth limbs and the slender beginnings of a woman's figure. Considering her age and the cadence of her growth thus far, she confidently anticipated being taller than her father in another couple of summers. By no means would this make any giantess of her. All of her relatives, it would appear—Shandeen, Hanoverian, and Skyan—were a trifle below galactic average stature. Nobody could tell her from what corner of the family she had received her comparative height.

There could be no similar question with regard to the color of her hair. Her mother Loreanna's was of a glossy, medium dark brown with striking auburn highlights—about the color of a well-aged copper token, burnished slightly along its edges and the higher features of the face. Her father Arran's was very fine and exactly the same color as a wind-rippled meadow of well-ripened grain.

Bretta's own hair color was an almost perfect blend of the two, a thick and brightly shining red-gold, hacked off, to a mother's despair, without any attempt at elegance, at her shoulders, which, like the bridge of her nose, had received a generous (and at the moment deeply resented) smattering of maternal freckles.

Bretta's mother, who, in what she considered proper company was inclined to affect sweeping floor-length gowns of pleated velvet (although she secretly preferred trousers), had long since given up on her daughter's choice of clothing. Today the girl wore a pair of frayed, faded work trousers fashioned of brushed kefflar washed too many times, in a shade of blue that had been traditional for far longer than a millennium. Bretta had chopped them off well above mid-thigh, and with even less ceremony than her hair.

Her suede vest, as she stooped low over her uncocked crossbow, gapped just sufficiently to offer a glimpse—had

there been anybody about to enjoy it, which there was not—
of a rounded fullness that was still more potential than actuality. The vest itself had been cut from the cured hide of an
animal of her own size that she had killed two winters earlier with this very weapon. The soft-soled slippers that laced
halfway up her ankles had been fashioned from the same
material. Each of the garments she presently wore had been
too large for her a year ago. They had fit her perfectly at
midwinter. Now they molded themselves to her body in a
manner local Skyan boys found impossibly distracting,
although if she had been aware of this—which she was
not—her immediate reaction would have been one of disbelieving scorn or embarrassed annoyance.

At her slender waist, swinging from the wide leather belt
which had been her first handcrafted project, hung the very
knife—its broad, spatulate, gleaming-edged blade exactly as
long as her strainfully outstretched hand from the tip of her
thumb across to that of her littlest finger—with which she
had, all by herself, flayed, field-dressed, and quartered the
antlered forest animal from the russet skin of which she had
fashioned her vest and slippers, sewing them with dried gut.
The knife, a gift from both of her parents, denoting passage
from babyhood, had been forged from the heart of a star-
fallen meteoroid, its generous handle crafted from a section
of the antlers of a beast identical to the one she had killed
virtually as her first act of young girlhood.

At an age when most children were struggling not to soil
their underwear, Bretta had learned that, in the forest (as
well as everywhere else), a good knife could make the difference between survival—even comfort—and an ugly
death. With her father's encouragement, she had disciplined
herself to care for her knife, and to groom it as carefully if it
were a well-beloved pet.

He had taught her all she knew of knives and other primitive weapons. Their use for fighting, in this age of kiner-
getic thrustibles, was an all but forgotten art which could
confer considerable advantage, if only of surprise. That he
had bothered to instruct her—in the use of thrustibles, as

well—spoke volumes, when "properly brought-up" females were supposed to be too fastidious and fragile to defend their own (Arran always added, "worthless") lives.

Ironically, one of these "primitive" weapons promised a material improvement in the hard lives of her woodsrunner neighbors. Among the commodities Skye exported to a galactic marketplace (others consisting principally of herbs of several types) were native fungoids of numerous kinds, some used for medicinal purposes, some for cooking, and some intended for a more exotic application, usually left undiscussed in genteel company consisting of more than a solitary gender.

The spores, suspended in a thick and sticky nutrient fluid in which she immersed the pointed tips of her quarrels, before launching them at selected trees in the surrounding forest, were those of giant "shelfshrooms," greatly prized everywhere they could be obtained, for their rich, meaty flavor and texture. The species could be counted upon to grow with astonishing rapidity, in a single season swelling to the width of her outstretched arms from fingertip to fingertip, jutting out from their arboreal host at least half that distance, and a tapering measure thick, without doing the tree visible harm. Harvested, dried, sliced thin, and sautéed, they could be substituted for smoked and salted meat and combined with leafy lettuce and ripe tomatoes, with no one the wiser except whoever had assembled the delicacy in the first place.

Long before the starship-raider Henry Martyn had made this rustic planet doubly celebrated, Skye had already been well-known in certain discriminating quarters for agricultural products such as these. The family of woodsrunners Bretta found herself assisting today had instructed her in all the secrets of the shroomer's craft. In return—and small recompense it was, she reckoned—she had invented this unique method of planting their spores for them. As the shrooms were inspected over the next several weeks and attended by the farmers, they would collect her corrosion-proof quarrels and return them to her.

More than anything, Bretta enjoyed this task because it took her away from the Holdings, away from four younger—and obnoxiously noisy—sisters, and afforded her time to think. It was a growing-up time that anyone her age, in any era, needed. Having once been fifteen himself, and having vowed to remember it well, Arran was correct in believing he understood the way his daughter Bretta thought. Nor, being who and what he was, was he inclined to resent what he had correctly deduced to be her principal line of reasoning these days.

After all, what could be duller than being the child of one's own parents?

It even failed to trouble her understanding father in the slightest that in the fondly imagined privacy of her own thoughts, she styled herself (in her mind, at present, fore-most) great-granddaughter to one Ianmichael Briartonson (locally pronounced "Bronson"), legendary Skyan woods-runner and outlaw chief, and, more importantly (at least to Bretta), granddaughter to the infamous old Ianmichael's martyred (and quite naturally, therefore—to any bright, fifteen-year-old human female—transcendently glamorous) daughter, Glynnaughfern Briartonson.

It was this beautiful "native" girl, of course, who by and by had become the wedded wife of Hanoverian war hero Robret "the" Islay, Bretta's paternal grandfather. By and by, she had also become the mother of Robret *fils* Islay, Donol Islay, and Arran Islay, in turn. It was a tragedy Bretta often reflected upon, that the pair of sons who might have recalled their mother best had been dead these past fifteen years. The first of them, Bretta knew, the younger Robret, had been but one of many victims of Tarbert Morven, the Black Usurper; the other, Donol of infamous reputation, had been the victim of his own evil treachery. Sadly, Glyn-naughfern's remaining living son was too young to remember her as more than the blurred memory of a face hovering above his cradle.

Moreover, given a history of dire times and desperate cir-cumstances upon moonringed Skye—not to mention the

mundane reality that the Briartonson family, however celebrated, had earned a meager living as humble woodcutters—
but few likenesses of Glynnaughfern were to be found.
Many, indeed, had known the young woman when yet she
lived, and to this day all remembered her well, enthusiastically regaling Bretta with tale after tale of her cleverness and
kindness. And yet—perhaps by this very process—the
bright and lovely peasant girl had, at the same time, somehow become an immortal, larger than life and legendary in
stature, and many more—who had never in truth cast eyes
upon her—now claimed nonetheless to have been among
her closest friends.

From time to time, Bretta's father had directed a considerable number of artists, both of the homegrown amateur
variety and professionals expensively imported from offplanet, to attempt drawings of his mother, based upon the
remembrances of older Skyans. It had become something of
a hobby with him, and the likenesses were now to be discovered in virtually every chamber of the Holdings. They
had also been combined, by some variety of *ulsic* craft, into
a formal portrait now hanging over the titanic fireplace in
the Great Holdings Hall.

It had been wise and beautiful Glynnaughfern, witnesses
upon all sides afterward asserted (usually in interminable
ballads imposed upon customers and stallkeepers in the village marketplace) who had altruistically given her selfless
love, and eventually her precious life as well (it was pro-
claimed in forced rhyme and imperfect meter) to bring the
curtain down upon a bloody war and obtain lasting peace
between two hostile peoples. The war in question had been
the prolonged and sanguine conflict between the Skyan
"natives" and two distinct "waves" of Hanoverian conquerors who had arrived about a century apart.

With chagrin, Bretta suddenly realized that she had somehow fallen into a reverie ("like a girl," she admonished herself) and was neglecting work which must be finished well
before the wan light of the deep forest glade began to fail
her. She could do much that many another individual could

not, but she could not see in the dark like a slit-eyed Skyan *jerrypouncer.* Three times in rapid order she cocked her crossbow, dipped a shaft in shroom spores, and sent the combination flying toward a tree she had chosen, creating a reliable bodily rhythm, before again allowing her conscious attention to the task to waver.

Nevertheless, there was, for a young person in her place, much to think about, and unlike most people's children, she had been taught to enjoy the act.

The Skyan "natives," of course, had not been native to the planet Skye at all, but simply descended from the first human beings to set foot upon the planet—not yet moon-ringed, if fireside tales were to be credited—in an antiquity so dim that nobody even recalled stories of it. That mountainous and wooded world, as lush as it appeared to be despite its small, cold seas, had given rise to no sapients. Its higher life-forms, no brighter than pets the newcomers had brought with them, were all completely alien—trilaterally symmetrical.

Recent archaeological estimations and attenuated folk-lore—principally arising from offplanet—generally agreed with what little local folklore there happened to be (collected, in the main, by Mistress Lia Woodgate, when she had lived here), placing initial human colonization of Skye at somewhere between nine hundred and one thousand standard years in the past, connecting it directly with an astonishingly widespread pattern of stories and popular beliefs centered upon humanity's having been outcast from an ancient, mythological mother planet.

And yet while mythology is one thing, reality is another altogether. In the beginning, as was well-known by those truly closest to her, the "sainted" Glynnaughfern Briartonson had been neither a willing nor an eager sacrifice to the cause of peace, love, and brotherhood upon Skye-under-the-Moonrings. What the young renegade had principally desired in those days was to murder as many Hanoverians as she possibly could, preferably with her own hands. As a fiery and capable combatant in her own right, she had only suffered the humiliation of being taken captive by Robret "the" Islay himself after leading an abortive raid upon some Hanoverian establishment he happened to be inspecting at the time.

By all accounts, the subsequent romantic collision between the pair was an exceedingly passionate and violent one. Legend held that it had proceeded, inspired by the generally frenzied circumstances of wartime, from something greatly resembling mutual rape, to a deep and lifelong mutual devotion, in the span of only a few hours. And in this case legend was not merely consummately correct, but had been recapitulated so closely in the meeting of Bretta's own parents that she entertained the idea that there was something genetic to the pattern.

Glynnaughfern awoke the next morning, it was said afterward, pulsing with her bruises and her satisfaction, but to the impossible discovery that she had fallen in love with none other than the chiefmost of her father's enemies and her own, as well: a foreign interloper who had been rewarded for his display of valor in some irrelevant war— by a faraway satrap who properly had no such right—with an abandoned Hanoverian title to the world that was their home.

As the soul-shattering tale of Glynnaughfern's capture and capitulation began to circulate among her former woods-runner compatriots, she was neither praised by her fellow Skyan "natives" nor loved for what she had done—even for what, presumably, had been done to her. Upon the contrary, enough of her own people began to regard her as a traitor of the most contemptible variety imaginable—a *bedroom* collaborator—that her all-too-brief life was subject, from that moment onward, to the gravest dangers at every turn, and she lived what little of it remained to her under the shadow of imminent death.

It was in the throes of childbirth, however, that beautiful and valorous Glynnaughfern had ultimately perished, the inevitable consequence, according to the dour pronouncements of her long-faced Hanoverian physicians, of almost a thousand years of biological isolation and genetic drift between Skyans and Hanoverians. The young woman had been surpassingly lucky, they had declared with a lugubrious disapproval—as they packed their carpetbags for the long journey overland to Skye's equatorial starport—simply to have survived two previous successful pregnancies (these having been attended by Skyan midwives, they failed to mention) along with some unguessable number of unsuccessful ones.

And so it was, as it often happens, that with the passage of time, her passion, for her own people as well as for her Hanoverian husband—and what came afterward to be regarded as her sacrifice for the sake of peace between them—came to be better and better understood and appreciated. No doubt thanks to her, in the end, Robret would prove a light-handed ruler who truly loved the world he had been given and respected its people and their customs. And, as also often happens in such affairs, it would be her children who would turn out to be her greatest gift to seal the bloody breach between two warring populations.

For in even harsher times yet to come, Skyans and Hanoverians would stand together side by side against another foe and bring him down—together side by side—to the most ignominious defeat ever recorded in the history of the galaxy.

And yet, myth and reality representing differing contours and textures of the same object, as they will, nobody (least of all, Bretta, herself) doubted that Glynnaughfern would far rather have *lived*, to enjoy seeing at least one of her sons grow up and sire six children of his own (thus far). Likewise she would have enjoyed spoiling her grandchildren and been proud (and unsurprised) to discover that, in terms of those grandchildren, everything had worked out vastly better than either she or her descendants might have planned, had they not, instead, merely followed the course their lives had plunged them upon, headlong.

For above all, her eldest granddaughter Bretta (who was not a whit less beautiful than her fabled grandmother, if the girl but knew it) belonged, from the top of her handsome head to the tips of her well-formed toes, and to the equally admirable innermost recesses of her being, to both worlds, Skye and Hanover.

CHAPTER XIV:
OF CHILDREN AND PARENTS

Someone was waiting for Bretta when she came down the hill at midday, bereft of quarrels save a prudent handful, crossbow slung over one sunburnt shoulder.

"Hullo, My Little." Her father winked. He, too, carried a sizable knife upon his belt, but in addition, had strapped his second-best thrustible to his right forearm. "I have come to tell you that our old friend and neighbor Hugh Toomey and his goodwife Selda have kindly invited us to luncheon." Glancing over his own shoulder to assure that he was not being overheard, he added in a somewhat softer voice, "after which your mother requires us to return home and prepare for supper. 'Tis a hard life, I confess, but *somebody* has to live it!"

Bretta laughed. The old friend and neighbor to whom Arran had referred was the very shroomer upon whose behalf she had spent this morning improving her already respectable marksmanship. It was his humble stacked-log home the tidy foreyard of which she and her father found themselves approaching as he spoke.

"Friend Hugh, indeed." She handed the man her empty spore crock, setting her crossbow down to lean against a knee, and gladly accepted the spraddlehorn dipper of well water he offered her. "I have started one hundred and fifty plants this morning. If the weather holds, I believe there will be time for a second crop before winter."

"Aye, yoong Bretta-me-lass." The peasant bestowed upon her his infamous and nearly toothless grin. Having come into the world without a master, in a long-abandoned Hanoverian Drectorship, like other "natives," he had violently resisted becoming a serf with the arrival upon Skye of Arran's father. Since the Battle of Skye, however, there had been no serfs upon this planet; while Toomey was a tenant upon Arran's land, he was nevertheless a free man. "An' if ye'er hoppen t'be attacked by hardwood trees, ye'll be that prepared, I'll wager!"

For just a moment, Bretta did not know quite what to make of old Toomey's jest. It is a rare fifteen-year-old, female or male, who can easily endure being made the butt of humor, especially by adults who may or may not be joking. Then she noticed her father watching her closely and recalled, through a hot haze of offended adolescence, just how long and how well this preposterously toothless figure before her had been their faithful and trusted friend. She burst into laughter that was genuine, for all that it had come a heartbeat late.

"Too right," Bretta offered. "Any I miss I'll count upon you to chew to death!"

This struck Hugh as the funniest thing he had heard in a long while, and as they all stooped low—Arran clapped Bretta upon the shoulder to let her know that he approved of what she had said—to enter the rude dwelling with its foot-hardened dirt floor, the man repeated it to his wife, a plump and prematurely aged woman with approximately the same number of teeth left as her husband.

Selda Toomey laughed as she spooned a thick and aromatic stew into wooden bowls she had set upon the table. The fact that they *had* spoons and bowls—and a table—was a source of pride to them, and this primitive hovel of theirs, a lifelong dream come true. When they had married, Bretta knew, they had dwelt under a lean-to over the hollow formed by the roots of a fallen tree. It was by no means, however, the source of Hugh and Selda's greatest pride.

"What news," Arran asked them both as he sat down upon

a bench beside his daughter and took his first bite of Selda's
stew, which was as rich with flavor as the old woodsrunner
couple was poor of wealth, "d'you have lately of Young
Hugh?"

In a way, this polite exercise was absurd, for it was he
who had brought them the news himself, only a few minutes
earlier, in the form of yet another autothille from the capital,
carried by the same ship the courier had arrived upon. Still,
they could all pretend that he had asked for Bretta's sake, for
she knew their son quite well. Only a year or two older than
Bretta, it had been Young Hugh, for the most part, who had
taught her everything she knew of shrooms.

Hugh sat himself down upon a tree stump roughly hacked
into the shape of a stool, since the couple (who imagined
themselves to be rich enough as it was, compared to the
manner in which they had begun life together) possessed no
other furniture. Selda assumed her usual proprietary pose
beside the clay brick woodstove upon which she worked her
daily culinary miracles. Before her husband could so much
as open his toothless mouth to answer Arran's question, she
herself spoke up enthusiastically, and as she did so, placed a
great round loaf of freshly baked bread upon the cleanly
scraped boards of the trestle table.

"Yoong Hughie's doin' right as rain, all thanks t'ye, sair.
He tells us in yon thilly-thing they've premoted him already
from scullery t'salad—an' Ceo's asked twicet herself for
morsel of selfsame stew ye're eatin' now, she has!"

Bretta glanced up from her own rapidly emptying bowl,
her eyes gleaming with appreciation and with happiness for
the old couple over their son's accomplishments—although
in a corner of her mind, she remembered that they were not
that much older than her own parents, ten or fifteen standard
years, at most, which would make them between forty-five
and fifty. There was many a citified pursuit—literature, politics—at which they would have been considered young.

In their pride—a pride Bretta had been brought up to
understand well and to admire—they had refused repeated
entreaties to come and work for the Islay family at the Hold-

ings. The life they lived here aged them so quickly, she observed, not for the first time, although they appeared more than content to work themselves to death in the knowledge that their son's life would be better.

Bretta knew her father believed such differences—not so much in wealth as in access to the benefits of technology—were a result of civilization's failure to respect the rights every sapient should be at liberty to exercise and which he himself had fought so fiercely to guarantee. Old Hugh and Selda, like fifteen quintillion others throughout the imperium-conglomerate, remained poor because for centuries the Monopolity had carefully stifled every opportunity with rules and regulations (promulgated for nothing more than its own sake), taken away everything they had in taxes, and then wasted it all—and stolen their children into the bargain—for its innumerable and senseless wars. There was nothing their Drector-Hereditary could do here upon Skye, nor even the Ceo herself upon Hanover, that could make up for that, or even change it soon.

Bretta loved Hugh and Selda Toomey well and often wished that she could do more for them, but one could not do favors for a woodsrunner—not of the kind they could never hope to repay—for they would never permit it. Also, there was the point her father often made, that you cannot help everybody for very long—even those who may deserve it—before you begin to need help of some kind or another, yourself. Moreover, he had instructed her from his own bitter experience that help of any variety is much more likely to weaken those who receive it, than ever to uplift them. The kindest favor one can do for a fellow being was to exchange values with him upon an equal basis, or leave him alone.

In this particular instance, Arran (who did not always listen to his own lectures) had been at pains to convince the Toomeys that they were doing *him* a favor—helping him to make a good appearance upon Hanover—by allowing their only son to travel to the capital planet to work his mother's culinary miracles, employing his father's ingredients, in the Ceo's shining kitchens. It was that "favor"—a useful and pleasurable fraud jointly perpetrated by a father and daughter—that Bretta was gradually "working off" in the shroom grove. That the Toomeys understood and permitted it only made the joke the better.

Afterward, Arran and Bretta deliberately took a long way home, strolling through the forest, enjoying one another's company. Arran's hands were tucked comfortably behind his waist in a manner particular to the deck-pacing officers of Deep-sailing vessels, especially those accustomed to wearing thrustibles upon their forearms. Bretta wore her weapon across her back upon a sling (not the best choice, tactically, had she not been well escorted) in order to carry a crock of shroomstew Selda was sending her mother. Arran often felt a pang of guilt that he loved this eldest daughter of his more than anyone else, with the exception of his wife. He had five other children to please him, but none of them was Bretta.

"I came out to meet you here this afternoon with a purpose in mind," he confessed.

"I reckoned that you had, Father," she replied, "despite the autothille from Hanover that you brought to the Toomeys. And good news that was, was it not?"

"Aye, My Little, that it was." Idly, he stooped to pick up a stick the length of his arm and employed it to swat at the ripened heads of weeds they encountered as they walked along. "But my real purpose, as you have in some part anticipated, was to remind you of something—some pertinent facts with regard to the life we Islays lead here—before I convey to you some news of my own."

A sense of deep foreboding swept unbidden through her body like a sudden chill. And yet—unlike virtually any other child of her years—she kept silent, merely nodding to her father in acknowledgment of what he had just said.

He cleared his throat. "As you understand well, Bretta, I was compelled by the ugliest of personal and political circumstances to grow up somewhat earlier in life than most children of our culture are generally accustomed to doing."

Bretta smiled, for this was more familiar ground to her. "Yes, Father, I know the story well of how, as the merest

youth, you arose perforce to become known to an entire
dumbfounded galaxy as the Deep-roving ship-scourge
Henry Martyn." Although her words may have been mocking ones—perhaps the only ones possible in these circumstances—they both knew that her admiration was genuine.

"I warrant that this is the Deep-roving ship-scourge's
wench—your own dear mother—speaking through you."
Arran shook his head to conceal a grin. That his eldest
daughter was actually proud of her father was more, at
times, than he could bear. "A Deep-roving ship-scourge, I
might add, who now prefers simply to be known as his beautiful and intelligent daughter's loving father."

Had these words been delivered in any less straightforward a tone, they would doubtless have elicited from her a
response common to those of her age, involving a finger
thrust down the throat, accompanied by a gagging noise. As
it happened, although it had been spoken as if in jest, Bretta
knew that her father's protest—allowing for an intermittent
painful longing (which she shared) to find himself back
under starsail upon the boundless Deep—was genuine.

"All of that was in the evil days of the Black Usurpation,"
she volunteered instead. "At the merest mention of those terrible times, Hugh and all of his cronies still avert their faces
and spit, and nobody needs any explanation of their bitter
feelings over that. As impoverished as they were before his
vile advent, Morven left them even more so. We still lack an
accurate account of the number of them he slaughtered. And
yet, Father, I have always thought it a trifle contradictory
that Skyans might prefer one set of Hanoverians over
another."

"You have always thought a trifle too much—belay that,
My Little, for it was an ill-delivered joke which I do not
mean, even in the slightest. Hugh and his folk—which is to
say, *our* folk, through your paternal grandmother—are possessed of a most sensible desire to know where they stand at
all times."

Bretta nodded her approval.

"This sensible desire upon their part is readily satisfied by nothing more difficult than the consistent rule of law upon *our* part, and the most energetic enforcement of their rights we can manage." With his stick, he struck a seed-pod from a stalk and watched it hurtle across the clearing they passed through to fetch against a treetrunk. "Failing either of these, they will rebel, and in their place, so would you or I. That is *exactly* what I did."

"Against everything and everyone, by all accounts." She approved of this, too.

He chuckled. "That's about what it amounted to at the time. Looking back, I suppose what made the Usurpation most unbearable to me, in an abstract sense disconnected from the suffering it caused, was the fact that Morven's brutal and illegal activities upon Skye had the tacit approval of Leupould IX, himself."

"While you, upon the same account, had no allies upon whom to rely in your struggles." There had been times, when she was younger, that being told of this injustice to her father had made her clench her tiny fists and weep with rage. "All 'Droomly hands within the Monopolity being turned against you, you were forced to build an army and a navy out of outcasts, criminals, and failures."

He shrugged. "Exactly like myself."

"Do not be silly, Father. You were even younger than I am when it all began, and bear responsibility only for having righted the wrongs perpetrated or permitted by others. This is also why you turned for help to aliens like the *nacyl* and the *seporth*. We don't see enough of them these days, you know."

He sighed. "I know, My Little. I did learn much from my disheartening 'educational' experiences, which I have always hoped to pass on to you less painfully. Which brings us, by the sheerest of coincidences, back around the barn and to the point: as a consequence of all I suffered in my youth, I have endeavored to see that, even at your tender age, you are as self-sufficient a creature as your mother and I can make you. You are aware of this, are you not?"

Bretta rested a well-educated hand upon the familiar

pommel of a tool and weapon that she could, at need, have
fashioned for herself, in all likelihood, had the knife not
been made as a gift from her parents. "Very well, indeed,
Father."

Arran paused to place a hand over his daughter's. "And in
every respect, My Little, every day, your mother and I have
discovered a more willing, more eager, brighter, and more
talented student than ever we might have wished for."

"Thank you very much, Father," she sniffed. "You are
about to make me cry."

"My sincere apologies." He had been close to it, himself.
"Never thank somebody for simply telling you the truth, My
Little—now where was I? Oh, yes—and because I had to
learn it all the hard way, you have been taught how to work
a full-sized interstellar sailing vessel, and can acquit yourself passably in every position of responsibility from common deckhand to overall command. I have even included in
your education certain hard-learned ins and outs of starship
gunnery that military and merchant captains know very little about."

"Yes, Father." Bretta wondered—and worried—what
Arran was leading up to. For his part, he was struck by her
uncharacteristically submissive tone.

"Now admittedly, My Little," he went on in an attempt to
reassure her, "your practical experience of starsailing and
gunnery has been limited. Over the years—and they have
seemed passing short to me—I have only been able to take
you upon outings in the near-spatial environs of our homeworld. For this reason, I will take you with me upon whatever mission the Ceo Lia has in mind."

There was a considerable pause while Bretta struggled
inwardly to absorb the unbelievably good news she had just
been given. Then: "You really mean it? Oh, Father, please
tell me you are not joking!" In an attempt to leap, dance,
laugh, and seize her father about the neck, all at once, she
very nearly lost the crock of shroomstew she carried.
"Where will we go? Is Mother going with us? Of *course* she
is! What will we do? Do we sail first for Hanover?"

"More than likely." Arran laughed, too, loving his daughter all over again for the game creature that she was. "And yes, your mother is going with us. As to the rest of it, we will have to see. The 'bad' news is that you must trade that twanger across your back for the thrustible I have been saving for you."

She laughed again. She knew the particular weapon in question well, and in plain truth had always more than halfway expected that it would be given to her someday. Now she wondered whether she would be required to wear a dress, and whether the thrustible—her thrustible—could be concealed within its sleeve.

Thanks to her conscientious and unconventional father, the girl had long known (and from more frequent exercise than her shiphandling practice) which end of a deadly kinergic thrustible was which. Like the *atatl, davesling, gladius, bowie,* and *fortyfive* before it, it was the personal weapon of the times. Still, this was a rare skill for any woman of Bretta's milieu to possess.

Bretta had a thorough theoretical grounding and considerable experience in many other technical subjects, and—at the insistence of her mother—she was well versed in all of the historical and literary subjects, too. She could also outrun, outclimb, outswim, and outfight any of the local boys she knew. In all of this—although it was at Arran's insistence she had become acquainted with various kinds of primitive weapons, powered, unpowered, Skyan, and otherwise—Bretta had been following all her life a particular example that her mother, Loreanna, might not even have been consciously aware she was offering.

In a civilization that otherwise consisted largely of deliberately self-enfeebled women, Loreanna Islay was another of those rare females who knew what a weapon was for and feared not to use it at need. She took pride and pleasure in maintaining her proficiency and, upon more than one occasion, everything she lived for had been preserved by what many of her overly tamed contemporaries would have regarded as an unseemly willingness to fight, mostly with the ancient chemenergic handgun Arran had given her. To this day, Bretta knew, she carried the small, black *walther pp* in a pocket of her dress.

Bretta was perfectly aware that her own existence was a direct result of a fiery romantic meeting between a daring, swashbuckling boy outlaw and the girl who became his equally daring bride-of-war. In its own way, the whole thing was more than a little reminiscent of what had happened between her grandfather Robret and her grandmother Glynnaughfern. Loreanna—packed off for disobeying her uncle—had been an unwilling passenger aboard a starship that Henry Martyn happened to have seized. She first became his prisoner, then secondly his woman, and at last his wedded wife and the mother of his children.

And yet, although the unique, cherished, and affectionate understanding often said to exist between a father and a daughter prevailed indeed between Arran and Bretta, his youthful exploits as Henry Martyn had somehow been set aside in her mind as something mythical. Perhaps it was simply too difficult to see a swashbuckler in the gentle soul who read bedtime stories to his baby daughter.

It had always been just as hard for Bretta to watch her mother knitting, for example, and to appreciate that those same small, capable hands had fought for life and death against many an enemy too despicable to mention in decent company. Upon more than one occasion, Loreanna had firmly refused to tell her bloodthirsty young daughter whether she had ever killed anybody, "in the old days."

Yet perhaps after all, this may have been a rare mistake in the girl's upbringing. To Bretta, as to everybody else, the fabulous star-raider Henry Martyn, and Loreanna his fearsome warrior-wench, had become figures out of fantasy. And although she saw and spoke with her illustrious parents every day, at the same time, they belonged somehow to another world and a different time.

CHAPTER XV:
ARRAN ISLAY'S DAUGHTER

In daylight, the moonring was often visible as a ghostly band across the sky.

Together, Arran and Bretta emerged from the growing shadows of the forest to find themselves at the edge of the great green meadow, upon the far side of which lay the Holdings. Sprinkled with the low blossoms of a dozen brilliant colors—which would eventually transform themselves into harvestable and delicious groundberries—the cover was less than ankle-deep this early in the year, and it was not very long before they stood within their own flagged foreyard.

Bretta looked back the way they had just come, the way she had taken—she did some multiplying in her head—many thousands of times since she had first turned seven or eight and had won the freedom to roam as widely as she did now. It was difficult to credit the story that an entire town, comprised of hundreds of flimsy false-fronted shanties, had once arisen in that broad green field, been utterly destroyed upon the historic night of the Battle of Skye, and every last trace carefully removed afterward by her parents and by thousands of eagerly cooperating Skyans. She had never found as much as a nail or button to show what evil the Black Usurper and his minions had wrought there.

Upon reaching home, Arran had excused himself almost at once, speaking vaguely of some chore that must be attended to, giving his daughter a hug, and a kiss upon her forehead, and telling her that he would see her once again at table with the rest of the family. Even at the age of fifteen, Bretta was neither unbright nor particularly naive. Their dis-

cussion of his glorious outlaw past had gone exactly as far
as it ever had upon a hundred previous such occasions, and
had shut off as abruptly as it always did when it had reached
a certain point.

Bretta could not help but understand from this pattern
that, for all of her life—or at least as long as she could
remember—her father had been concealing some painful
secret. She had watched this specter herself, creep up and
steal the joy of life right out from under him upon too many
otherwise happy occasions. Whatever it was, it had to be the
source, she had long ago reasoned, of the troublesome and
uncomfortable distance she could often feel between herself
and—not so much her *father,* perhaps, but—his heroic past.

She sighed as she always did whenever she felt defeated
in this manner, and, rather than head directly for the great
house, directed her steps to one of the outbuildings, where
the estate's spreighformery was maintained. Here, many
useful things were fabricated, a single atom at a time, and
there was an ample washroom she could enjoy without the
enthusiastic assistance of her four sisters.

She had given her father the crock of shroomstew, which
he had offered to deliver to the kitchen. Now she laid her
crossbow upon a workbench, along with her sheathed hunting knife, hip-quiver, and what few she had left of her quarrels. She had already locked the door behind her, knowing it
was unlikely that anyone would wish to use the workshop
this close to suppertime and that its several windows were
just grimy enough to assure her adequate privacy. Striding
into the washroom, she sat down upon a wooden bench to
remove her leather slippers. The red floor bricks were cool
upon the bare soles of her feet.

Almost half of the spreighformery washroom had been
given over to what might have been called a shower enclosure, had it actually been more enclosed. Bretta set both of
the showerheads running, directed partly at the floor and
more or less at one another, a luxury she sometimes permitted herself, until the air within the washroom hung heavy
with warm vapor. Unfastening her vest—its buttons had

been fashioned from pierced sections of the antlers of the same forest animal which had provided the hide—she hung it over a wooden peg set beside the plank-built door and stripped away her cutoff working trousers.

Then, as a guilty afterthought, she ducked back into the main room of the spreighformery to draw her knife and scabbard from her belt, relieved that her father had not seen her leave it this late. She had used the weapon once or twice today in the forest, and then eaten with it at the Toomeys'. The knife would never rust, and its scabbard was of a waterproof material that could be washed clean with soap and water. But Arran had taught his daughter to keep the blade virtually sterile, a sensible precaution that could someday save her life.

She set her knife aside upon the ledge of a large, glass-bricked window which could not be seen through, but which provided the shower with plentiful light, unwrapped a freshly manufactured bar of soap she had just taken from the spreighformery, and began lathering her tightly muscled and smooth young body. She used the soap upon her hair, as well (her mother would have yelped to see that), this being one reason she preferred to wear it short. Bretta was not entirely without the virtues that make a mother proud, however, being as fastidious about the condition of her nails—which she also wore short—as she was about her knife. She had never shown up at table with dirt beneath them.

In this, she followed Arran's example.

Thinking of her father brought her back to her earlier line of thought. Children, she had observed (still being one herself in many more respects than she was enthusiastic about acknowledging) are invariably more attentive to the after-bedtime whispering among adults than adults ever seem to remember they are. (Bretta had promised herself long ago that she would remember this when the time came, and maintain her privacy better than her parents had theirs.) The girl already suspected that, whatever her father's secret torment happened to be, it must have something to do with a terrible naval accident of some kind.

As far as Bretta was aware, her father had always avoided talking about whatever it was that troubled him, with anyone at all—even with her mother. This, in spite of the complete openness he had otherwise invariably shown his family and close friends with regard to so many other aspects of his unique life—it appeared all but impossible to embarrass the man or to shame him—including, ironically, most of his other boyhood experiences in the Hanoverian War.

On very little evidence, and rather too much speculation, Bretta had long ago calculated that "it" must be something that had occurred precisely upon the heels of Henry Martyn's final, triumphant, and celebrated clash in his long, bitter struggle against the Monopolity of Hanover and its evil accomplices. Whatever "it" was, she had observed, it appeared to have robbed her father of any lasting satisfaction that he might otherwise have taken in his wonderful—and wonderfully historic—victory, or in much of anything else, for that matter.

Having washed and rinsed her hair, she noticed in a nearby mirror that her freckled, upturned nose and the equally freckled upper surfaces of her shoulders were turning pinkish and beginning to peel slightly. A genuine sunburn was relatively rare upon damp and densely wooded Skye, but there had apparently been less cover at the top of that hill than she had counted upon. No matter, the damage was slight, and her mother would have something to put on it. Her vest had protected the rest of her, although she was starting to develop a tanned "V" where her cleavage . . . well, would *someday* appear, she fondly hoped.

From where it lay beside her knife upon the redbrick windowsill, Bretta picked up an enormous yellow bathing sponge, the spreighformer programme for which she had written herself, as a schoolgirl exercise. Such a capability was virtually unique at present, even within the Monopolity itself (she was somewhat smugly aware), and even among its dominant male population. This particular civilization had enjoyed much better days, her father had often told her, and it would enjoy better yet if young people could be persuaded to relearn the skills which had once maintained it and made it great. For that reason, and in that hope, he had doubled the size of the Holdings' library, always seeking ancient books, and those that had been translated from alien languages.

She bent to lather her long, smooth legs.

With a grim persistence that others often had good reason to regret, the girl's thoughts returned stubbornly to the path they had wandered from only momentarily.

It was in the Holdings' huge library that she had first received some inkling of her father's secret shame. There, she had overheard a visiting Phoebus Krumm speak reminiscently to her mother about some four hundred Jendyne naval cadets who had been press-ganged aboard alien starships which had somehow later proven lethal to them. This was confusing, not only because the two spoke in the lowest tones they possibly could, but because the Jendyne Empery-Cirot, in Bretta's understanding, had counted itself among Arran's enemies at the Battle of Skye. So who gave a spreighformed damn what had happened to four hundred of their cadets?

She had been about eight at the time, as she remembered, and had sneaked down to the library after bedtime for something to read beneath her bedcovers, employing a peculiar sort of hand torch that her father had just given to her. He had informed her that it had been his as a boy, so she had doubly cherished it, and still counted it among her greatest treasures. What had made it truly wonderful was that, rather than shedding any light of its own, within reach of its strange influence, it had caused something washed into the bedclothes to glow.

But first she must make good her escape with her literary booty, and she had been cut off by the unexpected entry of Phoebus and Loreanna. As Bretta huddled under the enormous polished hardwood desk that had belonged to his father, Arran—it was one of only a few instances in which she had seen him genuinely outraged—had accidentally walked in upon the conversation between his best friend and his wife, interrupting them angrily, with bitter words to the effect that they—presumably the four hundred Jendyne cadets—had given up what he had called their "unlived lives," against their wills, merely that he, a useless parasitical aristocrat, might retain the title Drector-Hereditary of Skye.

It could not have been much worse, Bretta had often reflected later with an understanding bestowed upon her by the passage of another several years, if her father had stumbled upon the two of them making love. Arran had stamped out of the library, the guilt and shame he felt having momentarily exhausted his vocabulary, shortly followed by the other two, and by the next morning's breakfast, it was as if the frightening and peculiar episode between them had never happened—although Bretta never heard anyone speak of Jendyne cadets again.

Just now, she resoaped her sponge, unsheathed her knife, and scrubbed its broad blade carefully—a considerable degree of briskness was called for, but one slip could easily cost her a finger—until no hint remained of its having been used this morning. With an almost equal care, she cleansed its synthetic scabbard, for she had violated a tenet of survival by sheathing the tool dirty. Later, she would dry both pieces and touch up the knife's razor edge with a pair of smooth, white, triangular-sectioned stones she had "created" here in the spreighformery, struck at an angle to one another in a polymer base. Setting the weapon aside momentarily, she rinsed herself all over, turned off both showerheads, and stepped dripping from her bath, reaching for a nearby towel.

Just as Bretta loved and appreciated her father, the relationship between her and her mother was remarkably well-founded and loving, lacking even a hint of the primitive struggle for power (oddly enough, often symbolically manifest through a painful and bitter rivalry over control of the daughter's hair) that sometimes rages unconsciously—or not so unconsciously—between mother and daughter. Having desired nothing so much as complete sovereignty over her own life, Bretta knew, Loreanna had granted her daughter the same sovereignty—or as much as she could bring herself to risk at any given stage of the girl's development and still feel she was a responsible parent—as early as she could.

Not that she and her husband had ever failed to make mistakes. They had simply determined in advance to make them—against the trend of thousands of years of human history and millions of years of parentage—upon the side of liberty.

And yet for some reason, it had never so much as occurred to Bretta to discuss this situation of her father's secret torment over the four hundred cadets at the Battle of Skye with Loreanna. The girl was afraid—it was one of her few real fears—to press the matter further than she had with either of them.

Nor could Bretta turn, as she had so frequently done with other childhood problems, to Phoebus Krumm. In the first place, he was not reliably present upon Skye. And in the second, she had been brought up properly, with manners, which principally meant, above all things, an absolute respect for the privacy of others which she would literally rather have *died* than violate. Yet her dearest wish was that her father would someday, somehow find a way to speak of his problem with her, with her mother, with almost anybody else. Her staunch belief was that by doing so, whatever pain it might cost him in the beginning, he would at last be able to set himself free from whatever it was that haunted him.

Then she herself would be free to integrate the disparate images in her mind of her father, Arran Islay, and of the wonderful and dreaded pillager, Henry Martyn. This was most important to her, for in many respects—not all of them negative, by any means—Bretta lived a rather solitary life. She truly loved both of her parents and even her younger siblings, treating them in a wholly proper manner. But even when she was surrounded by their warmth and noise, it often seemed to her as if she were alone. Those who knew her best often remarked that it was as if she were an only child. One or two rare, disapproving scolds were always quick to add "and an orphan, into the bargain."

Bretta wrapped a towel about her head in a characteristic manner many a husband comes to believe must be programmed into the female genes. Gathering her hunting knife, scabbard, suede vest, slippers, and her kefflar trousers, she quit the washroom, leaving damp toeprints on the bricks. In the main room of the spreighformery, she set her things upon the bench beside her crossbow and quiver, unwrapped the towel, and essayed a final few drying motions with it.

Outside, a flash of motion caught her eye for just a moment, but through the dirty windows it was indistinct, and she dismissed it, returning to her thoughts.

Few individuals of Bretta's acquaintance (save for her mother and father) being as well educated, intelligent, or strong-willed as she (for all of the egalitarian goodwill in the galaxy, she could hardly discourse upon starship handling, for example, §-physics, or astrogation with the illiterate son of an ignorant shroom farmer), Bretta's independence had always existed entirely upon its own terms. It was nothing that she had arrived at in any deliberate fashion; it was more of a condition into which she had been born. Nor, in the terms of another century, was she following some popular trend or traveling in some politically acceptable direction. Had she been familiar with the phrase involved, she would have asserted herself to be a "Bretta-ist," rather than a feminist.

The same rare, disapproving scolds favored expressions like "selfish" and "snotty."

Upon the other hand, from the likes of young Hugh Toomey she had learned many useful things and, understanding the quandaries of this sort that life would place her in, her parents—Arran principally—had brought her up as free of any consciousness of social class as was possible for one of her times and station. As a consequence, she was well loved—even "adored" would not have been too strong a term—by the humble people of Skye, and her love for them was fully as sincere. But as another consequence, she had always tended to amuse herself and to keep her own counsel at all times. Her parents often found it exasperating, but it was precisely the result they had been striving for.

Nowhere was any of this more evident than in Bretta's relationships—rather, in the dearth of them—with her contemporaries. To begin with, she was possessed of certain skills—knife-fighting for one, unarmed combat for another, not to mention her prowess with crossbow and thrustible— that boys of any era would have found impossibly daunting to discover in a female. In addition, Bretta habitually displayed a basic strength of mind and character, and a seriousness of purpose, which placed her vastly beyond those of her own age. And those few local boys who were not afraid of her *were* afraid of her father.

Owing to this, and for a good many other reasons as well, at fifteen, Bretta remained a virgin. In itself, this was somewhat unusual upon moonringed Skye. It invariably tantalized and frustrated Hanoverian scholars—as well as those of other imperia-conglomerate—that the planet of her birth somehow managed to retain the rough-edged frontier character it had possessed over the past millennium. (Naturally, it never occurred to any of these theoreticians actually to *visit* the world they pontificated over.) Its forthright and unaffected inhabitants practiced much simpler, more "natural" customs (it was not acceptable, for example, for a Skyan girl to marry until she had "proved herself" by becoming pregnant) than those of their "sophisticated" erstwhile rulers.

It would have amused native Skyans to hear their culture described as a "passionate" one. For the most part, they tended to think of themselves as Stoics. But it was largely true, nonetheless. By the starkest of contrasts, the Monopolity of Hanover's was a stifling moral atmosphere of severe cruelty, repression, hypocrisy, and exploitation. Girls whose families could not find advantageous matches for them, in business or the 'Droom, frequently remained unloved and untouched all their lives. And because of such coldly contrived marital relationships, they usually remained unloved even after having been "touched."

But upon moonringed Skye, Bretta's virginity made her something of an old maid, adding, if she but knew of it or cared, greatly to the Islay family mystique. Being her own father's daughter (and her mother's daughter, too, if the truth be told), she had a highly sanguine underlying nature. Moreover, her curiosity in this connection was just as great as that of any bright, healthy adolescent.

Nevertheless, the independent-minded girl was more than satisfied, at present, with her lot. Had any among her acquaintances ever had the courage to brace her about this directly, which they had not, she had long planned to say, "Any man I give myself to had damned well better be a better man than I am!"

And then she planned to add, "And at least *half* as good a man as my father!"

Of a sudden, the motion outside, which she had dismissed, became a shadow sliding across the window. It paused, peering through the dirty pane, trying for a moment to scrub at the accumulated dust which was on the other side of the transparency. The shadow had acquired a little color, by now, and some detail.

It was not a shadow she recognized.

Forgetting everything else and laying the towel aside, Bretta slid her knife from its scabbard just as a hand tried the knob and, finding the door still closed, began to lean upon it and push it repeatedly with his shoulder. Knowing the building and her habits, no one in the family would have done that.

Bretta stood beside the door, knife in hand, and flipped the bolt. The figure upon the other side tumbled through and fell hard upon the bricks of the floor. In an instant, Bretta was upon him, the point of her knife at his throat.

"Oh dear, I have been done unto again, have I not?" It was the Ceo's messenger.

Bretta kept her bladetip at his jugular. "What upon moonringed Skye d'you mean?"

"Two of your thithterth," the fellow told her, trying to see the steel that threatened his life, "the nektht eldeht, I believe, thent me to fetch you to thupper. I wondered why they theemed to be thupprething giggleth. Thethe ablutionth in the thpreighformery, they are a reliable habit of yourth, I take it?"

"They are."

Bretta was suddenly aware that she was naked, and straddling the chest of a strange man. She felt a flush of deep embarrassment heat her skin all over.

"And so will someone else—*take it,* I mean—once I get hands upon them!"

PART THREE:
JENNIVERE DAIMLER-WILKINSON
YEARDAY 232, 3026 A.D.
MARRE 29, 518 HANOVERIAN
OCTAVUS 22, 1595 OLDSKYAN

"Yes, I'll take off my kefflar so fine,
Likewise my stays," answered she.
"But before that I do, you false young man,
You must turn your back on me.

"Turn around, turn around, you false young man,
Turn around, turn around," said she;
"For it is not meet that such a youth
A naked woman should see."

So 'round he turned, that false young man,
Around about he wheeled,
And seizing him boldly in both her arms,
She cast him into the field.

CHAPTER XVI:
DICTATES OF FASHION

"Mother!"

Bretta was already uncomfortable in her heavy, too-feminine Hanoverian finery, having for the most part successfully avoided wearing it over the past sixty-seven days. Yet for a moment, that was almost unimportant as she breathlessly rushed to the mullioned windows of the captain's quarters, which, slanting over the round hull of the *Osprey* as they did, allowed her to see outboard and aftward.

She had noticed, from an abrupt shift in the color radiating through the equally elaborate skylight overhead, that the §-field had been reduced to that minimum which would maintain the vessel's attitude in orbit about Hanover and retain an atmosphere upon her maindeck and about her mast and spars. When she was underway, the §-field rendered her father's starship inertialess, and therefore capable of being hurled—by unthinkably vast and powerful tachyon currents streaming through the Deep—at velocities greatly exceeding that of light.

The *Osprey*, like every other interstellar vessel of her time and place, was, in her general appearance, rather like a tree, planted in a bucket. The "bucket," some eighty measures in diameter at its top and not much more than that from top to bottom, was the starship's hull, from which sprang the "tree"—her great mast—standing more than a klomme above the maindeck covering the bucket's mouth. The "branches" of the tree were the *Osprey*'s nine huge radial spars, set staggered in three levels along the mast, mizzentier, maintier, and foretier.

While the maindeck lay completely open to the Deep,

protected only by the §-field which, in addition to making
the act of starsailing possible, allowed mast, spars, and sails
to be worked by crewbeings attired for a "shirtsleeve" environment, there were lower decks meant for cargo, passengers, and a formidable array of projectibles bearing much
the same relationship to thrustibles that cannon did to pistols. Under an ancient starsailing tradition that even Arran
could not persuade them to abandon, *Osprey*'s crew
expected to sleep wherever they might, about the heavy
bases of the projectile mounts—or caliprettes—upon the
gundeck, even between cargo bales. Finally, at the lowest,
most aftward, extremity of the bucket, lay the liftdeck, hous-
ing the lubberlift and its many tens of thousands of klommes
of almost preternaturally strong cabelle.

All about the open maindeck stood the bucket's rim, consisting of the captain's accommodations and those customarily allotted to his officers and important passengers. The
roof of this superstructure became the quarterdeck, itself
rimmed by a stout taffrail (to prevent her crewbeings from
falling into the instantaneously lethal §-field), from which
the starship was navigated and commanded. Here, too, were
foundations for most of the vessel's standing and running
rigging. Upon the largest vessels—*Osprey* was not among
these—there might be a secondary level of luxury quarters
and another open deck, or poop.

Loreanna joined her daughter at the mullioned window,
placing a hand upon her shoulder and stretching upon tiptoe
to peer downward, which, owing to the unique geometry and
architecture of an interstellar sailing vessel, was the same as
aftward. Softly illuminated by the scene they attempted to
observe below, her face shone with excitement, as if she
were a girl her daughter's age.

Had they but turned round and crossed the room they
presently occupied, Bretta and Loreanna might have looked
out through similar windows, including those set in a pair
of "hatches," as Bretta had learned long ago they were
properly termed (although to her, they looked like ordinary
doors, just as most of the *Osprey*'s "ladders" looked like

ordinary stairs), onto the busy maindeck with its astonishing tangle of sheets, lines, and cabelles. There, hundreds of barefooted crewbeings scurried to and fro to do their captain's bidding.

Overhead, through the broad skylights, they might even have watched more of the crew, high aloft, standing upon the footcabelle and clinging to the spars. At the moment, they were taking in the ship's enormous equilaterally triangular sails, three to a tier—port, starboard, and dorsal or ventral—and the more scalene and numerous staysails spiraling fore and aft, from tier to tier.

Had Bretta been taking what she still thought of as her rightful part in things, it would have been another matter altogether, but this was simply another variation upon the processes she had been compelled to watch from a distance many times over the past several weeks, and it was not the view that either of the Islay women wished to see today. For the first time in her life, Bretta had an opportunity to observe a planet other than that upon which she had been born.

The breathtaking spectacle, aft and below, of the cloud-wrapped, gloomy surface of Hanover was almost, she thought, *almost* worth the two months and seven days she and her mother—but not all four of her sisters, who had remained home upon Skye with their little brother, in every case under tearful protest—had spent cooped up, for the most part, within these beautiful and comfortable but closely crowded quarters, traveling among the countless stars of the Monopolity in order to arrive here, just off the world that ruled them all.

Those seeing it from forty-odd thousand klommes above its surface, here in orbit, enjoyed something of an aesthetic advantage over those unfortunates who had to endure the demoralizing behavior of its atmosphere. (It had been said, upon more than one occasion, that Hanoverians sailed out to conquer an empire because they could not bear the weather at home.) Yet, through the all but eternal cloud cover which kept Hanoverian skies overcast most days of its extralong year, billions upon billions of lamplights brightening the planetwide city below made the world glow from pole to pole like a giant, pulsing jewel.

Bretta and her mother had not been advised as to how long it would be yet before they all boarded the lubberlift for the endless journey to the surface. Having endured the two-and-one-half-hour ride upon more than one occasion back home, she did not look forward to it very much. She would play cards with her mother, she supposed, or read, not being the sort to take a nap. Starships of her era and civilization never landed, being much too fragile of construction to maintain physical integrity within the gravity well of even a small planet. Instead, they placed themselves in orbit above a world at such a velocity, and in such a location, that they stood above one point upon the equator at all times.

From this so-called "synchronous" or "stationary" orbit, a starship's crew lowered to the surface a cabelle of fabulous strength—invented in the days when scientists and engineers were more curious and competent than lately—which crews upon the ground then fastened to gigantic bollards constructed for the purpose. It was upon this cabelle that the lubberlift traveled at velocities beginning with a slow walk, but gradually rising to about twenty-nine thousand klommes per hour. At no time did passengers experience any but the feeblest pressure of acceleration.

Failing this—if, for instance, the planet in question were previously undiscovered, unexplored, or unsettled—fusion-powered steam launches could be dispatched to its surface, assigned the task of building a proper mooring for their mother vessel. Upon occasion, owing to severe weather, hostile indigines, or reasons not afterward discovered, the launches never came back, and even when they did, Arran hated using his, as all starsailing captains did, because they consumed water, which could not be regenerated in transit. He was perhaps the first, however, to have put them to an effective use in combat.

Bretta knew that it was here, in orbit about Hanover, that they expected to rendezvous with Phoebus Krumm and his pair of small, plump wives, Tula and Tillie—provided, of course, that Arran's former first officer had received the Ceo's message wherever he had been and felt like heeding it. He was well capable of ignoring it, Ceo be damned, and if he did make his appearance here, it would be mainly to visit with the Islay family and to serve Bretta's father as he always had. She had known him well, all of her life, and loved him even better, thanks to his many welcome visits to the Islay home upon moonringed Skye.

Bretta, an oval hoop of embroidery still clutched (albeit entirely forgotten) in her hand, glanced over at her mother, straining, exactly as she was herself, to peer down through the many-paned windows of what presently served them as their sitting room. Bretta's father, she knew, was somewhere out upon the maindeck, or perhaps even aloft, commanding his well-drilled crew (and how she longed to be among them!) as they made ready to bring the Hanoverian pilot aboard.

Before Bretta's family could disembark, this highly talented and worthy individual, in his turn, would skillfully order all of the necessary maneuvers to bring Captain Arran Islay's splendid old "armed freighter" into the exact orbital position already assigned her by the Hanoverian Port Captain. As an *Autonomous* Drector-Hereditary, her father had diplomatic immunity, and, in consequence, there would be no quarantine or customs inspection. Thus far, no mention had been made of any kind, at any level of officialdom, with regard to the starship *Osprey*'s genuine identity as a captured fighting vessel, heavily weaponed, or of her genuine master, the notorious world-pillager Henry Martyn.

How ironic, Bretta thought, that this otherwise well-traveled brigand had never before had an occasion to behold at first hand this ultimate center of human civilization and the Known Galaxy. Nor had he ever, to her knowledge, evinced much of an interest in doing so. Although his principal adversaries had commanded their forces from here, his own struggles and concerns had been upon the edges of Hanover's broad domain. His wife Loreanna, however, had been born in the city below some twenty-nine years ago, within a stone's throw of the 'Droom itself.

Bretta regarded her mother almost afresh. This was one of those pivotal moments, she realized, that they would both remember vividly for the remainder of their lives. Petite, auburn-haired, and, her daughter admitted, more than amply freckled (what did men *see* in all these damned freckles, anyway?), by all accounts, and from every likeness she had seen, Loreanna had only grown more beautiful, to her husband and to everybody else, over the fifteen years since, as a girl even younger than Bretta, she had last had sight of her native world.

Now Loreanna had returned to the capital world with her husband and her daughter to become acquainted (among a good many other reasons) with a mother whom she had never hoped to know. Many of those "principal adversaries" Henry Martyn had eventually defeated so ignominiously would be here, as well—this time, theoretically, as his allies. If Bretta had informed her mother of what she thought of that particular arrangement, Loreanna would have agreed, with a grin, but would have informed her daughter that she was too young to be so cynical.

Deep in her heart, Loreanna had long since forgiven her uncle Sedgeley Daimler-Wilkinson for the more than significant role he had played in her past misfortunes and her husband's. She would be most interested, Bretta had overheard her mother confess to her father, to see whether she was morally or emotionally capable of admitting this to the old villain, face-to-face. Upon one hand, he had sent her off into exile for refusing to be a commodity; upon another, he had been responsible for her having met Arran; upon a third, he had not known that, and would surely have interfered, had he been capable. She did look forward to seeing him for the first time in more than a decade and a half.

Turning to ask a question about her great uncle and his activities since then, suddenly, for the first time since Loreanna had hurried in from the next room at her daughter's excited shouting, Bretta realized what her mother was wearing. A pang of—what?—disappointment, embarrassment, certainly not envy, passed through her, and for once she was at a loss as to what to say next.

"Mother . . ."

At least, being an as yet unspoken-for female of not quite marriageable age, Bretta was not required by the humiliating dictates of fashion to affect the—what were the stupid things called?—the *emzeebees* she saw now upon her mother's arms and the ridiculous clothing that went with them. (In any case, she had always thought it was supposed to be the other way around with accessories.) *Emzeebees* were the allegedly decorative physical restraints for upperclass women, which of late had somehow come into fashion upon the capital world.

"Yes, dear, what is it?"

"Slithered into fashion" would most likely have been a more appropriate expression, Bretta thought resentfully. It seemed more than a little ironic to her—in plain truth, it was so embarrassing that she could scarcely bear the sensation of the thing—that in an indirect way, her own famous freedom-fighting father and mother had been generally credited by the Hanoverian mass media for having been responsible for this most recent, egregiously slavish fad.

For in a broad way, the fashion upon Hanover had shifted sometime in the past decade from an overly elaborate foppishness of fabric, cut, and manner, to an affected Deepraider's style for men. Whatever it was that historically ignorant fashion designers happened to believe such "buckle-swashers" had worn over the past fifteen hundred years or so, was apparently being affected this very day upon the streets and in the offices and meeting chambers of the capital world. And yet fashion, as everybody knew, was not really about men at all. Among married women or the betrothed, it was the studied, ragged finery and glittering fetters of a sexually suggestive captivity that had currently become all the rage.

For practical purposes (as practical as fashionability here or elsewhere ever became) these fetters consisted, in the main, of mirror-polished metal bands no less than a couple of siemmes wide, fastened about the bare arms just above the elbows, and connected to one another by a light, faceted metal chain passing across an attractively naked female back. Naturally, the more extreme the statement being made, the broader the bands became and the shorter and heavier the chain. The truly dedicated sometimes added matching wrist-cuffs and chains that passed across the bare midriff, a "belly chain" about the waist, or even ankle-fetters, for the very latest word in "helpless" feminine captivity and compliance.

"*Emzeebees.*" Bretta wondered where the name had come from, and whether it referred to the style in general, or just the chains. At least it had nothing to do with her family, she thought. She had been utterly scandalized to see her own mother adopt this new and foolish fashion without a minute's visible hesitation. Somehow, the otherwise observant girl had managed to miss the glances, grins, and innuendo, between her parents, of a second honeymoon. On the other hand, they were not for her, and she had never been meant to see them.

"Excuse me, dear, what did you say?"

"Nothing, Mother. Never mind."

Loreanna, after all, had once been a *real* Deep-raider's captive, sexual and otherwise, and her buckle-swashing husband a genuine brigand of the Deep. It was a certain limited public awareness of these facts which had apparently created the basis for this idiotic fashion. If Bretta had only overcome her emotions for a moment and thought about it, she would have realized (in fact, she would have remembered) that her parents were perfectly capable of swimming against the current of fashion whenever they saw some good reason to. It was just that, at this particular moment, they saw *no* good reason to, and if the truth be told, were rather enjoying themselves, and each other, by means of it.

Abruptly, a brief flash of reflected sunlight caused the two of them to glance upward instead of down. As they did,

they saw through the space once occupied by the ventral
mizzensail—and descending upon them like the bird of prey
their own vessel had been named for—a tiny, hurtling shape
without sails, constructed of the same metalloid mesh from
which the *Osprey* had been fashioned.

It was a fusion-powered steam launch, but not one of the
Osprey's, as Bretta could tell immediately, not only from its
size and shape—noticeably different from the auxiliary vessels she was most accustomed to—but from the profligate
manner in which its operator tumbled it upon its longest axis
and braked abruptly, wasting uncountable leets of precious
water. This, then, she supposed, must be the Hanoverian
pilot arriving. Having an entire planetful of water below
him, at the end of a handy lubberlift cabelle, the fellow
would grow to feel that he had reaction mass to waste. And
he was doing precisely that.

Bretta wondered momentarily about the peculiar direction from which the steam launch had arrived—based upon
experience, her expectation would have been to see the pilot
boat approach their vessel laterally, instead of from overhead, or forward—and commented upon it to her mother. It
was only with some difficulty that Loreanna tore her attention away from the great spectacle outside.

"Is it possible that neither your father nor I explained this
to you, my dear?"

Bretta shrugged.

Loreanna shook her head, attempting to watch what was
occurring through the window while answering her daughter's question. She was not making a good job of either. This
was not the first time Bretta had seen her so distracted over
the past several weeks. Upon the other hand, the girl calculated, it had to be the very definition of distraction to be
returning home, after some fifteen years, to a mother one
had never known and a half brother one never even knew
existed.

In a somewhat shorter time than either of them had
expected, they felt a solid *bump!* transmitted through the
starship's metalloid fabric. Apparently the pilot launch had

docked in one of the launch bays of the boatdeck two levels
below.

"You have such a good memory," Loreanna was continuing, "I am certain you would remember if we had mentioned
it. The disembarkation procedure in orbit about Hanover is
considerably different, here where they have so much daily
commerce, from those at frontier ports of call more familiar
to you. Although I have been informed upon the very best of
authority—your own father, to be precise—that they follow
quite similar practices upon the Jendyne capital planet."

This was not the first instance of late in which Bretta had
found herself left out of matters and affairs to which she
might have ordinarily expected to be admitted. The most
painful example was her unexplained confinement within
these very quarters. Although before this voyage, it had by
no means been a daily occurrence, Bretta could not count
the number of times she had helped to work this ship, in any
one of hundreds of capacities, almost as if she had not been
born the daughter of the vessel's master, but just a common
able-bodied crewbeing.

Why her father had suddenly decreed, upon this first
occasion that they were actually sailing *somewhere,* that she
must remain a useless passenger—a "beast" in common
sailor's parlance—she could not say, nor would he. For
some reason, it had never occurred to Bretta to discuss this
with her mother; she had decided to endure stoically this
unjust, arbitrary punishment to which she had been sen-
tenced. She dared not press the matter with Arran, not out of
fear of his anger but out of fear of her own. Simply thinking
of her unhappy situation now had brought her close to tears
which she refused to show anyone.

"Lay-deez!"

Of a sudden, her bleak thoughts were interrupted—nor
would they resume again for some while—by sight of a
gigantic and familiar figure throwing wide both doors of
their little sitting room and spreading his arms wide. As she
had done all her life, she flung herself into the giant's
embrace without an instant's hesitation, burying her face in

his great curly beard as he made oofing sounds and
exclaimed about how much she had grown since he had seen
her last.

Behind were two fat little women and her father, beaming
as if it were a holiday.

Which, now, it was.

For Phoebus Krumm had arrived.

Chapter XVII:
A Show of Accessibility

Phoebus Krumm never changed.

Even the passage of fifteen eventful years had failed so
far to put a single white hair into his magnificently voluminous beard. It was a well-worn dictum among the family
Islay that the oceans might dry up, mountain ranges might
crumble into dust, stars might consume all of their fuel and
turn into supernovae, whole galaxies might collapse and
suck themselves down into black, gravitic oblivion, but
Phoebus Krumm abided, constant, immutable, invariable,
unalterable, and reliable.

Standing in the double doorway to the captain's quarters,
Krumm reached an interminable arm backward, past Arran,
to his two wives, Tula and Tillie, big-eyed as always, with
curiosity and excitement, who were bringing up the rear. Not
apparently related to one another, the pair of Krumm
women, whom Bretta had known all of her life, were
nonetheless of the same approximate size, shape, and
demeanor. Bretta was more than a trifle scandalized with
herself to discover that she was wondering why the man had
never thought to add a little variety to his life. "E'er we do
or say aught else, medears, will ye kindly show the girls,
here, t'yer facilities, as they are too bashful t'ask for them-

selves? By the Ceo's bladder, t'was a long haul aboard that lighter!"

Across the maindeck, leaning against the quarterdeck taffrail, stood the *Osprey*'s communications officer, Mr. Suprynowicz, the weaponlike barrel of his ship-to-ship laser resting upon his shoulder, speaking into a microphone which converted his words into light impulses that could be received at short range by other ships. No doubt he was exchanging remarks with the helmsman of the towing vessel which was presently pulling them into the desired parking orbit.

At the same time, directed more by long-standing experience than by their officers' shouted instructions, hundreds of briskly moving crewbeings upon the main- and quarterdecks and high aloft were busy taking in all sail and making other changes to the running rigging that would effectively put their vessel to sleep for as long as her master determined she should stand in orbit about Hanover.

All about the *Osprey* lay dozens of other starships, along with their auxiliaries, making the same changes for the same reasons, or making the same changes in reverse, preparing to leave behind that planet which the Known Galaxy turned upon in point of economic and political fact, if not in terms of astrophysical geometry.

It was one of the most distracting—and distracted— moments Bretta could remember in a long while, with so many interesting things going on all about her, both aboard the *Osprey* and outside her hull in the surrounding Deep, that she could barely keep track of them all. Not for the last time did she find herself yearning (despite her earlier desire to be out upon deck or somewhere aloft with her father) for the tranquillity—even for the boredom—of her faraway homeworld, and even more, for time to think about what was happening.

It was more than probable, Bretta thought now, that her mother privately disapproved of the Krumms' polygynous marriage, being herself well and truly dedicated to a single man alone. Nevertheless, as she had upon every previous such occasion, Loreanna stepped forward now, from where she had been standing beside the outboard windows, warmly taking Tula and Tillie's hands in both her own.

"Kindly permit me the inexpressible pleasure of welcoming both of you to what presently serves us as the Islay family home. And welcome, as well, my dear Phoebus. It has been far too long—as indeed it would be, had we last seen you only yesterday afternoon. Please, Tula, Tillie, be seated wherever you will. How have you all been? May I offer you anything? A cup of tea, perhaps?"

Outboard, a brightly decorated steam launch hurtled past within not more than a crossbow shot of the *Osprey,* its rapid passage utterly silent until the vapor of its exhaust reached the cabin windows, which it rattled. Farther away, Bretta could see a pair of similar utility vessels—by which she meant not ship's boats—identifiable by the huge reaction-mass containers fastened upon the exteriors of their hulls. Behind them they towed the sad, dismasted cadaver of some old Jendyne or Duggerine caravelle, perhaps toward a graveyard of ships.

Bretta could guess from the uncharacteristically rigid manner in which Loreanna controlled her movements at the moment that she had been about to throw herself at Phoebus, as well. After all, he had known her since she was at least a year younger than Bretta was now. The loss of spontaneity was just another price of growing up, she supposed. A consensus was quickly arrived at that a "nice cup of tea" would be more than acceptable to everybody concerned. Loreanna left the room for the sketchy galley facilities that their quarters afforded, joined by the two Krumm women before the girl herself could offer to help her mother. Bretta remembered her father's stories of how Krumm and his wives used to bake bread and cakes and pies and biscuits aboard the old *Gyrfalcon.*

This apparently suited Phoebus, who, with Arran beaming proudly at both of them, had set Bretta down in what he thought was a gentle manner upon the deck and pushed her back to his great arm's length as if to get a well-focused look at her. The door behind him still lay open. Through it, she could hear all the wonderful racket of a ship's busy and amazingly crowded maindeck just outside.

"Ye'll definitely do, lass—though you're getting that tall and full-bodied t'be flinging yerself upon old Phoebus lest he fear for his unsullied reputation!"

She could not help but laugh with him, and noticed that her father was similarly compelled. The man had this effect upon everyone who came within the sound of his voice, and that was some considerable distance, to be sure. Although her father had once told her that the first time he had heard that voice, it had been reciting a list of the many shipboard offenses that could get one thrown into the §-field. But now Krumm frowned suddenly, fingering the lace he had just found at the cuffs of her puffed velvet sleeves. With a similar expression, he turned a giant hand over—a more polite distance away—at the same sort of material spilling extravagantly out of her bodice front.

"But what's all this frivolous cupcake frippery ye've put on about ye? What's become of Bretta the Bloodthirsty, me thinly clad warrior-maiden? Bedad, at yer age, yer father here had just been chosen captain of his first starship!"

The style was far from new, unlike the bizarre habit her mother presently affected, but its intention was essentially the same. The skirts of her dress were enormous and swept the deck about her feet. Had she been considered of a marriageable age, its front hem would have been rolled up to the waist—or that appearance given by the dressmaker—to display each of her petticoats, layer by layer, and offer at least a show of accessibility. In much the same manner, her décolletage would have not been camouflaged with lace, but would have been cut low enough to expose the uppermost margins of her areolae. The entire matter of Hanoverian fashions was impossibly humiliating to the girl, and for once—in this context at least—she was happy to be only fifteen years old.

"So he was." In her defense, she turned back the lace upon her wrist to show the deadly lens of her thrustible.

"Krumm the Baker ought to know better than anyone else," she offered, "how unwise it is to judge a cupcake by its frosting."

Both men convulsed with laughter, Bretta joining them heartily, and were still wiping tears from their eyes when Loreanna and the Krumm women reentered with a loaded tea tray, full of questions about what the men had been laughing at. Phoebus pointed helplessly at one particular item of baked goods sitting, by coincidence, upon the tray, but was unable to answer them any further. How all three of the women had fit into the galley was the question Bretta wanted answered.

Past them, through the windows, a stately row of great Deep-sailing ships could now be seen, not far away, only a small part of the impressive military fleet the Monopolity maintained—a fleet, Bretta recalled with a thrill of pride, that her father had once defeated soundly. Every one of these enormous vessels could have made four of the little *Osprey,* although Bretta doubted that any Hanoverian dreadnought could ever claim a more willing crew than her father's starship, or a better-hardened, battle-craftier master. Nor could any vessel merely four times *Osprey*'s size boast of a greater weight of projectibles.

Never had she seen the Deep so crowded, although her personal experience, she admitted to herself, was somewhat limited. Aside from special warning and defensive satellites, contributed by the *nacyl,* which he had installed—a majority of them hidden in the rubble of the moonring—her father's ship was generally the only man-made object in orbit about Skye. Here, vessels were as numerous, it would appear, as the individual pebbles of which that moonring was comprised, and vastly more varied in their size, purpose, and style of rigging.

In due course, they had all contrived to seat themselves upon various articles of furniture scattered about the tiny stateroom, as Loreanna poured and distributed their tea with her daughter's assistance. Each of them went through the usual difficulties of balancing their teacups and saucers

while politely accepting sweet biscuits and small cubes of
pastry. Bretta had long since decided that this was a ritual of
some kind, most likely a trial by ordeal.

"As to your earlier question, Captain Krumm," Bretta
began judiciously, casting what she hoped was an accusing
eye upon her father, "you must ask the master of the *Osprey*
why he forces me to wear this impractical and demeaning
mantrap of an outfit, denies me the freedom of a deck I've
known since I was five, and forbids me to go aloft to work
his ship as I have done since I was eight!"

There passed a moment of surprised and embarrassed
emptiness. Loreanna raised an eyebrow, but remained silent.
The two Krumm women glanced at one another, maintaining neutral expressions. Unabashed, Arran arose and took
his daughter's hand—the hand that carried the dangerous
end of a thrustible along its back and a control yoke across
its palm—bent his head over it and kissed it. Bretta backed
away, utterly astonished and blushing to the lace in her
bodice.

"I had not been aware, melady," her father intoned
gravely, maintaining a studiously sober face as he did so,
"that I offended. If you had but told me—"

Bretta exploded: "I should not have *had* to tell you,
Daddy! You know I—"

"Pardon me, but you did not permit me to finish, my
dear," he admonished mildly.

Krumm chuckled, " 'Daddy,' is it, now?"

"Shut up, Phoebus!" Ignoring his old friend further, Arran
turned back to his daughter. "If you had told me, Robretta
Islay, I would most certainly have done precisely *nothing,*
for since when does a captain explain his orders?"

"Well, I—" Bretta could say nothing. Helpless, she
dropped her arms to her sides. Her father had restated a policy which had long seemed wise to her.

He nodded acknowledgment of her defeat upon this initial issue, and went on. "Did I not bestow upon you an
adult's responsibility, by arming you as I have?"

"Well, I—" Again she could think of nothing to say. He

was entirely correct. She did not resent that in itself—she was long accustomed to her father being correct about things and had come to rely upon it as any daughter has a perfect right to—but she hated to be proven wrong this way, in front of guests, and particularly in front of Krumm who, second only to her parents, was the single individual in the entire universe whom she was most desirous of pleasing.

For his part, the giant sat upon a ship's chest against a bulkhead, with his arms folded into one another. His expression at the moment was impossible to read. Perhaps he, too, was discomfited at being present during a family dispute.

"Is it not an adult responsibility to study the task ahead," Arran nodded at the enormous stack of textbooks she had brought with her to read upon the history, politics, economics, and customs of Hanover, which she had finished the first month of their journey, "and protect the physical well-being of her mother?"

"Well, I—" That, at least, was absurd: Loreanna required nobody's protection. If she were an evildoer, Bretta thought, she would almost have rather faced Henry Martyn than the woman who often signed letters, "Loreanna Martyn." To begin with, being thrust at must have been unpleasant enough, but Bretta was willing to wager that Loreanna's little antique cartridge weapon *hurt*. She glanced at her mother, but found no support or comfort in her eyes.

Arran gave Phoebus a significant glance. "And is it not mine, equally, both as captain and father, to protect that of the next Drector-Hereditary of Skye?"

"Well, I—*what?*"

He took a step toward her and seized her hand again, holding it in his. "My Little, had I given you the freedom of the deck, would you have learned all that you have by now of the planet below? Or would you have simply raced up and down the lines and ladders of this ship ecstatically, learning nothing you did not already know? More than that, would you have started acquiring, in the eyes of our crew to begin with, a certain quality of aloof dignity that I wish you to possess before you try your hand at commanding a starship, or a planet?"

"But I . . ." Bretta was confused and stunned. She, a female, to be her father's heir? Was that even legal? On the other hand, had Arran Islay ever shown concern over what was legal when it conflicted with what was right? And *was* this right? It certainly might have helped allay her boredom over the last two months if she had known that—against all Monopolitan convention past and present—Arran had intended to make Bretta his political heir. She could see now that Loreanna, of course, supported her husband in this decision and was speechless with pride in both of them. For some infuriating reason, all she could say was, "I already know these crewbeings, Father! They are my friends!"

Krumm seemed to be watching her carefully—even critically—now, but it was her father who continued speaking. "Precisely, My Little, which is why they must now begin to learn to know you all over again. But that part is easy enough; the difficult trick is to persuade the wild woodsrunner within *you* to settle down—only the merest trifle, mind you—to some serious business. Knowing you best by knowing myself, I believe that the experiences we are all about to have—whatever they prove to be—will help you do just that."

"And there is this, too." At long last, her mother spoke. "The Ceo sent your father and me a warning we have not told you of until now, that attempts might be made to interfere with our voyage or to injure or kill one or all of us."

Arran nodded. "Knowing that you were here with your thrustible—yes, and your mother with her little pistol—made my mind rest easy, believe me, and greatly aided me in seeing to the good reckoning and good conduct of the ship."

"So you have explained your orders after all, my captain." It was a weak rejoinder, and she knew it. She was beginning to grin at him and could not help it. She only hoped she had not failed some test it was vital that she pass.

Apparently not. Arran placed his other hand atop hers,

squeezed them, and smiled back. A glance showed her that her mother, too, was quietly beside herself with joy and pride, the faintest glimmering of tears showing in her eyes.

"So I have, indeed. And now, My Little, may we have our tea before it gets cold?"

Bretta folded the drinking siphon of her emptied teacup into the closed position and placed it back upon the magnetic center of its delicate matching saucer.

Far below the *Osprey*'s present orbital position, she observed another steam launch plunging into the dense atmosphere of the capital world, no doubt upon some tremendously important official business, as direct landfalls of this sort, she understood, were seldom permitted upon Hanover for any lesser reason.

But what was it Krumm had been saying?

". . . I grew that weary of hangin' about in orbit, an' when I heard that ye'd arrived, arranged t'come onboard with the pilot." Krumm sipped at a cup that looked ridiculously tiny in his hand, then took a professionally critical nibble at a sweet biscuit. "Nor, meboy, would I have handed me starship over t'some civil servant quite that easily, and come all lackadaisical-like, down t'tea."

Arran laughed. "No, my dear old friend, you most certainly would not. I believe I know you well. You would have hung upon the poor fellow's every move, breathed down his neck, questioned his every decision, and made his job twice as difficult as it is already. Pray let us change the subject: so you have been orbiting up here for an entire week and not yet been down to the surface?"

"Aye," Phoebus nodded, speaking round a mouthful of his dozenth biscuit and not hearing the good-natured irony in his younger comrade's voice. "With our good old friend the Ceo of Hanover payin' the position fees. At that, I'd vastly liefer be up here, than down there upon that great, gray, miserable surface."

Increasingly drawn to the spectacle outside—although equally concerned with the conversation in which she was supposed to be taking part—Bretta blinked in disbelief as a figure in some sort of protective garment wafted by the window upon a column of expelled steam. The many pleats and folds of what he wore reminded her of meat-maggots, or of pupae in the nests of insectoid colonies.

Arran laughed again, a phenomenon for which his daughter felt particular gratitude to Phoebus. "My dear fellow, that 'civil servant' whom you failed to recognize—no, no, blind me, that would have been *after* we took separate ships, back at the end of the war, would it not?—well in any case, that Hanoverian pilot, one Captain Ernest Hancock by name, is a onetime sailing master of this very vessel. Willingly would I entrust my life to his skilled hands, and in fact I have done, upon many an occasion. He will be joining us here for tea, just as soon as he has brought the *Osprey* down to the Ceo's Eye."

"The Ceo's Eye?" All of this was news to Bretta, whose recent education had chiefly concerned people and events upon the surface of the capital world. Again she chafed at having been overprotected like a child (or a Hanoverian woman) and kept in the dark. Still, she kept her peace until she could learn more.

Arran glanced up sharply, perhaps becoming aware of an error he had made. As if confirming her suspicion, he peered at the spines of the volumes she had brought.

Phoebus simply nodded. "Nobody drops his own cabelle t'Hanover, medear. Too much traffic, an' the prospect disturbs the creepie-peepies of Monopolitan Protection. (Of course, they're a type would like t'have everybody's *brain* confiscated, an' it may well be that they've *succeeded* upon this planet.) Instead, we'll heave to off this asteroid they've put in stationary orbit an' called 'the Ceo's Eye,' t'serve as a counterweight to the greatest lubberlift cabelle in the Known Galaxy. It's this we'll take down to the gloomy world below."

Now in the distance, she could just make out some gigantic object coming round the planet. In truth, she knew, it was the *Osprey* rounding Hanover, under the guidance of the pilot they had been discussing. In general, the faraway object was spherical in shape and covered with artificial structures. It must indeed have been an asteroid, and no less than several klommes in diameter.

Even so, it took her quite some while to realize that the apparent swarm of gnatlike particles, that cloud of tiny midges she could barely discern all round it, were not thousands of men in maggot-suits, nor even steam launches, but full-sized Deep-sailing vessels of two, three, even four great tiers of starsails.

" 'The Ceo's Eye,' " a thoroughly awestruck Bretta Islay half whispered to herself. She was beginning to get a fresh concept of the actual size, scope, and power of the Monopolity—along with renewed appreciation of her father's courage. Of course he would have been the first to remind his daughter that he had seen nothing of this intimidating spectacle when first he began his rebellion.

"And the bad news?" It was true that Arran knew his old first officer well.

Phoebus sighed. "It's merely that, all of us having arrived here about this glorified mudball in such remarkably good order, we've no choice before us but t'spend a considerable amount of time upon its miserable surface. We are all to be ushered in immediately t'see the Ceo Lia, long may she wave, but then it seems other matters, unspecified details connected with her summons, require more time t'resolve. Ye realize what we're dealin' with, don'tcha, melad?"

Osprey's captain shuddered, dramatically but with complete sincerity: *"Bureaucrats."*

"Aye, an' if I was a religionist, I'd be aprayin' now fer our immortal souls."

Chapter XVIII:
Civilized Captivity

"Please, Brougham, leave the small case beside the bed."

"Very well, Madame, as you wish."

The *yensid* butler picked up the box in question (containing a mate to the thrustible Arran had departed with that morning under his jacket sleeve) and placed it carefully upon the nightstand where Loreanna had indicated. As the alien moved about the room, helping them to unpack, Bretta observed him carefully. So little weight did each of his hundreds of short tentacles bear that they left no trace behind him in the thick nap of the bedroom carpet. She was grateful that she would not be called upon to track him across a forest floor.

It must have all seemed very strange, both to Brougham and Loreanna. The girl could understand that much, as she watched her mother and the old family servant attend to the careful unpacking of the many trunks and bags they had lately brought down from orbit with them from the *Osprey*. In theory, Bretta was assisting them, but the last time she had seen any sort of non-human, it had been a crew of *nacyl,* she had been only three or four years old, and she was having to suppress a tendency to gawk. For the moment, the three of them were working in a stately bedroom suite Loreanna had chosen for herself and her husband, rooms that had belonged to her own father and mother a generation earlier.

"And I suppose," Loreanna sighed, anticipating prolonged and frequent absences upon her husband's part, "you had best leave my sewing case at my side."

"Very good, Madame."

Bretta suspected that the *yensid* was in fact ecstatic to be of service to the Daimler-Wilkinsons once again, and, with the return of Loreanna, whom he had known and cared for, almost since her birth, was demonstrating—quite literally— an inhuman degree of restraint. No fewer than a dozen members of his peculiar species had maintained this great establishment immaculately for many years, in the complete absence of their human . . . would it be masters or employers?

Like those of every other room in the monumental edifice they presently occupied, the ceilings in this bedroom suite were not a siemme less than six full measures high, supported by walls wainscoted to above head height in some dark and ancient hardwood not native to Hanover, and covered the remainder of the way, up to the elaborately decorative moldings where they intersected with the ceiling, with a richly textured printed fabric. Upon the walls hung family likenesses going back many generations, and scenes depicting hundreds of planets upon which the Daimler-Wilkinson family had business and political interests. Everywhere, vases and small sculptures stood upon decorative stands.

The entire establishment was rather eerily—but at the same time rather agreeably—quiet, quieter, in any case, than Bretta (who had grown up among five noisy siblings and dozens of happy and uninhibitedly human servants) had ever known an occupied residential building could be. The whole place smelled, somehow, of generations of unlimited wealth, and of a restrained decorum in all things that it necessitated, bordering upon the superhuman. She wondered briefly and irreverently whether it was an aerosol of some sort that one could purchase.

These, Bretta thought, had been Clive and Jennivere Daimler-Wilkinson's private chambers. For her, walking through them was like visiting the royal tombs of some ancient, long-lost civilization, and the idea of sleeping here, was unimaginable. She had discovered that she could not make herself think of the wrinkled old crone, Owld Jenn, as the lovely young bride who had shared these rooms with her husband, Loreanna's father. She suspected that her mother was experiencing much the same difficulty, although her composure remained as it had always been, and she betrayed no outward manifestation of discomfiture. Loreanna had installed her daughter in her own old rooms which, just like everything else in the Daimler-Wilkinson town house, she had not seen for fifteen years.

"Thank you, Brougham. And now, Robretta Islay, while we still have time to discuss it before luncheon, tell me what it is that is bothering you, young lady."

Another recent phenomenon to which Bretta could not accustom herself was the inconsistent manner in which, momentarily surrendering all reserve, her mother had thrown her arms about the upright, inhuman form of the ancient caretaker, exclaiming through an uncharacteristic flood of tears how happy she was to see him, then, having regained control over the outward expression of her feelings, could speak of personal matters with her daughter as if he were absent, while at the same time continuing to direct him as he assisted her to unpack.

Bretta sighed, resigned to the fact that she did not know precisely what was troubling her—many things, she knew that much, hopelessly intertwined—and that, even if she did, she could never possibly get all of them out at once.

"Very well, Mother," she replied, temporarily settling, more or less at random, upon a single item, very likely not even the most urgent or important. "Why have we not accepted the Ceo's gracious invitation to reside with her in that great palace of hers while we stay here upon Hanover? I say, it would be *ever* so entertaining, for it is not at all the more or less humble executive mansion that I had been led by reading to expect. Why, Lia even has her own *archery* ranges, one indoors and another one outside! Why ever did Father decline?"

Loreanna took a garment from a suitcase opened upon the bed, casually refolded it to different dimensions, and put it away in the drawer of a nearby bureau.

"My dear, I thought that we had agreed upon this. In the first place, it would greatly disappoint Brougham and his entire staff. And in the second, as upon earlier occasions, your father senses in his former mentor's offer a not-so-subtle suggestion that he redeliver both his political and his personal sovereignty to the Monopolity. The entire conceit may simply be Lia's idea of a joke. Sometimes I believe sincerely that it must be. But at the very least, your father sensibly desires to retain complete control over his own comings and goings, which could quite possibly become awkward were we to stay with the Ceo."

" 'Awkward' is hardly the word for it," Bretta agreed with a degree of bitter enthusiasm, her understanding of political nuances being sophisticated for one of her age. "But staying here is little help for it, as far as I am concerned, having been informed in no uncertain terms that, upon the capital planet, unescorted females do not venture out to explore the city upon their own!"

Loreanna nodded, having in her own time chafed under the same restriction and understanding her daughter's resentment very well indeed. "My darling, it pains me inordinately to watch someone I love as much as I do you writhing so uncomfortably in what amounts to a kind of civilized captivity. I recall most vividly how much like torture it felt to me when I was younger. I appreciate that it must be incalculably worse in your case, as you have been accustomed virtually all your life to the complete freedom of field and forest. And yet now, to your dismay (not unlike many another individual before you), you find that you have suddenly become a prisoner to other people's expectations of you."

Bretta could say nothing to Loreanna because she was suddenly forced to bite her lower lip in order to avoid humiliating herself by bursting into tears.

"All I can add, my dear," her mother went on, preserving her daughter's dignity by pretending not to have discerned her severe emotional distress, "is that this is a principal reason that we dwell upon our lovely moonringed Skye—to which we shall return as soon as we are able—instead of upon this world."

"But Mother—"

Loreanna laid a nightgown she had been folding upon the coverlet and set gentle hands upon her daughter's shoulders, pressing her forehead to Bretta's. That it was possible only because she was wearing shoes with heels, while her daughter wore slippers without them, did not escape her. Sometime recently, she realized, not without a pang, while a mother's attention had been directed somewhere else for the briefest of moments, her little Bretta had become a woman.

"My dear, I am aware that you believe it unfair that these strictures do not apply to men like your father and Phoebus, busy preparing their respective ships and crews for whatever Lia may call upon them to do. I know you feel injured, still wondering at some level, why you cannot be in orbit with your father."

Bretta closed her eyes. "Mother, I—"

"Although you and I will probably find ourselves with absolutely nothing productive—or even particularly interesting—to occupy our time, we have no choice except to wait, grateful that, away from Hanover, with your father in command, we will no longer be excluded from this great adventure. In the meantime, you should understand that waiting in patience—without such hope in sight as a reward—is the one art practiced to perfection by Hanoverian women."

"Why," the girl stood back from her mother and grimaced in a manner known only to fifteen-year-old human females, "do I fail to be much comforted by this information?"

Loreanna grinned back at her daughter, and shrugged. "I assure you that we shall not be entirely without activities and events to which we may look forward. Although we shall visit with her privately sometime tomorrow, a public audience with the Ceo must be fitted for us into the official schedule of the 'Droom. All interested parties are scurrying even as we speak to rearrange their personal affairs to accommodate this 'emergency' conference. Among ourselves, we and the Ceo must decide upon the wisest course of action, and then strive to make it appear that we arrived at it during our public meeting."

Bretta did not reply to this, but Loreanna understood by what the girl did with her eyebrows that there was more to her discontent than the family Islay merely having chosen to take up residence at the Daimler-Wilkinson town house, or even the one-sidedly restrictive Hanoverian customs she found being imposed upon her. Sometimes, Loreanna readily appreciated, the only way to disentangle these things from one another and sort them out, was one item at a time.

"Very well, what is it, dear?"

Bretta threw her mother a significant glance, indicating the old *yensid* servant as he easily carried a trunk that must have been five times his weight across the room toward an open closet. Bretta had been informed that he and the rest of his species had evolved upon some faraway, primitive planet possessed of many times the gravity of Hanover, and this was one of the occasions it was obvious.

"You may speak quite freely before Brougham, my darling, as I always have done."

"You may, indeed," Miss Brougham volunteered, "for I am discreet—and quite deaf."

Both females stood for rather a long while in astonished silence, Bretta with a grin widening upon her face, and Loreanna having dropped whatever item of clothing she was handling, simply to gape. Apparently the old servant was absolutely giddy to have his former young mistress back after all this time, and for however brief an interval, along with a younger version of her whom he appeared to like just as well. This uncharacteristically jocular observation, which Bretta always recalled afterward, was the only way he ever chose to show it.

Bretta cast her eyes downward and scuffed a delicate, slippered toe upon the carpet. "It is just that everyone seems to expect me to be delighted at this cozy arrangement. Should I not be perfectly thrilled, after all, to be sharing accommodations with my long-lost and mysterious grandmother, not to mention a foreboding, equally mysterious half uncle whom I never knew before I had?"

Loreanna bestowed upon her daughter a most curious look. "Apparently not."

The Islay family had arrived at the Daimler-Wilkinson city residence late the previous evening, following a rather prolonged and tedious voyage down the cabelle from the Ceo's Eye in a multistoried lubberlift which boasted private compartments, and an even more prolonged and tedious voyage from Hanover's equator, aboard something reminiscent of their draywherry back home, except that there had been several such conveyances, all hooked together into a long chain. Their initial meeting with Owld Jenn and her son Woulf this morning at breakfast had been mercifully brief, yet long enough to leave an indelible impression.

Making up her mind (as always) to be straightforward, Bretta cleared her throat. "In my opinion, Mother, and with all due respect to you, neither of them seems friendly to excess, nor even . . ." The girl hesitated here, until Loreanna nodded at her to go on. "Nor even particularly *clean.*" This was a serious failing in the fastidious young woman's estimation, and among the worst condemnations she could level. In fact, it had taken less than an hour at the same table with the grim, crazy old woman and her barbaric son for Bretta to begin wishing fervently that her father had accepted Lia's offer.

"I see . . ."

Bretta had been grateful when her newfound relatives had been chauffeured away to some unnamed establishment of Hanoverian officialdom to continue being interrogated. Owld Jenn, it seemed, knew certain things the Ceo's government desperately wanted to know. But at present, she only knew that she knew them; she did not know what they were. It was a considerable problem. The girl was mature enough to be aware that time and increased familiarity might conceivably modify her initial opinion of the pair, but she rather doubted that they would.

Her mother went on, "I imagine that I might pretend to be offended by what you have just told me." Loreanna looked at her daughter. "Jennivere is my mother, after all. But you have been brought up to identify the truth unfailingly, as you see it. And as I see it, myself, I fear. I confess that I am having trouble of my own, reconciling that unpleasant and difficult old woman downstairs with the image of her I have always carried in my mind. And characteristically," Loreanna added, "it never occurred to you to go stay with Lia upon your own, although you would almost certainly have been welcomed by her."

Now it was Bretta's turn to gape. "Mother, I could *never* do that to you and Father!" She giggled, or came as close to it as she ever had. "It would be—I don't know, *unseemly*— disloyal, even. It would appear that I am just as much a prisoner to my *own* expectations as to those of anyone else!"

Her mother nodded, highly gratified with her daughter's judgment. "I'm glad you appreciate the fine points, my dear, resent them though you may. Even were we mistaken with regard to Lia's ultimate intent, which we may well be, your father is concerned with what might be made of it in the 'Droom, by friend and foe alike, did we appear to be as intimate with her as in fact we are."

Bretta wrinkled her nose. "You actually relish this political stuff, don't you?"

Loreanna smiled what Bretta thought of as her secret smile. "I'm afraid so, my dear, although I like being your mother and your father's wife a deal better."

"You do?"

"There is an ancient and extremely very romantic notion that somewhere in the universe there awaits you, whether he knows it or not, that one individual most perfectly suited to you, your ideal mate. I was fortunate to meet mine, and fortunate again to have done so when I was only a year younger than you are now. Thus at his side, I have spent somewhat more than half my life—which is appropriate because he *is* more than half my life—though I am but twenty-nine years of age. And in the fifteen years we have been wed, I have borne him six splendid children, beginning with you, my dear, so that I would have more of him to love."

Happily, it was not long before Loreanna's promise, that they should not be entirely bereft of events to which they might look forward, began coming true.

That very afternoon, for the first time in many years, and thanks in part to the Ceo's encouragement (as a young woman, Lia, too, had been an unwilling captive of Hanoverian civiliza-tion), there began a series of what would prove to be many courtesy calls of varying formality paid at the Daimler-Wilkinson residence.

Although Arran had not been told what the Ceo required of him (perhaps because she did not know, herself), it was clear that he would be expected to go somewhere and do something. Consequently, he and Phoebus were furiously busy at the moment, as they would be until they departed Hanover, with ship outfitting and recruiting. The most difficult part of any voyage was to find a suitable and willing crew. In his absence, his womenfolk were expected to receive calls, extend a welcoming hand to old friends, perhaps even to make new ones. Before Bretta quite realized what was happening, she was making the acquaintance of individuals who, before this day, had been Islay family legends.

"Believe me, I am utterly enchanted to meet you at long last, my dear Robretta," her mother's distinguished-looking uncle, Sedgeley Daimler-Wilkinson, informed her, bowing deeply over her hand and kissing it. Bretta managed not to blush. Perhaps there was something, after all, to be said for Hanoverian fashion. His gallant gesture would not have been the same had she been wearing her suede vest and cutoffs. And if Great-uncle Sedgeley noticed the thrustible her mother had insisted that she wear, he gave no indication of it.

Bretta wondered if her mother had felt awkward, making her uncle welcome in what was, at least technically, his own home. Presently, they occupied one of the Daimler-Wilkinson residence's many plushly furnished parlors or drawing rooms, there awaiting a late luncheon. From her lifelong study of history and countless family stories, Bretta understood that it was Sedgeley who had once borne the unenviable burden of informing a ruling Ceo of his utter defeat at the hands of a mere boy—her own father, Henry Martyn. If so, the old devil wore it well, for he appeared much younger than she had expected. Or perhaps there was something truthful, after all, to these stories about the Immortal School.

At the same time, she found herself thoroughly enchanted —or at least well entertained—by Sedgeley's companion, the wry and darkly handsome Frantisek Demondion-Echeverria. Seizing her hand in both of his and kissing it in a manner that differed greatly, somehow, from that of her uncle (and this time she had blushed, right down to her navel), the former Ambassador Plenipotentiary of the Jendyne Empery-Cirot had introduced himself as "merely an adept" of that same mysterious organization to which Sedgeley admitted he belonged.

Both had apologized for being out of fashion in their attire. Their dark velvet three-piece suits and many-ruffled blouses were quite as impractical as her own dress, but they were better, she thought, than the fake Deep-raider clothing she had earlier seen being worn upon the street below her bedroom window.

There were others at these initial gatherings, as well. Her father's own daughter, she found herself wondering how many among these illustrious figures were actually traitors who opposed whatever her father and Lia intended doing. How many, even those in high positions of great trust, were working in secret, perhaps on behalf of the Oplyte slavers themselves, whoever they turned out to be?

"And this good fellow, my dear," her great-uncle Sedgeley informed her as Demondion-Echeverria looked on, "is our mutual friend and fellow Initiate, Brother Leo. Brother Leo does not speak, having undertaken a solemn vow of silence, but you will soon discover that, at need, he can be most articulate, nonetheless."

Bretta noted that her mother wore a most peculiar expression. She lent special scrutiny to the man standing before her, a great hulking animal of a creature with dark curly hair, massive beard, and brilliantly azure eyes that may have been inspired or insane. Sedgeley was correct about him. Somehow he managed, without a word, to be as charming—and as sinister—as the former ambassador.

Suddenly, she realized who the man was—none other than Lia's father, the former Ceo Leupould IX, himself—and when he observed that dawning realization light her face, he responded with a dazzling smile and a sweeping bow that let his hair brush the carpet, no small feat for a man of his great size.

"I believe"—Demondion-Echeverria suddenly gave her a look of hunger that chilled her to the core—"that Leo would tell you that he, too, is charmed, Mistress Islay."

Whatever Bretta might have offered the man by way of a reply was lost in an uproar that began at the door to the drawing room and swept into the middle of the parlor before anybody realized what was happening. A slender figure wearing a deeply hooded cloak stood among them suddenly, followed awkwardly by poor old Brougham, who was long accustomed to preceding and announcing all guests.

The figure brushed its hood back, breathless, and radiant with exertion. "My dears, I simply *couldn't* wait to see you! I'm so glad you're here, at last! Where in the Ceo's name are Arran and the indomitable Phoebus? Pray forgive me for inviting myself, but I trust I haven't arrived too late for lunch!"

Belatedly, Brougham announced, "Lia Wheeler, Ceo of the Monopolity of Hanover!"

Chapter XIX:
An Almost Motherly
Interest

GURUHHHHHHH!

Unfortunately for the Ceo, her dramatic entrance was spoiled by a long, rolling peal of thunder that shook the house and rattled every window. The quantity of dust sifting down upon the gathering from the ceiling and fixtures overhead would have greatly distressed Brougham, had he been present to see it.

Wherever he had gone at the moment, he was certain to be frantic. Here, there was considerable expostulation and shrieking. When Bretta discovered that she was contributing to it, she stopped. A landscape hologram hanging upon a wall crashed to the floor. The former ambassador, believing they were under attack of some variety, broke a vase diving beneath the end table it had been sitting upon.

"By the Ceo's beard," exclaimed a conspicuously beardless Ceo, grinning at Demondion-Echeverria's posterior. "That must be a steam launch! Sedgeley, pray tell me that this pretentious pile of bricks *does* boast of a landing stage!"

"Indeed it does, Madame, albeit long unused." Sedgeley had leapt to his feet, exhilarated where his friend was terrified. "We should be in a poor fix did it not!" With his stick he prodded that part of Demondion-Echeverria's anatomy which Lia had been regarding. "Do get up, Frantisek, you embarrass yourself!"

His dignity unruffled, the fellow brushed at his unfashionable clothing as he arose and adjusted his masque. "I pray your kind indulgence, dear ladies, and Brother Leo.

Sedgeley, my valued old comrade, you would not be quite so alacritous to criticize, had you been brought up, as are we all in the Jendyne Empery-Cirot, an involuntary subscriber to the Coup-of-the-Month-Club. Madame Ceo, did I overhear you speculate that a steam launch has alighted upon the roof?"

Before they had become entirely aware of a noisy clumping from the hall, the double doors of the parlor swung wide to admit a variety of sapient forms. "Indeed, it has done!" roared a voice familiar to some within, as a cheerful, ruddy-faced Phoebus Krumm followed Arran into the gathering's midst. Both were attired as common starsailors and reeked of a hard day's labor and of the harsh solvents used to clean and repair the wire mesh of which starships were constructed.

Brougham entered immediately behind them. Bretta believed that for the first time, she was seeing the old alien servitor put off his guard, either by her father's precipitate landing upon the roof, or his and Phoebus's equally impetuous entrance. Perhaps it was merely the way that they smelled. Bretta realized suddenly that she longed, more than anything, to smell that same way, herself.

Oddly, Lia seemed surprised, and perhaps even a trifle displeased, to see them. In a flash, the girl consummated a pair of inferences that would have made her father proud of her: first, that the Ceo Lia had come here in order to persuade her or her mother of something in his absence; second, that he had a watch set, here at the Daimler-Wilkinson establishment or at the palace—considering their timing, the latter seemed likelier—to warn him of such an occurrence.

"Compared to the more conventional lubberlift," Phoebus added, "it has great speed and other features to recommend it, although the process tends to consume rather a deal of energy—do I understand that we're just in time for luncheon?"

". . . and for that reason," Lia informed the gathering, once they had all finished their midday meal and come back to the parlor, "by my direct command as Ceo, and under the aegis of the Monopolity of Hanover, Captain Islay, along with a select few companions, will embark at his earliest convenience upon a voyage I have every personal hope and expectation will alter the course of history."

Bretta understood that her "Aunt Lia"—which was to say, her late uncle Robret's unwed wife—was presently exhibiting one of the attributes of true leadership. Whatever seat she chose—in this case a green velveteen settee—immediately assumed the properties of a throne. Having, with all of her customary dispatch, recovered whatever aplomb she had momentarily lost upon Arran's unexpected arrival, she was now employing what Bretta understood to be her "official" voice. The girl wondered how her father would take the words "direct command," since he had refused to be considered a Monopolitan subject. This must be another gambit in the game of sovereignty they played. She did gather, correctly, that "under the aegis of" meant Lia would be paying for the expedition.

Arran opened his mouth, more than likely to protest his former tutor's provocative choice of words, but found himself interrupted by Demondion-Echeverria.

"I beg your pardon abjectly, Madame Ceo." The former Jendyne ambassador glared daggers at a man who, fifteen years before, had been his own antagonist as much as he had been Sedgeley's, and had unknowingly altered his own personal circumstances even more severely. "But I must ask, are you entirely satisfied you have chosen the most qualified individual to lead this historic voyage of yours?"

Arran shook his head.

Phoebus laughed.

Bretta was scandalized and had difficulty suppressing a derisive snort at this overdressed *dandifop* her great-uncle unwisely called friend. Who *was* the most qualified individual, if not the celebrated Henry Martyn, who, to recover a family legacy vilely expropriated from him as a boy, had managed to humiliate the two greatest imperia-conglomerate in the Known Universe, all but single-handedly?

At present, Lia was conveying essentially the same opin-ion to Demondion-Echeverria, and, naturally, rather the greater portion of what she might have told the man went unsaid. As an example, what would he have made of the fact that she maintained an almost motherly interest in the well-being of the last (albeit vigorous and expanding) branch of the family Islay? The amazing truth was that it remained a matter of considerable legal and academic dispute whether or not she herself was a member of that family. As she had observed herself upon occasion, it all hinged upon whether she was a widow or an old maid.

Over the fifteen years since her interrupted wedding, Lia had never laid claim to any right as the younger Robret Islay's widowed bride. Nonetheless—to whatever extent an all-powerful ruler can ever be seen as anything but that—Arran and Loreanna had always done their best to treat her as a part of their family. The Islay children had always bestowed upon their adopted aunt their colored drawings, clay and papier-mâché sculptures, and other unidentifiable accretions of yarn and plaster. And to give her proper credit, Lia had set aside an entire hall within her great residence as a museum for such objects.

In any event, Lia greatly appreciated the loving concern they had always shown her, and she appreciated it especially well because they had shown it before she came to be appointed Ceo of the Monopolity of Hanover. At the same time, she relished the trifling games of power she played with Arran. And yet Lia was unusual in that the loneliness and isolation of power did not trouble her.

What she did mind, more and more every day, was never knowing upon whom she could rely to tell her the truth. Being a scholar of history, she was not unaware that in this she was echoing her father and every other conscientious ruler of humanity's past. But even this daily occupational irritation could be ameliorated to a certain degree: all she had to do was activate the autothilles of Arran and Loreanna's half dozen children, which stood upon her desk.

As she had been with Sedgeley—only far more so in Arran's case—she was eager to give him every opportunity to redeem himself, not in terms of any transgressions of which the man may have been culpable against the Monopolity; having been at the receiving end of their tender mercies herself, she believed that Sedgeley and her father had needed taking down, and that Arran had been the perfect individual to do it. No, it was in his own eyes—and those of no others—that his redemption must be accomplished. It was unnecessary where his loving wife and adoring eldest daughter were concerned, and much the same was true, for that matter, of the woman who may or may not have been his sister-in-law.

For the past decade and a half, Arran's life might have been described as satisfying and productive. Many another individual might well have envied the young, accomplished Drector-Hereditary of Skye. And yet it was quite obvious to anyone who loved him that the man suffered a continuous, debilitating case of self-condemnation. Each and every day he had to discover, all over again, a way to live with what seemed to him the moral certainty that, in cold blood, he had "murdered" four hundred innocent Jendyne naval cadets. It was undeniable that Arran had killed many times that number in his struggle against his enemies. Yet this instance, and this instance alone, seemed to trouble his warrior's conscience.

The tragic incident had occurred as an unintended consequence of Arran's overall strategy during a final clash with the Monopolity and its allies. He had press-ganged the not-altogether-unwilling cadets into service aboard the eerie sailless fighting ships of the *nacyl,* his own alien supporters. (For their odd shape, these otherwise advanced and civilized creatures were known throughout the Monopolity by the considerably less-flattering appellation, "flatsies.") Unfortunately, the cadets had all died a horrible death soon after the historic battle they had helped him win, appearing to have succumbed to certain lethal energic emanations somehow associated with the odd alien vessels.

No one involved, neither alien nor human, could have predicted such a horror. Yet in the darkest moments of his moral torment, it had never helped Arran to understand that nobody else blamed him for what had happened, not even the cadets themselves, speaking from what they knew were their deathbeds. He was long accustomed to relying, in times of the direst need, upon his own judgment and upon nobody else's. In this instance, he simply calculated that everybody else was wrong about his guilt—if for no other reason than that they loved him and wished him well—and that he was right, and therefore guilty.

For fifteen years, with only the most minimal of interruptions at its onset, the Ceo Lia had made a high priority of maintaining an intimate and frequent correspondence with Loreanna. In all that decade and a half, Arran's loyal, loving wife had never betrayed her husband's confidence. Still, Lia was an astute woman, more than capable of observing and drawing her own conclusions. Making the fullest use possible of her own intelligence background and the resources of an entire empire, she had learned that it was this tragedy that prevented Arran from permitting himself to be the hero he richly deserved to be.

And what was even worse, from being the hero his *children* needed him to be.

But what she said now to Demondion-Echeverria was merely this: "Are not his feats still held by everyone, in every quarter, as evidence of an inherent strategic and tactical genius? Have I not personally known him for many years to be an exemplar of integrity and reliability? And are these points not good and sufficient reason in and of themselves, my dear Ambassador, to select him to lead this preliminary reconnaissance against the repulsive purveyors of the Oplyte Trade? Pray do not bother answering, sir, for that decision, I remind you, is ultimately mine in any case, and my questions are purely rhetorical in character: one of the few privileges of power in which I occasionally indulge myself."

Sedgeley's visage began to lose the look of apprehension it had assumed, as Demondion-Echeverria stifled a reflexive snort of his own. Bretta noticed that her father kept his eyes upon the carpet, some grim ratiocination pulling the corners of his mouth practically down to his chin. So there it was again, that seldom-seen but undeniable reaction of shame at any reference to his heroism.

"Which is the reason," Lia added, "that, anticipating his arrival here, I took certain steps to aid him. Foremost was to assure that, in addition to his family, whom he insists upon taking with him (although they would be most welcome to remain with me, did they but prefer it), Captain Islay has worthy traveling companions for the journey I purpose. For example (and I trust that in this, my choice has been correct) I summoned Henry Martyn's trusted right hand, the famous and formidable Phoebus Krumm, who, in this particular and perilous undertaking, should prove himself even more indispensable than usual."

The man managed to blush and stammer, "Me very own pleasure, t'be sure, Ma'am."

"And I assure you sir, that the pleasure is entirely mine." She turned to the rest of them. "I have never before met this not-so-gentle giant, but I have often viewed material concerning him in the mass media, smitten as they seem to be in recent years with 'brigandial histories.' For the most part, I have relied upon what my friend Loreanna has had to tell me about him in her letters."

"Which have not gone far enough in his praise," her friend Loreanna volunteered.

"Captain Krumm is known throughout the imperia-conglomerate—and his reputation is more than justified, according to what Loreanna tells me of her husband's opinion—for his starship-handling abilities. When Captain Islay first encountered him, he commanded a gundeck's mighty projectibles to sure and deadly effect. What is more, he is so large of frame, and muscular, that he wields a pair of outsized thrustibles originally constructed for issue to Oplytes!"

As well as did the considerably more diminutive Captain Islay, Arran's daughter knew, from one corner of her eye observing her mother smile quietly at the same time, and doubtless with the same thought. Of course, that was a different matter, they both realized, one of sheer, indomitably stubborn determination.

"We are likewise informed," Lia went on, "that Captain Krumm once enjoyed a narrow but successful escape from chirurgical and cheminergic alteration into an Oplyte warrior-slave, himself. It is asserted that he decapitated a number of the slavers with an oven 'peel,' a sort of gigantic metallic spatula gradually rendered razor-sharp through its continual sliding contact with an oven floor. It is our conviction that, upon account of this experience, he will prove that much more unlikely to allow his commander, his commander's family, and their fellow travelers, to suffer such a cruel fate as capture by the enemy they pursue. That is precisely chiefmost of the tasks with which we would charge him."

For his part, Bretta was aware, Krumm would never consider undertaking such a journey without his own family, his two wives of long standing, Tula and Tillie. These constituted yet another reason—and an insultingly salacious one—that the Hanoverian media could not seem to get enough of Krumm. Never mind the mundane fact that both his women were small, plump, middle-aged, and remarkably unglamorous to anybody but him. Most of the human populations of the imperia-conglomerate were monogynous, although this was chiefly due less to any virtue of moderation and restraint than to a need—Bretta recalled reading about it under the heading "Marginal Utility" in an economics textbook—to preserve the perceived value of politically and financially advantageous marriages.

Lia smiled as sweetly as possible at each of her listeners in turn. "And then, of course, there is our present—and our father's former—Executor-General, the wise, courageous, and highly capable Sedgeley Daimler-Wilkinson, esquire."

"What?"

"Did you say something, Sedgeley? We thought not. Sedgeley is that most insightful and resourceful individual who brought Jennivere Daimler-Wilkinson—or 'Owld Jenn' as she now styles herself—to our attention in the first place, for which we thank him profoundly and sincerely. Not only does he have unanticipated depths, as we have discovered more than once already, we know he will agree that, in this best of all possible worlds, no good deed should go unpunished."

Bretta could see clearly that her great-uncle now wore a nonplussed (not to mention openly apprehensive) expression upon his face. Such transparency represented a breach, she thought, for a professional diplomat of his reputed level. The girl regarded Lia with new appreciation. For Sedgeley, being torn out of his sybaritic life at the Immortal School and sent upon this perilous, uncomfortable expedition, would be rather like what he had done to his niece—and more importantly in this context, the Ceo's closest friend—fifteen years ago.

But Lia was going on. "Of late, it has come to our attention that these depths include a rather sensational career as a duelist in his youth, during a period when masques were fashioned in 'cutaway' style, first to facilitate, and then to reveal a fashionable scar." She leaned forward, more directly to address the one of whom she had been speaking. "Where you go now, Sedgeley, such an avocation may prove more valuable than any political skill you may possess."

Lia snapped her fingers, and a servant who had not been apparent before came forward, bearing a leather-covered case. Within lay something slender and silvery which made Bretta think of the slim rod running along her own forearm.

"Therefore, Sedgeley Daimler-Wilkinson, Executor-General to Lia, Ceo of Hanover, we present you, in the sight of all these others, this handsomely engraved personal thrustible—with which we command you to begin practicing each day, beginning this evening, until you and your company leave Hanoverian orbit."

The diplomat stammered. "Madame, I am not—I do not quite know what to—"

"Say nothing, then, good fellow. We have come to like you well and would greatly enjoy seeing you seize this opportunity to reestablish yourself. What is more . . . I shall take personal advantage of the moment to advise you that I was brought up to favor a stoic, rather than a hedonistic view, as I believe you were, as well. Your long, faithful service to my father made you wise and useful in the ways of power; however, I believe that you have been foolish, lately, squandering your capabilities upon a myriad of empty-headed bodily pleasures. I fondly hope that you will think upon this waste during your journey."

"Madame Ceo, I—"

"Also, my dear Sedgeley, I reckon that you have an old and unpaid debt of honor that you must be quite desperate to settle. Your brother Clive was not quite as lucky in escaping the Oplyte slavers as Mr. Krumm, here. Upon that account, the bizarre wretch once known as Jennivere will travel with you. She should serve you as a constant reminder of that debt, do you require it, the repayment of which—with interest—may well turn out to be the making of you."

Bretta squirmed a little with vicarious embarrassment. She supposed that it must have been a very humbling experience for a man in his late fifties to receive such a lecture from someone less than forty, and a woman, at that. The Executor-General had colored as it began, but now appeared to have himself in hand.

"For this and other reasons, we have commanded that Jennivere retrace, as nearly as possible, the unlucky pleasure voyage she began so long ago with her husband."

"But Madame Ceo," Demondion-Echeverria interjected, "when we questioned her, she was quite unable to tell us anything about where she had traveled or when—"

"To aid her, my dear Ambassador, we have consulted at some considerable length with an expert skilled in the evocation of lost memories, including such trivial data—that is, from the viewpoint of an unwilling passenger—as the visi-

ble stellar patterns from which navigational inferences may
be extracted."

"Ahh," Demondion-Echeverria nodded understanding.
"The ancient hypnosis. Mesmerism."

"Owld Jenn has already experienced a number of surprisingly productive sessions with this expert. Thirty years ago,
Jennivere Daimler-Wilkinson's ill-fated journey took her
from the dizzying heights of Hanoverian aristocracy to sub-
human depths of degradation and despair. Her one comfort
today seems to be the anticipation of revenge, and to this
end, we assure you, we shall lend her every assistance. To
begin with, at our order, her son Woulf will go with her."

Bretta must have made some kind of face, although she
had no recollection of it, for now the Ceo Lia turned to her.
"That will make one more like you, my dear, who is familiar, not just with weapons themselves, but, something far
more important in these overly fastidious times, the *idea* of
weapons." The Ceo shrugged. "And the pair, mother and
son, appear to be inseparable in any case."

"Lastly, we shall require that Sedgeley be accompanied
by his old friends and confidantes, Frantisek Demondion-
Echeverria who, as a refugee to Hanover, will now have an
opportunity to repay his adopted imperium-conglomerate,
and the formidable Brother Leo—no, no, Father, do not
break your vow to thank us."

"Madame Ceo . . . I implore you . . ." Demondion-
Echeverria spluttered, "I beseech you . . . I . . ." His face had
turned purple. Brother Leo's was pure white.

Lia straightened herself where she sat. "Dear gentlebeings, we fervently wish that we, too, were going forth with
all of you upon this great adventure. We could complain, as
others before us have done, that we are no more than a prisoner of our office. But in truth, we rather enjoy being the
Ceo, and in any event, who put a thrustible to our head and
commanded that we accept the position?"

The irony, Bretta knew, was that this was virtually what
Leupould *had* done.

"And now, one of the most dangerously exhilarating

temptations of power is the frequent and satisfying opportunity it presents one to command whole gaggles of poltroons and dimwits to stop jabbering over a task and get on with it.

"With due respect, it is to this temptation that I now allow myself to succumb."

CHAPTER XX:
EUNUCHS DRESSED AS CLOWNS

"Now, now, Father, you need not say a single word—even if you were inclined to do so. I happen to know *precisely* what you are thinking at the moment."

Lia buried both of her hands in the opposite fur-trimmed sleeves of her coat. It was not truly cold today, especially where she and her companions sat together now, but the perpetually leaden skies of Hanover—which made the rainy planet Skye appear relatively sunny and dry—always made her feel as if it were. She had never gotten used to it, and doubted that she ever would.

Brother Leo raised his massive eyebrows at his daughter, but, of course, said nothing at all. He had a secret wager with himself that Lia knew nothing of what he thought. And if she did not, then no one did, which was exactly as he wished it. The ugly fact that he was about to be compelled to spend the next several months in human company not of his own choosing filled him with disgust and dread. But he was not prepared to say so to his daughter now, nor—the prospect being far worse than that of the voyage itself—to explain why.

Instead, he pretended to gaze out through the one-way window at his elbow upon the dense traffic of passersby, both vehicular and pedestrian, both alien and otherwise. There were even one or two sapient species out there that he was unable to recognize, an indication that considerable time had passed since his abdication—along with an even greater number of events—so much that he had somehow lost track of it. The route they took this afternoon, however, was completely familiar to him, as he had often been a guest at what he still thought of as Sedgeley's house, during a happier time when he had been the ruler of more than he could possibly survey and called the Residence ahead his own.

They were being conveyed back to that very edifice now in his daughter's official unmarked vehicle, a glowing teardrop-shape of metalloid mesh, self-directed, entirely devoid of moving parts, driven by §-fields that forced air through a forward intake, accelerated it, and expelled it out the rear of the machine, thrusting them along efficiently and quietly, several siemmes above the cobbled street, suspended upon the same frictionless §-fields propelling them.

There was a time when he would have enjoyed this ride, but it was gone forever.

Lia had requested that her father accompany her back from the Daimler-Wilkinson establishment while Sedgeley and his friend Demondion-Echeverria took transport of their own to the same destination. Since that first day when they had called upon her with regard to the return of Owld Jenn to the capital planet, she had gently but firmly insisted that they stay with her at her Residence. The strain of remaining upon dry land, within an unnourishing atmosphere of mere air, under the full force of Hanover's rather oppressive gravity, was beginning to tell upon all three—an effect she had awaited patiently.

In the end, they would be more than eager to take ship and be quit of her.

Presently, she smiled. "You wish to know why, aside from reasons I have lately given in public, I urge my old pupil, Captain Arran Islay—your old enemy, the brigand Henry Martyn—to accept this all-important assignment I have offered him. It really *is* quite straightforward, Father. You see, he was brought up—partly by me—to detest the Oplyte Trade. If anyone lives who would deal it a mortal blow—and

can—it is he. And, sharing his deep hatred of the vile enterprise, as I do, I sincerely wish him every conceivable success."

Had there been reproach in what she had just said? In all
his time as Ceo, he had done nothing about the Trade, nor
had it even occurred to him to try.

She watched his frown, and chuckled. "Is that a trifle circular for you, Father?"

Her father shrugged, pretending to indifference. Apparently Lia had not meant to criticize him. And in all truth,
Brother Leo was more than a little curious about what it
would be like existing at close quarters with the boy who—
but no, Henry Martyn was the merest of scamps, compared
to the horrific things that haunted his nightmares these
days—had done, for more than a decade—and he actually
looked forward to spending some time with the young ras-
cal.

"All the same," Lia continued, as if completely unaware
of the way in which her father's troubled mind was churning, "I must confess that I wonder myself whether it is altogether wise of Arran to take his wife and daughter along
with him. As you know—and better than anyone else, I
should think—I have garnered rather a deal of personal
experience upon behalf of . . . well, shall we say, 'far-flung
interests' that you and I happened to share at the time?"

Brother Leo nodded, remembering.

His daughter went on. "Much of it involved long-range
reconnaissance and deep-cover espionage, operations the
benefits of which I experience today from the *consuming*
end of the gathering process, as it were, rather than from the
producing end. Yet I understand that process well, and by
every indication that I am aware of, Father, the present expedition is certain to prove to be an exquisitely dangerous
undertaking. Still, within the Monopolity of Hanover—just
as in any other imperium-conglomerate that considers itself
remotely civilized—not even a Ceo may question a man's
decisions concerning his own family."

There it was again, that bitter tone of reproof. Or perhaps

it was just his guilty conscience attempting to communicate with him. Again he peered at his daughter suspiciously and tried not to assume a pained expression. Again he wondered what all this was in aid of. Lia had arrayed herself against an institution vaster, and vastly more ancient, than the imperia-conglomerate to which it sold its one and only product. Conceding that the coming mission would be dangerous was like conceding that erecting the 'Droom had required a bit of stonemasonry.

"You know, Father . . ." As the conveyance turned at last into the broad semicircular driveway at the rear, unofficial entrance of the Residence, Lia began offhandedly as if the new subject she was about to broach were merely small talk she had just thought of. "It is quite characteristic of my early life that it never occurred to me to wonder at the time about my own case in particular."

He gave her an interrogative look. What in the Ceo's name could she be driving at? He felt himself far too old and tired for these games. He had lacked the energy and spirit for them since just before his abdication. If the girl had some issue to rebuke him over, he wished she would simply spit it out.

"Judging by his behavior, my father must have felt he had children to spare."

There it was, at last.

"He sent me out upon one desperately dangerous mission after another, to 'sink or swim' as I may. Not that I ever raised a complaint, mind you; I had been very stringently brought up never to do so. No one can deny today that I managed to survive, grow, and flourish, somehow, as a result, although I doubt that this was the object of my upbringing. And in the end, perhaps also as a result, my father even thought me qualified to take his place. Although might a daughter not reasonably judge that to be just another desperately dangerous mission?"

She gave him a sidelong glance.

Leupould was adamantly determined never to offer to his daughter—or to anybody else, for that matter—as much as the slenderest clue to the reasons for his behavior, either past or present. He knew perfectly well, now, what Lia was attempting, and he swore grimly to himself that he would deny her the satisfaction.

"Sink or swim," to be sure! And had *any* child ever proven satisfied, in the years that followed afterward, with the manner of its upbringing? Had any ever failed to blame its personal shortcomings and professional failures upon its parents? Had any never yearned for the chance to bring its manifold grievances before that selfsame vile culprit, bound, gagged, and helpless—precisely as Brother Leo found himself—whom he held most accountable for them?

"The object of her upbringing," she had prattled. By the Ceo's ballocks—strike that; make it *ovaries*—what other object could there be, except to be brought up? And if the orb and scepter that he had passed along to Lia were just the least bit tarnished, a trifle second-rate, well, she might prove fortunate enough never to learn the truth of that particular matter, might she not? Had he not done everything he could, himself, to assure that she never did?

At last their carriage drew itself to the gentlest of halts at the foot of a broad, sweeping, colonnaded staircase lined solidly from bottom to top with liveried guardsmen. Undaunted by her father's silence (which seemed only natural, by now) and his lack of response (which did not), she stubbornly refrained from dismounting when the door was opened for her, but instead, continued:

"I do know my own father, Leupould Wheeler, well enough to understand the one, all-important fact about him: that, without even a moment's hesitation, he would have thrown himself straightaway into the same danger he exposed his daughter to, had he but believed the action needful to preserve his concept of civilization."

Brother Leo sighed deeply as if in good-natured resignation, and nodded, wondering whether his daughter would ever have occasion to learn that, more than anything, what he was agreeing with her about just now was her choice of tenses.

"And now, Father," she told him over her shoulder as she allowed herself to be handed out, "with this expedition, you will have a chance to prove me right."

Lia's stirring (if somewhat sarcastic) call to action was one thing. The realities of preparing an excursion into unknown territory were quite another.

To begin with, there were crewbeings to recruit, for skilled hands almost certainly would not be replaceable beyond the farthest reaches of the imperia-conglomerate. Careful precautions of the belt-and-suspender variety must also be taken regarding sails, standing and running rigging, consumable supplies, weapons, and spares. A two-month pleasure tour such as they had just essayed to Hanover from Skye—not just through the Known Void, but through the Well Known Void—was not the same at all as the open-ended sally they purposed into what would inevitably prove hostile territory. Was that not the reason they were venturing out, after all, to accomplish things that would engender hostility?

In the end, after a great deal of consideration and discussion, Arran and Phoebus had reluctantly decided between themselves upon taking but a single ship, principally because their patron had described their present mission as "a preliminary reconnaissance." They would play the turtle then, in terms of tactics, rather than the tiger. And if need be, they would play the rabbit, unashamedly showing their heels to any well-found enemy they happened to meet, living to report to their mistress, and then to come back and fight another day.

That ship would be the long-legged, extraordinarily well-armed *Osprey,* with Arran in overall command and Phoebus acting as his first officer and chief gunner. Combining their two ships' crews would greatly reduce the need to recruit more. And best of all, for the most part, they could keep their designs "within the family," as it were, of long and well-trusted men and women.

During their necessarily prolonged sojourn upon the

cloudy capital world, the women of the Islay family, mother
and daughter, remained in residence at the palatial Daimler-
Wilkinson town mansion, which was certainly no more than
as it should have been, since Loreanna happened to be her
late father Clive's rightful heir. Clive's widow Jennivere
Daimler-Wilkinson might have disputed such a claim, but
had betrayed no inclination to do so, appearing well content
to let her daughter act as mistress of the house. Loreanna's
half brother, the wild youth Woulf, had been a houseguest,
along with his mother, at the family establishment even
before Loreanna and her family had arrived upon the planet.
As the mighty labor in synchronous orbit continued apace—
supplies, tools, and spares being shifted from one vessel to
another— boredom had set in below.

"You have managed, somehow, to ingratiate yourself to
some degree with my mother and to a lesser degree—
because the latter is absent most of the time—with my
father. Pray do not deceive yourself that it will be so easy
with me."

Bretta had been blessedly alone, high in the rooftop solar-
ium—the name for which, of course, was an utter joke upon
this world of eternal overcast—watching Brougham and his
minions scrubbing blast streaks off the transparency that her
father's steam launch had left the day before, arriving and
departing the platform not ten measures away. Briefly, she
wondered what those streaks must be composed of, since the
auxiliary vessel's exhaust byproducts consisted principally
of water vapor—she must remember to ask—but what a
spectacle it would have been, she thought, to have watched
the landing and takeoff from here!

To the tremendous annoyance of a suspicious and hostile
young Skyan, her new "uncle" (she still thought of him that
way, in quotation marks) had taken it upon himself just now
to deprive her of her long-sought and highly valued solitude.

Her brusque response was to an innocent opening remark
he had made. He replied, "My guess, Robretta Islay, is that
there is nothing at all easy about you."

She rather liked that, and had to rein herself in, to remain properly indignant with him. There was something about the clothing she was wearing which made that especially difficult. "In this, sir, you are quite correct, for it is the way my father has brought me up. Ours is a hard life upon a frontier world, not to mention aboard ship. It requires hard people to live it."

Woulf nodded agreeably. His manner was disarmingly open and frank, his speech better cultured than his appearance. "My life, and my mother's, have been soft by comparison, I suppose, spent in the relatively luxurious sewers and posh back alleys of the cities of a hundred worlds, where merely looking about too eagerly for a place to sleep can earn you a smile—from ear to ear."

He made a broad, curving, throat-slitting motion and a horrible noise she had first heard when, her hunting knife clenched in her bloody fist, she had penetrated the body cavity of the first large forest animal she had ever killed.

She was stunned.

He grinned.

She laughed.

Then they were both laughing and slapping one another on the back, tears running from their eyes, as Brougham peered at them distressfully through the transparency.

As Woulf wiped his eyes a final time, he told her, "Truthfully, niece, I am here because I overheard this stupidity about women not being permitted to venture into the streets of Hanover unescorted. I have also heard something about life upon the planet Skye, and understood that this absurd rule would be intolerable to you. So I thought to ask whether you desire an 'escort' in an exploration of the city that you would invariably attempt, with or without such."

Ceo blast his baby-blue eyes—the curse was a result of Phoebus Krumm's influence, the only aspect of the fellow her mother deplored—how could he *know* her that well? For the first time, she gave her uncle an evaluating look.

Woulf was not a big man—he scarcely stood as tall as Bretta—but he was quick of reflex and well muscled. She

had even noticed with approval that there were hard spots
upon his hands which spoke of honest toil. She approved
less of the fact that it was difficult to tell which part of him
was tanned and which was dirty with an urban kind of grime
that never seemed to wash out. His hair was dark and
shoulder-blade long, but not as clean as it might have been.
His clothing was subdued in color and hung about his body,
almost in tatters. Only his light, soft shoes and the long, flat
scabbard upon his hip with the dark, knurled metal hilt protruding from it, spoke of any care or grooming.

"How exceptionally thoughtful of you, Uncle." And she
discovered that she meant it. By the Black Void itself, were
those *dimples* she felt forming in her cheeks, entirely of their
own accord, like malignant organisms of some variety? First
freckles, then *this*. And just exactly what was happening to
her, beneath the lacy bodice of her dress? "I accept your
offer, sir, most gratefully— provided that the very first place
we shall stop will be a tailor."

More than anything, the accord that eventually developed
between Bretta and Woulf was a matter of cultural contrasts— between the pair of them, and between them and the
world in which they found themselves unwillingly. Arran
Islay's daughter was, above all, a hardworking, stoic frontier
girl, from a hardworking, stoic frontier world. The worst
epithet she had ever thought of to employ against another
human being, and her version of an obscenity, was "useless."

Over the next several weeks that she whiled away in her
uncle's company, Bretta discovered the worldwide city of
Hanover to be quite an interesting place, despite her initial
prejudices against it, with its many historical monuments,
museums, interplanetary zoos, botanical gardens, aquaria,
and other attractions. There were buildings to see that stood
several klommes tall, and subterranean habitations to explore which had been dug just as many klommes deep.

Together, they slipped into the visitors' gallery of the
great 'Droom of the Monopolity itself, crowded appendage
to appendage with human and alien tourists alike, and expe-

rienced a guided trek through the Ceo Lia's palace as mere anonymous tourists. Bretta surprised herself again and again, finding that she especially enjoyed visiting shops of every variety imaginable which abounded within the planet-enwrapping city. For her own part, her mother, astonished at all of this sudden enthusiasm, bestowed upon her a generous allowance. Bretta was quietly determined to spend every Hanoverian clavis of it.

Upon the other hand, the girl soon found herself severely disimpressed with the *people* who inhabited the Hanoverian metropolis, and came almost to feel as if they were all spoiling it for her deliberately. If they would just go away, she thought (and became perhaps the trillionth individual ever to do so), it would be grand. She tried—with a remarkable degree of maturity—to be tolerant and make allowances. But as a matter of plain fact, she found her revulsion with the great city's inhabitants increasing, virtually by the hour.

For one thing, none of them smelled much better than Woulf or his mother did. Nor was it particularly long before she came likewise to despise their studied ineffectuality and their effete, overly civilized mannerisms. Bretta abominated helplessness—she hated it even more than uselessness—in any sapient being. The stylish, feigned helplessness of the affectedly fettered Hanoverian women she encountered in her explorations of the city revolted her utterly. As for the lisping, limp-wristed responses of their— theoretically— male counterparts, she found that even more revolting, if such a thing was possible. She caught herself making excuses to avoid shaking hands with every individual she was introduced to; she could not bear the moist softness of their overly pampered flesh. And afterward, she could never bring herself, in ordinary conversation, to refer to these self-emasculated urban specimens as "men."

How pathetic and ridiculous they all were, in their masquerade play-party costumes which her father and mother had inadvertently inspired. To Bretta, it was as if the entire planet of Hanover were inhabited by eunuchs dressed as clowns!

And perhaps most intolerable of all, these wretchedly affected creatures, not one of whom could have survived upon his own for as much as half an hour, were he dropped into the deep everblue forests of her increasingly beloved Skye (Bretta was unaware that, fifteen years earlier, under different circumstances, her father had fondly imagined exactly the same event) actually believed that they could look down their elevated, snotty noses at vital frontier worlds like her own!

Young Woulf, by unmistakable contrast, appeared to abide in a quiet—if somewhat grubby and bedraggled—strength. To Bretta, he might as well have belonged to a different plane of existence, or at least a different species of animal, altogether, one that she—and several increasingly suicidal tailors in rapid and acrimonious succession—had difficulty finding suitable attire for.

It was at the commercial establishment of the last of these desperate souls that she received an urgent message from the Daimler-Wilkinson mansion—implying that her father was maintaining some sort of watch over her, as well.

"This is Robretta Islay speaking," she informed the portable view screen at present hanging before her eyes. Beyond it, she watched a silent struggle taking place between Woulf and a fitter. Both of these worthies seemed to be taking it personally, in their own characteristic ways, that the sleeves of a velvet jacket outfitted with lace cuffs could be rolled up to his elbows only at the cost of destroying both the desired sartorial effect, and the garment itself.

The screen resolved itself into an image of her grandmother. "Robretta, my child, wherever you happen to be at the moment, you must return home immediately!"

A sick, paralyzing fear coursed through the girl's body as she suddenly thought of everything that could happen to Arran, working upon his ship in orbit.

"I greatly fear for the safety of your dear mother," Owld Jenn told her, however. To Bretta, the old woman seemed uncharacteristically lucid. Perhaps it was on account of an adrenaline-charged terror that she was in danger of losing her only daughter for a second time. "They say she is about to be arrested!"

The screen went blank.

CHAPTER XXI:
NOBLE SAVAGES

Together, Bretta and Woulf hurried out the door of the shop into the street, the latter trailing pieces of the suit which the tailor had been fitting to him. Behind them, the tailor shouted at them, shook his fist at the sky, and cursed.

Bretta hailed a passing conveyance-for-hire, while Woulf disposed of the remains of his suit. They leapt in, she spoke the name of the family mansion, and they were off—until, a few blocks later, when Woulf cried, "Stop the machine!"

He turned to her in his seat, laying a hand upon her arm. "I have seen many an urban constabulary, Bretta, and remember all too well the way they work. In a city upon one planet I recall, I watched them burn down an orphanage in order to 'save' the children within, who were all killed by the fire they set. Will you believe me when I tell you they were all given medals for their 'valor'?"

She raised her eyebrows.

He nodded confirmation.

"That message from my mother was cut off by whatever jackbooted thugs are trying to arrest your mother. It is standard operating procedure and all a part of state terrorist tactics. Most likely they have the town house under siege by now, surrounded by a hundred thrustibles. And they will have their plainclothes agents out, trying to find you—which is why I thought it wise to get away from that threadmonger as quickly as we could. Now, contact your father if you can, from that street screen. Then will we continue to the mansion."

It sounded like good advice to Bretta, and she had every reason to believe him about the police. Woulf was as wise in the ways of the town as she was in the ways of field and forest. She observed his face, however, understanding that the bright, clean avenues they traveled now were territory quite as alien to him as to her. Woulf, she knew, had arisen from the raw underbelly of that most human of institutions, the megapolis. He had survived in many such, upon many worlds, in many imperia-conglomerate. But his home ground was the gritty, utilitarian, dark, and seamy part of the urban arena where tough-minded values and skills had saved his life and his mother's upon many an occasion. It was an environment Bretta had been aware of only from her reading, but Woulf's were the same tough-minded values and skills, she could not help but persuade herself, that she herself had been brought up by her parents to practice and cherish.

Of a sudden, Bretta warned herself: history demonstrates clearly that to thoughtful individuals everywhere, and in all times, shared values have always been a powerful aphrodisiac. So, for that matter, she thought, have shared dangers.

Mindful once again of what she carried beneath the sleeve of her dress, she stepped from the machine and dropped a coin into the communicator, giving it a code her father had given her in case of an emergency like this. Neither Arran nor Phoebus answered. Instead, she saw a card upon the screen that told her the device she was connected to had no visual component. And she heard a voice.

"This here's corvette Osprey, *an' Third Officer Savage ye'er speakin' to."*

"Fionaleigh, is that you?"

Not "armed cargo vessel *Osprey,*" Bretta noticed, but "corvette." Her father had put his crew upon a wartime footing. The answering voice had been that of Phoebus Krumm's longtime first officer. The woman had also been her uncle Robret's mistress upon Skye, in the dark days of the Black Usurpation. Now, apparently, she was integrated into the *Osprey*'s complement. Bretta wondered how her long-dead uncle's unwedded wife felt about that. She never even considered the possibility that Lia might not know; no such possibility existed.

"An' who else would it be, Bretta me lass, answerin' squawker wi'me name? I'd say ye'd grown foot, but wi'this comset, it might'swell be growin' from yer head. Now tell Fionaleigh what she can do for daughter o' Henry Martyn."

Bretta told Fionaleigh about the message she had received from Jennivere Daimler-Wilkinson. Arran and Krumm were with Sedgeley, as it happened, down here upon the planet's surface, at the 'Droom, speaking with some of Lia's political allies. The *Osprey*'s third officer was in possession of a screen code that would reach them in extreme need, and she promised to attend to it straightaway.

She made Bretta promise to be careful.

Bretta rang off, rejoined Woulf in the conveyance, and immediately broke her promise to Fionaleigh, ordering the machine to resume its progress, and to stop at the next street over from the Daimler-Wilkinson establishment. She had suddenly remembered something her mother had told her recently about the house.

"The foundations of the building go back," she told Woulf, as people and lampposts flew by her window, "almost to the original settlement of the planet—some believe that was about nine hundred years ago. It would appear that this world was, from time to time, not entirely as sedate and civilized as we see it now."

"I see," Woulf replied. "You regard *this* situation as 'sedate and civilized'?"

Bretta shook her head, ignoring the digression. "At the rear of the back garden of the house there is a gazebo— although why anyone would wish to sit outdoors upon this drizzly ball of rock, I cannot imagine. In any event, the gazebo boasts a trapdoor in its floor, opening upon a tunnel leading directly into the cellars of the house. It was intended as an emergency escape route. I rather doubt that its builders ever visualized its being used to get back *inside*."

"I doubt it, too," Woulf agreed. "Be that as it may, what have you for weapons?"

She showed him the lens of her thrustible. He was suitably impressed. Then she told him, "Turn away, if you please, while I retrieve another item we may require."

Woulf obeyed, hearing the rustle of her skirt and petticoats. When she told him to look again, she held a sizable knife before his eyes, one that nearly triggered a killing reflex within him, although he managed to control it.

"I wish I had my crossbow with me, it is quiet. But I had to leave it home."

The conveyance stopped; Bretta paid it. Together, they slipped through a back gate. Bretta was astonished at how silently Woulf was capable of moving. They could not see the front of the house, of course, but there were armed men at the back, standing about as if they had nothing to do. Their attention was focused upon the house itself; the gazebo had been deliberately constructed to be disregarded, in order to screen its users from the scrutiny of just such marauders.

Inside, Bretta had a bad moment when she could not seem to find the trapdoor, and an even worse one when she discovered that it had been painted shut, many times over. Woulf's big black knife whispered from its sheath, however, and together they cut at the paint-filled joints in the floor until they were able to pry the trapdoor open. Immediately a musty smell wafted up to them, and a dense curtain of ancient cobwebs waved like seaweed in a gentle swell upon the ocean.

It was dark down there.

"Ladies first," Woulf offered, raising a single, sardonic eyebrow.

"I have always wished I could do that," she replied. The clothes she had been forced to wear made her feel utterly ridiculous. But, knife in her left hand, thrustible at the ready upon her right, she swung her legs over the edge.

*   *   *

Loreanna was furious.

The formal charges were as perfunctory and ridiculous in character as it had been possible to make them, and it was clear that even the bored, unshaven ruffians, in their soiled, ill-fitting rental uniforms, who had delivered the autothille to her did not believe a word of them. The entire situation had been carefully calculated, without a doubt by bitter and long-standing foes of the Daimler-Wilkinsons, the Islays, or perhaps even the Wheelers, merely as an insult. Great men—and women—tend to attract great enemies. The only thing more absurd than the charges themselves—if such a thing was possible—was the attempt to arrest Loreanna at her family's home in the capital city.

Nevertheless, the document claimed, for some fifteen years, as a citizeness and subject of the Monopolity of Hanover, one Loreanna Daimler-Wilkinson had willingly given "aid and comfort" to a known and self-declared enemy—that would be her husband and the father of her six children—of the imperium-conglomerate.

"Aid and comfort," indeed!

Loreanna paced the decoratively tiled floor of the foyer, which she had become determined to hold against intruders like a castle keep. In her left hand, she gripped a thrustible that she had yet to strap to her forearm. With her fingers clenched round the long, brightly polished axis of the weapon, the arm and wrist straps flailed whenever she moved, like the thongs of a whip. She had not, however, similarly forgotten the pistol in the pocket of her dress.

When those unkempt louts had first appeared upon her doorstep, enveloping her in the cloud of alcoholic exhalations that accompanied them everywhere, she had surprised their leader (and herself) by giving him a good, solid shove in the solar plexus, sending the fellow tumbling, literally head over heels, down the seven-stepped stoop, onto the pavement. As a girl, she had seen the same thing done by her uncle to a salesman who refused to go away when Brougham had asked him to politely. Their forebears, Sedgeley had told her afterward, had ordered the top step of the stoop fashioned narrowly for exactly this purpose. Sales-beings were expected to apply at a side door, which opened onto a blank brick wall.

While this short-lived excitement had been going on, Loreanna learned afterward, her *mother* had somehow persuaded Arran's surveillors to let her know where Bretta and Woulf were. (Loreanna would not previously have wagered a milliclavis upon Jennivere's ability to tie her own night-gown strings in an emergency.) She had apparently contacted them and they were coming now. Loreanna hoped they would have the good sense to stay clear of the hood-lums outside.

She also hoped they would contact Arran, and that he would soon arrive with Phoebus and perhaps even representation from Lia. She was certain these charges did not originate with the Hanoverian government. In the Monopolity, however, despite the most strenuous efforts upon Lia's part to discourage it, torture continued as an art form practiced by the aristocracy. Loreanna knew that if she let herself be taken off by these hireling guttersnipes, she would be systematically, scientifically maimed in some hidden basement, by experts who were maintained in luxury by their patrons, the way painters and sculptors once were, until she confessed to the trumped-up charges or died resisting the impulse.

She had borne six children well enough without recourse to drugs, but she was uncertain how much *unnatural* pain it would be possible for her to withstand.

For once she was almost grateful that going about armed upon Hanover was a privilege of a wealthy and powerful elite. Even the Monopolitan police—invariably recruited from among the lower classes—not to mention goons like these encroaching upon her doorstep, were forbidden the use of thrustibles or other weapons, powered or otherwise, and were forced to rely upon muscle power alone. Clearly they had not expected her to be able, and willing, to defend herself. The fact that she possessed the means of self-defense (and, like the rest of her family, would have, regardless of what law or custom demanded) was something they had not taken into account. Perhaps it would buy her time she needed.

There came another pounding at the door, for perhaps the fifth time in an hour, and a rudely corresponding rattle at the doorknob. *What effrontery,* she thought. She strapped on her thrustible, adjusted the knurled collar of the collimator for minimum thrust at maximum dispersion, aimed for the doorknob, and squeezed the yoke, delighted to hear a howl of pain from the idiot hanging on to the other side of the knob. Next, she heard a series of seven dull thuds as the same idiot became a victim of her ancestors' sense of architectural humor.

With any luck, he had broken his neck.

They groped their way through sheet after dusty, musty-smelling sheet of cobwebs within the unlit garden tunnel into the basement. More of a gentleman than either of them had suspected he might be, Woulf had squeezed past her and preceded—before them, he shone a tiny electrical torch no bigger than her little fingernail, which had been hidden inside the hollow handle of his knife—through a warped tube of timeworn bricks oozing with nitre, gleaming in the lamplight.

The notion came to Bretta, as she followed with her weapons at the ready, that Woulf's rough urban background differed greatly from her own childhood. Yet he seemed much more like the Skyan boys she was accustomed to than anyone else she had encountered upon this vaunted capital planet. She had discovered that she was having difficulty remembering that the individual in question was in fact her mother's half brother. Then again, she had found it impossible to think of Owld Jenn as her grandmother. More and more she wished she had never had occasion to meet the irrational, unpleasant old woman. But "Uncle Woulf"—somehow this phrase piped falsely whenever she thought about it. Of course the fact that he was a dark, smooth-skinned, muscular young man of about eighteen or twenty, with regular features and a wicked eye, had absolutely nothing to do with it.

Absolutely nothing.

Woulf's tiny torch, in fact, lit very little round it. The farther they went, and the more damp cobwebs they accumulated in their hair and upon their faces and clothing (how she longed for rough-and-ready attire of the kind—perhaps excluding shorts—she had been accustomed to all her life upon her native world!), the larger grew the spiders skittering through Bretta's nervous imagination.

Despite her better judgment, Woulf had begun to intrigue her the longer she compared him with Hanoverians. The young fellow was fully as city-bred in his own peculiar manner as her great uncle. Yet he was without question very different in countless ways from the elderly, charming, urbane, witty, but—at least in Bretta's view—neither very masculine nor very admirable Sedgeley.

Woulf was no prancing sissy like those she saw all round her. She was embarrassed by their recent, trendy affectations to her father's youthful profession, and several times she had caught Woulf attempting to conceal his own expression of contemptuous disgust. This seemed to happen whenever they came face-to-face with some egregious example of Hanoverian foppishness. They would catch each other's eye and laugh, while passing strangers looked at them oddly.

At long last, they reached the end of the tunnel. To their dismay they found no door—it might have been worse: they might have found yet another brick wall—but a thick, age-darkened expanse of the local hardwood that colonists, new to Hanover a millennium ago, had decided to call "oak." Their eyes and knives and fingers found no hidden catch or hinges. The thing appeared to have been nailed into place. Woulf had to kick at the heavy panel again and again, raising clouds of moldy-smelling dust that choked and blinded them, and there was no room in the passage in which Bretta might lend him her assistance.

She was surprised when the wooden wall gave way of a sudden, and made a mental note to avoid getting upon

Woulf's bad side. They made their way through the splintered doorframe—and their own personal cloud of dust—into the mansion's enormous cellar. Bretta felt a trifle guilty about the havoc they had wrought. This was not some dark, dank subterranean recess, not in any house kept by Brougham and his staff, but a warm, dry, relatively well-lit space for storing various foodstuffs and supplies. The stone floor was even, the walls sealed and whitewashed, and there were no vermin. They might have made a fine meal, down here, of what they could find sitting upon the shelves.

This was not the first time that either of them had ventured into such a place. Woulf was unaware of it—at least she hoped that he was—but in the weeks since he had first begun escorting her out into the city, upon more than one occasion she had followed him and watched from hiding as, deep within one of the mansion's many cellars like this one, the young barbarian warrior had practiced strenuous martial exercises for hours without resting, or thrown one improvised bull's-eye after another with the massive knife he carried at all times. Afterward, she had watched him honing its razor edges with a hard white stone. Unlike the overly sophisticated innocents all round her, Bretta had recognized at once the stark significance of the long, heavy black slab of heat-treated steel he wore upon his hip. In his hands, it was as if the great edged weapon were nothing more than a toy dart that he had taken from a pub somewhere.

Bretta found herself wondering whether he might ever have killed anybody with that big knife of his, perhaps in order to save his own or his mother's life. Rather like her father, Woulf appeared to be uneager to volunteer such information, and she had been brought up with a strong disinclination to ask. She also wondered how and where he had planned to carry it if the tailor had been permitted to finish him a suit of clothes. But she discovered, to her self-embarrassment, that although she had been well trained in the use of primitive weapons herself, the idea that he might have killed with it aroused her.

She might have to talk with her mother about that. More

than likely, Loreanna would tell her, matter-of-factly, that, just as men were inclined to prefer young, pretty women— "pretty" representing an estimate of a female's reproductive health—so a woman tended to be attracted to that male with a demonstrated capability of defending his mate, their off-spring, and the family cave. Anyone offended by such a basic, visceral fact was probably unfit to reproduce.

Finding their way as quickly as they could, upward through the building's underpinnings, they hurried through rooms and down corridors, always heading toward the entrance foyer at the front door, where they expected the most trouble.

They were proven correct. As they slammed into the entryway, Loreanna whirled. Her eyes grew wide but her jaw was firm and the set of her mouth was positively grim of purpose. She did not recognize them, but aimed both pistol and thrustible at them. Bretta saw red light from the thrustible's designator and knew she would be the one to absorb the brunt of the weapon's pure kinetic energy, while her mother's antique Walther stitched Woulf's body like a rag doll. If everyone in ancient times had been able to thrust—no, the proper word was "shoot"—like Loreanna Islay, mankind would never have given up firearms.

"Mother, no!"

Woulf, covered unrecognizably from head to foot in a filthy shroud of cobwebs, and waving his long black knife, came to an immediate halt. Bretta crashed into the back of him and barely avoided stabbing him with her own fighting blade. Sliding, instead, she knocked his legs from under him. He slipped upon the tiled floor, somehow landing atop Bretta, who had fallen just behind him.

"It's only us!"

In the meantime, old Jennivere had suddenly materialized from nowhere and seized Loreanna's elbow, attempting to push her thrustible upward. *Do not thrust my boy!* she cried, but her quivery voice was drowned out by a great thundering crash as the heavy front door was smashed inward, the fragments nearly hitting Loreanna. Upon the threshold just outside, beside a kneeling figure manipulating whatever device had been used to shatter the door, stood a pair of ill-uniformed hoodlums, improvised truncheons raised high over their heads.

One of these thugs leaned in to strike Bretta's mother a killing blow to the back of her head, but reeled backward himself an instant before he could connect, crashing against the broken doorpost as if he had been struck by an invisible vehicle. Blood streamed freely from his mouth as he slid down the wall. From where she lay, Loreanna's daughter had thrust the invader nearly through.

The second hireling made a similar attempt, but there was a dark blur in the air between him and the foyer floor, and he stood, abruptly, staring down in astonishment at the middle of his torso, where it appeared that a knurled blue-gray metal handle had blossomed. Woulf's laborious practice sessions in the cellar had fulfilled their purpose. A great length of razor-sharpened steel now impaled the invader like an insectoid in a collection. He toppled forward and landed across the threshold with a thump, his shirt standing in a peak high above his shoulder blades like a tent. Bretta could only imagine (feeling ill as she did) what falling upon the handle of the knife had done to him.

Woulf was back upon his feet within an instant and, with a sucking noise, recovered his weapon, cleansing its blade upon his victim's clothing. He had pulled the second body inside while making sure the first had fallen down the stoop, and was about to secure what was left of the door when Bretta got in his way. The technician she had briefly seen had vanished, but he had left his infernal device upon the stoop. As she retrieved the object, she saw at least a hundred men outside upon the street, apparently milling about in confusion.

She let Woulf slam the door then, and helped him brace it with the foyer coatrack.

"Well," he observed, "at least *that* is over with!" Of a sudden, the young man discovered that he was completely covered with a solid blanket of cobwebbery and other filth.

Making noises to articulate his disgust, he tried to wipe the stuff off, which only served to pass it from one hand to the other.

Bretta stifled a giggle and a feeling of euphoric hysteria which she was certain must be mostly a nervous reaction to having been in a real fight for the first time in her life, and having killed a man—but Woulf did look very funny.

"I am afraid that you are wrong," Loreanna told him, wiping splattered blood from her face, "although I am more than proud of both of you and very grateful into the bargain. My eldest daughter and my newfound brother have together saved my life. But Woulf, my dear, I greatly fear that this is only the beginning."

They were startled by a noise.

In a foyer corner, Owld Jenn drooled and cackled.

CHAPTER XXII:
THE SHADOWS BETWEEN THE STARS

Bretta Islay moved like a shadow through the quiet lower spaces of the *Osprey*.

All she really sought here, belowdecks, was blessed solitude. And yet, although the places she explored during this period reserved for sleeping—termed, for the sake of everyone's convenience, the "nightwatch"—were as familiar to her as her own bedchamber back at home, they always remained new to her. She adored the way they felt to her, the way they looked, and especially the way they smelled. It was only one of the ways she knew she was in love with her father's ship: her fascination with the *Osprey* never faded.

A continuous inspection of the smallest recesses belowdecks was a stark necessity of survival upon the interstellar Deep, and not only because vessels wore themselves

out or people grew lax. Despite bitter cold and hard vacuum,
there was a surprising number of vile *things* that spawned
and grew and bred within the darkest shadows between the
stars which, attaching themselves to any passing, ill-kept
starship, were likely to feed upon her, or upon her crewbeings.

Although Bretta's desire was sincere, to assure herself, as
a responsible crewbeing and member of the Ceo's expedition, that everything was as it ought to be aboard the *Osprey,*
she also relished the opportunity to climb out of her stifling
Hanoverian garments and get back into the vest and cutoffs
she wore at home. No absurdly pleated, lace-trimmed velvet
sleeve concealed her thrustible now, where its engraved and
polished axis gleamed upon her forearm in the lamplight.
Her trusty hunting knife slapped openly against her naked
thigh.

A very great deal had happened over the past 107 days,
with little time or space (a peculiar but genuine necessity,
she had discovered) in which to subject it to the full reflection that it merited, and she had much to think upon.

To begin with, Bretta had killed a man, another human
being, when she, Woulf, and her mother had held the arresting minions at bay while help was being summoned in a
rather roundabout manner—thanks to Fionaleigh Savage
aboard the orbiting corvette—from the 'Droom. Within only
a few minutes, Bretta's father and Phoebus Krumm had
come swerving and swooping up the boulevard, each of
them hanging from an open door of the vehicle they had
commandeered, thrusting enthusiastically at a startled and
demoralized enemy who had broken at the sight of the two
Deep-captains bearing down upon them, and cravenly scattered. Uncle Sedgeley had made the only live capture of the
day, adroitly employing his own thrustible to break the leg
of an escaping villain.

Otherwise, eight disanimated bodies lay upon the pavement before the house.

Unfortunately, their single captive had proven to be nothing more than a drunken hooligan hired straight out of an

alcohol emporium, and possessed not the least scrap of information useful to them, although it made Bretta shudder to imagine how, precisely, that fact had been ascertained with any degree of assurance. Somewhat to her surprise, any amount of remorse or of emotional distress she was supposed to have suffered upon having successfully defended herself, her mother, and their ancestral home had so far failed utterly to manifest itself.

Halfway down a ladderway, Bretta paused in her ruminations. Within its special niche, a ship's glowlamp had apparently gone out, a rare occurrence aboard a vessel of this type and vintage. Opening its transparent case upon reluctant hinges, she found that the lamp's core had rattled loose somehow from its connection to the mesh-fed power supply. Tightening it carefully until it glowed once again, she closed the case, turned the catch, and moved on.

Eventually, the matter of Loreanna's putative "crimes" of treason against the Monopolity had been settled when it was discovered that the arrest warrant displayed the electronic signature of a Hanoverian colonial magistrate who had never set a foot upon the capital planet, and had been deceased, according to the outraged Ceo Lia who had inherited him from her father, for at least three years.

They had never learned precisely who it was—which of their many and various presumed enemies—that had mounted the attack. Upon the other hand, such a frontal assault upon them had not been attempted again, and events for all of the Islay family had moved afterward in a manner astonishingly similar—albeit associated with a greater degree of caution upon all their parts—to the way they had before. They had been presented formally to the Ceo Lia at the 'Droom. Bretta had discovered that she could not dance—and then that she could, thanks to the unpredictably protean Woulf. They had attended some theatrical performance, which, although it had been presented in the language she *thought* she had grown up speaking, she had failed to understand one word of.

They had visited more shops and museums.

As all things must, however, Bretta's social whirl upon Hanover, such as it had been, came finally to an end, and to her surprise, the no-nonsense backwoods girl found herself—with the notable exception of being compelled to deal with the mass media upon an almost daily basis—almost regretting it.

After twelve weeks onboard what she felt was as an overpassengered *Osprey,* she was beginning to know why. (Reflexively, she rapped a fire extinguisher lightly with her knife handle to determine that it had been refilled up to the proper level, and marched onward.) She would almost rather deal with the media.

The Islays and their traveling party continued to believe that the real reason for their coming expedition remained a secret. Who would likely have believed what they purposed to do—to undermine and overthrow an institution older than the 'Droom itself—in any case? Yet it was unavoidable that they should nonetheless depart Hanover amidst a tremendous clamor. A virtually breathless public interest in most of them reached back more than a decade, and nearly everything about them seemed calculated to excite the general curiosity.

Captain Arran Islay, for example, was vastly better known to everyone as that (presumably) former interstellar brigand Henry Martyn, who had embarrassed the Monopolity of Hanover fifteen years ago, and yet now appeared to be serving it in some as-yet-unexplained capacity. He had brought with him his wedded wife, the lovely Loreanna Daimler-Wilkinson Islay, herself the former ward of the abdicated Ceo Leupould's discredited right-hand man. Apparent complications such as these were exquisitely thrilling to the vast hordes of obnoxious media pontificators who wished above all to be perceived as profound and subtle, and had begun following each member of the Islay party everywhere they tried to go.

Under any other circumstances, their predicament would have been comical. (Bretta had believed it was comical under *these* circumstances, but wisely forbore to say so.)

Both Arran and Phoebus had been compelled to resort to masques, hired decoys, verbal obscenities the parasitic media dare not record, let alone transmit, and outright physical threat, in order to shake the vermin off.

Loreanna simply stayed home, within the Daimler-Wilkinson establishment, content, for the nonce, exploring artifacts and memories a decade and a half old.

Bretta, who refused to make of herself a prisoner of the mass media or of the house, could tolerate no such recourse. The already romanticized Islay couple's eldest daughter, a slim, attractive barbarian wench just old enough herself to become the object of many salacious rumors, had heightened her own visibility to the point of ecstatic unbearability, by thrusting a man to death with a personal kinetic energy projector, a villainous instrumentality that no right-thinking, correctly brought-up young Hanoverian female would even have *contemplated* possessing, let alone becoming proficient with, and actually using.

As she reached up to inspect for a particular sort of parasitic dustmote above a doorsill, the villainous instrumentality upon her forearm glittered reassuringly.

But there was even more to outrage and delight the jaded sensibilities of the capital world. To Hanover, the infamous Captain Phoebus Krumm had brought with him both of his small, plump wives, Tula and Tillie. Although every sort of marriage custom was practiced upon the centerpiece of the Monopolity, which drew its inhabitants from virtually every sapient species and all parts of the Known Galaxy, for the most part, humans—who comprised the media's principal clientele—were generally monogynous, although, it was to be admitted, not particularly happily, nor yet particularly faithfully. And from the reports of various media rating services, it appeared that all of them loved hearing about the Krumm family, and—even better—imagining what they did in bed together.

Even the Ceo herself, upon whom a disheartened media had long since given up as a source of shocking scandal, titillating rumor, or even mildly interesting innuendo, could never have kept a secret (had she been so inclined, which she was not) of the melodramatic return to Monopolitan civilization of Jennivere Daimler-Wilkinson. For weeks they had reveled in publishing her likeness as it had been almost thirty years ago, radiantly magnificent, before that tragic and perhaps even foolish sojourn with her husband, and as it was now, that of a shriveled hag, half-mad with every indignity that had ever been inflicted upon her.

It was the very stuff—quintessential, unrelenting misery—that any journalist's dreams were made of, and it was reiterated so often that it was said (perhaps in jest) that hearing the first syllable of the victim's name now triggered a regurgitory reflex among those with a weaker constitution than others.

For some reason that nobody would condescend to explain to the frustrated snoops who had apparently convinced themselves that they had a right to know everything about everybody—and to tell every bit of it to everybody else—Jennivere Daimler-Wilkinson (now known to an empathetic public as "Owld Jenn") seemed to be accompanied everywhere by a famous high-society brain-poker. The media had never been able to make anything of that. But fortunately, for the practitioners of a trade whose watchword for a millennium had been, "If they won't tell you, make it up!" Jennivere had a grown son with no known paternal connection, who could be linked through prurient insinuation with his very mediagenic and underaged half niece, bringing the whole affair tidily back upon itself.

Satisfied with her informal inspection of this cargo deck, Bretta took an outboard ladderway to the next deck below. Exactly as upon the deck above, a full circle of black, hulking spherical shapes, each a measure and a half in diameter—the starship's mighty projectibles presently standing quiet watch at their gunports—lined the outermost circumference of the vessel's hull. Phoebus always joked that, aboard Henry Martyn's ship, *every* deck was a gundeck.

All that remained for the media to discuss at an interminable length were the mysterious—and undoubtedly corrupt— circumstances under which the Ceo Leupould's disgraced and exiled Executor-General had suddenly been restored to power, returning with him, to a counterfeit semblance of respectability, his old political crony and apparent mentor in the often-exposed debaucheries of the so-called "Immortal School" (to which, as a point of fact, many a retired and formerly celebrated media personality belonged, as well), none other than the presently stateless former statesman and onetime Jendyne Ambassador Plenipotentiary to the Monopolitan 'Droom, the sinister Frantisek Demondion-Echeverria.

Quite strangely, Bretta thought as she tiptoed carefully across a gundeck littered with the softly snoring bodies of several dozen sleeping crewbeings, no mention whatever had been made in the mass media of the former Ceo Leupould himself, or, as he preferred to be called these days, "plain old Brother Leo," although one would certainly think of him, very nearly foremost, as a fertile subject for sensational stories. Perhaps there were decent limits, after all, even for such vermin as found employment within the media. Or perhaps Brother Leo simply knew where too many bodies were buried—or possibly soon would be.

Arriving at that cylindrical enclosure in the center of the gundeck which was but an extension—and the foundation— of the klomme-high mast of the *Osprey,* Bretta ducked, lifted her foot, and passed through an oval hatchway, its heavy valvelike door propped open and chained back, and, from a metalloid mesh landing inside, descended a skeletal spiral stairway to the next deck, below.

Those two old Deep-raiders, Arran and Phoebus, and their distinguished patron Lia, had not been without certain propaganda countermeasures of their own to fall back upon. In their craftiness, the three of them had finally offered to the media an explanation for the expedition. It was the Ceo Lia's wish, they announced, that they begin a search for the ancient homeworld of all humanity, the legendary planet "Terror" or "Yurt," or whatever it had been named.

Likewise, they set a widely publicized date for their

departure, while Phoebus offered an extraordinary display of readying his own starship, the armed carrack *Tease,* for the historical undertaking to come. Then he and Arran saw to it that they and their several associates departed two full days *earlier* than anyone in the media had expected of them, and only aboard Arran's famed corvette, *Osprey.* Fionaleigh Savage would command Phoebus's carrack upon a decoy mission to the famed star-raider's sanctuary of Sisao and Somon.

The traveling company they carried with them aboard *Osprey* was a most peculiar assortment of individuals. Arran commanded both the starship and the expedition, Phoebus assisting as his second-in-command and gunnery officer. Representing the Monopolity of Hanover officially, Lia had sent her Executor-General, and at Sedgeley's urging, she had also promised Demondion-Echeverria certain rewards, political and otherwise, should he acquit himself well in her service.

She had also sent her own father and predecessor— although with what understanding between them, nobody knew. Jennivere was to act as a kind of "native guide" to the expedition, a hypnotist having helped her to recall the way.

Even here, many light-years away from that personage, Bretta felt an urge to shudder at the memory. They had only met upon a few occasions, but the hypnotist had disturbed her deeply, in many ways. Firstly, she could not be certain which gender the creature favored, a phenomenon altogether different in quality from the merely effete manner of Hanoverian men. The hypnotist had offered no clue whatever to whether he, she, or *it* was male, female, or even something else. To a straightforward girl raised upon a planet of equally straightforward farmers and foresters, such uncertainty was more than merely disconcerting.

The woman (at some point, Bretta had arbitrarily decided that it was a female) had been unpleasant to look upon, as well, possessing coarse, stringy hair that stuck out upon every side, except for an obscenely naked forehead— ornately tattooed—that seemed to reach almost to the crest of her skull. Her eyes bulged from their sockets like halves of the lightweight balls Bretta and her sisters batted back and forth with paddles across a table. She never seemed to blink. Her irises and pupils never left the precise centers of her eyes. She never spoke above a whisper, or without slow, melodramatic gestures entirely unlike those Bretta had been brought up making. Perhaps the creature was not even human, but some variety of alien that someone working for Lia had discovered.

The worst of it, she thought, was the way that the Ceo's hypnotist *had* with her grandmother. Bretta did not care at all for Jennivere, and was not in the least ashamed to admit it, at least to herself. But at the same time, she was human enough to pity the old woman. To have somebody like that brain-sifter nudging, nuzzling, whispering in one's ear continuously, from morning until night, to have somebody's damp, spidery fingers lying upon one's arm or skittering across one's cheek . . . Bretta shuddered again, just thinking about it.

The creature might as well have come with them; it *felt* as if she were here.

Having left the central shaft, crossed another of Arran Islay's gundecks, taken a ladder below to the next deck, and successfully avoided stepping upon anyone for a third time, Bretta made her way through another oval hatchway cut through the ship's hollow mast. Resting her hands upon the metalloid railing upon either side of the spiral stairway, she slid downward and around, making a full circle before she reached a similar hatchway leading to the next deck below.

One by one, this ill-assorted handful of individuals had started to make whatever adjustments they were capable of making to one another. To give them proper credit, each of them occupied quarters, at the moment less luxurious and far more crowded than most of them—with the notable exceptions of Woulf and his mother—had ever been accustomed to. They had all been compelled, as well, to accommodate themselves to the unique rhythms of the ship herself, rising with her daywatch, eating by her rigid schedule, learning to stay out of the way of her complement of more than three hundred hard-driven, busy sailors.

At the same time, Arran and Phoebus drilled their crews without ceasing, insisting upon the highest possible standard of performance—a standard upon which the survival of all might soon come to rely. The primary emphasis, naturally enough, lay upon the speedy and accurate employment of the vessel's unusual number of projectiles, and the accompanying tactical aspects of starship handling. From moment to moment, the girl believed that she was seeing her father "come alive" again. He flourished under the strains, pains, and disciplines of a shipboard command. He even unbent sufficiently to let her take an occasional watch, serving as an unofficial member of the officers' mess.

It was all that she had ever wanted, and even now, she smiled at the thought.

Taking a long metal pole from its brackets upon a bulkhead, she poked it upward, deep into a ventilation shaft. There was a kind of, well, of *moss* the crewbeings called it, that dropped from such recesses, and made a short meal of any unwary sapient it fell upon. The stuff was rather rare, but very dangerous.

As a direct but unfortunate consequence, however, of Bretta's newly found usefulness aboard her father's starship, more and more, in her vacant off-duty hours, she had found the crowded passenger quarters of the interstellar vessel unendurable. Try as she might, she could not learn to abide her grandmother, the merest shell of a human being who, to all appearances, never bathed, whose rare, lucid moments were completely unpredictable, and whose behavior at other times was . . . well, absolutely disgusting. It seemed only natural to detest her.

And then there were certain other annoying little exercises in the art of interpersonal relationships. From the manner in which he seemed to leer at her whenever he thought that she was unaware of it, Bretta believed that Frantisek Demondion-Echeverria—a "dirty old man" if she had ever seen one (which she had, in old dramathilles)—

would have loved to trap her in some dark corner some-where.

Even her great-uncle Sedgeley's urbane, witty, and ingra-tiating manner was beginning to rasp upon her country girl's nerves. And the silent Brother Leo was beginning to seem more sinister to her than charming. She wished that she could be quartered among the *Osprey*'s junior officers, some of whom were female, rather than with her suddenly—and quite unwelcomely—extended family, distributed in cabins about the torus formed by the rise from main- to quarterdeck.

Upon the other hand, few ordeals actually last forever, and after three and a half endless Skyan months (not a minute soon enough for Bretta, nor for the remainder of the ship's company, she was willing to wager), the *Osprey* had arrived at last at her initial destination, an unexplored stellar system within a reasonable margin for calculatory error from the statistical center of historic Oplyte distribution, a location within the Deep that agreed roughly with the infor-mation the Ceo's hypnotist had been able to extract from Owld Jenn.

Now, in the cabelle tier, deep within the lowest reaches of the starship, where kiloklomme after kiloklomme of neatly coiled skyline was stored for the *Osprey*'s lubberlift, Bretta suddenly heard a grating noise, as if something hard and heavy had been dragged across a sandy surface. Startled at first, she immediately wondered what crew member of the nightwatch had cause to climb down this far belowdecks, to a portion of the starship that remained all but completely unused except when she stood in orbit about some port-world—and why.

Believing herself safe aboard her father's own corvette, where she had once teethed upon belaying pins and learned rough-edged work chanties for her nursery rhymes, it never occurred to the girl to draw her knife or ready her thrustible.

All at once, a visage that she very nearly failed to recog-nize, that of a strangely transformed Woulf, flashed into view, catching her by surprise. Without passion or expres-sion, he snapped his knife upward, directly out of its scabbard, and struck her a vicious blow upon the temple with its steel pommel.

Bretta never knew that there could be so much pain. It flooded through her body, weakening her at every joint, turning her stomach, making colored lights flare behind her eyes. Woulf struck her again before she could sag to the deck at his feet, and again after she had done, reducing her to a floating semiconsciousness that left her paralyzed while failing to relieve her of her agony.

"This is just to remind you that incest is a game the whole family can enjoy!"

He then began to slash her meager garments until she sprawled unclothed before him, a torrent of blood beginning to redden, and then to blacken, what little vision remained to her. Bothering only to expose the necessary part of his anatomy, he took her brutally, comprehensively, and, at astonishingly brief intervals, again and again. Bretta quickly learned that there could be vastly more pain than a simple, smashing blow to the head. No portion of her body did he leave private to her, or untorn, no portal left unbroached. Had she been able, she would have screamed, or fought, or vomited, or wept, or died.

She was helpless to do any of those things.

At last, believing her dead or seeming not to care in any case—in fact she had felt and heard everything that had happened to her with a clarity and poignancy that she would have previously believed impossible—Woulf lifted Bretta's broken body and stuffed it into a canister meant for trash disposal.

"Nothing personal, child, not *very* personal, anyway. Fifteen years is just too long to go without relief. I must speak with my employers about that."

He threw the bloody remnants of her clothing and accoutrements in on top of her. Then Woulf adjusted his clothing and stalked away as Bretta's ignoble casket sealed itself, rolled down a rampway between a pair of canisters like it, and was automatically ejected through the *Osprey*'s otherwise impermeable §-field.

The Ceo's misgivings, especially where Bretta was concerned, had proven too well justified. It would be, however, a long, agonizing time for those the unfortunate girl had left behind, before Lia came to know anything about it.

CHAPTER XXIII:
A CEO'S SECRET

"Bretta!"

Loreanna's voice echoed unavailingly throughout the lower gundeck. Like others aboard the ship, she was beginning to grow hoarse with calling for her daughter. She betrayed herself by no outward manifestation of fear or grief, but Phoebus had noticed that her hands trembled, and she wrung incessantly at a handkerchief.

"Bretta Islay!" That voice would be Sedgeley's, issuing from the mast well. He had surprised his niece—and Krumm, in the bargain—by knowing his way round a starship very handily. Perhaps he had been a yachtsman in his youth.

It was the *Osprey*'s youngest officers who had first missed Bretta at the "morning" meal. She was the sort of individual who would be missed. Her family and traveling companions had next assured themselves that she had not merely overslept—an idea the girl would have regarded as insulting had she known of it—but no amount of shouting throughout the ship had elicited a response.

Acting quickly, Arran and Phoebus conducted a more and more frantically fear-driven search of the whole vessel. The captain's hands trembled as well, more from rage, Phoebus suspected, than anything else. What he was apparently looking for now was an object for his burgeoning anger. Before beginning to search this morning, he had strapped upon his forearms both of the outsized Oplyte's thrustibles he had worn through the late war. Phoebus, too, carried one such. He had experience of boats' projectibles that boasted of less power.

Most of their effort this day had been wasted before it had been spent. With better than fifteenscore of diligent crew members conducting their search tier by tier, deck by deck, in every recess and locker of a starship they all knew blind-folded, it soon became obvious that no trace of any kind remained of the girl. Arran's response—twice—was to set them searching all over again. At the end of it, even those who loved her best had no choice other than to assume that their worst fears upon her account had somehow come to pass.

Not knowing for certain was by far the worst of it. Phoe-bus suspected this was only the beginning, that it would con-tinue to be so for years to come.

"The poor darling must have been wandering about the all-but-deserted vessel during the sparsely peopled night-watch," Tula Krumm theorized for the benefit of her hus-band. Hanoverian was not her native language (although she had been speaking it almost exclusively for more than twenty years) and her pronouncements in it tended to be a trifle stilted, for all that they were sincere.

She touched Loreanna upon the arm.

Tillie (whose own command of the official Monopolitan tongue was little better) nodded sadly. "That appears to have been her habit of late. A girl-child of this particular age requires her privacy and freedom. I certainly did. Why, I remember my own adolescence as if it had been only yes-terday."

Their husband agreed reluctantly. By now he had started to worry more about the girl's mother and father than about the girl herself. Something inside him, something he did not like very much, was starting to give Bretta up for dead. It was a terrible, nauseating feeling he seemed to have no con-trol over. "An' in the darkness of the maindeck—unbelievable as it may seem—she must somehow have lost her footing an' tumbled into the lethal §-field."

Phoebus Krumm was well acquainted with that danger. For many years, as an officer aboard the carrack *Gyrfalcon*—where he had first met a very bright but badly frightened young stowaway who had signed himself into the ship's complement as "Henry Martyn"—it had been one of his duties to instruct newly press-ganged sailors in that danger. It was the first thing every crew member learned. The possibility of such an accident as this had not, however, been made clear to *this* lot of passengers. Krumm would have felt guiltier, but the fact was that upon shipboard, Bretta knew what she was about.

"We have been through the entire vessel three times," he told his wives, although his words were actually addressed to Loreanna. In his decades upon the Deep, he had lost many a comrade to accident, disease, and war, but could not remember feeling worse about it than he did at this particular moment. For fifteen years he had loved Arran and Loreanna as if they were the very children he had never been able to beget. He had watched their glorious Bretta growing up, and it was all that he could do to keep himself from breaking down in the deep, lugubrious sobs that were customary to his people. "Let us betake ourselves up to the maindeck, an' see what our poor captain would have of us now."

For most of the morning, Woulf made a show of helping crew and passengers search for poor, lost Bretta. Those aboard the *Osprey* did not suspect him of having harmed her and cast her overboard, and they would not—until he had an opportunity to gloat about it. It was an opportunity he looked forward to. For the moment, he had retired to a place of hiding he had prepared by breaking into one of the steam launches upon the boatdeck, in order to take stock.

Out of habit vastly longer than any one of these mere mortals all around him might have imagined possible, he squatted with his knife in one hand and a hone set in the other, touching up the edges of his fighting blade. He was always happy when he could combine business with pleasure, and last night he had accomplished both most handily. In one stroke—so to speak—he had dealt a mortal blow to the morale of this insane expedition, while at the same time, *consuming* one of the most delectable morsels that had ever come his way.

How old had she been? Fifteen, was it? Certainly no record there. He'd had them a deal younger than that, over the past nine hundred years. But still, none sweeter.

He wondered, idly, how the others might react, did they know the truth about him, but he did not care. There was too *much* truth about him for little minds like that to absorb all at once, anyway. Learning it—or even merely the truth about his age—might easily have killed them where they stood.

He laughed at the thought.

It amused him to think that Loreanna—speaking of delectable morsels—could not guess that he was not her younger half brother, not Jennivere's son, after all, but, in fact, the most professional assassin the universe had ever known, energetically working for her enemies. He was also ninetenths of a millennium older than she, preserved by his keepers for the great majority of his existence in a form of electronic stasis unknown to the remainder of the galaxy.

He had begun his career nearly nine centuries ago—he enjoyed thinking of himself as an "uncivil servant"—in the employ of a secret government agency, the very existence of which had been forbidden by the highest laws of the ancient nation-state that had created it. And him. And now, from time to time, he was revived and began to live again, but only when his services were required.

The *Osprey* was within range of the stellar system where men were forced to become Oplytes. His own mission nearly over, now, he was upon his way home. This time, he had been awakened and dispatched to assess the threat represented by the Monopolity of Hanover's new Ceo, Lia Woodgate Wheeler. For one thing, she had publicly denounced the Trade upon one too many an occasion for the taste of those he served.

He was also to look over her predicted ally, the infamous skyrobber Henry Martyn. Fifteen years before, that one had been famous for granting freedom to slaves of all sorts. Although such an emancipation was impossible for Oplytes, it clearly established Henry Martyn's attitude, and demonstrated that he was just as great a threat as the new Ceo. It had also created a highly undesirable precedent which must be discouraged at all costs. In the end, Woulf would have to decide the best course, and kill one or both of them if necessary.

An earlier, more subtle attempt, which his employers had believed wonderfully clever—at destroying the warrior with guilt—apparently had failed.

But Woulf knew now that it was he who had miscalculated, owing to the internal biases of the culture of which he was now a part. For all of their baroque trappings and byzantine relationships, these were simpler times than those he had been born into. He tended to make things more complicated than they need be. Arran was all but crippled by his guilt—he simply bore it well.

Yet, in another respect, Woulf was like many another subject of the several imperia-conglomerate. Without being aware of it, he had come to believe that no mere woman could control the destiny of an interstellar empire. Instead, he had calculated that her father's abdication must have been some kind of ruse. Thus, rather than simply killing Lia or Arran as his employers wished, he had "reasoned" that the cleverest way was to follow Brother Leo and observe him.

More cleverness—and another failure.

There were reasons why Woulf felt a considerable distance from—if not an actual superiority to—those who foolishly believed they controlled him, and often substituted his own tactical judgment of affairs for their orders. For one thing, he had managed to remain completely human over the centuries—as human as he had been to begin with—while they and their successors had not.

For another, they were unaccustomed to extending their

own lives by the same process that had been used to extend his. The very notion of attempting such a thing—on the rare occasions it arose—appeared to terrify them. It was their habit to employ him, whenever they deemed it necessary, and then to pass him on as a kind of grisly heirloom, to another horrible generation. To them, he had become a mysterious and powerful being no fewer than nine centuries old. And yet, he knew (and knew that his keepers knew, as well) that he had only lived through—and learned from—fewer than thirty of those years.

They tended to forget that he was not an organic robot like the Oplytes they produced. For reasons that always seemed good to him at the time, he would do things upon his own. They could never have predicted that he would risk everything, seeking a moment's animal pleasure with young Bretta, and then murdering her afterward. Nor, because they did not understand a species they no longer belonged to, would they have believed he had done it for reasons of his own devising more complicated than the pleasure he had seen as a fringe benefit.

The simple fact was that Woulf—even by his own estimate—was allowed far too much latitude of judgment by his operators, although there was hardly any alternative. What set him apart, if nothing else did, was the fact that he was the only individual in the Known Universe who remembered humanity's homeworld.

He had been a covert agent there, trained by one of the powerful nation-states that had controlled the planet. Ultimately, he had been assigned to a community, shared by several nations, based upon the homeworld's large natural satellite.

It was this, of course, that had saved his life, while the people who had "created" him had perished. All life upon the homeworld had been obliterated by a hostile exchange of thermonuclear devices. Upon the moon, they had watched in horror as their home planet had enveloped itself in radioactive clouds.

A few thousand scientists, technicians, and workers, living in a colony specifically established to develop a faster-than-light starship were the only survivors.

And Woulf.

Not only was everything they had ever known and loved now dead and beyond reach, they were marooned for the rest of their lives upon a lifeless ball of rock.

"I fail," complained Demondion-Echeverria, pausing to take a whiff from the ornate narcohaler he had resumed using upon being forced to leave his beloved Immortal School, "to comprehend this lethality business everybody has been babbling about." This fellow knew much, Phoebus realized, but precious little about starships—or parents confronted with the death of their eldest child.

Upon bales and bollards, they sat in a circle upon the maindeck, outside the captain's quarters. It was better than being cooped up inside. Here they could feel that they were outdoors, although the §-field made a haggis of the sky.

Phoebus sat upon a great cleat, massive forearms resting upon his knees, fumbling with a large blue Skyan marshmelon he had not yet decided whether to eat. (Sedgeley's position was similar, face buried in his hands; it was clear that the old rogue had adored his great-niece; perhaps he was only discovering it now.) Phoebus had missed both breakfast and lunch, and still had little appetite.

Glancing uncertainly at Loreanna, who nodded a brave affirmative, he took a breath, and addressed the former ambassador. "Ye know, Mister Demondion-Echeverria, do ye not, that a subtle but powerful energy field, which forms the technological basis for all Deep-travel, an' other applications besides, like thrustibles an' projectiles, surrounds this here vessel an' renders her inertialess?"

The fellow sniffed delicately. The motions he made were languid, owing to the drug, but his eyes were as clear as his elocution. "I had heard some such."

"Well," Phoebus told him, "it is only in such an 'insubstantial' state of existence that the *Osprey* an' other starships like her may be driven before the otherwise trivial tachyon currents of the Great Deep, an' may by this means attain velocities greatly exceeding the otherwise limiting speed of light."

"Why, yes, yes. It all comes back to me now."

Phoebus gave the man a look, but he had apparently meant what he said without sarcasm. "At the same time, the §-field forms a protective bubble about a ship, retainin' warmth an' atmosphere, so hundreds of crewbeings may live an' work upon an open deck, no hull to enclose them—in what was once called a 'shirtsleeve environment'—unencumbered by special garments of any kind."

Demondion-Echeverria nodded uncertainly. He was by no means stupid, but had found no reason before now to know these things and probably intended to forget them again as soon as possible. "I believe I follow you, Captain Krumm. Pray continue."

"Good on you, Mister Demondion-Echeverria." He glanced at the Islays, rigidly in control of themselves. "What me wife Tula says must have happened to Bretta—indeed, what all yer companions with knowledge of ships have had uppermost in their minds—is a common shipboard accident at the best of times."

Arran closed his eyes a moment, then inhaled and straightened himself.

"I am afraid I still do not understand." Demondion-Echeverria began to take a whiff upon his inhaler, but forgot it with Krumm's next words—and actions.

"Then consider this."

Of a sudden, Phoebus caught everyone's attention by hurling the melon high over the quarterdeck, past the taffrail, and out into the surrealistic §-field. As it struck, they witnessed a loud report and the dazzling flash of §-field annihilation. The melon had been converted instantaneously into energy.

"Her slender body would have disintegrated, without pain, in less than a second." Phoebus knew the thought would fail to comfort a mother and father who wanted their daughter back more than anything else. Each was likely taking inventory of every time they had denied her something or spoken to her crossly.

"What an abominable waste," replied Demondion-Echeverria, earning him a look from Loreanna that would have had a more observant man watching over his shoulder the rest of his life. Arran's face assumed a dangerous expression.

"You are absolutely certain, then, that this is what happened to Mistress Islay?"

Phoebus sighed again. "Not at all. I am not bloody *certain* of bloody *anything*. But it must have happened to her. The only other way t'get off a starship upon the face of the Deep is through her launch ports or her garbage system."

At that moment, Woulf stepped out upon the deck.

The ambassador's raised eyebrows represented another question, which Arran, standing beside his wife with one hand lying upon her shoulder, decided to answer. Phoebus was very glad to hear him speak up. The captain had not uttered more than three words all morning long, and they had been, "Search it again!"

"You see, although small masses such as Krumm's marshmelon may be tossed out with impunity, large masses—a starship's daily accumulation of garbage—may not, as it engenders unwanted fluctuations in the §-field. Yet, it must be gotten rid of, or we should be even more crowded together than we are now."

Phoebus nodded. "Some older vessels handle the problem with a system that pulverizes and disposes of small quantities of refuse every minute, day an' night. Others, *Osprey* fer example, do it all at once, usin' disposable insulated canisters, capable of creatin' momentary lacunae—holes—in the §-field."

"I have seen these canisters myself," Woulf volunteered, "when . . . when Bretta showed them to me, upon a tour of the ship." He cast his eyes down sadly.

Jennivere, who had said nothing, was aghast. "Is this not . . . messy? Do we not litter the Deep? We cannot simply throw things *away,* there *is* no away!"

Krumm headed Arran off. "Madame, 'away' is all there is. When infinity begins t'fill up, let me know an' I will stop. Meanwhile, if there is no *away,* where in the Ceo's name will ye go when I tell ye yer opinions are not solicited?"

"Phoebus—" Loreanna warned him, as Woulf gave him a dark, hostile glare. The stress upon everyone had apparently begun to tell, even the mighty Krumm.

"Still . . ." Arran and Loreanna had remained relatively calm, refusing to accept the idea that their graceful, intelligent daughter could have been so clumsy and stupid as to perish in such an ignominious manner. "I would point out that for Tula's theory to have merit, Bretta would have had to fall *upward,* over the waist-high quarterdeck taffrail, something I find utterly unthinkable."

Gravity aboard the *Osprey,* or a useful facsimile of it, was maintained through a deliberate inefficiency programmed into the §-fields that rendered her inertialess. As long as she had headway, the deck remained solid beneath her crewbeings' feet. Phoebus nodded. Despite the fact that Bretta was nowhere to be found aboard the ship, the same thought had occurred to him, as well.

"Either that," Arran's wife argued reluctantly, "or . . . or Bretta would have had to suffer her . . . her misstep high amidst the vessel's many spars and complicated rigging. But I . . . but why would she, when it was not her watch aloft?"

It tore at Phoebus's heart watching Loreanna, whom he remembered as a girl her daughter's age, handling her loss with a clear mind and no emotional display. Even Hanoverians had characteristics, he had discovered, that were admirable. Had it been his own daughter, he would be howling at the Galactic Core. Given the way he felt about the girl and her parents, it might come to that.

"To be sure," Loreanna added, "one may for the most part wander freely about the decks during the ship's nightwatch. That sort of exercise is to be encouraged for many good reasons. But I gather that it is usually not done to go aloft without a specific purpose in mind and authorization from a superior officer."

"You are quite correct, my dear," Arran told her. "Even were it so, I cannot conceive of Bretta having lost her footing or her grip in so familiar an environment. Who knows better than I that she is as safe and comfortable aboard a starship as she is in her own bedroom at the Holdings upon moonringed Skye?".

For a long moment, everyone was silent. Then Arran began again. "For that matter, think about what Phoebus has just clearly demonstrated: that §-field annihilation, while instantaneous, is invariably accompanied by a loud bang and a bright light which could not have been missed by the watch-upon-deck."

Amongst the company, at that point, in the absence of a solution to the mystery of Bretta's disappearance, a somewhat hysterical argument commenced over what was wisest to do next. Some took the tragedy as an excuse to return to Hanover. Others saw in it a reason to push on. Krumm's mention of the canisters belowdecks inspired Demondion-Echeverria to suggest—and then to demand—that they search the nearby Deep in case that was what had happened. Arran pointed out that falling into the top of a garbage canister was an even more athletic—and unlikely—feat than falling over the quarterdeck taffrail.

Krumm agreed with considerable reluctance, adding that they were already a lightyear from where, according to the records of the watch, three disposal canisters had been ejected automatically in the middle of the night. There was simply too much uncertainty about the position, too much volume of the Deep involved, to go back and look. They could search forever, cubic measure by cubic measure, and never find anything. He was not certain the ambassador understood.

"A boy has never wept, or dashed a thousand krim!"

"What?"

Loudest of all was Jennivere—Owld Jenn—that individual among them (as is often so in human affairs, especially politics) with the least sensible contribution to make to their discussion. And yet whenever anybody told her to remain quiet—as her own daughter happened to do upon this occasion—her bastard son Woulf threatened them with a murderous glare, a slap toward the knife upon his hip, and something rather closely resembling an animal growl.

At last the situation had become intolerable.

"Does no one see what is happening, here?" Without warning, the former Ceo astonished everyone by breaking his long-held monkish vow of silence with a mighty roar. "D'you genuinely fail to understand that *They* have agents, everywhere?"

Surprisingly, Woulf answered first. "What are you talking about, you old—I will be buggered! The old fart spoke! But what did you mean by what you said?"

Leupould regarded the young urban barbarian, with his tattered clothes and primitive weapon, with a visible degree of distaste. "I meant, you poor, ridiculous creature, that, whatever befell the beautiful, and by all accounts exceptionally adroit, daughter of our esteemed captain and his wife . . ." Here, he ground to a halt, paused as if to gather strength, and then continued with an unwontedly stubborn set to his bearded mouth, "it was by no means any accident!"

Arran, desperate and disoriented by the loss of his eldest and favorite child—although he had refrained so far from displaying it—discovered suddenly that he agreed with Leupould. It seemed to snap him into some form of clarity. He strode to the man and seized what served upon a monk's robe as lapels.

"Brother Leo, let me warn you that I will stop nothing short of physical violence in order to have you explain *precisely* who and what you meant by 'They.' "

"As you will, Captain Islay—or perhaps in this mood you would prefer 'Captain Martyn.' And although I confess freely now that I have been all but *paralyzed* with fear for more than a decade by what I am about to tell you, and worn down by bearing the burden of it all alone, it is not *you*, my

boy, who inspires such fear. Do whatever you will, I have
been ready to die for years.

"But I warn you in turn, boy, after hearing what I have to
say, that you will *never* be able to look upon the universe in
quite the same way, ever again."

CHAPTER XXIV:
BENEATH CONTEMPT

Arran pushed Brother Leo away from himself. "Say on, and
be done with it!"

"And be damned to you, as well? Is that what you were
going to say, my boy?"

Brother Leo lowered his bulk onto a box he had been sitting upon earlier. "I am well aware that everyone—each of
those round us at the moment, for example—has always
been curious about the reason I relegated control of the
Monopolity of Hanover to my daughter, Lia Woodgate. I
will tell all of you that reason now, and whatever you ever
imagined it to be, you are in for a surprise."

He had everyone's attention now. "The crucial event," he
informed them, despite the visibly manifest emotional distress it was beginning to cost him to do so, "immediately
followed your brilliant and stunning military victory, Captain Martyn, over the forces of . . . of the status quo. Brilliant. And stunning."

Arran shrugged.

"I implore you, sir," the former Ceo told him. "No false
modesty upon your part. We were—*I* was—humiliated. And
yet it was but nothing to what came afterward. It is altogether beyond my capability to convey to you the . . . the
degree of personal shame with which I confess that, in the
privacy and in the presumed safety of my own innermost

quarters, a most unprecedented phenomenon occurred. I, the invincible Leupould IX, Ceo of the Monopolity of Hanover, was—in effect—issued a peremptory summons to appear before the rulers of an interstellar empire neither I nor anybody else had known existed heretofore."

Phoebus wondered where all of this was leading, but refrained from saying so.

Leupould continued. "I am neither willing nor able to discuss with you the mechanical aspects of this summons. However, when I ceased to be within the privacy and safety of my innermost quarters, and suddenly found myself somewhere else, it became clear to me that this unheard-of political entity, this empire, commanded new and powerful technologies we had not even as yet imagined."

The big man's voice had begun to waver, and his knees could be seen to shake beneath the cover of his robe. What had also become clear was that to the core of his being, even after fifteen years, Leupould was still frightened and humiliated.

"I, Leupould Wheeler," he sobbed, "ninth Chief Executive Officer to bear that ancient name and distinguished title for the Monopolity of Hanover, had been summarily—and literally—called upon the carpet like a negligent pupil before his headmaster, to account for my failure to stop Henry Martyn's Rebellion!"

This should prove interesting, Woulf thought—although his mind still lay upon events more ancient than Leo could imagine—to hear the events of the last time he had been revived, from a point of view directly opposite his own. And yet, despite himself, he found that he was thinking about Earth's moon.

In the sunlight it had been too hot for human existence, and it was too cold in the shade. Micrometeorites and deadly radiation swept the unprotected surface constantly. Without fresh supplies of air or water, it was anybody's guess whether the colony could be rendered self-sufficient before they all died.

But before any of that could even begin to happen, even before it became clear that the dust was *never* going to settle, back on Earth, another issue had to be settled first. People had begun looking around for somebody to blame.

Some scientists, technicians, and workers claimed that the Earth had died because of the existence of so many different governments. Not only were they always fighting with one another, none of them had had any real control over the dangerously unpredictable *individual*. On Earth, by the end of the first quarter of the twentieth century, most people had been free to think, to say, or to do anything they wanted. That, obviously, was what had made the destruction of humanity's homeworld possible. If mankind were to survive upon the moon, then a single, absolutely powerful dictatorship needed to be established, immediately.

Others argued that, upon the contrary, it was the existence of government itself which had destroyed the Earth. Governments had always stolen and diverted resources from the individuals who generated them. They had always converted the products of peaceful effort into the assets of war. And now the same sick system was about to be imposed upon the surviving Lunar remnant of humanity.

The latter group, although somewhat smaller in number (as might have been expected) than the former, were (as might *also* have been expected) better armed and faster upon the draw. They had herded all the members of the former group into the prototype starship they had been working upon together, sealed the controls, and aimed the ship at a stellar cluster upon the edge of the galaxy.

It was a source of eternal—cosmic—embarrassment to Woulf that mere amateurs had gotten the drop on him. For once in his life he had expressed a political opinion. As a consequence, he had been one of the authoritarian evictees.

He knew well the humble origins of the scattered cultures loftily styling themselves "imperia-conglomerate." They had learned nothing, but remained true to their nature. Aboard the experimental ship, they had broken into one viciously quarrelling splinter group after another. The preprogrammed ship couldn't stop, but could put lifeboats off along the way. One by one, each group had been kicked out by the others. By turns, each of them lucky enough to find habitable planets had established settlements throughout the Cluster. Suffering many an epochal rise and fall in the process, they had eventually evolved into the various polities now familiar to dwellers within the Known Void.

Bretta.

As a boy, Arran had lost his mother, his father, two brothers, his best friend, a beloved teacher (for a time), but he was unprepared to accept this death.

A part of him wished simply to give up and die along with his daughter Bretta—Arran had long since stopped feeling guilty over the fact that she was his favorite; how could she not be, being everything she was?—but he reminded himself now that he was the father of four other daughters and a son whom he deeply and genuinely loved, for all that he loved Bretta best, and a husband to Loreanna, who was the only thing in the entire galaxy he loved more.

It was upon their account, he told himself, characteristically allowing himself no credit for a spirit that everyone else understood perfectly well to be unconquerable, that he presently compelled himself to continue listening to the blubbering of this flesh-mountain who had once ruled so much of the Known Deep. It would appear that, having spoken not a single word for many years, Leupould now intended to talk them all to death, before he actually told them anything.

Arran had been paying only half attention, with his other eye upon the ship. In his own comparative youth, the former Ceo had been telling them, "plain old Professor Leo Wheeler" had been a competent and widely respected academic.

Arran squirmed where he sat, anxious to be anywhere but stuck here, with this whimpering ape's self-pity. Everybody present appeared willing to accept the former ruler's claim—Phoebus, Tula, and Tillie Krumm, Uncle Sedgeley,

Demondion-Echeverria, Woulf, even his crazy old mother—if Leupould would only assume that they all knew he was an unhappy fellow and get along with his story.

". . . an esteemed, well-published lecturer in the fields of history and galactography," Leupould went on. "I affected scholarly and esoteric masques, the likenesses of *jeffhummel, walterbloch, vonmises, walterwilliams.* Heady days, I tell you—acclaim from my superiors and eager-minded students—headier nights, if you take my meaning. Owing to my academic past, as Ceo of the Monopolity, I relished my role as the imperium-conglomerate's governor—my background, you see, having made me appreciative of the magnitude of my domain."

Everybody present was willing to accept him, that was, save the captain's lady. As a girl, Arran knew proudly, for the sake of an erstwhile captor—the freebooter Henry Martyn—she had come to love; Loreanna had confronted this pompous clod upon his own territory at the height of his power. Now, nearly prostrate with grieving over their missing daughter, she surprised even the husband who knew her by lifting her eyes, smoldering with rage, to do it again.

"Tell me, what is the point of all this?" she demanded of the onetime Ceo of the Monopolity, crushing a handkerchief in her fingers to keep from shaking her fist at him. "Where in the name of the—where is it getting us?"

There were nods and murmurs of agreement from every one of Brother Leo's impatient listeners, including the three Krumms and even—in their urbane and subdued manner—from his friends Sedgeley and Demondion-Echeverria. Only Arran's wife's mother sat quietly, still steeping in the first officer's reproof.

"My ascent to the high seat at the center of the Hanoverian 'Droom," as if he had not heard Loreanna, Leupould went on, "was an unforgettable—and indescribably pleasurable—experience. I was assuming control over the largest, most powerful civilization in history. I controlled the destinies of something on the order of fifteen quintillion human (and a rather surprising number of alien) lives. And from that unspeakably glorious day, until my abdication, the only masque I ever condescended to wear was a golden likeness of my own face."

Loreanna began to object again, but Leupould bowed his shaggy head and raised both hands, palms outward. "Madame, I beseech you, permit me to tell this in my own way. It is the only time I ever have, and the only time I ever shall."

Loreanna blinked with astonishment, causing Arran to smile a bit despite the grimness of recent events. To his wife, who had miraculously remained a young girl in her heart (it was his hope that she would forever), "Madame" had always been someone else—someone much older—who was probably no fun at all.

She nodded at Leupould.

He took a heartfelt breath. "I have meditated on it a great deal over the years. No, the fact is I have dwelt upon it endlessly. Although I was subjected to many other abuses at the time—underlining the point, as it were, that they could do anything their whim dictated—I have come to feel that the worst of the outrages inflicted upon me by this heretofore unknown agency was that they revealed to me a trifle more of reality than I wished to know."

It was Sedgeley's turn to blink, in openmouthed shock. "They *tortured* you?"

He smiled. "They accomplished worse than that, old friend. Has it never occurred to you to catalogue the mortal indignities that may be visited upon a person without damaging the flesh? I shall carry such a catalogue within me to the end of my days. And I have no choice but to peruse its pages every night."

He shrugged. "That was but a trifle, compared to making me see a simple truth. Perhaps that is all tyranny consists of, compelling us to understand that which we do not wish to understand. My friends, the 'Known Deep' proves not to be well-known after all. I was, perforce, made all too well aware of the actual position the 'Droom—and the 'mighty, dreaded, and fearsome' Monopolity it mistakenly believes it controls—occupy in the scheme of things."

Seen in different light, Arran had possessed that knowledge almost from the day of his birth. The 'Droom and the Monopolity, like every authority that mankind's natural weakness had ever given breath, were of no importance whatever—not to genuine human beings with genuine lives of their own to live.

That had been the point of what Leupould called Henry Martyn's Rebellion, and the proof, had anyone demanded it, was the brutal manner in which Leupould had coldly used his own daughter, first as a spy, then to take his place upon a throne he had rejected, whereas Arran would have given anything he possessed—the entire Monopolity of Hanover, for that matter—simply to have his daughter back.

Yet there remained some, perhaps even a majority of every sapient race, who knew no better and had *need* to ask. In this case it was Demondion-Echeverria who spoke. "And what, precisely, would that actual position be, Leo?"

Leupould looked up at his old colleague and fellow Initiate, the former ambassador. His expression, and his tone, were astonishingly gentle. "Why, a most embarrassing one, my dear Frantisek, precisely the same as that of the Jendyne Empery-Cirot. It was demonstrated to me that I ruled nothing more, in the actinic light of objective reality, than a pretentious, self-important military, technological, social, and cultural *backwater.* In truth, our much-vaunted Monopolity of Hanover was no less a rude frontier settlement, in its way, than the Islays' rough-hewn moonringed planet Skye, the difference between them being that the Islays always knew what they had, whereas I had not."

So disturbed was the man as he told his tale, he failed to realize that he was insulting Arran and Loreanna. To learn more, Arran let it pass without comment, as he most likely would have, anyway. He and Loreanna had lost their daughter. They needed to know why, and Brother Leo was claiming that he knew. Whatever insults had been inflicted upon the Ceo by these unknown malefactors, Arran reflected, in some respects—from every account he had heard of this man who had been his enemy fifteen years ago—they seemed to have improved him considerably.

"My friends, our 'Droom is no more than another smoky village campfire," Leupould went on, apparently warming to his subject, "surrounded by capering, ululating savages attired in absurd totemic disguises of wood, metal, and straw."

Sedgeley fingered his masque, a subtle *dumas,* then quietly took it off. Demondion-Echeverria watched and folded his arms in stubborn refusal to follow suit.

Leupould leaned in, focusing upon the Jendyne. "All about the Monopolity of Hanover, which we now perceive in proper, if uncomfortable perspective, lay a myiad of other presumably respectable imperia-conglomerate. To my newly enlightened sensibilities, they now appeared to be—and remain so today—no more than the grass-hut compounds of the unclothed natives of a barbaric planet. To my horror and chagrin, I discovered that I had become mortally ashamed that any of us—the Monopolity included—had ever made so much of ourselves."

He looked round, appealing to something he desperately hoped was in them. What he got was an observation from an impatient Tillie Krumm: "Loreanna is right, Leo. This may all seem profoundly philosophic to you, but where in your daughter's name does it get us? What does it have to do with our poor Bretta?"

Was it a flare of Ceo-like temperament Arran saw quickening in Leupould's eyes? If so, it died at once. "Madame, I was coming to that, I beg you to bear with me. Where was I? Oh, yes: it would appear that the role all of them serve—the many imperia-conglomerate—is that of nothing more than a market. I was told we live merely to purchase and consume a single product, propagated by a vastly greater—albeit heretofore unknown— civilization. And what might that single product be?" he asked his traveling companions rhetorically.

"Oplytes," Phoebus replied quietly.

"Give that man a narcohaler!" Leupould shouted with such false joviality that Arran found it almost obscene. "How ironic it is—and no doubt highly profitable—that the same savages who purchase the product (meaning us, in case it had somehow slipped your mind) unwittingly supply the raw material for its manufacture. We breed, they harvest— and sell our own children back to us!"

Loreanna flinched, but otherwise said nothing. She had been deprived of her father by the very process Leupould had just described, and, indirectly, of her mother—for all practical purposes. Nor was the disappearance and probable death of her daughter significantly less connected to the Oplyte Trade.

Arran decided to caution the man, but before he could, Leo resumed. "The most entertainingly ironical aspect of the entire situation is that to this supposedly wise, more sophisticated civilization, the Trade is but a minor enterprise. I would guess that most of its subjects are unaware it exists. Its victims, whose lives are so precious to us—to someone among us—are no more than the equivalent of trade-axes, colored glass beads, and plastic trinkets!"

Sedgeley, who had been quiet through the bitter tirade Leupould had so painfully refrained from indulging himself in for so long, was astonished. And enlightened. "No wonder the Traders never cared to manipulate the politics of the imperia-conglomerate. Just as long as we continue fighting amongst one another—"

"And purchasing short-lived but expensive Oplyte warriors to do the great bulk of our fighting with," supplied Demondion-Echeverria, chuckling to himself.

"The mundane everyday details," the Executor-General finished, "of our respective political housekeeping arrangements remain less than unimportant to them."

"Then Arran," suggested Loreanna, whose thoughts her husband had wrongly presumed to be elsewhere, "that is, 'Henry Martyn'—constituted a threat of the most dire order to the Oplyte slavers, not merely because he freed entire captive populations, but because of the philosophy of political and personal autonomy that he not only advocated, but put into vigorous practice everywhere he sailed. If that were ever to spread widely enough, why, in time they might cause peace to break out uncontrollably throughout the galaxy, both Known and Unknown."

"Madame, you describe the case precisely," Leupould told her. "It was made clear to me that they consider the politics of the imperia-conglomerate trivial beyond expression, utterly beneath their contempt. It is all the same to them if we continue squabbling over details of how to burden ourselves, and one another, with taxes and regulations. But should we contemplate not doing it at all, thus depriving them of a reliable source of revenue, they will show themselves and compel us to go on doing what we have done, for perhaps, ten thousand years."

"Come, now," Phoebus demanded. He looked from left, to right, to left again, from one of his wives to another, and bestowed upon the gathering a mighty shrug of disbelief. "Ye're sayin' these buggers've been around that long?"

Leupould shook his head. "I cannot say with confidence, Mr. Krumm. To be sure, it would illuminate a considerable portion of history that is irrational and perverse. Is it not a comforting idea that we may not be responsible for *all* our folly and brutality? For now, permit me to testify that nothing we know can in any way compare with the power that could humiliate me—absolute ruler of fifteen quintillion souls—in so cavalier a manner. As a scholar and former Ceo, I am unaware of any resources anywhere, of any kind, capable of changing that situation within our lifetimes, or those of many generations to come."

"An' the power t'humiliate"—the first officer shook his head—"is what scared ye outa yer 'Droom, hoppity-skip with yer tail atweenst yer legs, is it now?"

Leupould roared. "I was not 'scared' out of anything, you cretin!" He subsided. "Of anything. I beg your pardon, Mr. Krumm; none of this is your fault. It is simply that—oh, my—for all my life, I have been unwilling to settle for anything less than the biggest and best of whatever it was I happened to be interested in at the time. This was true of my character as a child, it was true of my character as a student, it was true of my character as a professor and a private citizen-subject of the Hanoverian imperium-conglomerate."

He took a deep breath.

"And I assure you it was no less true of my character, once I had been selected to succeed an aging Ceo who was less than satisfied with his natural heirs, and ascended to the highest office that the Monopolity of Hanover has to offer. In my view (and I know that some of you may find this a trifle odd), I would far rather do entirely without—and have often made a point of doing just that—than to accept anything less than the best of whatever it was I desired."

"Bravo," Loreanna said sarcastically. "So now, childishly disappointed at having learned your true place in the scheme of things, you shoved what you had been forced to see as your spoiled, second-rate kingdom off on your long-suffering daughter, and cravenly retired from life and the affairs of the 'Droom."

"I am quite incapable, Madame, believe me, of being insulted any further than I was by the humiliating knowledge that I was not a second-rate power, as you suggest, but a *hundredth-rate* or a *thousandth-rate*. I contemplated suicide."

"Poor baby," commented Phoebus.

Sedgeley asked, "And your vow of silence?"

"Was no more than a parting gift," Leupould informed him, "to the proud Hanoverian people I had ruled. I could do nothing to protect them from the predations of the slavers. I could protect them from the knowledge that had destroyed my life. To spare their dignity, I would take it with me to the grave."

"Leave them unprepared to deal with reality," Loreanna observed without sympathy.

Leupould turned both palms up and shrugged in a gesture of resignation. Whether this confirmed what Loreanna had accused him of, or was intended to signify that he could argue with her no longer, he offered no particular indication.

"Why," Arran demanded suspiciously, "have you now decided to break your vow?"

Leupould gave him an odd expression and a noise that was almost a laugh. "Because, my boy—would you prefer to be addressed as Captain Martyn?—to the last cell of my body, I believe that, one by one, or all together, we are about to die. Thanks to my impetuous daughter, and to Sedgeley and Frantisek, too, we have blithely invaded territory—this sector of the Deep—each cubic siemme of which is held by an enemy unimaginably more powerful than we are!"

Phoebus stood suddenly, alerted by a subtle change in the colors of the §-field surrounding the ship. It appeared that Leupould's grim prophecy would be fulfilled as soon as it was made. Arran noticed what had happened almost as quickly. Together, without a word to each other or to their companions, they hurried up the six-step ladder to the quarterdeck from which the vessel was commanded. Not for an instant had Arran forgotten his missing daughter or the bizarre tale Leupould had told, but he had more immediate problems to deal with.

Arran looked up from a binnacle-like instrument bolted to the deck that he was consulting as Phoebus stared straight into the naked §-field, judging events directly—thanks to decades of experience—by patterns he discerned there.

"Believe it as you will, Phoebus!" the younger man shouted at his first officer. "They must possess some means of shrouding their own §-fields, for the rapespawn are hard and very hard upon us, and we have had virtually no warning!"

It appeared that the *Osprey*'s far-reaching §-fields had somehow been detected long before those of the larger vessels now approaching them. Arran wondered: was this part of the superior technology that Leupould had warned them of?

"Call General Quarters!"

Without answering his captain, the first officer shouted orders, firstly to the lesser officers commanding the gundecks, secondly to those upon the maindeck who would convey his desires to the starsailors aloft. For the first time since their "Adventure of the Missing Third Forge," more than two years ago, Henry Martyn's famous fighting ship *Osprey* was preparing herself for war.

From upon the maindeck and aloft, there came a mighty cheer from more than a hundred willing throats whose owners knew well what they had signed on for.

From below, through the very fabric of the starship herself, those upon the maindeck could hear the rumbling of the gunports' heavy covers being slid aside.

Despite himself, a thrill of inexpressible joy coursed through Arran's body. "Phoebus, I know the cut of these sails," he cried. "By descriptions I have heard from rare souls who escaped their clutches, it would appear we are pursued by the very slave-taking curspawn that we ourselves have been looking for!" He peered into the instrument. "I make it six—seven—eight four-deckers!"

"By the Ceo's black guts, I make it eleven," Phoebus declared, showing some of the same euphoria Arran was experiencing. "*Osprey*'s fallen under a vicious an' concerted attack by at least eleven projectible-bristlin' four-decker dreadnoughts—the largest an' most powerful vessels of war known t'humanity!"

Arran grinned; it was not a pleasant sight. "Bedad, it is surrounded that we are then, with never a chance to obey the Ceo's command to 'show our heels'!"

PART FOUR:
ANASTASIA WHEELER
YEARDAY 339, 3026 A.D.
MAYYE 18, 518 HANOVERIAN
TERTIUS 14, 1596 OLDSKYAN

AND AS HE FELL AND AS HE TURNED
AND AS HE FELL CRIED HE,
"OH GIVE ME YOUR HAND MY PRETTY YOUNG THING,
MY BRIDE FOREVER YOU'LL BE."

"FRY THERE, FRY THERE, YOU FALSE YOUNG MAN,
FRY THERE INSTEAD OF ME,
SIX PRETTY MAIDS YOU'VE ANNIHILATED HERE.
AND THE SEVENTH'S ANNIHILATED THEE!

"FRY THERE, FRY THERE, YOU FALSE YOUNG MAN,
FRY THERE INSTEAD OF ME,
SIX PRETTY MAIDS YOU'VE ANNIHILATED HERE.
GO KEEP THEM COMPANY."

Chapter XXV:
The Night-Black Deep

Silence, darkness, *pain*.

Had it occurred to her to wonder about it, she could never have said who she was. She lived, if it could be called that, suspended somewhere between an awareness that was not quite consciousness, and an unconsciousness that was not quite death. Her skull smashed like an egg, bleeding inside and out from a dozen wounds, cruelly used and even more cruelly cast aside, she drifted away from the corvette *Osprey* onto the velvet breast of the night-black Deep. Over the hours that followed, she came close to drifting away from life itself.

"Daddy?"

It was an ironic mercy that her breathing was infrequent and shallow, for all the air she had was what had been sealed in with her. She slept fitfully, troubled and half-awakened from time to time by pain and an odd, disquieting sensation as the canister fell end over end. She imagined presences, and conversations.

"Mama!"

Then a *bump* she never felt, and a push to which she was insensible, and her eternity of drifting, whether she was aware of it or not, was over. Her rescuer—unintended, as it happened—had arrived just in time to save her rapidly faltering life. Soon there would be air and light and warmth again. The refuse canister had been salvaged from its aimless tumbling through the Deep.

Her all-unwitting rescuer, merely one of hundreds of thousands of such entities where it had come from, had no way of knowing—or more importantly, of understanding—

what a kindness it had accomplished, any more than it was capable of being aware of how closely it resembled one of the manta rays of dead, lamented Earth, or that it plied the absolute cold and bitter vacuum of the Deep in the same way that long-gone mantas swam the ocean. The injured girl's unknowing savior was a highly intelligent—albeit nonsapient—animal.

Its species (which, but for the strangest and most extremely unfortunate of circumstances, likeliest would never otherwise have been discovered by the decadently incurious imperia-conglomerate) was an astonishingly ancient one, older, indeed, than many of the stars under the cold, pale light of which it lived and bred. It had evolved out of the rich complex of organic molecules always to be found drifting in attenuated clouds throughout the interstellar Deep.

Perhaps the most amazing fact of all, regarding the bizarre creature that now patiently nudged her canister toward the gigantic disk it considered its home—sparkling like a billion diamonds as it wheeled against the velvet blackness of the Deep—was that it was *domesticated,* and had been so for countless generations. Indeed, for all of that time, it had been particularly trained to perform such homely tasks as this one, for its even more bizarre keepers.

Which was why the creature steered itself, now, toward a specific sparkle among billions in the great disk (how it managed to accomplish the required feats of navigation and astrobatics remained a mystery, even to its masters), understanding only that it would be fed, groomed, and praised for what it had discovered.

In the beginning, naturally, she believed that she was experiencing an endless series of nightmares from which she could not awaken herself and escape.

She lay within an irregularly shaped space, considerably smaller than her bedroom at home—if she could just remember where that had been—totally unable to move, for the most part unable even to feel, and yet wracked now and again by unbearable pains in her head and . . . elsewhere. The air she breathed was warm and laden with peculiar but not unpleasant odors. Time appeared to go by slowly, whole hours seeming to pass between a pair of heartbeats, loud in the utter silence of this chamber. Sometimes, when she awakened upon her own, the space about her was darker than she had ever known a space could be. At other times, she would be fed, sponge-bathed, or turned over by one of some unknown number of grotesquely deformed monsters, no two of which were similarly misshapen.

She was not particularly frightened—it was not much of a nightmare as nightmares go—but she was uncertain whether she never saw the same monster twice, or her memory was damaged and functioning so badly that she could not remember it. After all, she still could not remember what her own name was, where she had come from, or who her people—if she had had any—had been.

But she *could* hear.

"Hanebuth, I believe she's truly waking up, this time!" hissed a voice. "None too late: I didn't know a person could lay unconscious this long and live!"

"She may *not* live," replied another, seeming to be more in charge of things than the first. Her vision was badly blurred—was she going to be blind?—but by the deadened sound of their voices, she realized that they were in a small room with very rough or softly covered walls. "It's a great pity none of us is a doctor. Why have the mothers never captured a doctor? Fetch her some water, will you? There's a good fellow. I'll keep an eye on her."

She heard a rustle of fabric.

"Then again I may live," she informed the second voice as the owner of the first departed. She was gratified to find that her voice, while weak and strained, continued to serve her nonetheless. "Just to prove you wrong. How—how long, precisely, did I lie unconscious? Am I going to live? How did I come to be here? Who are you, and where, by the Ceo's brass astrolabe, is *here?*"

With these words it all came back to her, her name, her

family, her home, their long journey away from it, first to
Hanover, then to—its end, for her. Bretta suddenly recalled
every vile intimacy that her half uncle Woulf had inflicted
upon her, her futile struggles to stop him, every injury that
he had given her by way of punishment before she had been
compelled to submit to his wishes anyway.

Awash with bitter anguish, black fury, and an overwhelming experience of shame she could not account for,
Bretta attempted to sit up, and was terrified to discover that
she could not. She then attempted to wipe away whatever it
was that was obstructing her vision and was unable even to
move her arms—or her hands. Fighting down the mind-
shattering panic of feeling trapped within her own body, at
last she fell back—at least that was the sensation of it,
although what she had actually done was relax and quit trying to rise—and, unable even to turn her head away from her
unknown captor, she began to sob uncontrollably.

"There, there, now . . ." A hand had suddenly been laid
upon her. Bretta flinched, and would have slapped it away.
And then she realized that this was merely the owner of
the second voice, apparently attempting only to comfort
and console her. "Please . . . I won't touch you again.
Please don't injure yourself further, Mistress. Don't worry
about your vision, or try to see me, for I'm quite ugly, and
the sight of me surely wouldn't be conducive to your healing."

Bretta heard the fellow chuckle in a wry, self-deprecating
manner that failed to disguise the depth of his genuine feelings regarding his appearance.

"Why, you are speaking Hanoverian," she informed him,
sniffing back her tears. Abruptly, a violent shudder coursed
through her broken body as she experienced another brief
flash of hated remembrance. She must learn to *control* this
weakness, she decided, and turn it into strength, if she were
ever to have her revenge.

And she *would* have revenge. Woulf had made a mistake,
allowing her to live.

"Truth is, Mistress, I'm speaking the Coordinator's English. But you've no reason to understand that just now. To answer some of your questions (if you'll just lie quietly for a while, for you've been very badly misused, which I'm sure you don't need me to tell you), I'm Hanebuth Tarrant, esquire, at your service."

Somehow she knew that he was bowing.

Bretta took a long, deep breath, experimentally, and although she felt some considerable pain through her rib cage, she was pleased that it did not tremble through her as she let it out again, the way a breath will, sometimes, when one has been crying. "A good, solid Hanoverian name, Hanebuth Tarrant, if I do not mistake myself. 'The Coordinator's Anglitch,' is it?" She had suddenly become aware that she was hungry. "Why can I not see clearly? How extensive are my injuries? When may I eat? Where are we? *And where are my weapons?*"

"I say, Mistress, I have never before encountered anyone— excepting for myself, perhaps—who asked quite so many questions. This place, it's—" Here, the voice hesitated, its owner attempting to sort out all her questions. "Well, this is where we are, Mistress, hidden deep within the twisted, rocky fissures— extensively resculpted, I might add, by countless patient hands over many centuries—of a tiny worldlet, one of many millions, belonging to a uniquely planetless one-star system, composed entirely of such tiny worldlets."

"And—"

"And you have been here, Mistress, let me see, now . . . six, seven, eight, nine weeks—your many and very grievous injuries having been attended to as competently as we were equipped to do it—being otherwise nursed gradually back to as near a semblance of robust good health as we have been able to contrive!"

Bretta could almost hear the blink and nod of relieved satisfaction that accompanied those words. Despite herself she giggled, partly from her severe emotional and physical weakness, partly from the sprightly and amusing manner of Tarrant's speech. His accent—although it had clearly been altered by some later circumstance—was completely typical of the urban lower classes of Hanover, who took a certain pride in the elaborate and colorful way they spoke.

"As to the balance of your questions, you can't see because I don't wish you to, this being, as I indicated, a matter of courtesy and modesty upon my part."

She began to speak.

"Pray do not interrupt me, for I've been dreading this, and you should demonstrate a modicum of consideration. You have a very well fractured skull, Mistress. I am enormously surprised that you survived it—which, despite my careless earlier words to an associate, I believe you have. You cannot move, because you have been restrained for fear that you will unset one or more of the many broken bones you arrived here with: both humeri, both radii and ulni, one clavicle, several ribs (I didn't count 'em), one femur in three places, the tibia and fibula of the opposite leg, most of the fingers of both hands. Whoever did this, Mistress, you put up quite a battle and should feel unashamed. You have a number of unspeakable soft-tissue injuries I don't know how—"

Bretta interrupted him. "Will they heal?"

"I think so, Mistress. Thanks to many an oversight upon the part of our malefactors, we've some good equipment here. Still, I'm a ship's officer, not a—"

"Then pray stop all this 'Mistress' nonsense. I find that I dislike it quite as much as my mother dislikes being called 'Madame.' And undo whatever you have done to my eyes, sir. My name is Robretta Islay, eldest daughter of Arran 'the' Islay, Autonomous Drector-Hereditary of Skye and of his wedded wife, the former Loreanna Daimler-Wilkinson. My friends—and Mr. Tarrant, for your many troubles and kindnesses upon my account, I reckon that you must be at least a dozen of those, all by yourself—my friends call me Bretta. And I believe I have a better character than you credit me with. I would thank the person who saved my life, whatever his appearance, face-to-face."

Suddenly exhausted by the effort of speaking, and despite her ravenous hunger and the myriad of questions that remained to be answered, she fell asleep.

* * *

When Bretta next awoke she was alone, her chamber cheerfully illuminated by a simple, old-fashioned antenna-lamp such as her father had once given her, irradiating several sizable sheets of structural polymer attached to the walls.

The walls themselves were very rough, and although they had been painted with a clean white sealant of some kind, were filled with bubble holes of all sizes, much like the big blocks of reddish and blackish lava, from the lovely and violent Tamara range of volcanoes in the Skyan southern hemisphere, that her mother kept in a decorative garden to one side of the Holdings Hall. The little bedroom could boast of no particular shape; it was, perhaps, roughly that of a potato. And it was only about twice as capacious as the garbage disposal canister into which her half uncle Woulf had callously stuffed her body.

She experienced another lurid, unbearable flash of anger, and a churning hunger for vengeance more physically overwhelming than any emotion Bretta had ever experienced before. Then, just as abruptly, a pang of sympathy, love, and regret coursed through her body at the remembrance of her poor mother and father—what must they be thinking and feeling of her just now, that she was dead?—which was almost canceled out by a sudden realization that she could see!

"Hello?" She was uncertain how her voice would carry or that anyone was listening.

A door of a kind, with a curtain of a kind, could be seen beyond the foot of whatever it was that was serving her as a bed. Whatever it was, it seemed to be soft. There were what appeared to be silken bedcovers across her legs—queerly luxurious, she thought, remembering what Tarrant had told her, for cave dwellers living inside an asteroid—but she could see that both of her arms were wrapped tightly in some sort of light, coarsely woven fabric, from the base of her neck to the tips of her fingers. Her peripheral vision and returning tactile senses informed her that her head was heavily bandaged, as well.

"Hello?"

"Hello!" a voice replied from behind the curtain. "I see you're feeling better this morning. You fell asleep, right in the middle of our talk last night."

"You can see me." She smiled and, running her tongue about inside her mouth consciously for the first time since she had awakened in this place of blessed refuge, wondered that she was not missing teeth, along with every other injury that had been inflicted upon her. And how in the Ceo's name had she escaped without a broken nose? "But I cannot see you. I apologize most abjectly for last night. I did so want to learn more—and I was hungry, and still am, for that matter. But pray, will you not let me *see* you, Hanebuth Tarrant?"

"She remembers our name, does she?" Tarrant murmured. "She remembers our name, indeed. And I did bring you a bit of breakfast, which I had planned to place beside you as you slept. Although upon reflection, I suppose you would have had some trouble feeding yourself, all swathed up in bandages as you are. Ah, well, never mind all that now. I will indeed come in, do you but desire it. But I warn you, Princess Bretta, brace yourself. For I am not a pretty sight."

A metal tray with a steaming bowl upon it preceded him through the parted curtain. She could not see his hands because they were hidden beneath the tray. How very odd, she thought: judging from the height of the tray, there must have been two or three steps down to whatever served them as a corridor outside.

And then she realized that she was wrong.

"As you may perceive, I am not tall." Indeed, the entity speaking to her could have been no more than sixty or seventy siemmes in height—only two-thirds of a measure. The top of his head would not have reached to the middle of her thigh. Every one of Bretta's little sisters was taller than Hanebuth Tarrant. "To be absolutely truthful, Princess, I was never particularly tall to begin with, but I do believe you will agree that this is carrying a good thing to extremes."

"At first it was 'Mistress'—of which I had believed I disabused you." It was extremely painful to laugh with her ribs as tightly bandaged as this. In truth, her exasperation with him was wholly fictitious. "Why do you insist upon calling me 'Princess,' when I am only the eldest daughter of an Autonomous Drector-Hereditary, and nothing more? And what did you mean by, 'to begin with'?"

"I call you Princess, Princess, because—as any fool can see—that is exactly what you are." He set the tray upon a sort of stool beside the bed. "And by, 'to begin with,' Princess, I mean that I was not always as you see me now."

What Bretta saw was a tiny caricature of a human being, only a little over knee-high, but with the hands and feet—and, most hideously, the head—of a normal-sized man. His fingers appeared abnormally long, with large joints, and ended in talons. His knees and elbows, too, seemed oversized in comparison with his stick-thin limbs. Hanebuth Tarrant was almost hairless—a mere half dozen coarse strands stood away from his shiny scalp—his skin had almost a scaly appearance, and he was the green-brown color of a soldier's uniform.

However, what Bretta noticed first about Hanebuth Tarrant were his ears, which were extraordinarily large and pointed, just like those of a storybook elf, and his eyes, which were also very large, brown, and filled with wisdom, suffering, and an endless reserve of humor. She wondered whether she was going to have eyes like that, now, considering what she had suffered. Somehow she rather doubted it. Soulfulness failed to go properly with their brilliant color.

He blinked. "I believe I heard you say that you're still hungry?"

"Ravenous, if you would know the truth. I think that I had dreams about eating."

"Well, I hope this does them justice."

Tarrant helped her sit up first—those frail-looking limbs of his were singularly strong and gentle—then set the tray across her lap, and began to feed her with a flat-bottomed plastic spoon. What he gave her was more like a rich, spiced gravy than anything else. Bretta did not wish to know where it had come from or what it had been made of; she only knew she wanted more of it than he had brought. She wanted bread, as well. And, after a few spoonsful of the hot, salty broth, with its wild, dark, earthy flavors—could those be *shrooms* she felt and tasted?—she also wanted something sweet and cold to drink.

But she was too polite to ask.

"Let us be as swift and merciful about this, then, as possible," he told Bretta as he went on feeding her. "Indeed, Princess, despite my wonderfully hideous appearance, I am actually a human being. That is to say, I was human, until some or all of these obscene and unspeakably painful transformations had been performed upon me in a vain attempt to turn me into an Oplyte warrior-slave."

"You are an Oplyte?"

"Not quite—look at me, Princess. Consider me a half-baked Oplyte and leave it at that. I can tell you that the Oplyte transformation process is less complicated and lies upon a higher technological plane than most people would believe. Most people have always envisioned vast darkened plains under leaden skies, upon which helpless victims were lowered in their manacles into bubbling vats of thickened, vile concoctions. Not unlike this soup, perhaps. Or they have imagined repeated injections and complicated bloody surgeries that transmuted innocent human captives into the mindless monsters we know too well."

Bretta was startled when another hand—this one was thick and powerful-looking, with only three clawed fingers and a thumb—thrust itself through the curtain to deliver a metal plate upon which sat a small loaf of coarse bread and a wide-bottomed cup. Her host, her nurse—whatever he was—gave her a sip from the cup. Fruit juice of some kind, and cold as the very Deep itself; could these strange people read her mind? The bread, too, was exactly to her liking. She returned to the soup with a refreshed palate and greater delight.

"In truth," Tarrant continued, "were the procedure all that complicated and expensive, it would have been rejected many centuries ago. Instead, the process involves nothing more than a single injection in the carotid artery. From there, an inconceivably miniscule machine—what is elsewhere known as a 'nanotechnological device'—travels through the bloodstream directly to the brain. There, it anchors itself and begins to alter the pituitary and other glands."

"How d'you know this?" she asked round a mouthful of dark, coarse bread. Tarrant was probably surprised—his eyes told her that he was—that his story did not deter her appetite. But then, she felt nothing but contempt for the females in Hanoverian dramathilles who fainted constantly, and upon the slightest stimulus. Her appetite had always been a vigorous one, and anybody who could gut, skin, and quarter her own game was unlikely to have a weak stomach.

"Because they *told* us, Princess. They're boastful of it. Most of them relish seeing the terror in their victims' eyes as the horrifying realization dawns upon them of what is about to become of them. Once the evil device has been implanted, every captive is installed—tidily stashed away—inside a coffin-shaped cage of wire mesh, convenient to hand, yet out from underfoot. From time to time, within the warehouse-caverns they fill in this nightmarish manner, the piteous shrieking of two hundred thousand prisoners at a time—stacked dozens deep so that they must urinate and defecate and vomit upon one another, and hundreds claustrophobically across—is very little short of deafening."

Bretta shook her head to stop the feeding momentarily. Even her strong young constitution had its limits, and she was close to reaching them, now. But at the same time, she was absolutely determined to hear more—to hear it all.

"Upon other occasions, the silence is profound and unutterably more terrifying." Lost in the tale he told, Tarrant had not noticed the effect that he was having upon her, in large measure because she would not *let* it show.

"They hose us off with a combination nutrient and cleansing solution, but do not otherwise feed or attend us. Bright floodlights are never turned out. The helpless victim watches himself become an Oplyte. Over the next weeks, his intelligence and personality are obliterated by the thing inside his head. Struggle as he may—and there is nothing to struggle with or against—he gradually loses his mentality, his very identity. Meanwhile, he also acquires enhanced muscular strength, an animal ferocity, and a perverse willingness to obey."

The silence within Bretta's rough bedchamber was also profound by now, and a bit terrifying. Her own wounds, she thought, however grievous, would heal in time, and, whatever else happened, now or in the future, her life would go on. But what must it be like to carry memories like *those* around in one's head? Hanebuth Tarrant's wounds, inside and out, would never heal, and the fact that his life would go on, like hers, must not have been much comfort to him.

"Now you would know," he said, anticipating her, "what went wrong. Why did I not become an Oplyte? Why did I become what I am today? How did I make my escape and come here? I do not know the answer to the first two questions, Princess. In individual instances, the process apparently fails in one way or another."

"And your escape?"

"I escaped because we were never closely guarded, and my cage lay at the outside of a layer near the top. It was not particularly difficult. The vast majority of captives are somehow paralyzed by the transformation process. I was not. That, in my case, is one of several things that went wrong with the process. When I grew strong enough—I tested my strength many times a day—I wrenched my cage open, clambered down the side of the stacks, and crept away."

Bretta's mind was filled with bleak and terrible images, her heart with pity.

"Not knowing at the time that there were many others more or less like me—more or less like each of my fellow unfortunates waiting impatiently to meet you—I subsequently contrived to escape my careless captors altogether. We failures of the system comprise what amounts to—and what has, in fact, amounted to for many centuries—a widely scattered 'civilization' of such fugitives."

She opened her mouth, but could not think of anything to say.

"You have arrived, Princess, at the hidden system of the Oplyte slavers, where evil transformations have been performed by the billions for a thousand years!"

CHAPTER XXVI:
BASIS FOR SELECTION

Bretta slept a long while after her first conscious meal. She reckoned later it had more to do with all that she had learned than with anything else.

It seemed to her that she had awakened, at least to some degree, several times when she had been turned or otherwise attended. She tried to accept the necessity, without emotion, that strangers must assist her to complete certain bodily functions that had otherwise been entirely private to her since she was three.

When she awoke the next time, she was alone. She believed it to be an hour that her hosts considered nighttime. It was unsurprising that they would keep the same watches as upon shipboard. But it was not as dark as it had been upon previous occasions. Had she said something to Tarrant about it, or only imagined she had? For that matter, could she have imagined Tarrant, as well?

"Knock . . . knock . . . knock," a voice informed her slowly. It was not one that she knew. "May . . . I . . . please . . . come . . . in . . . Mistress . . . Tarrant . . . has . . . other . . . business. . . . I . . . am . . . here . . . to . . . provide . . . you . . . food . . . and . . . look . . . to . . . your . . . dressings. . . . He . . . informed . . . me . . . that . . . you . . . are . . . not . . . afraid . . . to . . . look . . . upon . . . us."

She smiled, but the faintest thrill of fear passed through

her. What would the appearance be of someone speaking in such a peculiar manner? "Well, I was not afraid of him, as it turned out. What would you be like, if I may ask?"

"Of . . . course . . . you . . . may . . . Mistress. . . . I . . . am . . . like . . . *this.*"

The curtain parted and half a man entered. The other half, of necessity, remained kneeling outside, for the proprietor of both halves, as well as of the slow, careful voice she had heard, could have stood not a siemme less than three full measures tall, and perhaps half as wide. He also had but a single eye—of a startlingly brilliant sapphire hue (although it was also a trifle bloodshot)—set precisely in the middle of his broad, corrugated forehead, above a great hooked nose that sported but a single nostril. A Cyclops, then. For a moment Bretta entertained the notion, once again, that she was dead, or at least engaged in the hallucinogenic business of expiring from a fractured skull.

"I . . . know . . . that . . . I . . . speak . . . dreadfully . . . slowly . . . Mistress . . ."

And indeed, the fellow did. It demanded monumental patience of her to wait through his sentences. Bretta decided that the best way was *not* to listen consciously until he had completed one of them, then go back and reconstruct it in her mind, in the manner of a child who has been asked, "Have you been listening to me?" In that way, it was almost like hearing a normal individual speak.

"It is merely a part of what They did to me, all of which Tarrant says he has explained to you. And I appear outlandish, Mistress, even to myself. But you will discover that I am hardly unintelligent. I was a §-physics engineer before this happened—and you will remember what they say of us engineers—now I can *literally* look through a keyhole, with all of the eyes that I possess!"

Bretta laughed, as she was meant to, suspecting that Tarrant had taught him this good-natured way of dealing with his infirmities, and that she would soon be seeing the same sort of thing in others hereabouts, although she had been given, as yet, no idea of how many of them there were. The witticism the cycloptic giant had mentioned was among her father's favorites: "An engineer is a man with a mind so narrow that he can look through a keyhole with both eyes."

But the one-eyed giant was speaking again. The girl was able to catch up immediately with what he had been saying to her. "I am called Vokhiwa Kanvor, Mistress, originally of the Gesellschaft, although I am not a Gesellschaftian subject. Both of my parents were itinerant Garcian missionaries, you see, and I happened to be born to them when they were there. Forgive me for going on so."

She almost laughed, although not in a cruel way. "Not at all, Vokhiwa Kanvor."

Bretta finally thought to return Kanvor's laboriously prolonged greeting as warmly as she was able. She and Woulf—of hated memory—had watched a gaggle of Garcians capering through the thoroughfares of Hanover wearing the colorful, loose-fitting habits they were known for, playing and singing some ancient hymn of theirs about going somewhere in a bucket. Although why anyone would wish to bother writing a song about a lubberlift was entirely beyond her comprehension.

And Phoebus Krumm, if she remembered correctly, had originally hailed from the Gesellschaft, one of the many smaller imperia-conglomerate within the Known Deep, although he had been apprenticed outworld at a comparatively early age—or sold, depending upon how one looked at it, and who one happened to be—to a Hanoverian baker just across an interstellar border from his native world.

Both of his wives were Gesellschaftian, as well.

"I would shake your hand if I were able. I am Robretta Islay, daughter of—"

The giant held up a shockingly pink palm. The remainder of him, where he was not covered with a coarse brown kefflaroid sacking, was an exquisite pale green, exactly like one of those sharply flavored apples she adored that broke like glass when she bit into them, and were filled with a rich, sweetly sour juice. What she could see of his complexion was smooth and shiny, almost waxen.

He blinked his eye. Watching him do it was beginning to give Bretta a headache. "Do not bother, Mistress. Tarrant told us all about you. You are Robretta Islay, eldest daughter of Autonomous Drector-Hereditary Arran 'the' Islay of Skye and his wedded wife the former Loreanna Daimler-Wilkinson. This afternoon we drew cards to see which of us might attend you in his absence, and—"

"You lost." She laughed again. "My sincerest condolence, friend Kanvor. I offer you my solemn promise that I shall endeavor not to be a burden to you."

His single eyebrow threatened to scurry away, right over the top of his head. "No, no, Mistress, I won! It is an honor, merely to hear your voice! You do understand, do you not, that most of us (and we are hundreds in this drift alone, thousands throughout the asteroid) have not seen a woman for many years? The cruelest part of my curse is that, with this slow metabolism, I am exceedingly long-lived, and so for me, it has been something more than two centuries."

"You are," Bretta answered, almost as slowly as Kanvor, and for the first time since she awoke here, beginning to feel a bit afraid, "every one of you, *male?*"

Kanvor shyly averted his eye. "Each and every one of us, Mistress—or at least," he amended sadly, "most of us were to begin with. Sometimes the process . . ."

"I believe that I understand," Bretta interrupted in as kindly a manner as she could manage, before the shy and gentle giant could embarrass himself any further. And she believed that she did understand, knowing all too well of her grandmother's life-shattering experiences. The Oplyte slavers' female captives were disposed of elsewhere, in a very different and considerably more ancient kind of marketplace. Which meant that each successive "generation" among these pathetically twisted refugees consisted of nothing more than those freshly arrived newcomers who had managed to escape from one decade to the next.

And now she had come to share that life.

She shuddered, but attempted to conceal it for his sake.

"How many are there of you, altogether, friend Kanvor, throughout this system? Do you know?"

"Well, Mistress," Kanvor answered in his ponderous and inexorable manner. "Our friend Pwee Nguyen keeps such facts and figures as we happen to possess, inside his head. He would be the one to ask for accurate estimates. You will be introduced to him in good time—Tarrant will see to that—but just now he is sleeping. He is an idiot savant, you see, and he sleeps most of the time."

" 'Pwee Nguyen' " She rolled the curious name round her tongue as Kanvor inspected her bandages and dabbed with a warm, dampened cloth at her face and feet, the only portions of her not concealed by dressings. She must remember, in the future, not to break so many bones at once. "Can you give me a guess, just to think about before I have an opportunity to consult this sleepy friend of yours?"

"Well, Mistress," Kanvor answered with an infuriating deliberation, "the Oplyte Trade, so I have been reliably informed by those among my friends and colleagues able to overcome their aversion and study the phenomenon— though I was myself unwilling to credit what they claimed for it at first—is said to amount to billions of individuals stolen from their lives each standard year."

" 'Stolen from their lives'—an adroit turn of phrase, friend Kanvor. But surely you meant to say 'millions.' " She, too, reflexively doubted such numbers.

"You are exactly the same as I was," he chuckled. It was an eerie, slow-motion sound, as of somebody chopping wood with a hand-axe. "No, Mistress, 'billions' is what I said, and 'billions' is what I meant. Had I meant to say 'millions,' I would have said 'millions,' but what I said was 'billions,' because—"

She laughed at what she thought of as his glacial loquaciousness. "Very well, friend Kanvor, I understand. But what would you have told me after you told me that—had I displayed sufficient intelligence to leave well enough alone?"

He smiled, presenting Bretta with perhaps the strangest sight, so far, of all, for what should have been the poor fel-

low's upper two front incisors had become fused together—
even now she could make out a faint trace of the seam—
giving her something of an idea of how he might have ended
up with but a single eye. The process must have been indescribably bizarre—and extremely painful.

"I would have requested that you consider the fact that the
Monopolity of Hanover alone claims to have fifteen quintillion subjects. That being the case, then who, I ask you,
except for the families of the victims, is likely to miss—or
raise much of a fuss over—a mere seven-*millionths* of one
percent of that?"

"I see," she replied. "I had never thought to look upon it
like that, statistically."

"Nor do most individuals, I greatly fear me. What is even
more astonishing, Mistress, is that we have reason to believe
the Trade has been going on for centuries—possibly as long
as a thousand years. Unbelievable as it may seem, that
would bring the possible number of its victims into the tril-
lions."

"I believe that I understand," she mused, mostly to herself,
beginning to think every bit as strategically as her father ever
had, although she was completely unaware of it. "And so the
rate of failed Oplyte transformations could be comparatively
low—and the percentage of them who manage to make good
their escape utterly · insignificant, in comparison to the
numerical vastness of the galaxywide slavery operation—
and yet individuals like you and Tarrant could still exist in
extraordinary numbers throughout this entire system."

"Ceo's *name,* Mistress." The giant blinked his eye. "Did I
say all of that?"

"You told me, whether you realized it or not. Most likely
it is simply uneconomical for the slavers even to take the
necessary precautions to *stop* escapees, let alone hunt them
down afterward. And if you have all hidden in warrens like
this one, I doubt that you can be discovered as readily by
your former kidnappers as they can take fresh captives from
the open Deep. Tell me, have they manifested much of an
interest in reclaiming their embarrassing failures?"

Kanvor shook his massive head. "No, Mistress. Did Tarrant not tell you that this system consists, uniquely, of nothing but a clutter of millions of asteroids?"

"Somehow I knew that," she answered, wishing that she had some method of scratching the many itches that had begun making themselves apparent here and there. She felt as if she had been cast—like a leaf or a collected insect—in some sort of thermosetting resin. And perhaps, beneath her bandages, that was precisely what had been done. "But I don't remember his telling me, no."

"The great majority are of a densely metallic composition, rendering any instrumental search all but impossible—and, no doubt more important to the slavers, prohibitively expensive. What a very peculiar thought that is, that economics might influence their vile calculations in such a manner. I think me that it may betray a useful vulnerability. Mistress, before now I was only conscious of the evil done to me. Now you have taught me to see it in a new way."

" 'Follow the money,' " she quoted the ancient adage. "Excellent, friend Kanvor, I am delighted that you understand me. The point, my mother always says, is not that one may happen to be miserable or afraid—that can happen to anyone at one time or another—the point is to be constructive about it and not to wallow in it. Personally, I do not intend staying here for the remainder of my life. And, friend Kanvor, I believe I am beginning to have a plan."

"It was named by its discoverers the 'Vouhat-Letsomo System,' one of the last to be found in an initial wave of exploration of the Known Deep, roughly nine hundred years ago. It is home to a culture that calls itself the Aggregate, the oldest continuous civilization, quite paradoxically enough, which . . . I have ever . . ."

The speaker, Pwee Nguyen, the "idiot savant" Kanvor had earlier described for Bretta, threatened to fall asleep again in the middle of a sentence, until one of his comrades nudged him, none too gently, and his grotesque eyes popped open. It was one of the oddest sights Bretta had ever seen, but she tried not to show it; she was becoming quite an accomplished practitioner of that sort of polite deception. Apparently, among Pwee Nguyen's other talents, he had never forgotten a single historical fact—even the most obscure and trivial datum—he had ever heard, although he appeared to have difficulty staying awake.

". . . which I have ever heard of. As usual, I implore you to excuse me, one and all, for I have slept only sixteen hours today, instead of my accustomed twenty."

At Bretta's insistence, they had moved her from her makeshift bedchamber to a larger cave to facilitate this gathering. This had not been accomplished without some degree of pain upon her part. In particular, her shattered left collarbone seemed capable of generating the most exquisite agony she had ever known.

Tarrant, back from whatever errand had taken him from her side, fussed over her endlessly, making ominous, not-quite-subvocal comments with regard to her several fractured ribs and the possibility of punctured lungs and internal bleeding.

Bretta looked closely at Pwee Nguyen once again, scarcely able to believe what she saw, even after having listened to the fellow for over an hour. His eyes were dark and enormous, each perhaps the size of two fists held together, set in the sides of his head like those of a barnyard fowl. She remembered an old children's tale: the lids, at least, that covered those great eyes were, indeed, the size of saucers. And like a fowl's embryo within its shell, the rest of Pwee Nguyen's facial features appeared minuscule and only crudely formed.

His head seemed to narrow to a point at the top, although that may have been an illusion propagated by his hair, which was bright orange, cut skin-close at the sides, and stuck straight upward at the top. His shoulders were impossibly narrow, as was his chest. He grew outward gradually, tapering as it were, until his stomach and fundament were quite fully rounded. Like many of those Bretta was meeting here today, his limbs were quite thin and almost seemed stuck on as an afterthought. Pwee Nguyen's skin was a bright lemony yellow.

"But you were speaking of the Aggregate, my friend," Tarrant prompted him gently.

"Ah, yes," Pwee Nguyen sighed, "So I was, was I not? Very well, the Aggregate is apportioned into many so-called 'Alliances,' the densely crowded populations of which occupy a single asteroid per Alliance in our planetless Vouhat-Letsomo System. We free spirits, of course, live within the shadows of its edges, upon and within small rocks that even they reject as suitable for habitation."

There was general laughter at that remark.

"Overall, their massively overpopulated culture is a dictatorship of a brutally consistent ruthlessness unknown elsewhere in the Deep, even within the worst of the imperia-conglomerate. Its ultimate rulers are almost unknown to the teeming billions who happen to be unfortunate enough to be governed by them."

In addition to Pwee Nguyen, Bretta, Kanvor, and Tarrant, they had been joined by a number of their fellow involuntary troglodytes, to whom she had been earlier introduced. Nibwelt Glint-Ritchbengen was even taller than the cyclops, but he was almost impossibly thin and seemed to have no pigmentation of any kind. And where Pwee Nguyen was supposed to have been an idiot, but was proving not to be, the albino stilt-man did not impress her as being very bright.

It was more difficult to tell with the armor-scaled and powerful Swader Hornyak, who, despite his rather intimidating aspect—the fellow had a zigzagged reptilian crest upon his skull—was exceedingly cheerful and good-natured.

Perhaps he was simply happy not to be like his friend Shong Cowl, who had grown an extra pair of arms, or poor Ragan Stengaard, whom Phoebus would have described, in his straightforward way, as a basket case with a trunk. Indeed, the unfortunate fellow had a long, flexible, muscular proboscis with which he handled objects, and upon which he moved himself through the twisting passages of the asteroid, thanks to its almost nonexistent gravity. He and all of his comrades had once been human, and many appeared to be Gesellschaftian, like Kanvor.

"Every person within the culture is continuously super-vised by a 'Cell Leader' who has been given an absolute life-and-death responsibility for the productivity and behavior of five other human beings. This responsibility is exercised upon a 'better safe than sorry' principle. If one steps out of line even a bit, he can—he will—be killed outright, death being administered 'prophylactically,' by his Cell Leader at the very scene and moment of the 'crime.' "

"Tarrant," Bretta asked, intensely curious, "how does he come to know all this?"

"Hundreds of cautious, patient years, Princess. The normal-looking among us sneak about, asking questions. Members of this culture are trained—bred—to obey, so they believe they must answer us or die. Pray continue, Pwee Nguyen."

The so-called idiot savant nodded. "Cell Leaders report on a regular basis—every hour or so—to their 'Brood Moth-ers.' Do not be deceived; a generous proportion of Brood Mothers, perhaps even a majority, is male. It is from their ranks, generally, that the crews of their Deep-raiders are made up. Brood Mothers wield the same life-and-death 'prophylactic' authority over Cell Leaders."

She glanced at Tarrant, remembering how he had referred before to "the mothers."

"Brood Mothers, in turn, are required to report every few hours to their 'Perrish Elders,' who, of course, may be the youngest members of the group. Note that their records spell it 'E double-R,' a somewhat pointed ambiguity. Perrish Elders report with only slightly lesser frequency to 'Burrow Mayors'; Burrow Mayors report to leaders of the Alliances, viewed as the fundamental subdivision of this society. These one-asteroid Alliances are organized into 'Localities'—in general separated by the system's Cassini divisions, an astrophysical term, of which there happen to be twelve, if I recall correctly—and Localities, finally, form the entire Aggregate, of which I spoke at the beginning."

"They sound like colonial insectoids," Bretta said spontaneously. "And I would guess that there are no true individuals remaining within their culture, nor probably does there remain the faintest trace of individualism in its gene pool."

"How . . . do . . . you . . . reckon . . . that . . . Mistress?"

"Because, friend Kanvor, it is the only result possible after something like nine hundred years of stringent . . . let us call it, *'unnatural* selection.' What did you say, Pwee—*bother,* he has gone to sleep again. Did he not say that Cell Leaders are encouraged to kill those they supervise—how did he state it, 'if a person steps out of line even a little'? And what is stepping out of line if not a manifestation of individualism? I called it 'unnatural selection.' The basis of selection, of course, is a person's utter compliance with the least whim of their society. I could almost feel sorry for them—almost."

"Why?" It was the first she had heard from Stengaard. He was entitled to ask.

"Because," she told the trunk-man, "dealing with them is going to be too easy."

Shong Cowl objected, spreading wide all four of his arms and taking up what little room was left within the chamber. "What do you mean by 'dealing with them,' Mistress? Do you mean that we ought to fight them? Just how? And with what? If that were possible, do you not imagine that over nine hundred years, we—"

"How? Why, as ardently as we are able to. And with what? With the only *truly* dangerous weapon in the galaxy." She would have tapped her head had it been possible. "The trouble is, just as you have no doctors in this place, none among you are fighters. I am a warrior by inheritance, by choice, and by trade." Well, she thought, that was at least partially true. Potentially, anyway. "And yes, I believe I can get us out of this nine-hundred-year mess. But . . . you were a sailor and shipowner, Hanebuth. Kanvor, an engineer. You, Pwee Nguyen—"

Pwee Nguyen awoke at the mention of his name. "An idiot savant, just as I am now, Mistress. I have only been altered physically, as far as I know." She laughed.

"My friend, could you have told me that *before* you were altered?" All of them laughed with her; they knew their comrade better than Bretta.

"Probably not, Mistress, I . . . you have given me something new to think about." The strange-eyed bird-man blushed deeply. "Perhaps now, I am only a savant."

Tarrant was holding his sides, and there were tears starting in his eyes. "Bedad, Princess, we've been trying to tell him exactly that for ten bloody years!"

"And happy I am to prove useful," Bretta replied. "My point is that, in addition to whatever else you were, you should have been brought up learning to defend yourselves. To neglect one's offspring this way amounts to child abuse."

"Have we not authorities to protect us?" Hornyak inquired with feigned innocence.

"Very funny. Self-defense means just that: *self*-defense. It is not just another occupational specialization, like sailing or engineering, but an individual bodily function which, like breathing, eating, sleeping, or making love, cannot be delegated. Look around you. See what happens to you when you try."

The reptile-man winked at her. "But all the imperia-conglomerate forbid it." She was beginning to perceive that, like schoolboys, her companions were long accustomed to such discussions. They had little enough else to do with themselves.

"True. Such a capability, and the self-sufficient mentality that goes with it, spreading throughout a populace, threaten the state. That is why it is so viciously suppressed. But as I said, look around; see what happens as a result. Our enemy is one example, which is why I said I almost feel sorry for them.

"I fear me they will be all too easy pickings for the daughter of Henry Martyn!"

The view had proved worth the effort.

"We are uncertain, but believe that the vessel was alien. The seats within were of an outlandish shape and too small, even for me. The backs were bifurcated, with too much space between the halves to keep a man from falling through. Something odd sat in those chairs, let me tell you. And before you ask, Princess, we do not *know* what the Aggregate does with its non-human captives. Just imagine a flatsy or a *yensid* made into the equivalent of an Oplyte!"

Although she doubted the ability even of the Aggregate to take a *nacyl* vessel that did not wish to be taken, and knew better than anyone that the *yensid* had never built ships of their own (although, she thought, they were often passengers along with those they served), Bretta nodded. It was all she could do, and the spectacle beyond the huge, curved window (it was that window of which Tarrant had been speaking) defied any words she might have thought to use.

Tarrant had been explaining to her how he and his friends had found the crystal-domed transparency in a ship hulk drifting through their asteroidal neighborhood. It was a common enough occurrence of its kind. Desirous only of raw material—human beings—for manufacturing slaves, the Aggregate was otherwise profligately wasteful of its combat prizes. But it was exactly the sort of common occurrence that was responsible, to a considerable degree, for the escapees' ability to survive here. They had salvaged this transparency, carefully shaped a surface penetration to match it in a rock-bubble lying just beneath the asteroid's surface, and set it in place in order to create this view.

This cave was a most popular place among the asteroid's population. Aside for an odd bull's-eye or peephole—both terms of Tarrant's choosing—usually set in an airlock door, Tarrant had told her, it was their only view to the outside.

"Why, thank you, Hanebuth," Bretta answered Tarrant at last, referring to the chillingly repellent vision of an Oplyticized *nacyl* or *yensid* that he had put into her mind—and intending precisely the opposite of the sentiment that she had expressed. "I greatly fear me that I can imagine it all too well."

To her it seemed appalling, rather than amusing, to mentally transpose the horrifying changes wrought upon human beings to non-human entities like old Brougham and his kind. Perhaps Tarrant and his friends here believed it funny because, in some ways, what had been inflicted upon them was so much worse. Nonetheless, she found it difficult to appreciate the joke. She would rather gaze out through this transparency she sat in, bulging a full measure up, or outward, above the asteroid's surface. Thought of as an opening through a wall—however rough and pockmarked—it was much like sitting in a window seat.

Gathering the full measure of whatever dignity circumstance had left to him, Tarrant arose to his total of threescore and six or seven siemmes. "If I have somehow given you offense, Princess, I most humbly and abjectly beg your pardon." Somehow, the little man made it feel more like an accusation than an apology.

She smiled at him. "My father says that people laugh at whatever it is that happens to frighten them the most; whenever they decide that there are certain things *too* serious to laugh at, they begin an inexorable slide into despair and madness. I think it likely that this elucidates a great deal of rather unpleasant history. Pray be seated, Hanebuth; you have not offended me. You simply happen to have lived in different circumstances than I and, as a consequence, different things strike you as funny. Who knows, should I linger here a year or a decade, I could easily wind up with very similar proclivities."

"You are wise, Princess," Tarrant told her, "and forbearing beyond your years."

"Thanks, Hanebuth, for all that your words of praise run with sarcasm." She attempted to shake her head. "My *father* is wise; I have merely paid attention."

The truth was that she did not wish to argue with Tarrant just now; she only wished to look. It was difficult believing that she had somehow managed to survive out there, where the liquid within one's eyes would boil, explode, and freeze, all in the space of only a minute or two. And yet, what Bretta saw beyond the marvelous curved transparency was one of the most breathtaking sights that she had ever beheld—although, initially, she had been rather disappointed.

Her first words upon approaching the window had been, "Where are they?" Except for the many faraway stars, there was nothing else in sight. The Deep-black sky completely failed to be filled with hundreds of thousands of great, rough, many-cratered boulders, tumbling about end over end, crashing into one another.

The Vouhat-Letsomo System was wholly composed, she had been told, except for its rather unremarkable yellow primary and the occasional comet soaring crosswise through the local ecliptic upon wings of frost and vapor, of bodies too small properly to be called planets. Upon the other hand, her home system possessed no asteroid belt of its own, and the ring for which the planet Skye had become moderately famous was composed of fragments—most of them about the size of her thumb—too small properly to be called asteroids. All that Bretta really knew of asteroids she had seen in a number of action-adventure autothilles.

Tarrant had laughed.

Bretta had taken no offense at this, for whenever Tarrant laughed like that, he looked very much to her like a picture-book elf or one of the "little green men" of ancient flying-saucer legends. All that the fellow lacked, she thought, were colorful slippers with their pointed toes curled upward, perhaps a little hat with bells dangling from its corners, and a forest shroom to sit upon.

Or a helmet with antennae sticking out.

"They *are* there, Princess," the little man told her, happily unaware of the unflattering manner in which he was being imagined, "with just about a thousand klommes between them, upon the average. I know what you believe they ought to look like, but they do not, I'm afraid, and never have. From here, they look just like the stars, and one is compelled to watch them very closely—or to record and compare their likenesses—before one can discern any difference." He lifted a long, thin, preventive index finger when she began to look unhappy. "But there is another way, and that is simply to wait patiently for a few more minutes."

Bretta had but little choice in the matter anyway, since, bandaged up as helplessly as she happened to be at present, she could not move until Tarrant had ordered her moved by his colleagues. This, in spite of the manner in which it conflicted with her physical, self-reliant nature, she was willing to accept with a certain amount of philosophical resignation, having considered all the most likely alternatives. When Tarrant's requested few minutes had elapsed, however, she was rewarded with the astonishing, heart-stopping sight that she saw now.

Viewed from within, casting the eye upward, downward, or outward from the system, the Vouhat-Letsomo asteroids appeared to be nothing more than empty space. Observed, however, almost from the outside—from just above the plane of the ecliptic, where millions of such bodies could be looked upon at once—which Bretta and Tarrant were able to do once the asteroid they occupied had rotated a few degrees, Vouhat-Letsomo presented quite another appearance.

From that perspective, the system formed an unimaginably grand, silvery, sparkling disk, stretching from one edge of the bubble-window to the other, as far as the eye could see, filled with minuscule glittering lights that changed every instant that she watched them. At the center of the disk, the system's primary was suspended within a golden mist, befogged by the innermost layer of asteroids.

"Silence always speaks of the most sincere appreciation." The little man nodded with satisfaction. Bretta's earlier vision of him outfitted with the trappings of a jester now made her feel ashamed of herself. She never failed to be astonished at the amount of dignity that Hanebuth Tarrant carried with him at all times. "I asked them to bring you up here, Princess, as a token of my sincere gratitude. What I desired to thank you for was the manner in which you lectured the others tonight. I, myself, have been here far too long, but I have *never* given up—as something like fifty generations of the rest of us seem to have done all too easily—upon getting out of this place and going home."

"Going *home*." Bretta wished—not for the first time nor for the last—that she were not wrapped up in bandages and plastic bracing. She found it grew increasingly uncomfortable—hot and itchy—and even worse, that she was beginning to feel like a white, glistening pupa of one of those insectoid species she had mentioned earlier, coddled and carried from chamber to chamber of the colonial burrow by worker bugs. "You are most welcome, Hanebuth, but that is not the actual reason you had me brought up here so laboriously, is it?"

She glanced back at the window—the girl's eyes were virtually the only thing that she *could* move—and as she did, she thought she saw some large, dark object cross it for an instant. But because Tarrant said nothing, she dismissed it as the kind of thing that happens—shadows flitting past the corner of one's awareness—when one becomes fatigued. And she was fatigued. It had been a long day for her—all four or five hours of it so far—and she was as weary as if she had run each and every measure of it at her best speed.

Upon the other hand, they had not hurt her quite as much this time, she believed, bringing her up here, as they had earlier in the day. Perhaps that only indicated that she was becoming accustomed to the pain. A bleak thought, that. Pain was certainly not the sort of thing she had ever wished to become accustomed to. A wave of acidic hatred for Woulf swept through her. There followed a considerable silence, during which Tarrant seemed to be working up his courage.

"I confess that it was not the reason. Princess—my new friend Bretta Islay—I have not made anything at all of your apparent age, which I would estimate to be an unusually poised and accomplished seventeen or eighteen. Nor do I intend to, at least in front of the others. But out of my own bitter experience, I wished to offer you a warning—in private—so that you would not be quite so disappointed, as I have often been, myself, with your fellow human beings. For you will soon discover, I fear, that there is opposition to the plan you purpose."

She recoiled with surprise. "Opposition? Why?"

He shrugged. "For one thing, people are natural conservatives, Princess, and tend to resist change for its own sake, for no better reason than that it *is* change, without regard to whether it happens to be change for the better or the worse. They are inclined to forget how miserable their circumstances have become—I suppose, in a way, that this is the obverse side of the coin of human adaptability. In any case, they appear to prefer whatever suffering they endure today, to which they have grown accustomed, to any paradise that unknown circumstances may drag them into—kicking and screaming—day after tomorrow."

There it was again, the same fleeting impression she had earlier had of a great expanse of *something* passing between her and the light outside. She glanced at Tarrant; his head was turned, back the way they had come getting up to this chamber. He appeared to be contemplating the nature of his fellow escapees.

"But that is . . . insane." Bretta could not think of any other word for preferring to stay here, a prisoner of the Aggregate (admittedly upon a long tether), to winning free into the open Deep, with the prospect of returning home.

"Oh, I wouldn't go quite that far," Tarrant argued mildly. "I'll gladly concede that it's all too human. And perhaps to do them a little more justice than I have, the overwhelming majority of my associates here, and upon other nearby asteroids, as well, sincerely believe that they can never escape this strange system, even if they had the ships to do it in—which they certainly do not—because almost the very moment they attempted it, they would be killed."

Before she thought of it, she turned her head—and was highly gratified to discover that she could do so, even the slightest bit. Nor had the equally gratifying fact escaped her that Tarrant had estimated her to be two or three years older than she actually was. She had torn her attention away from the glorious window, to look the little man in the eye. "Why, pray, might that be?"

"That they would all be instantaneously killed, or merely that so many of them believe so?" Tarrant directed Bretta's attention to the view outside the window once again. "I suppose it doesn't matter. For some among them—for the weaker of heart or mind or resolution who seem always in the majority—it simply means they will never have to attempt it, and that, in itself, is enough."

Bretta nodded, understanding well. How many times had her father warned her: it is moral weakness, rather than villainy, that accounts for most of the evil in the universe—and feeble-hearted allies, far rather than your most powerful enemies, who are likeliest to do you an injury you cannot recover from?

"But there is also this: within this unique system we are *camouflaged,* so to speak, both optically and electronically, by millions of ever-tumbling, metallic asteroids. Look out there, Princess: who can find a single given sparkle among a myriad of them? It's a great wonder that their ships can ever find their way home. Breaking out into the open Deep surrounding the system, however, we would be detected in an instant by the Aggregate—they possess the superior technology with which to do it—and be as instantly destroyed by their many patrol squadrons, if for no better reason than to keep the many imperia-conglomerate from *ever* learning of the system's significance and location."

Now there could be no mistaking it. Something large and very swift had crossed the window outside, just as she had blinked her eyes. But she had seen its shadow upon the opposite wall. She looked a question at Tarrant; he nodded.

"Indeed, Princess, you were not mistaken. What you just saw is *quite* real. It is a living creature of the Deep, such as that which brought you to us, here. That minute that you're able to walk again, I'll take you to see them."

Bretta had retained only the dimmest recollection of having arrived here, and wondered whether half of what she remembered was not delirium. "What is it?"

Tarrant shrugged his tiny shoulders. "How can I answer that? I suppose that, in repose, it looks something like a huge bird, or some kind of great, flat fish. It lives and breeds and dies out there by the millions, protected in some way by these asteroids, just as we are, breathing the vacuum round them as if it were air. I am informed that it is quite a remarkable specimen of evolution."

"I should hope to shout *that* from the rooftop! Is—can it *think,* Hanebuth?" How had such a creature come to rescue her? She had been inside a garbage canister. How had it ever guessed that she was inside and *wanted* rescuing?

He shook his head. "It isn't intelligent—I mean, it couldn't have had this conversation with you—but it can be trained. We keep a . . . well, call it a 'stable' of several dozen of the creatures here because they help us to salvage useful items—such as yourself—from out there. I expect that, kept by all the people like us within this system, there are several thousand creatures like it. And many millions more, of course, that have never been tamed."

She nodded, deciding she must learn more of these animals as soon as she could. Something told her that they could prove important. "But we have been distracted."

"So we have, Princess."

They had been discussing the supposed impossibility of escape. She felt her blood rise a trifle at the memory and decided to make the most of it, as she had seen her father do now and again. "What would you have me do, then, Hanebuth, remain here like fifty generations of poltroons who gave up on being alive?"

"Upon the contrary, Princess." Tarrant raised both hands, palms outward, although it was obvious from his unsuccessful attempt to hide a grin that he had seen through her counterfeit tantrum. Perhaps she needed practice. "Has anyone ever told you you're beautiful when you're angry? I thought not. The truth is your face turns red and gets all screwed up—not a pretty sight. All I wished was to tell you how the land lies. And persuade you to stay whatever plans you're making—temporarily—until you know more of our situation."

"Well—"

Bretta would have folded her arms and sulked except that it was not in her nature, her arms were already folded, and Tarrant was unlikely to have noticed. She began to laugh, instead. Before long, Tarrant was laughing, as well.

"It is not as if I planned to go tomorrow. I assume these bandages are coming off someday? Until then, you are right, I need to learn more. Let us begin with you, if it is not too personal or painful. What brought you to this system?"

He rubbed outsized hands together. "I asked for that. It's a story you were bound to hear anyway, and it has pleasant moments. Bid me stop if I bore you."

"In one sense," she replied with arched eyebrows, "helpless as you see me now, I am indeed *bound* to hear the story. Is this what is meant by a captive audience? Still, I have every confidence that you will not bore me, Hanebuth."

"You flatter me beyond my ability to endure it, Princess. As it happens, I was taken and brought to this system while making a vain attempt to return to home and family in the Monopolity of Hanover after decades of 'exile' in a fabulous, faraway system that many today believe exists only in mythology and legend."

She settled more comfortably into her window seat. His "exile," he said, had followed the theft of a starship aboard which he had worked as an ordinary crewbeing.

"The most amazing thing about the whole adventure"— he grinned at Bretta, relishing the anticipation of what he was about to tell her—"is that the ship in question, the

voluptuous *Lion of Hanover,* was the official conveyance of
Leupould IX, Ceo of Hanover. Even better, she was hijacked
at lenspoint by *Anastasia Wheeler,* the rebellious elder sister
of none other than Leupould himself!"

Bretta smiled, not so much at Tarrant's revelation as with
a remembrance of home. Like many a child with good hearing and a better memory, she had managed to overhear her
parents more than once, discussing what little was known of
the so-called "Anastasia Incident." The hijacking of that
Ceo's yacht by his own sister had been *the* scandal of the
generation just prior to that which had enjoyed being scandalized by the more notorious exploits of Henry Martyn.
The full, shocking details were still known only among the
highest Hanoverian echelons.

She said so to Tarrant, who laughed and nodded. As one
of *Lion*'s crew who had survived more than a year's epic
journey, he knew "the rest of the story."

"The whole thing started," he said, "when Anastasia—
you two would have gotten along famously—refused a
suitor whom her brother, in absence of their dead parents,
had selected for her. Somebody wealthy or powerful or both,
be assured. Anastasia was of an age considered by many to
be that of an 'old maid.' "

Bretta was aware that her mother, Loreanna, had been
sent off to a faraway, frigid colony world for having done
much the same thing. In a way, she ought to have hated her
great-uncle Sedgeley for his villainy, but in another—it had
been upon that journey that Loreanna had been captured by
Henry Martyn.

"How old was Anastasia?"

"I cannot say, Princess; he had been Ceo only a year or
so. Unlike yours, her hair was black, cut in a style known as
a 'valiant,' her eyes enormous, dark and haunting. She was
a tiny thing—I, myself, was taller then—standing no higher
than your shoulder, and wielding a 'haler longer than her
forearm.' "

He cleared his throat.

"You may know that arranged marriages are common

between unfortunate daughters of ambitious families and repulsive but financially attractive bridegrooms."

"Yes, Hanebuth, and politically attractive ones, as well. We marry for love upon the frontier—at least upon moon-ringed Skye—we woodsrunners do. I am alive today because my mother avoided exactly such an arranged marriage."

"You don't say! Well, the story goes that Leupould, newly ascended to the seat of power upon the basis of merit alone, and lacking the advantage of a powerful family, was anxious to acquire it at any cost, especially if it would be paid by his sister. Anastasia, however, expressed in no uncertain terms her absolute unwillingness to submit to the customary Hanoverian marital arrangement."

"Good for her!" Bretta would have clapped her hands had they been free to move. Given Anastasia's circumstances, she hoped she would have acted as well.

"Instead," Tarrant continued, "Anastasia 'allowed herself to be seduced into adventure'—those being the words her brother chose to describe it at the time—by nothing more than a nearly forgotten trunk of musty family records."

Bretta laughed. She had heard that much the same had happened to her father, and, having at an early age thoroughly explored the extensive cellars of the Islay family Holdings herself, she could well believe it so. Perhaps, instead of banning weapons, they should have tried outlawing attics and basements.

"Somehow, in the heart of a capital city dedicated to preventing it, she learned to wield a personal thrustible with a respectable degree of skill. Somehow, she even arranged for clandestine lessons in starship handling and interstellar navigation. And with Leupould's unwitting assistance, she came to know key people at the Ceo's private landing pentagram. When the time was right, it was nothing for her to board and commandeer her brother's personal starship."

Bretta was coming to like this Anastasia Wheeler more and more. Why—she had most likely demanded in her brother's name—should *men* be the only ones to have all the fun? Especially given society's attitude toward her, the ready availability of a ship, and a chest full of nine-hundred-year-old navigational charts? Bretta thought that the woman might be in her late fifties or sixties by now. Maybe someday, when this was over and another adventure had begun, they would meet.

"Having easily overcome the *Lion of Hanover*'s crew, more by force of personality than by force of arms, Anastasia navigated her stolen prize out of the capital system, out of the Monopolity itself, out of the great stellar cluster in which the Monopolity is but a tiny floating particle, and into the vaster Milky Way that the cluster slowly circles, toward what she had come to believe from family annals was the birthworld of humanity, a planet at the edge of the galaxy proper, rendered uninhabitable in ancient times by hideous weaponry."

"I have heard that story," Bretta said, trying to recall who had told it to her.

"So have we all, Princess, at our mothers' knees. And indeed, the human beings who dwell upon the single large, natural satellite that those Wheeler family annals had instructed her to look for, still call their dead planet 'Earth.' "

CHAPTER XXVIII:
BALANCE OF TERRA

"Princess," Tarrant told Bretta, "I swear to you upon all that I revere, that I myself have seen the shrouded world where humanity is supposed to have evolved."

Although she had begun to feel a trifle weary, she nodded encouragement, eager to have him continue. For a moment she could at least forget where she was and what had happened to her. She had grown up with Skyan yarns of "Lost Yarth" and had become conversant, later, with the more erudite Hanoverian theories (no likelier to be correct than folklore, in her mother's scholarly opinion) regarding mankind's planetary origins. She had even managed to read more in her great-uncle Sedgeley's library at the Daimler-Wilkinson establishment upon the capital world. This was exactly the sort of subject that interested her most.

"But—" Tarrant advised the girl, clearly still awestruck, even after many decades, by his unique experience, "it was only from a very considerable distance. We could guess from the weird colors our own §-field was taking on that the planet is a veritable fountainhead of deadly ionizing particles, and on that account remains as inaccessible as every ancient legend would have us believe. It hangs there upon the velvety black Deep, pearly white, as empty of life and expression as a blinded eye, its atmosphere and its soil rendered lethal to all life-forms in some long-forgotten war, by instrumentalities which are, at least within the imperia-conglomerate—gratefully—equally long-forgotten."

Bretta knew, because her father had told her, that this common belief of the lower classes with regard to ancient doomsday weaponry was untrue. Their ancestors had possessed nothing very unusual, simply too large and far too numerous.

Nor were they quite forgotten. Arran himself had resorted to one against a pursuing enemy corsair at the very beginning of his war upon the Monopolity. They were often carried as self-destruct devices aboard freebooters' vessels, as a means of avoiding capture. (And if more starship captains were to follow such a prudent custom, Bretta thought, the Aggregate would soon be out of the Oplyte business.) Imperia-conglomerate generally refrained from using them upon one another, out of fear the same sort of weapon would be used upon them in retaliation. This agreement-by-default had first been tried upon mankind's homeworld, so the tale went, and for that reason was called the "Balance of Terra."

Someday she would ask someone why the thrusted planet

had so many names! But she was too tired to ask now, very hesitant to interrupt, and Tarrant was going on . . .

"And yet Anastasia and her reluctant Hanoverian crewbeings—yours truly among them—soon discovered something more astonishing even than that. Over the near millennium since our particular ancestors had abandoned that unlucky system and its brutally murdered homeworld, the descendants of the surviving individuals who remained behind had 'hanoverformed' the now-lifeless planet's only moon. Hard as it may be to believe, over a stretch of several centuries, and at an unspeakable cost in lives and precious resources, the smaller of the two worlds, that which had never before known any life of its own, had been rendered not simply habitable, but downright hospitable to unprotected human beings."

Involuntarily, she yawned.

"Do you wish to retire," he asked solicitously. "May I get something for you?"

"I wish you would not, Hanebuth," she answered. "Pray continue, if you will."

Then let me confess to you, Princess (Tarrant went on), that the enormous technological prowess—not to mention the sheer, unrelenting stubbornness—that must have been required by that achievement was such that, even those of us sufficiently sophisticated to comprehend and appreciate the unspeakable effort, for example, represented by construction of our own mighty 'Droom, or the orbital insertion of the Ceo's Eye about Hanover, stood openmouthed in admiration.

Sadly, Anastasia conceded to her crew, as we openly approached the living world—and gave the widest possible berth to the dead one—that the many skills and steely determination that were demanded by even the least of these undertakings were no longer to be found within the decaying Monopolity of Hanover.

As a wag among the *Lion*'s crew put it, Hanover's future was all in her past.

But in an instant—even as we hung slack-jawed in the *Lion*'s rigging, admiring a mighty thunderstorm, brilliantly illuminated from underneath by sheets of lightning, sweeping across vast golden prairies and verdant forests that our obsolescent charts would have had us all believe were merely barren oceans of frozen lava—we were surrounded by a belligerent swarm of tiny fighting vessels we first took for steam launches, circling about us and thrusting explosive bursts of some kind into our path, obviously warning us to heave to.

We were taken by surprise and considerably abashed to be so, especially our captain. But naturally, we were happy to do as they demanded, and lucky as it proved, for the only ships remotely like the *Lion of Hanover* that they had ever seen before were of the warfleets of their deadliest enemy. Being a generous and kindly folk, however, willing to exercise restraint even at the possible cost of losses upon their own side, they had held their thrust until they were able to determine why we appeared peculiar to them. You see, Princess, they were also a circumspect people, and we were not *precisely* like their foe.

They looked like anybody to us—anybody human, so to speak, as we had encountered no alien species that day, although, as it turned out, they happen to abound within this culture. Their *accoutrement* did strike us as rather comical, consisting as it did of close-fitting one-piece outfits, soft leather helmets with huge goggles which they never used, and long white silken scarves trailing almost to the deck. But of course that sort of eccentricity was to be expected of foreigners. Certainly we must have looked as silly to them in our striped shirts, beribboned caps, bare feet, and ankle-length white kefflar trousers.

What was not expected was that they would speak perfectly intelligible Hanoverian—with surprisingly few differences, even of pronunciation or of accent—insisting all the while that, in reality, it was their *own* language, English.

The individuals who had threatened and then welcomed us, named themselves "interceptors," their particular unit being the "Bader's Raiders." They were not, as it happened, a part of any government. As a division of some entirely private organization called the "Sea of Tranquility Militia," they had been taking their regular turn among other such groups at orbital patrol when they caught sight of our sails which, for reasons I will discourse upon later—reasons, Princess, you may not wish to credit—they thought a considerable novelty.

They had hailed us, they asserted upon being welcomed aboard the *Lion of Hanover* by her upstart captain, by means of a contrivance they called "radio" and also with some other device which (although none of us believed it at the time) they insisted was capable of sending messages more swiftly even than a starship sails. Not being equipped to do so, of course, we had not heard them hailing us, but had at last responded to flashes of coherent light from their little one-passenger vessels, first in traditional Hanoverian ship-to-ship code (which, like our language, they called a different name—"Morse"—and claimed to have been using for centuries), then by means of voice-modulated laser.

The origins of that particular device, I'm afraid, have long since been lost in the obscuring mist of history. Some believe it once to have been a weapon.

After all that time upon the Deep, stopping rarely at uninhabited worlds to replenish our stores of food and water, we did not have much refreshment to offer. They took tea with the officers and afterward were shown round our ship, which they admired greatly. Each of them—a dozen men and, believe it or not, half a dozen women—wished to know every detail of her working and showed no reluctance to give us similar information regarding their fighter-interceptors.

Conferring with someone on the ground using devices within their helmets, they told us the *Lion* would be towed—if it did not displease us—to a position where she would not obstruct commercial traffic. We had unknowingly arrived at a bustling port where orbiting vessels appeared few and far between only because they actually put down upon the surface. Each of us would then be taken—only if we wished to be—to visit that surface and its people. Earth's long-dead moon had become an unlikely but energetic center of a revitalized interstellar civilization which called itself the "Coordinated Arm."

Princess, how can I begin to describe for you the civilization Anastasia and her band of adventurers—yours truly again included—discovered upon the resurrected moon of ancient Earth? It was for me the most fascinating of exercises, simply examining their strange culture and comparing it with our own.

Their history of our species from the beginning of time until the death of the Earth varies considerably from what schoolchildren are taught within the Monopolity and diverges altogether, naturally, after that point. Yet like the imperia-conglomerate, they retain the immortal works of Shakespeare, Conan Doyle, Steele, Roddenberry, and Snodgrass. They lack the literary efforts of such creative giants as Laurel Stover or Elizabeth Eastdale, who flourished among us well after our ancestors left Earth's system. But they have still other storytellers—Heinlein, Anderson, Wilson, Piper, Boardman—whose monumental *corpi* were apparently lost, or perhaps even suppressed, by our civilization.

Much the same is true where music, other arts, and science are involved. Not much of painting or sculpture did I see, but they've a way of making music hang in the air before one's disbelieving eyes. Technologically, they're more advanced than the Monopolity of Hanover, but I swear this tells only half the tale, being merely a consequence of the rare political economy we discovered there.

Perhaps the best way is to swear to you that the people of the Arm awaken every morning looking forward to whatever the day may bring. They spend their waking hours at whatever pleases them, confident that nobody will tell them what to do, how to do it, or confiscate the fruits of their labors—nor any part of them—when they have been completed. At night they go to their beds somewhat reluctantly, as if unwilling to concede that another wonderful day is over.

They pay no taxes: "Theft is theft," I must have been told fifty times my first week there, "no matter who does the stealing or how many wish it done."

Now, Princess, we had each of us aboard the *Lion of Hanover* been hand-selected in the first place for the honor of joining the Ceo's crew. We had been detached from the Monopolitan Navy, in part because none of us had ties— families and the like—that might interfere with our duty, which was to serve the Ceo's whim whenever and wherever it might strike him. Only our old first officer had a wedded wife at home, and he did not like her much. All of us were able-bodied starsailors, and—believe it or not, this was considered to be as important as any other qualification—we were all of very much the same height, which meant that we looked well, lined up upon the maindeck for inspection.

That last, alone, will tell you what's become of the Monopolity. We were all somewhat slighter of stature than the average, I suspect, so that the Ceo, who was quite a big man, himself, might look even bigger, by contrast, for the media.

Once we had glimpsed the least of what awaited us upon Earth's moon, none of us was particularly eager to return to the Monopolity. I don't believe the Ceo himself could have found it in his heart to blame us—he might even have wished to join our number— although by your expression, I suppose I could be wrong.

Back home, none of us could ever have hoped for anything better than the positions we presently occupied, growing old—did we remain lucky—in the service of the Ceo and his toy boat. In the Coordinated Arm, a man belongs to *himself,* first and foremost, and then to whatever class he can successfully aspire to. And—much more to the point, I do believe—everyone who finds some way to make himself even the least bit useful within that civilization eventually becomes, by the standards all of us were accustomed to, obscenely wealthy.

What is more, Princess, although you must believe that I am by no means overly anxious to be thought by you a liar, it took me five very long, nervous years simply learning not to whisper the undeniable fact I am about to impart to you, that the Coordinated Arm is, for all practical intents and purposes, *stateless*.

No, Princess, they are not what we usually mean when we say anarchists, although they frequently and cheerfully refer to themselves by that very word. Their society is spontaneously ordered, they say, and therefore voluntarily productive, prosperous, and free. It is not so much that they don't believe in stop signs, if you will; it is that those stop signs are all the *private property* of the intrepid gentlemen adventurers who built, own, and maintain the roads. Should you fail to obey them, you will simply not be invited back again.

By all of this, what you are to understand me to mean, Princess, is that the Coordinated Arm is absolutely devoid of all of the many mandatory customs, statutes, ordinances, or divisions of caste that always seem to be of so much comfort to stuffy Hanoverians of every class who have been educated to believe there is a place for every individual in society, and every individual in his place.

Not so the people of *this* place.

The mountains of the Moon are unspeakably promethean. Upon the sheerest face of one of them they have carved their only sacred monument, in letters so tall, and graven so deep, that it may be read from three hundred klommes away. It is a "Bill of Rights" from one of the old Earthian nation-states. Even now, Princess, I weep to think about it. What it has to say, in just a handful of brief sentences, is that—as far as rights are concerned—there is no such *thing* as society, that there are only individuals whose liberty may never be restrained.

These people—you know, Princess, there is no collective name for them—they laugh whenever you call them Coordinated Armians. They have but one law, enforced by everybody, that upon possible pain of death (imposed by the intended victim at the scene and moment of the crime), you are never to start a fight. Everything they consider justice consists for the most part of various procedures, formal and

informal, for determining who struck the first blow, as
opposed to who retaliated, with whatever degree of severity,
in innocent self-defense.

In the Coordinated Arm, self-defense is *always* innocent;
no questions are ever asked, regarding the degree of force
chosen and employed to achieve it.

Ah, but I perceive that you grow weary of my socio-
political dissertation—or perhaps your many and grievous
wounds have tired you again—and that, in either event, all
you want to know is what eventually became of Anastasia
Wheeler and her reluctant Hanoverian crewbeings, perhaps
even, dare I hope, yours truly? Well, Princess, be assured
that they all lived happily ever after.

Eventually, every member of the *Lion of Hanover*'s
hijacked crew found a place for himself. If you will not
object to my discussing the subject, the girls of the Coordinated Arm were tall (I guess that they still must be, for
that matter), long of limb, fresh-faced, and remarkably
beautiful, not unlike yourself, Princess. But, unlike most
Hanoverian women, they were very bold—unabashedly
straightforward in the open expression of their desires—
so much so that I am ashamed now to confess that I
remained a bachelor, and, for the most part, rather disap-
pointingly chaste, until it no longer made much of a difference.

As far as I am aware, however, each and every one of my
old shipmates—save for me, of course—still dwells upon the
Earth's moon to this very day. Some, I suppose, have ventured off by now to one of her many colonies within the arm
of the galaxy from which the culture derives its name.
Because I kept in touch with most of them, I know for certain
that they have all long since acquired wives and families,
businesses, a certain *standing* that they could never have
achieved back home in the Monopolity. In this astonishingly
open society called the Coordinated Arm, even the least
among us—and I reckon that must have been me, for I was
the youngest member of the Ceo's crew, no different from the
rest of my shipmates in any significant respect—began pros-

pering beyond the wildest dreams of traditional lower-class Hanoverian avarice.

I have neglected to describe the embarrassing commotion that the media made over us. I greatly fear that they are no better within the Coordinated Arm than anywhere else I have ever been. To hear them tell about it, it was as if we were all living fossils, painstakingly chipped out from under the ice somewhere. To be sure, at least for some of us, the humiliating interviews and . . . well, something they called "commercial endorsements" offered us an initial stake in the civilization in which we had, by choice or otherwise, enlisted.

For others—and I was one of them—it also brought a possibility of real employment. To obtain her initial stake, Anastasia had sold the *Lion of Hanover* to the wealthy owners of some famous shipping line or other, quite generously sharing the astonishing price she had bargained for with her crew. In part because it was the only thing I knew, and in part because I had come to love the old girl, I was the first hand who signed on with the *Lion*'s new owners.

To my unending regret, they only kept the poor old *Lion* about as a sort of mascot—a "logo" they called her—merely employing her for her striking likeness in their advertisements (as I said, we had made quite a sensation in the media) and to convey their biggest, most important (or most temperamental) customers upon brief, purposeless excursions round the dead Earth and back. And she, the gallant vessel in which we had dared to traverse half a galactic radius!

I endured that nonsense for as long as I found it necessary, in order to get my bearings within this new civilization. From the *Lion of Hanover,* I eventually transferred to another ship—they let you do that, you know—starting my life all over again as a seasoned hand aboard the ordinary cargo vessels of the Coordinated Arm. There was a great deal to learn about these ships, and I was determined to prove equal to anything that was required of me.

And now, Princess, for the strangest, and to me, most

incredible part of my story: in a relatively short time, simply by learning as much as I might, whenever I found the opportunity, and by working as assiduously as I believed possible, I discovered that I had somehow climbed my way up, rung by rung, to a commission! I need not remind you that this was an achievement that would have been utterly unthinkable, let alone impossible, within the complicatedly stratified Monopolity. I daresay that for a good long while, I was more than a trifle scandalized by the notion of such "social mobility," as they call it.

But almost despite myself, I eventually became an experienced and widely respected ship's captain. Scarcely before sufficient time had passed for it to seem possible, I discovered that I was offering employment and shipboard training, first to the sons, then to the grandsons, of many an old comrade from the *Lion of Hanover* who apparently remembered me in a kindly light. (I had contemplated buying the old girl back, but by then preferred the starships of the Arm.) For years, I contentedly plied the Deep with them and others, amidst an apolitical "empire" but little smaller than that ruled by the Ceo himself.

Think, Princess, for a moment, upon what it signifies that I, who had been nothing more than a common deckhand, was now providing opportunity for so many others. How much prosperity and progress are the Monopolity and other imperia-conglomerate throwing away, with both hands, simply by denying this freedom to their own subjects, by means of confiscatory taxation, crippling regulations, and a rigid social hierarchy? Rather than risk the stagnation that invariably results from such a policy, the Arm will countenance none of it.

Our ambitious and capable Captain Anastasia, in the meantime, had become involved in politics. In a way, that was understandable, as she had been born to it. Bitterly opposing anyone who, using the threat of war as an excuse, wished to establish the kind of unanswerable authority under whose absence the Coordinated Arm had so thoroughly prospered, she eventually became its primary political leader—to any extent that they have one—or Coordinator. As far as I know, to this day—without the aid of any unanswerable authority—she conducts a bitter and protracted war with something called the Clusterian Powers. It was they whom Bader's Raiders took us to be, that first day we arrived.

When at long last I began to meditate upon retirement, I discovered, to my surprise, that somehow—simply by making the same sensible decisions, on a day-by-day basis, that anybody else would have made in my place—I had become the wealthy owner of a handsome and lucrative merchant fleet. Having never married, and remaining still in remarkably good health, I was prepared now to consider doing other things with my life. Again to my surprise—although, thanks to the advanced medical capabilities of the Coordinated Arm, I could reasonably look forward to living vigorously enough for many another decade—all I really wanted was to see my homeworld sometime again before I died.

I suppose I could have taken a big ship and a full crew back with me, on a somewhat more voluntary basis than Anastasia had. It would have been more than satisfying to show the people I had known in the old days—those of them as still lived—what I had made of myself. But I was unwilling to make such a possibly irrevocable decision for a crew of mine that Anastasia had for us.

Besides, this was my voyage home and nobody else's.

Unfortunately, the jaunty little personal spacecraft by means of which I chose to make that voyage, proved unequal to the task I had demanded of her. My little vessel's electromechanical breakdown was highly unusual and truly an unlucky fluke. But the most embarrassing fact, that she was unarmed, had been my very own—and as it turned out, extremely ill-advised—personal choice.

Thus, while she drifted dark-ported and without headway, so agonizingly close to home, I fully expected to die a star-sailor's death, succumbing slowly to eventual freezing, suffocation, starvation, or even thirst. I had avoided it so many years, so many decades, that it almost seemed proper. I confess, Princess, that I have subsequently wished many times that I had died such a death.

Instead, my little vessel and I were found and seized by minions of the Aggregate.

Chapter XXIX:
The *Windhover*

Tarrant held the likeness before her face.

It was like nothing Bretta had ever seen before.

She sat up in bed, weeks before she had thought she would be able, a combination of undemanding gravity, good food, healing potions, and devices she had also never seen before, implanted in her bandages, having worked wonders.

Both her arms and her legs were still immobilized. Only her right thumb and forefinger were free of bandages, and they were bruised so black that she was afraid to see what the rest of her looked like. It had not retarded her healing to have found friends in this bizarre place—or for them to have found her—bizarre friends, surely, but friends nevertheless. So numerous were the more terrible fates that might have befallen her that, despite her injuries, she felt fortunate beyond her ability to express, or even comprehend it.

Bretta could hardly wait to visit the creature—she kept wondering what they were called and promptly forgetting to ask—that had rescued her. And she was still touched to the core of her being that, having noticed how much she had enjoyed this special observation chamber of theirs, with its rare and wonderful great window, her hosts had willingly deprived themselves of its use for a not inconsiderable period of time, converting it into a bedroom for her convalescence.

She could see several of the Deep-breathing creatures

now, a klomme or so away, playing together like triskel pups or mock-dolphins in Skye's Great Briny Loch. These must have been young, for they were relatively small as the things went—somewhat less than three measures across—and very nearly transparent.

For all that it was a sanctuary for the desperate, this place was simply *full* of marvels, the accidental leavings of a thousand heretofore unheard-of civilizations. The thing Tarrant displayed now was quite unlike an autothille and more like a simple card. It was as flexible as heavy paper or plastic and could as readily have been folded. However, within the eye-deceiving depths that it seemed to possess (the edges, held carefully between Tarrant's fingers, allowed her to estimate that it was in fact no thicker than a few pages from a book) there hung suspended in the night-black Deep an object shown in three dimensions, even more wonderful to behold than the object that was depicting it.

Watching, with an expectant look upon his green-brown wrinkled face, for her reaction, Tarrant turned the card over. Now she saw the depicted object's *other* side, again in full perspective, standing sharply against a background that included the curved edge of a blue-green, partly cloud-covered planet and an unfamiliar starfield. Beyond, in the greater distance, hung a gray-white, gangrenous-looking globe that could only have been dead Earth. The first side of the card had shown no planets at all, and a completely different array of constellations.

But look what lay in the foreground, upon both sides!

"This was my little starship," Tarrant informed her with a bittersweet expression of pride. It was he who perched upon the windowsill this morning, as she remained resting in the bed they had moved there. "As I watched them do it, the monsters tore her to pieces about my ears, simply so that they could get at me. What did they get for their effort? A colossal waste of grace and beauty.

"She was called *Windhover.*"

He propped the likeness against her crossed wrists that she might study it.

"Why, she is like a child's toy," Bretta observed, "the kind that comes back when you throw it? You are right; she was inexpressibly beautiful. How large was she? Here is a window with somebody looking out—would that be you?"

He shook his head. "The previous owner."

"As may be. From wingtip to wingtip, I would guess she measured roughly the same as my father's *Osprey* does across the diameter of her maindeck from taffrail to taffrail—a matter of some eighty or ninety measures. In any case, she appears to have very little in common with the ships that our civilization builds."

Conspicuously careful to avoid contact with her, or even proximity that she might find threatening, Tarrant leaned in to reexamine the likeness with her.

"An excellent guess, Princess, you've a sharp eye." The sad little man sighed the sigh of a long-lost love. "The traditional thing to say is that she was 'yar'—I have not the slightest notion why, or even what it means. The poor darling spanned ninety-three yards from her starboard running lamp to her port, making her a trifle small for her power class. Yards are an Arm standard—a yard is three feet and a foot is twelve inches, extremely practical, as it is almost impossible to mishandle the decimal—about 91 percent of a Hanoverian measure."

" 'Yards, feet, inches,' " Bretta repeated. "And 'yar,' whatever it means. I believe I have seen the first three in any number of books that I have read, along with miles, pounds, and ounces. Whatever 'yar' was, Hanebuth, she was it."

Indeed, the little craft seemed to consist of nothing more than a pair of long, tapering, smooth wings with rounded tips, as brilliantly white as if she had been covered with a trillion diamonds the size of sandgrains. The wings formed a graceful angle where they met. Although *Windhover*'s likeness had been taken in harsh light, Bretta could find not a seam anywhere upon her exterior. The leading edges of her wings and her softly pointed bow (where a beautifully curved transparency continued the sensuous lines of her hull) were as fluid and elegant as those of a well-worn streambed pebble. However, all her trailing surfaces were upright, perpendicular to the broad planes of her wings.

Tarrant nodded. "You see, now, Princess, why I wished to show you this hologram of my little ship, so that you might have some reason to believe that I have been telling you the truth, as many another individual has not, to my dismay. Despite appearances, her basic operating principle is not dissimilar from that of our vessels. She surrounds herself with a §-field, as our ships do—"

Bretta nodded. "In order to cancel her inertia, that aspect of her mass which prevents her traveling faster than light. And in order to compensate," the starsailor within Bretta continued, almost automatically, "for some of the more inconvenient side effects of vile Relativity. Believe me, Father made sure that I was well acquainted with that all-important principle at a very early age. I know of an alien race, Hanebuth, the *nacyl,* who have ships like this one, although they look rather more like bananoids, I think, than boomerangs."

To Tarrant's obvious astonishment, and unlike anyone else he had told his tale to, she had believed him at once, without need for further evidence or persuasion. It was only another step to believe in an entire civilization that traveled about in ships without sails. And why should she not believe him, knowing, as she did, of her father's friends the *nacyl* and their speedy vessels?

Nevertheless, Bretta was almost impossibly grateful that he had brought her this picture to look at. At this particular moment of her life, she felt the need of something beautiful to contemplate, and with all due respect and gratitude, it was neither Tarrant nor his friends. Nor was she likely to find it, just now, in any mirror. Of a sudden, she felt herself becoming strangely excited. She adored sailing vessels, but this was something novel, something perhaps more personal. No wonder Tarrant had come to prefer these magical vessels of the Coordinated Arm. She wondered what the larger ones could be like.

"Indeed, Princess. She was given the name—although not

by me—of a little predatory bird that can accomplish some highly unusual maneuvers in the air. Or *could;* it is most likely extinct by now, having died with ancient Earth. What made *Windhover* different from the sail-driven vessels of what we Hanoverians smugly refer to as the Known Deep— indeed, what makes all of the starships of the Coordinated Arm different—is that, instead of awaiting the whims of the tachyon currents of the Deep, she generated her own stream of tachyons—"

"Action and reaction—Newton's Third Law—like a child's balloon, blown up but not tied off, and released from the fingers so as to blast its noisy way about the room!" The idea had flashed instantly through her mind. "Rather like a steam launch, except that it uses particles instead of whole molecules. Tachyons come out of these aftersurfaces, right here, do they not?"

With a nod, she indicated the flat, upright portions of the starship's wings.

"You're passably quick, Princess. If I don't mistake myself, I've seen your like but once before. I trust you'll not take it amiss if I say, from the first, despite any difference in age or appearance, that you've reminded me of Anastasia Wheeler. And you're quite correct. *Windhover* drove herself along at many multiples of the best speed our poor tachyon-jammers are capable of. The arduous journey that took more than three years of our lives aboard the *Lion* required less than three weeks to retrace aboard my swift little vessel."

"Hooray!" Bretta's outburst was entirely spontaneous, for Tarrant as much as for the *Windhover.* Here was a little man—or perhaps a not-so-little man—who apparently thought nothing much of sailing the radius of the galaxy, alone. His ardor for his late, lamented vessel was catching. He must have loved her greatly, as who could resist doing, simply laying eyes upon her?

Even now, he laid an affectionate finger upon her image in the hologram. "She was a racer when I purchased her, which accounts for her pleasing shape. She was designed for the pleasure of her turn of speed alone, and for nothing nobler or more significant than an afternoon of galloping out to the Centauris and back again, over and over, endlessly, in lovely little nine-light-year loops."

Bretta raised a skeptical eyebrow. It was one of the few gestures that she was presently capable of making. "People *do* that in the Coordinated Arm?"

Tarrant laughed and nodded with the remembrance of a better time in his life. "With a war on, and all, do you mean? Indeed they do, upon Saturdays, Sundays, and holidays, Princess. It is an extremely popular pastime for both participants and spectators. They also race genetically reconstructed horses upon the grassy maria and shoot metallic game silhouettes with pistols at a thousand paces.

"But we were speaking of the *Windhover,* were we not? Naturally, her winglike architecture had nothing to do with flying. It provided long-armed leverage for tight turns demanded by the course. I've seen three- and four-winged racers, but they're obsolete, the general experience being that they cannot be manufactured lightly enough—that's not quite correct, but it'll do—to take full advantage of newly improved propulsive systems. A matter, I'm reliably informed, of the squares not being able to keep up with the cubes."

Intense as it had been, Bretta's concentration suddenly doubled as she completed a logical connection she felt she should have made minutes ago. "Tell me all you can of her propulsive system, Hanebuth, and I mean *all* about it."

He grinned. "It cannot be seen in this picture without an instrument I no longer have—perhaps I can find a magnifying glass for you this afternoon if you desire—but, as I told you earlier, your surmise was right. These aftersurfaces here were covered edge to edge with powerful tachyon-generating cells."

Bretta leaned forward. "Now tell me all about the lethal radiation these things shower upon their unlucky crewbeings, or spew behind them in their grim wakes. Why is their use tolerated? I have it upon the best of authority that strong men will sicken and expire horribly from only a few hours' exposure to them."

He blinked. Bretta knew he must have expected many an ardent question from her with regard to his little ship— indeed, he had finally grown almost accustomed to her curiosity about technical subjects—but never one such as this.

He shook his head in a continuous denial. "Why, none whatever that I am aware of, Princess. Believe me, I have logged hundreds of thousands of hours aboard such vessels. Of course the §-field boundary is instantaneously lethal whenever it is intersected—which happens to be the case with *any* vessel capable of interstellar flight—but that is much less of a difficulty with this sort, where both pilot and passengers remain safely within a protective hull."

But instead of satisfying her curiosity, all of Tarrant's reassurances only encouraged Bretta to press her victim the harder—and by his puzzled expression, unaccountably—for a considerably different sort of information than he had apparently believed she would be eager to receive regarding the *Windhover.*

She realized that by now she must appear very nearly hysterical to the poor bemused fellow, but she had the most excellent of reasons for it, and there was so much at stake— provided, of course, that she ever managed to return home. "I want to know, Hanebuth—I desperately *need* to know— about deadly emanations of a variety possibly never heard of before within the Monopolity."

He shrugged helplessly. "How can I tell you of something I know nothing about?"

"I've recently met a whole *planetful* of people whom that would not deter in the least." Without any further hesitation, Bretta told Tarrant everything that she had ever managed to learn about the alien energies that her unhappy father believed responsible for killing his twentyscore of press- ganged Jendyne naval cadets.

Having absented himself from the Monopolity, indeed from all of the Known Deep, for several decades, her new

confidant had understandably never heard of the exploits
and adventures of Henry Martyn. He had to be discouraged
firmly several times from steering their conversation toward
a direction that Bretta presently regarded as irrelevant. So
abjectly did she miss her father—her mother, as well—so
firmly had she suppressed it until now, that it taxed her
resolve severely simply to complete her account without
bursting into tears. After she had finished, he thought a
while, and then asked, "These alien starships—you are quite
certain that they were constructed and operated by *flatsies?*"

"It is true, Hanebuth. Your turn to believe me. I have
autothilles, at home."

He joined her in her somewhat rueful laughter. "Well,
they sound to me as if they're propelled by physical principles identical to those I've long been familiar with. Do *I*
appear to be dead of radiation poisoning? Look at me—
rather, trust that I remained relatively healthy and regular of
feature until the damned Aggregate got hold of me. I swear,
Princess, I know nothing of such dangers inherent in the
ships of the Coordinated Arm. Such dangers don't exist, as
I ought to know, having had a lifetime's experience with
their technology."

Bretta sat silent for a long while, desperate to think
clearly, wrestling for self-control against overwhelming
pangs of homesickness. Then, because she needed to trust
someone, and having earlier chosen to believe Tarrant, she
changed the subject. "How is it you still retain a likeness of
your little Deepcraft?"

He grimaced. "You mean, having been so ignominiously stripped of all my clothing and possessions, and
funneled through the Oplyte process? A shrewd question."
She would have shrugged. "Some years ago, Princess, following my escape and having made a place for myself
here, I offered modest rewards for any fragment of the
Windhover the community might happen across. Such
goods are a staple of commerce among us. Just now, we're
all looking for a particular doll—I don't want to know
why. Ultimately, I received several items, the most wel-

come being this carton of holograms I brought with me this morning. I first made them to display to family and friends when I returned to Hanover. Would you care to see more of them?"

Although his bearing remained dignified, Bretta could see that Tarrant was pitiably anxious to share these tattered remnants of his former life with someone he believed might appreciate them. For her own part, increasingly, she was interested in seeing something tangible of this Coordinated Arm he described.

"I would greatly enjoy doing so, Hanebuth," she told him sincerely. She pointed to another hologram. "Now who is this? Would this be Anastasia, herself?"

She was finding (although for now she had decided to keep it to herself) that, from one of the longest "afars" in recorded history, she had begun to admire the Coordinated Arm, and respect the ideals it stood for. It sounded like everything her father had fought for all his life. The more she learned, the more it seemed to be an entire civilization composed of woodsrunners. She wondered how Uncle Sedgeley and his establishmentarian colleagues would like that!

"Indeed, Princess, it is—upon the overceremonialized occasion of the simultaneous launching of a thousand unbeinged scout probes toward the Cluster. For reasons that will be clearer later, it was, for all that, an important event. I was present, myself, soliciting patriotic donations from beside her upon the platform."

The Coordinator appeared just as Tarrant had described her, older in this likeness, taken decades after she had stolen her brother's yacht. She was a bit grayer and stouter than Bretta had imagined. Her hair was just as the girl had imagined, cut off sharply all round, a few siemmes above the woman's shoulders, the squared corners curving forward along her prominent cheekbones. In one slim hand she held the long narcohaler that Tarrant had said was her trademark.

"And who might *this* be?" Bretta pointed to a tall, dark figure in the background—standing protectively just behind the Coordinator—that of a handsome young officer in military uniform, wearing a weapons belt, plaided kilt, and leather sporran. With his left hand, he seemed to be leaning upon a cane.

"Now, let me see . . . I seem to recall being introduced to this young man, a Captain Nathaniel Blackburn—'Nate' I think she called him, her only full-time Intelligence op. He lost that leg, and probably his girlish laughter, in some particularly awful battle somewhere. It was Blackburn who tidied up the mess with that little music entertainer, Chelsie Bradford, and later on, those delightfully nasty serial killings of the network anchors." Tarrant went on chuckling at the idea of murdered newspeople. After her recent experience with the media upon Hanover, Bretta could hardly find it in her heart to blame him.

But for some reason she could not put a finger on, she found this young man interesting. She realized that she felt the same way toward him—toward his broad shoulders and well-drawn jawline—that she had upon first sight of the *Windhover.* The feeling was most embarrassing, uncomfortably warming odd parts of her body beneath her bandages. She hoped it was not discernable to Tarrant.

Perhaps not: "I took this just before my speech. I'm no speechmaker, so it was a memorable day all round. I'm unsure whether I regret that I have no likenesses of myself before I was—" He cleared his throat, having revealed more of his feelings than he intended. "You understand—or perhaps I failed to mention it—that in this war Anastasia fights, the Arm suffers a serious disadvantage?"

"And what is that?" It seemed to her the Coordinated Arm was fighting a rather leisurely war if it could afford such diversions as starship and horse races.

"Unfortunately," Tarrant replied, "the Clusterian Powers know just where to find the nerve center of the Coordinated Arm: Earth's moon, Anastasia's office."

She smiled abruptly. "The second star to the right and straight on till morning."

"Yes, Princess," he returned her smile, remembering,

"They have retained Barrie, too, but for some obscure reason, Peter Pan is invariably portrayed by a—"

"You were saying?" They had digressed; there were things Bretta wanted to know.

"What was I saying? That the forces of the Coordinated Arm appear not to have the foggiest idea where these Clusterians are to be found. Their best guess is that the Powers— the Arm's name for them; nobody knows what they call themselves—are located here, among these very stars. That would place them not far— relatively speaking—from the Monopolity and other imperia-conglomerate."

"This 'best guess' having to do with past history?"

"It might well be one of the imperia-conglomerate we know, as far as that goes. They send guided missiles, full of germs and nuclear explosives, and whole shiploads of prefrontally lobotomized suicide troops—not Oplytes—who never expect to return home and have been conditioned to expire whenever captured."

Not warrior-slaves, Bretta mused to herself, and yet the moral signature, the distant, impersonal cruelty of the style, nevertheless appeared familiar.

Bretta's weapons had been returned to her just that morning. The axis of her thrustible had been broken in her fight with Woulf. Her knife—little could damage that; she believed that he had never even noticed it—hung now upon an unwindowed wall, along with tatters of her clothing found within the canister.

She would have liked to see her thrustible repaired, as she was planning to have a use for it. Tarrant had informed her, however, that the leaders of the Aggregate insisted upon an hysterical weapons-destruction ritual, whenever their own heavily armed minions—instructed to scour the asteroid system for them constantly—happened across such objects. Which meant that thrustibles—or even any replacement parts for them—were virtually impossible to come by.

She would never give up looking, of course, and in the final analysis, she knew just where to find all the weapons she needed. She would simply *take* them, from an enemy utterly unprepared to resist her. For upon no better evidence than her feelings (her parents would have lectured her sternly about this) she had decided that the enemies of the Arm, and of Anastasia—and of handsome Captain Nathaniel Blackburn—were her own: none other than the Aggregate.

Tarrant arose. "Rest, now, Princess. Is there anything I can do for you?"

"Yes, Hanebuth, hand me paper and pencil, if you will. I believe I can make these fingers work well enough to sketch something you could have made for me."

"Indeed?" As the drawing took shape, Tarrant grinned, his expression one of wonder that no one here had ever thought of this before. "This we can do. We suffer no lack of materials for that sort of thing. It should play hell with a Deepsuit if the arrows are hollow-shafted. How strong do you want the bow?"

"It's called a prod," she answered, admiring the picture she had drawn of the crossbow she had left behind at home. "And the 'arrows' are bolts. Or quarrels."

"I see," Tarrant answered, a hand upon the drawing, the other resting his chin.

"I believe that just now I prefer the latter."

"Then so do I, Princess, so do I."

PART FIVE:
LOREANNA ISLAY
YEARDAY 340, 3026 A.D.
MAYYE 19, 518 HANOVERIAN
TERTIUS 15, 1596 OLDSKYAN

He fell into the §-field,
And flashing, ceased to be;
No living thing wept a tear for him
Least of all his beauty so free.

She put on all her milk-white sails
And she ordered her ship under way,
And she sailed till she came to her father's world
An hour before it was day.

She alighted upon her golden cabelle
And boarded a fast-traveling dray,
And she rode till she came to her father's gate
An hour before it was day.

CHAPTER XXX:
THREE TACTICAL ELEMENTS

"See t'that mizzentier stays'l!"

Given no more than an instant's warning, Arran and Phoebus cast all else aside, ordering idlers below and their well-drilled crews to battle stations. Arran's first words of command set the *Osprey* turning like a top, albeit at a rather sedate pace. He had several good reasons for doing so, worked out fifteen years earlier in circumstances nearly as dire and pressing as these now appeared to be.

At the same time, he directed his vessel toward what he reckoned was the opposition's greatest strength, thereby regaining for himself the element of surprise. To the enemy, *Osprey* would look like an auger boring straight at them.

Aloft, one of the crewbeings slid down a line in answer to the captain's shouted command, securing a halyard that had somehow broken loose. It was a dangerous action to take, this close to the coming fight, carrying him, as it did, into the lethal range of the bow chasers. Yet, taking confidence from the discipline with which the fellow knew the *Osprey* to be managed, he never hesitated. Arran felt a momentary swell of pride in the knowledge that this valorous and sensible conduct was quite typical of his crew, rather than the exception.

Beneath his feet, Arran could feel, more than hear, the low rumble of projecteurs opening their gunports and pivoting their great weapons this way and that to assure themselves that all was in working order since the last drill.

Briefly, he was aware that, with the exception of Loreanna, who had lived with him through many everlasting moments like this, and Phoebus's wives, of course, his passengers—Loreanna's mother and half brother, the former Ceo, Uncle Sedgeley, his friend Frantisek—must be wondering what was happening. Well, let them find out, he thought, the same way he and Loreanna had in their time.

All about him upon the quarterdeck where he stood, upon the maindeck two and a half measures below, and high overhead, dozens of crewbeings scampered about at apparent cross-purposes, and in seemingly violent disorder. Such an appearance of chaos was, of course, altogether deceptive. In his mind's eye, Arran could clearly discern his enemy's crewbeings similarly scrambling across their own decks, swinging upon lines and cabelles from point to point, all the while desperately striving to obey the harshly shouted commands that their own astonished officers—certainly well enough prepared for *Osprey*'s flight, but never for her bold counterattack—had probably never expected to be issuing.

And well might they *not* be, he grinned to himself. As the galactically renowned boy-captain Henry Martyn—in part out of an inherent genius no one among his family and friends had ever suspected he possessed, and in part due to the assiduous and demanding tutelage of Phoebus Krumm and many others—Arran had developed his own personal style of strategy, consisting of three elements.

"Ease off half a point, now!" he commanded the helm upon the quarterdeck, relieving a lateral strain upon the entire vessel's structure which correcting for the ill-set sail had engendered. He was satisfied to hear *Osprey* groan, as if with gratitude. It was unhealthy for a ship to engage others in combat with stressed keels or other members, as it magnified the devastation of her enemies' thrusts. It was worse when that vessel spun about her axis as his did now. And should all of the projectibles upon one side of a badly strained vessel happen to thrust in concert—Henry Martyn had always been well-known for giving his projecteurs their heads in battle—the consequences could be disastrous.

Loreanna would know that groan; the others would think it the end of the world.

Now he paced the quarterdeck in short, ferocious laps,

waiting—which was invariably the most difficult part of any battle—for his plans, laid long ago upon Skye and elsewhere, to produce the consequences he desired. At some forgotten point within the past few minutes, he had somehow strapped his thrustibles where they belonged, upon both forearms and wrists, although he could not recall doing so, nor who had brought them to him from his quarters below.

Unconsciously he clenched and unclenched the fists he held stiffly at the outsides of his thighs. When this day was finally through—provided that he survived it—his arms would sorely pain him, and he would wonder why.

The first element of Arran's strategy was *drill*.

There had been a time, long ago, when the formidable fighting vessels of the Monopolity of Hanover had reigned supreme throughout the Great Deep, for no other reason than that their crewbeings had all been better trained and more scrupulously practiced than those of any other imperium-conglomerate. The standards they had been expected to live up to had been high and absolute. To Arran's great fortune (and in the same instant, to his aesthetic regret) that time was no more. An inappropriately fastidious concern for mere appearance had replaced one for actuality and substance within the once-great Monopolitan Navy.

Still, no one happened to be more aware of that navy's glorious history than Arran, nor more insistent upon a fit and ready crew of his own, prepared to act together as a unit upon deck, at the projectiles, and aloft. The key to his success was the degree of coordination he had thus engendered among them.

Peering into the phosphor-lit depths of the binnacle-like device he had begun using at the onset of the attack, he shouted another order as he saw that they had made a serious error—possibly of ship handling, but far more likely one of tactics—allowing their slowly forming sphere of encirclement about him to lump up upon one side, inviting panicky flight through a weakened opposite side that they would presumably attempt to turn into a trap for the *Osprey*.

It was truly the most childish of ruses, and had there been

sufficient time to spare for the luxury, he would have felt
mightily insulted, and said so.

He failed to take the bait, however, and continued to steer,
instead, toward the greatest number and concentration of
enemy vessels. Who among them could possibly predict
what he intended to do, even now? Given the character of
the master they most likely served, such a tactic as this was
well beyond the reach of their imaginations. By now they
must be absolutely frantic with confusion.

Arran's second element was *maneuver.*

No commander in the rather lengthy history of the
imperia-conglomerate had ever spent more time or effort in
the evolution tactics which would remain reliably unpredictable to his enemies, and at the same time quite effective
at disabling or destroying them. In general—this was especially true in these overly cautious times—all that this
required, more usually than otherwise, was an indomitable
audacity such as he displayed upon this day, in the face of
seemingly hopeless odds. Nobody could be riper for defeat,
Arran had always calculated, than some captain who com-
placently expected victory, as a kind of entitlement.

Also, in the two years since they had last seen battle,
Osprey and her crew had not been idle. Arran had taken her
out upon short-range experimental and practice excursions
at least monthly. (He felt a brief, painful twinge at the memory of his beloved eldest daughter, now lost to him forever,
who had enjoyed nothing more than to accompany him upon
such outings.) In this way, despite the passage of a relatively
peaceful decade and a half, Henry Martyn and his infamous
minions had retained and improved their well-honed fighting skills.

He was more than grateful, too, that he always brought
his wife along and counted upon her now, as he was certain
Phoebus did upon his wives, to calm the others and encourage them—at weapon-point if necessary—to behave themselves. "Chasers, look ye sharp, now! Gundecks, tell yer
crews t'fire as they bear!"

That would be Phoebus, acting as his chief gunner, having handed off his duties as first officer to a grumbling sailing master. What he was shouting now was more by way of authorization, at this point, than orders to the lesser officers belowdecks, in command of their own weapons crews. His well-trained projecteurs knew with precision what was expected. This particular maneuver was called a *sutherland* for some reason lost in the mists of history, and it ranked high among the many that the *Osprey*'s crew knew best. He believed that they could have performed it as required, even had the word never been given.

Or in their sleep.

They were preparing, at the moment, to take the best advantage that they might of the *Osprey*'s stately whirling motion, intended to bring more weight of projectiles to bear upon the enemy than perhaps he was accustomed to—and to offer the temperamental weapons a chance to cool off a trifle between thrusts.

"Steady as she goes, now!" Arran encouraged a visibly nervous helmsman. Or perhaps it was only he who was nervous, requiring the childish reassurance of issuing a command. In any case, the obscenely colored, irregular blotches that marked the nearest part of the enemy fleet in the §-field about the ship had begun to resolve themselves into the identifiable signatures of individual vessels. "Mind you let the other fellow veer off if there is any veering to be done!"

He nearly bit his tongue then, dreading that some cretin would remember those words and write them down, adding to what he felt was his already rather overripe legend. It didn't help cases that he had many an illustrious—and altogether all too literate—passenger below who, lacking for any colorful experiences of his own upon which to expostulate, would help to spread the tale.

"Aye," replied Phoebus conversationally, albeit at the top of his lungs, for the benefit of the crew. "An' we shall give him sufficient reason to do so!"

Arran cringed, knowing too well the way Phoebus enjoyed his discomfiture at being what some idiots would choose to call a hero. He took what minuscule refuge he might, at the moment, in contemplating the third tactical element which had made him one such, which was an almost ridiculous superabundance of *weaponry*.

Merely to cast an idle eye upon her, no starship handler would ever have suspected that the *Osprey* was a vessel of some eighty-two projectiles' strength—not reckoning upon the weapons carried by her auxiliaries. As the boy-captain Henry Martyn, Arran had first ordered additional projectibles placed between each pair already standing upon the gundeck. Thus, where the gundeck of an ordinary fighting starship *Osprey*'s size would usually have carried a dozen, each looking rather like an outsized spherical iron pot about the height of a tall man, *Osprey* carried twice that number. Moreover, each of the working decks below, that generally never saw a projectile in vessels of *Osprey*'s class, had been converted into additional and unsuspected levels of utter lethality.

One manifestation that might have alarmed a more informed observer with regard to the *Osprey*'s true potential for destruction, was an unusual amount of sail that she bore upon the unusually long spars about her unusually high mast.

The sophisticated fabric from which these had been fashioned—among the highest technological achievements of the imperia-conglomerate, as well as the most ancient—like those of any starsailing vessel, not only permitted any ship to be propelled through the Deep upon the tachyon breezes, but converted other subatomic particles passing through them into useful power, lighting and warming the vessel. Arran's starship required half again the ordinary square measurage of sail, in order to satisfy the voracious appetite of her many projectiles.

Even the trio of conventional bow chasers aimed aloft, forward, through the skylights of the officers' and passengers' quarters, had been doubled in number, and two pair of completely unheard-of *stern* chasers added upon the lift-deck.

"Away all boats!"

Osprey shuddered delicately as this order was obeyed.

Lastly, as a part of his third element of overarming himself, Arran had devised (at the time, desperation had been driving him) an unprecedented use for his steam launches (of which *Osprey* carried an unusually high number), equipping each with its own full-sized ship's projectile. These he sent out to buzz about his enemy's vessels like so many stinging insectoids, harassing them in the defense of their mother ship, and, as often as not, single-handedly achieving their obliteration. Upon the capital world of Hanover, during his war with the Monopolity, it had been demanded that Henry Martyn be tried and executed if only for this highly innovative—therefore heinously "unfair"—tactic.

The trouble, Sedgeley Daimler-Wilkinson had replied blandly at the time (and perversely enjoyed telling Arran about it later) lay in *catching* him first.

The *Osprey*'s launches were fusion-powered, employed steam as a reaction mass, and consumed prodigious amounts of water which his defeated enemies were required to replace—it was stage-whispered in the capital—drop for drop, with blood, if the implacable Henry Martyn deemed it necessary. Just now the enemy captains, staring into analytical instruments much as Arran was doing, or directly into the §-field as older hands like Phoebus were wont to prefer, should be wondering why a single target had suddenly become a baker's dozen—outnumbering their own warfleet, had they but stopped to reflect upon it, by two.

Arran wished that he were aboard one of the little vessels now, as he had sometimes been a decade and a half ago, just about to encircle the would-be encirclers. How well he remembered the terrifying and thrilling manner in which the single projectile in the bow, supposedly recoilless, had shaken the launch and all aboard her until the very teeth in their heads had rattled. If he were lucky now, the enemy would believe that, confronted by overwhelming numbers, *Osprey*'s huge complement of lifeboats had abandoned her in cowardly disarray. If he were extraordinarily lucky, they would go on believing it till it was too late and his hornets were in amongst them, stinging, stinging, *stinging*.

Silently he sent his launch commander, Mr. Richard Tompkins, the best of hunting.

Meanwhile (Arran found himself musing during an unoccupied half second), for the representatives of a highly advanced supercivilization that they were supposed to be, the captains of the opposing vessels—or whatever admiral or commodore happened to be in charge of *them*—seemed singularly uninspired. Just as he had hoped they might—but not really dared to believe they would—they had simplemindedly continued their dull-witted textbook englobement of his *Osprey* and her twelve auxiliaries, as if they were unaware that the entire tactical situation had just been altered by the launching of the latter vessels.

What this told him—although he lacked the time to consider the matter further at the moment—was that, unless he was making an error of complacent judgment himself, the captains opposing him were locked helplessly into some rigid bureaucracy (or worse yet, bureaucratic mentality) that was controlled at an arm's length—and probably upon pain of torture and execution—by a book-educated pseudoauthority in tactics who was not present himself today and had nothing personal to lose by their defeat. Nor, in theory, win or lose—as long as they could prove they had gone by the same book themselves—had they. Success became an object secondary to avoiding being held to blame for failure. This was just what had happened to the once-formidable Hanoverian Navy.

Belowdecks, Arran heard the weapons officers urging patience upon their eager projecteurs and their crews. The spirit of the coming battle was well and truly upon them, although, to a degree, their greatest chance for success lay in ignoring it, and waiting until the moment was objectively correct. It had taken him and Phoebus many years, simply teaching this principle to their officers.

He looked up, confirming by the color of the §-field what he had already glimpsed within the depths of his instrument, and ordered that his crews aloft gather inboard, close about the klomme-high mast, where they would not become the accidental targets of their own ship's bow chasers. He had seen more than one crewbeing caught by a bolt of pure kinetic energy sufficient to obliterate a starship, and blasted through tier after tier, until nothing but a thin red paste remained upon the ragged edges of a long rent through the last of the staysails.

The ship's bow chasers might not be employed in any case, as it could persuade the enemy too soon that they intended to fight. Upon another hand, Phoebus might decide at any moment that there was some reason to alter that part of the plan, and Arran was more than content to leave that to his first officer.

All at once, the *Osprey* shook like a freshly bathed triskel, as a bolt of energy from one of the ships ahead found her somewhat sooner than Arran had expected. Most likely it was an impatient lucky thrust from the very sort of bow chaser he had been contemplating. They tended, upon other vessels than his, to be a little lower-powered than most ships' projectiles and collimated a trifle narrower for greater range. He had not awaited much in the way of discipline or gunnery from these creatures who would rely, instead, upon their numbers.

For the first time today, he became conscious of having to force himself not to worry about his beloved Loreanna (and the rest, he supposed grudgingly) belowdecks.

"Stand easy!" Phoebus shouted, just as his underofficers had done to their own projectile crews. It was ironic, he and Arran had often observed to one another, that having spent so much effort to instill a fighting spirit in a ship's crew, her commanders were required to work so hard to suppress it until the proper moment. "Hold your thrust, now, wait fer ye little pots t'bear!"

This initial assault, which seemed to have done the ship no harm, went unrepeated and without an answer from a patient Phoebus who would wait, no matter the cost, until he was sure of his mark. Another projectile thrust, more attenuated this time, seemed to confirm Arran's judgment that the first had been a matter of luck. His Bretta had been a better projecteur than that when she was nine or ten. *Osprey* stood on, spinning, headed for the narrow gap between three larger ships, where he reckoned she could wreak the greatest damage.

Without warning, the situation changed completely, as the *Osprey* shook from half a dozen blasts delivered from three sides along her beam ends. She was well among the foe now, deeply among them, giving thrice as good as she got with every broadside. Preoccupied with his own concerns, Arran had not heard the order to fire, but from the thrumming he could feel through the wire-mesh deck beneath his feet, he knew that each time an enemy vessel turned into the sights of each of the projectibles below, the projecteur would pull a lanyard, expending the full force of the mighty charge his machinery had been gathering.

The screaming had begun now among his own crew, some already turning to injured groans. There would be the damage done to *Osprey* by her enemies, and the ever-present possibility of a burst projectible or ruptured core-port which could kill a crew and turn the whole deck into a living hell. (He had been there when it had happened, himself.) There was no way of telling when a projectible might fail, or any preventive measure that could be taken against it. It was simply one of the risks of manning a fighting starship of this era.

A shock wave through the deckmesh and shower of enormous plastic-covered wire splinters caused him to turn for an instant, despite his training to the contrary. The taffrail behind him had been shattered by an enemy thrust. In another instant, a long cabelle, part of the vessel's running rigging, fell from high aloft like a great ponderous snake, bringing a single human body down with it, to smash itself upon the quarterdeck not a measure from where he stood.

The starship shuddered hard as Phoebus returned the deadly compliment, to slightly greater effect, he thought, than the enemy had been able to manage. A scurrying maindeck crew quickly cleared away the damage. Never allowing himself to be moved—naturally, he had known the dead Skyan crewbeing since she had been a child—he peered into the navigational instrument, turned and looked at the §-field, and hoarsely shouted another order closing the distance between the *Osprey* and what he thought of, from long habit, as her nearest victim.

The encircling sphere had begun to collapse as the eight other vessels of the enemy fleet, hungry for what they imagined would be part of an easy victory, attempted to close in for what they thought would be the kill. He grinned, knowing from experience that the idiots would do themselves vastly more damage with this foolish maneuver than they would ever be able to do to him. The deck lifted beneath his tingling feet as the *Osprey* was struck in her stern. He was not the sort of captain to call continuously for damage reports. As always, whatever happened, he would stand on and count the cost afterward.

And then, as if to prove him right, the other two ships he had attacked, in a belated and clumsy attempt to close with him, collided with one another, their §-fields merging like soap bubbles, their spars and sails and cabelles entangling with one another, their masts shattering like paper toys. They were close enough to see, now, and he knew that the occasional bright sparks he saw upon the §-field margins were unfortunate crewbeings thrown into it and annihilated. Phoebus thrust again and again into the tangle, taking both vessels from the fray—there was a horrendous explosion and fire upon the maindeck of one of them—possibly denying the hated enemy any further use of either of them, forever.

Meanwhile, their first opponent sheered off abruptly, the hot and heavy concentration of *Osprey*'s bellicose attentions having dismasted her below the foretier, throwing a deadly rain of broken cabelles, sails, and spars onto the tiers below and to the maindeck, collapsing a portion of her §-field upon itself, and engendering a dangerous overload and feedback that must have set every metal object upon the ship coruscating with what was known as St. Lucas' Fire.

Although he had never much cared for steering only by what could be seen over his shoulder, even Arran could tell by the hot, sickly pulsing at that spot within his own §-field—the colors formed a halo about the naked-eye image of the rapidly failing vessel—that he and Phoebus had hurt the enemy badly.

Osprey had passed through the theoretical boundary of the sphere they had attempted to form about her. Shouting a warning to his gunnery chief and first mate, Arran issued orders to reverse the vessel's course and reengage the foe.

Three down, he thought.

Eight more to go.

CHAPTER XXXI: HEAT AND CLAMOR

The *Osprey* made a wide, soaring loop.

This time, with the tachyon wind at her best point of sailing, she sped relentless, down toward the least of her foes, hungry for a quick kill. Four from eleven was a third; if *Osprey* were ruthless, the remaining two-thirds, captained by unimaginative fools, would find discretion was the better part of survival.

Meanwhile, a reckoning had come due. Arran's harriers had all come back with only the minor sort of casualty that might result—a sprained ankle, a jammed thumb, a bloody scalp cut—had they been launched for recreation at a picnic. It had been his armed boats which had forced the collision between enemy vessels, using hastily decollimated projectibles against their §-field envelopes to thrust one of them sufficiently off course that disaster ensued. A daring risk that, but most delightful to a captain. Mr. Tompkins was to be commended.

Aboard the *Osprey* there had been one fatality, the young woman—part of Arran's memory was going mad trying to recall her perversely disremembered name—jarred from the starboard mainspar, who had fallen to a grisly death at his feet. There had been the usual insults to decks and rigging; the enemy were astonishingly bad projecteurs. Belowdecks, breakage had been limited to what starsailors were inclined to describe casually as "the odd dish here and there."

A dismaying exception was their lubberlift, which had been smashed within its framing and would require rebuilding almost molecule by molecule. For the remainder of this voyage, did they desire to make a planetfall, it would be by steam launch. The liftdeck itself had been sealed, frozen and airless—the stern chaser crews had escaped—and would call for extensive repairing, as well.

And, although Arran had not noticed it at first, there had been one other minor casualty upon the quarterdeck, when some thirty siemmes of the wire that the vessel was constructed of had been driven through his left bicep, missing the bone and any major blood vessel. Krumm himself had tied it off only a minute ago. No more than that could be attempted until after the present engagement ended.

"Mr. Krumm," in lieu of the sailing master, acting as first officer, who had gone aloft to inspect damage, Arran addressed his friend. "Greatly loath as I am to trouble you just now, would it please you to tell me off a boarding party?"

"Aye aye, sir." Phoebus raised his eyebrows, but obeyed. They had not discussed such a possibility, but Henry Martyn was famous for what appeared to others to be spur-of-the-moment improvisations in the heat and clamor of the battle. Allowing for that proclivity, Phoebus made preparations, as a rule, well in advance of any anticipated necessity. Upon this occasion, it was merely a matter of barking a single command, and a dozen grim-looking but jocular crewbeings materialized at the break of the quarterdeck, ready, eager to be issued thrustibles, take their place upon the taffrail, risk their lives by leaping onto the deck or into the rigging of a hostile vessel. Arming his common hands this way (an obvious enough tactical recourse, in his mind) was another "unfair" practice that had set the 'Droom howling for Henry Martyn's blood.

Now Arran looked to his own weaponry. It was a long while since he had wielded them at full power against anything but inanimate targets. He had sparred with Phoebus and his eldest daughter at reduced settings, trading his harmless slaps for their gentle pushes. Something always felt different about that, however, something subtle, he could not describe. Thrustibles partook of the same technology that spun a §-field about a starship, altering many of its basic physical properties. Perhaps they took a different sort of hold upon the fabric of reality at different power levels. Where the §-field about a starship made mass possible without inertia, thrustibles made inertia possible without mass, and separated *action* (energy set in motion in one direction) from *reaction* (an equal amount of energy set in motion in an opposing direction).

Thrustibles consisted of a power module the length, width, and thickness of a hand, gently curved and attached to the forearm just below the elbow, and an axis the diameter of a little finger, extending from the power pack, along the top of the forearm (where it was attached at the wrist) to just forward of the second knuckles. The axis terminated in a small lens through which both a designator beam and the primary energies of the weapon were transmitted. Near the lens hung a yoke, a palm-piece the forward edge of which served as safety and designator switch. Squeezing upon it threw a scarlet beam. Pressing upon its end with the thumb released a bolt of pure, unidirectional kinetic energy. Such a thrust could last only an instant without destroying the device. Along the axis (some long-forgotten engineer having made a virtue out of necessity) a secondary, or spillover §-field served as a highly effective defensive shield.

Usually near the lens or the power pack, a dial adjusted the destructive energies of the weapon from a penetrating beam the diameter of a needle, to a manwide ray capable of breaking ribs, fracturing the sternum, rupturing the diaphragm, stopping the heart. Somewhere in between, it was possible to punch a fist-sized hole in an antagonist and see daylight through him before he fell.

Manufactured just for Oplytes, Arran's weapons differed from the ordinary thrustible. Neither polished nor embellished, they were finished in a matte gray-green. Their power packs were thick—one hand lying atop another. The axes, which had required shortening to fit Arran, were not cylindrical, but flattened, and at the working ends, the primary lenses were flanked by a pair of lasers, angled so the thrusteur could instantly estimate his range to the target.

Now it became time to issue instructions to the eagerly awaiting boarding party.

"Mr. James, you will gain control aloft. There is no time for niceties. Any crewbeing who will not surrender, thrust and cast into the §-field. Take Karlan with you—those mustaches of his should frighten the watch out of the rigging—and Holder, with his shipwife, 'Dangerous Pat,' as she is called belowdecks."

The man with the impressive mustache looked mildly insulted—although with fighting in the offing, it was hard to tell about people's expressions; perhaps he was merely playing along with the captain's jest—but the woman grinned.

Louis James was a young, dark, slender officer who had come by his gentle disposition naturally. He had been compelled by the exigencies of a strenuous existence to study ruthlessness as if it were a subject in a textbook, and had passed with marks that were more than satisfactory to his captain. He nodded at Arran and gave a proper answer, then looked to his thrustibles and stood ready.

"For my own part," Arran told them, "I shall want Lieutenant Nadja with me upon the enemy quarterdeck, along with our deceptively kindly Mr. Famularo, and my ship's technician Mr. Gibes." Nadja, he knew as a woman of few words who understood well how to put what she believed into action. He had sparred with her once or twice and respected her considerable skill with a thrustible. Gibes was a man who could twist two wires together and make them into a weapon or transportation home.

"Mr. O'Brien, you shall be needed, too, does it please you. Take Farnham, whose game temperament inspires all those about him, Heil, and Cooley to the maindeck with exactly the same instructions I just gave Mr. James."

"Aye aye, sir!" O'Brien grinned up at him through a bandit's mask of battle-soot.

Unable to resist, Arran grinned back at him. "Mr. Lukes."

"Aye, Captain." Lukes, a new crewman, was a hand so cool in the heat of battle he was known by all his fellow beings in his last berthing as the "Ice Man."

"Mr. Lukes, take you the Knoxes and Mr. Irakliotis to the liftdeck of the enemy vessel. When you receive word from me, release her lubberlift, severing the cabelle inboard. Are we able afterward, we shall take it to replace our own."

"Aye, sir!" Lukes smiled. It was the sort of task that he relished—the enemy's lubberlift would never be taken without a fight—and the sort of company he liked keeping. Contemplative Christopher and cheerful Jeffrey Knox happened to be first-rate starsailors, feared by every opponent whom they had ever permitted (from sheer *generosity,* Jeffrey was always quick to explain; from pure *civility,* Christopher invariably corrected him) to live through defeat. Leo Irakliotis, late of the Ceonine University of Hanover, was a storyteller and philosopher, who also knew more about the subatomic workings of §-fields than anyone else living in these strange, scientifically incurious times.

"Next to last, but far from least, Warrant Officer Suprynowicz."

"Captain?" the man answered Arran, as always, in a misleadingly languid voice.

"As comm officer, all will depend upon you. As soon as we are in range, take that laser-cannon of yours and begin telling my opposite number that we surrender."

"Captain?" The word alone was an unusually articulate question.

Arran laughed. "I would not have you lie. Simply *begin*

the process of telling him that we give up, employing as loquacious a manner as possible—imagine that I am paying you by the word—but do not ever quite finish. Let the captain draw whatever conclusion he will. While he is thus preoccupied, we shall board his starship and spoil his whole day for him, if not his entire career."

This time the laughter was shared all round and lasted the boarding party as they climbed up, onto the taffrail, holding onto lines and stanchions, and waited. Arran knelt where he was perched to have a last private word with his first officer, who had remained with both of his feet planted firmly upon the quarterdeck.

"With the course corrections that I will rely upon you to make, we should not *quite* collide with our opponent, but meet them perpendicularly, our two vessels crossing at the mizzentiers. Stay with her, Phoebus. I mean to have my way with her, to take her captain prisoner, steal her lubberlift to replace our own, and turn her into something her fleetmates will wish they had never seen."

"Sir?" There were times when Arran could puzzle even his old friend and mentor.

"I will send the boarders back, and come myself at the last, after which we shall wish to separate as rapidly as possible. Lay in our course to place her between us and her mates. We will then make good our break, away from the fight."

Phoebus nodded. "I believe I understand, Captain. You may rely upon me."

"Good." He began to get up, then thought better of it, kneeling again. "Phoebus?"

"Yes, my friend?" The choice of words sounded ominously to Arran like a farewell.

Looking this way and that, Arran reflected—out of a habit that he had long ago fostered to calm himself at such nerve-wracking moments—that his audacious design depended, like that of any other boarding party, upon a fact that when two §-fields intersected, they coalesced, as it was often explained, like two enormous soap bubbles, becoming one great §-field, centered upon a locus that depended upon which of the two vessels had the greater generating capacity. Through such a window of §-intersection, which could be maintained only for minutes before the least of the vessels' generating capacities became overloaded—but which might, by incompetence or misadventure, as easily last only a fraction of a second—he and his crew would leap aboard the enemy vessel.

Arran cleared his throat, "Er, never tell Loreanna that I did this, will you?"

Krumm laughed heartily and slapped him upon the back, nearly pushing him off the rail where he knelt, and out into the §-field. "As I say, rely upon me!"

Suddenly, from the least sapphire spark, there bloomed a rapidly growing circle with blinding edges of pure azure. The §-fields of the starships were coalescing. In a moment the edges had disappeared as two §-fields became one. From *Osprey*'s battered taffrail, Arran delivered himself of an ecstatic war shout, echoed by his henchmen, and, seizing a line, leapt onto the dorsal spar of the enemy starship's mizzentier. Securing the line, he suffered a shock—but hardly an unexpected one—as the pull of gravity rotated a full quarter circle.

Enemy crewbeings shouted alarums to one another, scurrying to repel Arran and his boarding party. The enemy officers were considerably slower to begin barking orders, and more than a trifle hysterical, if Arran was any judge of such matters. The mizzenyard he balanced upon vibrated with the contradictory strains of both vessels, locked grimly together, starsails and helms set to cross-purposes, and with irregular thumps as his forces landed upon it behind him.

Mr. James, mustachioed Karlan, Holder, and "Dangerous Pat" were already swarming up the staysail sheets toward the maintier and points aloft. Arran knew that their success up there would guarantee that of the entire boarding party.

"Forward, my hearties!" Arran shouted. "Fight your way *inboard!*"

Nadja, the only female Arran had ever known to make effective use of two thrustibles, Famularo, and Gibes, were right behind him as he knew they would be, followed by Mr. O'Brien, "Mad Michael" Farnham, Cooley, and Heil, who had proved it a small galaxy by hailing from the same planet as Holder and Krumm. The eight of them were already depopulating the mizzentier of its starsailors, using their thrustibles to pluck them from spars and rigging like so much ripe fruit.

Mr. Lukes, along with Chris and Jeff Knox and Mr. Irakliotis, were out of sight already, having swung directly to the maindeck to force their way below. Although he intended taking control of the quarterdeck and maindeck, Arran had chosen this route along the mizzenspar for himself and his eight accomplices, in order to share the vital task of mopping up aloft with Mr. James and his party.

Before Arran was altogether prepared for it at a conscious level, he had already blocked a challenging impulse with the protective axis §-field of his left thrustible. The reflexive return thrust that had saved his life so many times before, caught his adversary—a shaven-headed ruffian in striped shirt and kefflar trousers that may once have been white, hanging amongst the mizzen staysails like a flea in a hammock—in the chest. It seemed to Arran, who had not quite grown accustomed to the new ship's orientation, that the villain rocketed sideways, abruptly, past him and to the right, screaming as he did so and making a horrible broken-melon noise as he plunged onto the maindeck, headfirst.

Behind him, somebody—probably out of sympathy—laughed grimly. But Arran scarcely heard either sound, for he was already preoccupied, defending himself against another contender, an officer this time, standing spraddle-legged upon the quarterdeck to Arran's "right" (Arran shook his head; now the fellow appeared to be below him), blocking, thrusting, blocking, and thrusting again.

Arran felt, rather than heard, the thrum of a near miss close beside his ear. Then a well-sent thrust took his enemy in the face, Arran's Oplyte-sized thrustible flattening the officer's head for an instant, raising its internal fluid pressure until, with a dull explosion, it burst in a thick red mist that gave rise to a momentary eerie sparkling within the §-field margin behind the man. The headless corpse pitched over the break of the quarterdeck onto the maindeck.

All about him, now, he heard the deliciously dangerous thrumming of many thrustibles, although, had it been his own starship under attack, there would have been a deal more. In part, his plan to board depended upon a reluctance of captains to arm their common hands, and, once again, the risk had proven justified.

Yet before Arran could so much as draw a ragged breath, two more foemen beset him, this time obliquely from far overhead, upon the portside mainspar, and from midway along the same dorsal mizzenspar that Arran and his men now occupied.

The first thrust, of middling collimation, struck Arran upon an upraised left forearm, where the fury of the kinetic blow was absorbed as before by his axis field. The man was a dazzling thrusteur, an idle portion of Arran's mind realized with admiration. No fewer than twentyscore measures stood between them.

Almost simultaneously, he was forced to take a second thrust—craftily attenuated to seven-eighths width, with the objective of simply pushing its victim from his foothold upon the spar and outward into the deadly §-field—upon his right forearm, which he had hurriedly crossed over his abdomen as he balanced precariously upon the spar with his knees bent to lower his center of mass.

Quickly, Arran lashed out with both of his thrustibles braced at right angles to one another. He squeezed the yokes across both palms, saw from the corners of his eyes that the designator beams illuminated both of his enemies, one a trifle sloppily at hip and thigh, the other centered squarely upon the chest. In the next fraction of a second, Arran thumbed both of his trigger buttons.

The starsailor obstructing his way upon the mizzenspar slid backward and thumped, more likely dead than unconscious, against the ankles of a wide-eyed comrade whom Arran thrust without taking aim as the fool stared at him, mouth agape.

Arran's original opponent, whom the *Osprey*'s master had frankly never expected to strike with his first thrust, but merely to distract, plummeted without screaming into the §-field, where he vanished in a brilliant flash and sizzle.

"Captain!" Nadja and Cooley shouted together. *"Look out!"* A thrust from behind Arran's back slammed into the spar beneath his feet, shredding its surface. But it came with a ghastly scream and the stench of burning flesh. Arran whirled in disbelief. From the nearby quarterdeck of the *Osprey,* the mild-voiced Suprynowicz had used his comm-laser at close range to blast this would-be assassin off the cabelle he hung suspended from like a spider. The man fell to the deck like a comet and smote hard, burning with black, greasy smoke.

It seemed a long way—half a klomme at the least—from the outboard extreme of the dorsal mizzenspar where he had landed, and where the retracted studdingsail booms were lashed, inboard to where the spar intersected the mast. "Fail to take her, my braves," he shouted, "and we shall not see home again!"

They might not, anyway, he thought, but wisely kept the news to himself. Warding off the enemy, killing wherever they must, they made a slow, fighting progress. At last, they arrived at the railed platform which circled the mast and which, by means of a lever, could be made to carry them downward, aft, to the maindeck below. Arran's party scoffed at such sissified contrivances—at least when they had boarded an enemy vessel—and swarmed to the ratlines instead, their bare starsailors' feet slapping the metalloid mesh almost in unison.

Arran took seven steps up the ladder to the quarterdeck, where he thrust a pair standing beside the binnacle and tiller ball. He meant to be burdened in this struggle with no prisoners except one, and had given orders to his crew accordingly.

Once the maindeck had been secured, he set O'Brien at the helm and Nadja to guard him, with orders to hold upon *Osprey* at all costs. O'Brien nodded, knowing the cost might include his life. Nadja nodded, assuring him it would not.

Arran strode to the mast and, ignoring the uproar behind him, studied it. Failing to open an access port with his fingers, he stepped back to thrust its hinges. The door clanged open, exposing rows of control knobs, switches, and gauges.

In addition to driving a vessel through the Deep and gathering particles for the starship's energy needs, starsails combined those particles, quark by quark, into atmospheric gases. Ships' crews varying by species as they often did— and therefore in their planets of origin—some latitude of mixtures was to be desired. These were the knobs, switches, and gauges that controlled it.

Arran flipped a switch and swung a lever as far to the right as it would go. Then he flipped other switches and swung levers to the left. He had shut off all gases except oxygen, and stepped up production of that to the maximum. A light flashed as if the vessel knew something dangerous had been required of her. He punched an override. Adjusting his left thrustible to an oscillating needle, he heated the edge of the access plate to a dull glow, welding it shut.

Meanwhile, Dangerous Pat had slid down to his side, breathing hard but grinning. "Mr. James's compliments, sir, and the vessel is secured aloft. Those as we let live are confined in the foretier platform, tied by their own cabelles."

"Very well, will you be so good as to inform Mr. James that his presence is required upon the liftdeck? You will enter with Mr. Lukes's party and cast off."

Although the look she gave him was poignant with worry, she snapped him a cadet's salute. "That I will, Captain. And I presume you will be joining us, sir?"

"You presume too bloody much," he told her, as he must, but was privately flattered by her concern. "Gather up Nadja and O'Brien, too. Now get you aloft!"

In minutes, James—Arran saw with gratitude that his crew had all come with him—had vanished belowdecks. He had no report of Mr. Lukes's success, but had given him too few men to spare for that. Like refuse canisters, the lubber-lift could be cast off without disintegration. Unlike most lub-berlift trips, this one would take place without the cabelle being secured to the liftdeck.

Of a sudden, the enemy starship lurched, there being no one at the helm to assist Phoebus in keeping the two vessels properly aligned, and the §-field intersection became an eye-watering cobalt circle once again as they drifted apart.

Arran swore to himself. As oxygen began replacing nor-mal gases, he had planned to find the captain to gain some knowledge of his enemy. But here was a warning that it was too late. All he had time for was to hurry to the helm and turn the steering ball under his palm until the starship was aimed for the small fleet whose captains idiotically believed that they were coming to her rescue.

The §-field intersection dwindled dangerously to a daz-zling circle merely measures wide. Rotating a handwheel, Arran locked the steering ball in place. Feeling the thump of the lubberlift depart, Arran ran to the taffrail to seize a line. Aiming aloft, he thrust at a mainsail, being rewarded with the sight of another circle—fiery yellow—eating its way outward, from his point of aim.

He leapt for the *Osprey* as the azure circle closed, col-lapsing with a *bang!*

CHAPTER XXXII:
THE BUTCHER'S BILL

Where was Arran?

A worried Krumm watched the azure-bounded area of §-field intersection dwindle.

Where in the name of the Ceo was Arran?

Phoebus had held the *Osprey* upon station as long as he could, given the condition he suspected her to be in. Whatever course the enemy vessel pursued was gradually but inexorably tearing her away, despite his best efforts to the contrary. Still, he watched both §-field and binnacle, and fought the tiller ball.

From time to time *Osprey*'s many projectibles still roared, shaking her fabric, as the weapons came to bear and their operators believed they had the range. At this distance there was no way to tell whether they were having any effect.

Where, he asked himself, in the name of the Ceo's bloody bowel movement, was Arran?

At the opposite curve of the quarterdeck, across the expanse of maindeck that it encircled (vast or cramped as it seemed by turns to those who worked and lived upon it), Jan Cipra, a member of his own crew from the *Tease*, waved at him and whistled, calling his preoccupied attention to certain colorful signs and portents visible within the §-field to those who knew to look for them.

"Red field behind," the starsailor's doggerel ran unbidden through his thoughts, "lends peace of mind; red field ahead, mark it with dread." Like a lot of starsailing lore, it didn't mean a damned thing, but had been passed from old hand to fresh for centuries. He'd heard they gave a written exam for the master's certificate upon Hanover. He wondered if that meant anything, either.

Phoebus nodded broadly so that Cipra could see that he understood. The indications, much more complicated than any old starsailor's rhyme might lead its listener to believe, were that the remaining seven vessels of the enemy fleet had finally managed to turn, sort themselves into what they no doubt fancied was a tight attack formation, and were now bearing down hard upon the *Osprey*.

It would be some considerable time before they got here. What kind of idiots were these? Their tactics were generations obsolete. Clumped together like that, the fools made a tempting target. He licked his lips, idly wishing he had one of those atomic bombs that Arran had once used against a pursuing enemy. It had been a self-destruct device, as he recalled, wrenched from the fabric of the ship that bore it, and used instead, to destroy a predator. Remind us to ask *Derabendsvater* for half a dozen next *Gesellschaftsnacht,* he grinned to himself. Then, for a moment, he wondered: might the tiny fusion reactor of a steam launch be made to explode like such a weapon?

Only in very badly written fiction, he decided.

But where was Ar—without warning another kind of explosion caused him to whip his head about. He was gratified that one of the projectibles had not burst, as he had believed might be the case (he had seen them do that). The bitter-edged circle of the §-intersection had suddenly closed itself with a bang!

More concerned than ever, now, for Arran's well-being, Phoebus was about to interrogate himself once again—obscenely— regarding the whereabouts of his captain, when he was suddenly struck a blow across the full width of his broad torso so powerful and unexpected that it sat him straight down upon the deck.

"Permission to come aboard?" Lying beside him, an embarrassed expression upon his face, was Arran, having been blown at Phoebus like the cork from a bottle.

"Ceo blind me, boy," Phoebus roared, "if y'still don't know how t'make an entrance! Reminds me of that adventure we had upon what you called the Glass Planet!" With less effort than might have been expected of a man of Phoebus's age and weight, the *Osprey*'s muscular first officer regained his feet upon the deck, gave his fundament a rub, and, with a shoulder-wrenching jerk—the shoulder being Arran's, not his own—assisted his young captain in regaining verticality.

"Now there's a story the Explored Galaxy is not yet ready to have told." Arran laughed for the sheer joy of being alive. Like many another man, he was able to forget, for a brief moment in combat, the grim situation they found themselves in, as well as the death of his daughter. "Are all of my people safe?"

Freed at last of the drag of the enemy vessel, the *Osprey* required some considerable retrimming of her sails—a task that was greatly complicated by the damage she had lately suffered—which Phoebus attended to with a couple of shouts aloft and a spin of the tiller ball before he gave his captain an answer.

"Aye, yer boardin' party's safe an' sound an' well ahead of yer esteemed self. We've just recovered 'em in that castoff lubberlift of theirs. Clever, that—how can y'miss thirty-odd thousand klommes of cabelle afloatin' through the Deep?" He nodded toward the discolored §-field, of a sudden growing sober. "An', we've company comin'. I take it, then, that the ugly deed is done."

Arran nodded, ritualistically dusting off his hands. He looked about the main- and quarterdecks, assessing the destruction and approving what was being done for it. His vessel was like an insect colony that had been kicked over, in the manner that her relatively tiny denizens hastened over her, restoring her to her previous condition. "The ugly deed is done. We should be seeing the spectacular—if regrettable—results any moment. Ceo, how I hate killing a starship! Although it still remains to be seen whether I timed it right."

As they spoke, a giant, ragged-ended fragment of yardarm came crashing down onto the maindeck, followed by a feeble and belated, *"Look out below!"* Arran shook his head in astonishment, disbelief, and amusement—and caught Phoebus in the corner of his eye with precisely the same expression upon his face. "I expect the flyin' pies'll be next, sir," the first officer wryly observed.

Arran shook his head again, and laughed, despite himself.

The *Osprey*'s tens of dozens of energetic crewbeings scurried this way and that, repairing the damage aloft, clearing the quarter- and maindecks of battle debris, doing needful work belowdecks, and otherwise attending to the many hurts done to their gallant vessel in the desperate struggle she had just survived—as quickly as they could before she was called upon to survive another. Some few lined up to let

the ship's surgeon—in fact, the ship's cook, Mr. Curry—
glue and bandage their minor injuries. It was a testimony to
them—or perhaps even more, to the captain they served—
that having been treated, they returned immediately to the
task of setting the starship to rights.

And still the enemy bore down upon them, slow but inexorable.

They watched in fascination as the boarded vessel, still
lying nearby, became a sharply bounded sphere of fire, her
incandescence tightly contained, so that she looked like a
small white-yellow sun, or a child's balloon brightly lit from
inside. Neither had ever seen an electric lightbulb, which
was what she most closely resembled; that technology was
a millennium in their past.

The boarding party, now regathering upon the maindeck,
presumably for further orders or dismissal, also watched the
result of their handiwork, and with openmouthed awe. They
had each understood, in a rough way, what their captain had
been about, but had not had time or opportunity to visualize
the thing fully. Almost despite themselves, each of them
imagined the same thing happening to their own ship and
shuddered at the horrible images it brought to mind.

Between them—before the boarding of the enemy vessel
had commenced—Arran and Phoebus had laid plans to
make their own starship appear much worse damaged and
far more vulnerable than she truly happened to be. And from
the enemy's point of view, Arran's venture must have
appeared a failure, as well, followed as it had been by an
exceedingly hasty retreat by all hands. This, quite naturally,
had brought them in close. Arran had steered the captured
vessel directly at the spot where he had reckoned the
remainder of his enemy would gather before striking at the
helpless *Osprey* in their cowardly (or sagacious—he supposed that it depended greatly upon how one looked at it)
manner.

As usual, Henry Martyn the Scourge of the Known Deep,
had guessed aright. Within minutes, the fireship—so she had
been called in all of the ancient tales of ocean ship-battles in

which Arran had first read of such a desperate and savage tactic—was in amongst her former sisters of the enemy fleet, her fiery §-field intersecting and coalescing with that of one unlucky vessel after another, spreading the hellish, horrible, *contagious* conflagration Arran had established within her own §-embrace, to her fellow starships. Of the seven remaining enemy ships, three turned and fled, one already in flames and doomed. His other four victims remained—two of them colliding—and burned.

And unnatural fire lit the otherwise eternal night.

The *Osprey*'s entire crew, upon deck and aloft, including the courageous men and women late of the boarding party now gathered at Arran's feet, gave up an enormous cheer as the two colliding vessels exploded into an even greater ball of flame, unbounded by any confining §-field. Had they but stood a few klommes closer, those aboard the *Osprey* might even have heard the explosion as the gases that it liberated rushed past them. Deprived of oxygen, the fire quickly died away, but not before it had consumed every last molecule of both starships. A future astrophysicist or stellar chemist might stumble upon that cloud of oxidized particles and wonder what natural forces could have produced it.

With his giant first officer, Arran joined the cheering of his valiant crew both heartily and sincerely. It was true that he sorely hated killing a starship, but certainly not killing the murderers, slavers, and fools who had crewed it and its fleet sisters. This was merely something—exactly like spraying for the killer-mosses that sometimes spawned belowdecks—that had to be attended to from time to time, in order to make life possible for those others who troubled themselves to remain decent creatures and employ their intelligence.

In fact, he was hungry. He had neither his breakfast yet nor spoken to his wife. When he had assessed the toll upon ship and crew, he would see to both.

For his own part, Woulf had enjoyed the battle—for all that he had helped kill hundreds of officers and sailors in the attacking fleet who were nominally on his side. It was the first sizable engagement in which he had fought in a length of time that would have amazed those who thought they knew him.

It was not the first time he had killed hundreds of officers and sailors. That was the last time he had been revived and given, among other assignments in a remarkably busy period, the unlikely task of eliminating four hundred Jendyne cadets and making their prolonged, painful deaths appear to be a result of radiation poisoning.

The idea was to break the fighting spirit of Henry Martyn, who would blame himself for the demise of those he had pressed into ships using technology—superior to that of the Monopolity—which badly needed suppressing, as it threatened a balance Woulf's keepers had depended on for centuries. It would also discourage cooperation between humans and the aliens who had developed it.

Among thousands of cluttered warecaves his employers casually maintained, crammed as microgravity allows with the rejected booty of a thousand years and a billion hijacked ships, he'd found his weapon—created by an alien race no one had ever heard of before or since—a "death-ray"—in fact, a handheld industrial X-ray, apparently employed in the construction and maintenance of spacecraft. It had functioned well enough when he had tested it upon a few dozen surplus captives, doing its deadly work in utter silence, manifesting a useful range of a hundred meters, horribly killing in hours those he had aimed it at.

They'd been in a rush to have him act, violating all precedent by lending him one of the precious high-speed scouts they'd captured in their endless war with the Coordinated Arm. The little vessel had taken him to Skye—flown by one of the Aggregate officers he'd seen earlier today—in a fiftieth of the time tachyon sails would have required, then to Hanover for some tidying up there.

What a shame all their clever plans had been wasted, failing abjectly to make a visible change at all in Henry Martyn's—Arran Islay's—attitude or behavior.

But that was then; this was now. What Woulf had liked

most about today's work was that he had not been forced to
sneak about, but did his slaughtering openly, a smile on his
lips, a song in his heart. As he gutted them, the look of
astonishment upon the faces of the "enemy" officers who
recognized him, had been worth the risk of volunteering for
the boarding party at the very last instant.

He had liked it nearly as much as what he was planning
now to do with Loreanna.

"The good news ye know." Phoebus spoke softly but
without whispering. Nearly everyone aboard the *Osprey*,
from officers to the lowliest deckhand, was aware by now
that she was a deeply wounded vessel. Three hours had
passed determining how deeply; Arran had still not had his
breakfast nor spoken with Loreanna. "We've but one fatality
an' no serious casualties t'speak of—a circumstance I'd say
borders upon the miraculous, were I the sort t'believe in miracles."

Arran nodded cautiously, having a fair idea of what was
coming next. He, too, had been aloft and belowdecks,
inspecting his injured starship. Now he stood beside the
tiller ball and binnacle, the former standing askew where it
was attached to the damaged quarterdeck. At the moment
they were hove to, starsails reefed, to all intents and purposes motionless, permitting *Osprey* to drift where she
might, the nearest navigational hazard billions of klommes
away.

Phoebus forced himself to continue, his accent thickest
when he was most unhappy. "Well, here's the other, then,
an' bad news it is." He shoved huge hands deep into his
pockets—among the folk he sprang from, it was a gesture of
helplessness—wincing as if he felt pain for the *Osprey*. "The
impact we took fairly destroyed the liftdeck altogether. We
had t'bring the lubberlift ye stole alongside t'disembark yer
boardin' party over the taffrail. I reckon the damage below
results from no fewer than three simultaneous thrusts. Had
t'be accidental; the enemy hadn't that many skilled projecteurs among his number."

Arran nodded agreement. "That was the impression I had. I assume you secured the lift at the boatdeck. Pray continue then, and get this wake over with."

"That weren't the worst of it, I fear me." The first officer cleared his throat as if he felt a need to apologize for what he had to say next. "As ye know, the foot of poor *Osprey*'s mast is stepped within the liftdeck. The truth is that, the mast bein' a hollow cylinder, three full measures across at the foot, it pretty much *is* the liftdeck. Given the damage I saw below, I'd guess that, were we taken aback, it'd push the mast straight out, through the bottom."

Feeling years older, himself, Arran rubbed his temples. He had reached the same conclusions as Phoebus—for who had trained him to begin with?—and, staying as tactically alert as he could (when the fireship burned itself out, the enemy might well return), he was formulating ideas for repairing the damage.

"That certainly is bad news. Why do I have a suspicion there is more to come?"

Phoebus answered him grimly. "Because, Captain, ye've seen everything I've seen. We are all lucky to be alive—if ye call this livin'. T'begin with, there's a long, hairline fracture in the mast itself, meanin' one I can stick me fist into, runnin' in a lazy spiral from the liftdeck to the maintier crotch."

"If I remember correctly," Arran remarked, "the expression is 'shiver me timbers.' "

Neither man laughed. "It'll keep travelin', higher an' higher, right up to the figurehead, do we take much strain upon it gettin' wherever we're goin' next."

"Plus the usual broken spars and rigging," Arran added to his officer's report. Suddenly aware of how long it had been since his last sleep, he arose stiffly, determined, whatever happened, to stay upon his feet as long as he possibly could. His first duty would be to order Phoebus below for food and rest.

"Aye, plus the usual spars and rigging," Phoebus repeated needlessly. Of a sudden, there was a crafty glint in his eye, and he spoke quickly. "I'll take the conn, now, sir. Ye're in need of sommat to eat and some sleep, I'll wager. Tell me where t'go an' I'll see that we get there, if in a gingerly fashion."

Arran laughed. So much for his own strength of character. "Very well, my old friend, you win. And I surrender. But, before you set any course, was I correct in assuming that we continue to carry our stolen lubberlift—which may well prove to be the silliest captured prize in the history of Deep-sailing—under our proverbial wing, with all of its lengthy cabelle tidily coiled up somewhere?"

"Aye, sir, that we do, at the level of the boatdeck, as ye guessed. An' failin' anything better t'do with it, I had the hands wind the cabelle—all thirty thousand klommes of it—about the lubberlift itself. There is a port in the top of the contrivance that, fitted with a flexible tube, still allows us access."

Arran nodded. "Very well. Then have them pay out our old cabelle, which cannot be in good shape after the pounding undergone by the liftdeck, and wind it, one turn laid neatly atop the previous, about the mast upon each of the decks above the damaged one, including the maindeck, and aloft to the maintier crotch."

"Aye, aye, sir." That had been Phoebus's plan, as well.

Arran arose stiffly, unaware that he had sat down in the first place. "I will be awake, well before you have finished, but in case I have misestimated, when the winding has come within half a measure of the uttermost extremity of the crack, have somebody cut a perfectly circular hole in the mast, finishing the crack off in order to prevent it from traveling further. Then finish the winding."

"Aye, sir, and then . . . ?"

"You ought to have our dorsal forespar fished; I believe we have spares, and as I say, no dearth of cabelle to do the winding. Then we will discuss what it is best to do next. Keep a sharp eye for the enemy and a crew at each projectible."

At present, beyond such repairs as he had ordered, he had not an inkling of where they should go or what they should do. All his charts were useless; *Osprey* had sailed beyond their lavishly embellished margins. In her present condition, their poor vessel could not even pursue the fleeing remnants of her vanquished foe (and a good thing it was they did not know this) to whatever port they called home. He was uncertain whether his broken ship could reach a planet of whatever star was nearest. All they had to steer by were time- and pain-blurred memories of an aged madwoman who happened to be his mother-in-law.

While Phoebus hurried off to do his bidding, Arran had a word with those among his officers who fancied themselves navigators. Some, for lack of any better employment, had already been making stellar observations. The nearest system was that toward which they had been headed before the fight, the same to which his enemy had just escaped. He was interested to learn that it was composed entirely of asteroids—averaging less than a thousand klommes in diameter—and there was not a single major planet within reach of *Osprey*'s instruments.

Such a phenomenon was not altogether unique within the Deep as Arran knew it, but it was far from commonplace. The system was unusually large, as well, almost a light-year from one readily discernable edge to another. After only a moment's consideration, he decided, at least for now, to steer his injured vessel, once she had regained some strength, toward that portion of the system farthest from the enemy's apparent objective. She would hide there, among the rocks.

As soon as a course was laid and appropriate orders given pending repairs to the mast, Arran, not willing to face the noise and confusion the news was bound to generate, sent Mr. Suprynowicz below to explain to the passengers how *Osprey* had managed to drive off her assailants and escape into a nearby star system with only minimal losses to her own side. However, as his trusty comm officer would be pointing out just about now, even minimal losses were still losses.

While the *Osprey* had managed to inflict rather an astonishing amount of damage upon her erstwhile foe (especially given the overwhelming odds against her surviving any exchange of discourtesies at all), they would all be greatly dismayed, below, to learn from Suprynowicz that the starship had been severely injured by the fight, and that the poor, battered vessel would now be forced to seek some sort of temporary shelter in order to render herself Deepworthy again.

There would be endless fuss originating principally with three among the passengers, former ambassador, former Ceo, former right-hand henchman, used to giving orders (and who might even prefer following them rather than having patiently to endure their consequences) until they had resigned themselves to the situation.

Even that, Arran knew, would not end it. There would follow debate, far in advance of necessity, with regard to what they should do after repairs were made to the *Osprey*. Should they return to Hanover? Or continue their ill-fated—and so far futile—expedition? There was no question in Henry Martyn's mind. He would brook no disagreement, nor hesitate to become the first captain to toss a former Ceo (to contemplate but one example) into the §-field.

Arran grinned to himself. *Osprey*'s liftdeck was destroyed and, with it, her facility for trash disposal. All that remained was the §-field. He had an idea how to occupy the energies of his otherwise worthless passengers in a more constructive—and instructive—manner than he had previously thought. Why throw the former Ceo into the §-field when you could enjoy the luxury of commanding him—and his overdressed colleagues—to throw the garbage out, instead?

Chuckling with satisfaction, Arran handed the conn over to a helmsman upon deck, thrust his hands into his pockets—among his people, an expression of lighthearted nonchalance—and, whistling a sprightly tune he'd learned upon Hanover, climbed down the narrow steps from gallant *Osprey*'s war-splintered quarterdeck to her cluttered maindeck, and, from there, stepped into his own quarters.

Chapter XXXIII:
A Neglected Spouse

Loreanna sighed.

How peculiar appearances can be, she thought to herself as she gazed out through the mullioned windows of the captain's quarters into the apparently bottomless—and to all appearances empty—Deep presently surrounding the *Osprey.*

She half knelt upon the upholstered lid of a window seat, heedless of the unsightly creases it was pressing into the fabric of her dress, attempting to avoid wishing consciously that her lost daughter were here beside her to talk to. She found that she missed Bretta—and she knew that the girl would have been gratified to learn it—quite as much as an adult companion, as a daughter.

Yesterday, from half a light-year away, this planetless asteroidal system—for so it had been described to her—to which their badly broken vessel had limped so painfully in order to lick her wounds, had appeared to be a very solid and substantial thing, a bright, sparkling, lenticular disk whirling in slow motion against the velvet blackness of eternity. Yet now that they had found their way into the heart of it, there seemed to be nothing left of it at all.

Loreanna was perfectly aware, of course, of all the scientific reasons for such an impression. It was all a matter of perspective. Viewed from half a light-year away, each of those millions of points of light blended into one vast, beautiful shape, brightest at its center like any solar system, divided by conflicting forces of gravity within it into colossal multicolored bands exactly like those that comprised the moonrings of her beloved homeworld, Skye.

Viewed from within itself, this system—millions of tumbling stones varying in physical magnitude from the minute to the gigantic, and averaging a thousand klommes' distance from one another—seemed not to exist at all. As the *Osprey* hung well inside the outer boundary of the system, Loreanna knew that did she but cross the diameter of the starship and gaze out through identical bevel-edged windows gracing the quarters occupied by Phoebus and his wives, she would discern a hazy band of light lying across the sky, but that it would bear next to no resemblance to the splendid disk she had seen the day before.

Upon the other hand, at least in terms of the instrumental limitations of the day, the basically unsurveyable distances involved, and the sheer number of objects that must be minutely scrutinized, the *Osprey* was as well hidden among the acrobatic boulders of this odd system as any wild Skyan tuskporker lurking in deep cover. Surely that was well worth giving up a splendid vista for. They could be hove to within only a few minutes' sailing of the enemy's greatest strength—instead of the entire diameter of this system, as they presently reckoned themselves to be—and neither see them nor be seen by them.

Nevertheless, it struck Loreanna as extraordinarily peculiar that they should consider themselves concealed, hanging nakedly out here in the Deep as they happened to be at the moment. At the least, she thought, they ought to have moored themselves to one of these floating monoliths—not one of which had she so far seen as anything more than another little star in an impossibly star-filled firmament— hauled in and huddled close beside it, if that proved necessary, pretending to be a part of it. Although she trusted the tactical judgment of her husband and his formidable and accomplished first mate, the entire matter flew straight into the face of common sense. But then, so did most of the facts of a presumably objective reality, in particular all those associated with traveling through the Deep, did one but examine them closely enough.

The odd thought suddenly struck her that they might not

be the only ones in hiding out here. It was quite impossible to tell, and no one would ever know: there might very well be millions of similar refugees similarly hove to within this system, concealing themselves among an equal number of its "flying mountains."

Loreanna had neither seen nor spoken with her husband—nor even with Phoebus, for that matter (there were moments when the expression "first mate" felt more than a bit ironic to her)—for more than a hundred hours. Since they had set course for this system, both men had labored ceaselessly—and as strenuously as the crews that they drove—first to hold the poor *Osprey* together, for she was a horribly wounded vessel, then to try and heal her many injuries.

Overhead, upon the surface of the quarterdeck that served these chambers for a roof, she could hear members of the battlewatch pacing back and forth. All the while their weary shipmates drudged and strained at spars, lines, and cabelles, these crewbeings, the worst hurt in the recent clash, were charged with keeping a wary eye out for more of the marauding slave-raiders. She had heard that Phoebus was keeping all projectiles fully manned belowdecks, as well.

All of this meant that for many of the noncombatants aboard the *Osprey,* an unusually hectic period had ensued. It made Loreanna very angry to be left out of things when she knew the ship so well and they were as shorthanded as this.

What injured and disturbed Loreanna most was that, upon many a previous adventure—that frightful business last year of the "quantum leapfrog," for example—she had been accepted as her husband's full partner, sharing all of the risks, bearing her fair share of the hardships. She could not imagine why Arran saw fit to limit her now, in such a manner, when he had never done so before.

For the sake of their survival, above everything else they must return the *Osprey* as rapidly as they could to her former fighting condition. Even some of the ship's passengers, supernumeraries whom Loreanna had long since grown accustomed to thinking of as completely useless, had been

recruited by her husband or his officers to assist in the struggle to repair the damaged vessel.

It turned out, for instance, that the former Ceo Leupould
himself had been considered a first-rate yachtsman in his
youth, racing small ships from point to arbitrary point within
the confines of the Hanoverian system against the grown-up
children of wealthier and more powerful families than he
had come from.

Even the foppish former ambassador, Frantisek Demondion-
Echeverria, had once commanded a small, armed, single-tiered
sloop-of-war, boasting of perhaps nine projectibles, helping
patrol the frigid outermost frontier of the Jendyne home system
he had later represented as an interstellar diplomat. Service of
this kind was required of anyone who sought higher office
within the Empery-Cirot.

Thus, with the dubious assistance of these oddly assorted
companions in misadventure, a greatly preoccupied Arran
and the indefatigable Phoebus had begun laboriously to set
their broken ship to rights. Just now, they were either aloft
somewhere, pretending to be regular crewbeings, or deep
within the hull of the hurt vessel, doing what they could
about her battle-smashed liftdeck.

Loreanna, meanwhile, had found herself left to herself for
too many long stretches of time. Although perfectly capable
within her own milieu, there was little here usefully to
occupy her hands or mind, and it was all that she could do
to keep from plummeting into a state of paralyzed mourning
over the most tragic loss any parent can suffer. Why was it
that men invariably—and so utterly selfishly—reserved all
of the most reliable distractions for themselves?

If poor Bretta had only lived, she and Loreanna might
well have put up a united front, demanding and receiving
their rightful portion of the vessel's duties. However, as it
was, ever since the girl's disappearance and presumed death
(*there must be something unlucky about the name Robret,*
Loreanna thought for a moment, then chided herself for having given rise to such a superstitious thought), she had experienced a considerable difficulty feeling any enthusiasm for

anything, let alone continuing the human female's endless struggle against irrational societal conventions that had occupied so much of her previous existence.

At the same time, it would have helped her to have a husband to cling to in this darkest of moments. The death of her beloved firstborn daughter had unhinged her as badly as could be—worse even than she had ever understood that a person can be unhinged—and the only time she had seen Arran lately was when he returned to their stateroom at odd intervals for a sketchy meal, usually too exhausted from his labors even to talk, let alone for anything else. Sometimes he even spent the night aloft, among the spars, cabelles, and starsails.

Loreanna glanced down at her figure, still clothed in the exaggeratedly lascivious fashions of the capital (although she had long since put away her ornamental fetters). For a woman of her stature, her legs were surprisingly long and well turned (as workingmen were wont to express it), and the fact was that childbearing and maturity had been exceptionally kind to her. Her behind remained small and attractive, her waist remarkably slender; her well-shaped breasts, raised and almost indecently exposed within the constrictive bodice of her Hanoverian dress, were rather fuller than when she and Arran had first met.

At a conscious level, Loreanna knew perfectly well that her husband loved her and found her even more desirable than when he had first made passionate love to her more than fifteen years ago. She also understood, with a crystalline clarity, that he was working himself and his crewbeings to death to save her life.

All that kept her moving presently—or alive, she was inclined to think from moment to moment—were thoughts and images of her surviving children at home and of her husband. And her husband was too busy at the moment even to acknowledge her existence. She knew it was childish of her—and it made her squirm with guilt—but it was how she felt. In the future, did they but prevail against the current circumstances, she would have this out with him and never again be left in unproductive solitude. For the moment, then, she would simply persevere. The very best of wives, Loreanna would let Arran do what he must, without yet another worry to distract him, and endure what she could not correct.

She heard the teakettle whistle forlornly at her from the next room, but did not hurry to answer its plaintive call. It would shut itself off before long, and she had had quite enough tea for lack of anything better to do with herself.

She thought that if she were to begin eating in the same way she had been drinking tea—as she had begun to feel a temptation to do—she would swell up until she looked like one of the Krumm women, or perhaps even her uncle's fat sisters. And then Arran would have the very best of excuses—her own visible lack of self-respect—to ignore her, possibly for the remainder of their lives.

Not that he would long lack company. She had seen the way women upon the capital world had given their sidelong glances to her romantic and dangerous husband.

At exactly that moment, there came a knocking upon the stateroom door—the door leading directly out onto the maindeck, a scene of so much purposeful activity that Loreanna, feeling useless herself, could not bear the sight of it. She arose from where she sat upon the window seat and went to answer the knocking.

Through the many-paned transparency, she saw her new half brother Woulf, appearing unusually neat and well scrubbed. Shipboard life with all of its attendant disciplines, Loreanna thought, seemed to be doing the boy a world of good. Not that he looked that much like a boy. He was, in fact, a man full-grown, not tall, but remarkably muscular, almost handsome after a somewhat sinister manner, well-spoken—although inclined not to speak at all, most of the time—and with a surprisingly winning smile, when he chose to display it.

He offered her a broad grin now, through the transparency, and, returning it merely by reflex, she showed him in. "I bid you good morrow, half sister," he said, doffing a broad-brimmed imaginary hat that she was certain boasted an enormous plume, and bowing in a manner intended to be comical. "Discovering no better employment elsewhere for myself—I have been ordered to remove my inconvenient presence from so many quarters of this vessel I have lost count of them—and not seeing you anywhere about, I thought I would look for you here."

"Well," she replied, closing the doors and ushering him inside, "here I am—having in essence been told the same thing, myself. Would you care for a nice cup of tea?" She felt strangely glad—and vaguely guilty—to see him.

"No, no thank you. I had been wondering, instead, whether you would care to take a turn about the ship with me—naysayers to the contrary—in order to observe how the repairs to her are proceeding. Understanding rather more about such Deep-faring technicalities than I do, I had hoped I might persuade you to explain to me some of what is being done. It all looks extremely interesting."

Loreanna's heart leapt. She had been cooped up within these chambers for far too long, basically ever since, she realized, they had departed from Skye. And their stay upon Hanover had been little less confining, although Bretta had seen parts of the city—upon the arm of this young man, come to think of it.

"I should be positively delighted, Brother dear," she replied. "Please wait for just a moment while I find a jacket and perhaps some more appropriate shoes."

Woulf nodded. Loreanna turned and stepped into a sleeping cabin she had not shared with her husband for days, looking for the short velvet jacket that matched the gown she had chosen this morning—it would be unseemly for the captain's lady to display her unprotected throat and all but naked breasts to the crew—and something without heels to catch between the spaces of the deckmesh.

Suddenly, a shadow passed through the room. She whirled, believing that someone stood within the doorway, but was mistaken. At the segmented windows, outside, upon the hull of the starship—apparently protected from the rig-

ors of the Deep by a temporary extension of the §-field—
Uncle Sedgeley, of all people, dangled upon a line, wielding
a container of the plastic coating used to preserve the metalloid mesh of which the vessel was fashioned, and clothed in
the attire of a common starsailor. The Executor-General to a
great Ceo and his successor swayed to and fro, happy as a
lad with a new toy. Having caught her attention and waved
at her, he grinned like a marine mammal and swung out of
sight again. Blast it—even Uncle Sedgeley had found some
useful task to do!

It was so unfair!

She smiled ruefully at the thought, realizing that she
sounded just like Bretta.

"Ready?" Loreanna jumped, nearly startled out of her
wits. The young urban barbarian who happened to be her
mother's son loitered just outside her bedroom door, leaning
casually against the frame upon one jauntily upraised elbow,
looking round at her private things as if he owned the place
and all within.

It occurred then to Loreanna that, despite any blood relationship the two of them shared, they bore not even the
slightest resemblance to one another. At twenty-nine, she
knew exactly how she looked, brown-haired, freckled across
her nose and cheeks, pretty (she was aware) and . . . well,
nothing if not absolutely wholesome.

By all means handsome enough in his own sinister way,
at the same time, somehow, Woulf seemed to be darkness
personified, with that distinctly olive cast to his skin that
sometimes caused people to think he had not bathed, and
deep-black hair that hung in languorous shiny curls all about
his well-shaped head.

Woulf's eyes were so dark that the irises could not be distinguished from the pupils. At all times they looked impossibly, almost inhumanly large. And the manner in which her
half brother chose to attire himself, all in a light-absorptive
black, served only to emphasize the apparent darkness of his
being. It seemed so much more than merely superficial. Perhaps it was some sort of protective coloring or threat-

display, needful for survival in the environment in which he had been born and come to manhood. Whatever it was, that light-devouring quality appeared to reach down, through his bones, into his very marrow.

Into his very soul.

"Er . . . yes," Loreanna answered a question she had almost forgotten for a moment, uneasy, all of a sudden, to have someone looking—looking into what? Looking into a personal and intimate portion of her private sleeping quarters. Greatly accustomed as she had become, from time to time, to living the cramped shipboard life, she had never resented it quite this way before. It occurred to her to wonder why the feeling pulsed so strongly within her. "I was just coming."

"So to speak," he added for her.

She flushed furiously—and was furious with herself for flushing—at Woulf's adolescent and overly suggestive play upon words. "So to speak," she answered, attempting to do it in a light, bantering tone. She pushed past him into the sitting room and immediately toward the door to the maindeck. "Shall we?"

"Indeed," he replied, maintaining the wry expression he had started with. Without warning, he reached up in a casual, and presumably brotherly manner to tuck a stray curl of her hair where it belonged. Loreanna reflexively shied backward at this unwonted familiarity, and what she saw then, upon his face—for no reason that she felt competent to fathom—was a look of triumph. "We shall."

From that day forward—and despite any misgivings she might have felt initially—Loreanna and Woulf went strolling about the ship every morning. Together they took the opportunity to inspect the *Osprey,* to see what the battle had done to her, and to learn what was being done to repair it. They saw the great spiral crack running about the mast from the maindeck to the maintier crotch and, they were told, right down to the almost obliterated liftdeck. Already, highly skilled workers had begun to refabricate the mast, which proved to be an extremely complicated process, and a dangerous one, at that.

It began with very powerful, foul-smelling, poisonous solvents—Phoebus forbade any spark or open flame aboard the starship while this procedure was being carried out—used to clean and strip the polymerized coating off the metalloid mesh a handspan either side of the crack. Next, powerful retractors were set into the fabric of the mast, spanning the damage, and cranked tightly to draw the broken mesh ends together, narrowing the crack. Artisans adept at welding metalloid materials then joined the ends of each and every individual element of the mesh, an energy-intensive undertaking that drew massive amounts of power from the starsails, set up to soak up particles from the surrounding Deep.

Phoebus had ordered the full suite of starsails set, and in such a manner that, in terms of imparting any motion to the *Osprey,* they worked at cross-purposes to one another, leaving the vessel motionless. Even the ship's nine great stunsails—ordinarily used, in the special circumstances that allowed it, to increase the ship's speed—had been unfurled upon their retractable booms to gather and transform the energy they provided purely as a secondary function.

At that point, the captain had been compelled, after all, to tether the *Osprey* to a nearby asteroid, so that her suite of sails could be adjusted to provide her with a degree of traction, in order to brace the mast as straight and tall as might be, before whatever flaws or crooks it had acquired were made a permanent part of its fabric by the welders. That part of the mending done, the affected area was covered once again—first the wirelike elements of the mesh, then the open spaces between the elements—with a protective polymer.

Similar techniques were employed to rebuild the shattered liftdeck. The *Osprey,* like any other well-run vessel, carried spares—various materials and fixtures—to be installed or adapted following virtually any disaster which did not destroy the starship altogether. The recent battle had nearly accomplished that. *Osprey* was like a water-borne conveyance suddenly bereft of her transom. Yet she, her officers, and her crewbeings had survived, where others had not, and now the *Osprey* would be reconstructed, if not altogether reborn.

The original .liftdeck of Arran's vessel-of-prey would have been a trifle too small to accommodate the larger lubberlift of the starship they had lately plundered and destroyed. As facilities to house the replacement were rebuilt, the *Osprey* took on a broader-beamed, narrow-waisted, somewhat "voluptuous" aspect (as Phoebus put it with a leer) that Arran said he found displeasing. Crewbeings trimmed and then extended the battle-destroyed sheaves of metalloid mesh that made up the liftdeck, just as they had healed the fracture in the mast.

Siemme by siemme, measure by measure, the smashed stern took shape again. Amenities would be sparser than before. For example, there was no method by which the complicated machinery of the waste-disposal system—which had been altogether lost through the breached hull—could be replaced. From now on, all garbage and other refuse would be dragged up to the quarterdeck—by none other than Leupould, Demondion-Echeverria and Sedgeley, who had been surprisingly helpful in other ways, as well—and put over the taffrail into the §-field, as it was done in earlier days of starsailing. No matter, the *Osprey* would make do, and, wherever necessary, do without, until she returned again to her homeport.

Slowly, a feeling of hope began to suffuse the vessel's officers and crew.

Careful to stay clear of the bustling workers and their often dangerous tools and materials, Woulf walked the *Osprey*'s less well occupied decks with Loreanna and spoke with her about nothing in particular for hours upon end. In the increasingly burdensome absence of her husband, she had at first found the daily attentions of this handsome young fellow somewhat consoling, and rather flattering.

And after all, she made excuses to herself, who could possibly be safer, with regard to one's reputation and self-respect, than a lady's younger half brother?

Step by step, however, day by day, Woulf grew more familiar in his manner with her. That business with her hair had only been a beginning to it. She was acutely aware of feeling increasingly uncomfortable with Woulf's boldness, but at the same time, she seemed strangely unable to do or say anything about it.

Exactly, she realized, as if the whole situation were occurring in a bad dream.

CHAPTER XXXIV:
THE LADDERWELL

She laughed.

For the first time in what seemed a very, very long while, Loreanna Islay laughed.

Woulf's jocular observation was certainly not the most outrageously witty remark that she had ever heard. He was most likely content to leave that sort of endeavor to their uncle. *Their* uncle! She realized it again: she had a *brother!* If someone had happened to ask her an hour later exactly what her half brother had said, she could probably have not remembered. All she knew was that she was in the company of someone she liked—at least she thought she did; he still made her nervous at times—and who liked her, and that she had someone to drink another cup of tea with, in an endless series of cups of tea.

They had just returned from another of their several explorations of the *Osprey* in the past few days, this time down to the boatdeck to inspect the vessel's steam launches. By an odd combination of circumstances, Loreanna had never ridden in one—most shiphandlers, her husband included, regarding them as prohibitively costly to operate without sound reason, and risky, as well—always having employed the lubberlift to travel from planet to ship and back again.

Somehow, somewhere, Woulf had apparently learned to pilot such auxiliary vessels as these, and, having reached the boatdeck by a little-used outboard ladderwell connecting the captain's quarters (and nobody else's) to the spaces below, they had sat together for some time, side by side upon the oddly tilted acceleration couches, as he explained the launch's control systems to her. Loreanna had found the whole lesson utterly fascinating—very different from sailing a starship—and she longed now for some practical experience in the Deep.

They had just returned to the staterooms she shared—*theoretically,* she thought with a moment's wash of resentment—with her husband, and having left Woulf in the sitting room in order to change out of the rough-and-ready clothes her daughter had left behind, into apparel that was less modest in its way, although considerably more formal, she was now preparing another cup of tea.

She leaned over awkwardly to pour tea in his cup, strangely concerned—she could not fathom why; he was her *brother* after all—not to display her breasts to him too frankly. Her back was to the doors and mullioned windows looking out upon the maindeck. Woulf sat facing those windows, politely (she thought) gazing past her to watch the crew at work healing their vessel's many wounds.

Of a sudden, he raised his eyebrows. "Beg pardon, Sister, but if I am to be expected to drink that, I shall be compelled to make, er, adjustments, if I may?"

She smiled back at him. "By all means do, Brother. You know the way by now." She poured tea for herself and sat, enjoying it after having been upon her feet most of the day and especially after their long climb up the outboard ladderway.

Woulf nodded, arose, and went quickly through the door

into the sleeping accommodations, which was necessary to reach the sanitary facilities which for some reason lost in the mist of antiquity were referred to aboard ship as "the conrad." Almost in the same instant, the outer door banged aside, and a grim-looking Arran stalked in from the maindeck. "A word with you, my dear, if I may?"

Perplexed at her husband's apparent anger, she blinked up at Arran. "Of course, my darling—with regard to what, if I may inquire?" She gestured to him, inviting him to sit beside her upon the settee, intending to offer him a cup of tea. However, equally without words, he curtly refused and remained standing.

"Some of the crew have told me that, despite my clearly expressed wishes to the contrary, they saw you below this morning, upon the boatdeck, with that Woulf."

Not particularly surprised, now, Loreanna forced herself to shrug. ".Yes, and . . . ?"

"Yes, and you are to immediately *cease* your purposeless meanderings all about this vessel, and in particular, in company with that half brother of yours. I do not care for him and trust him less. That to one side, Loreanna, *Osprey* is far too dangerous a place at present for mere idle recreation, and I—"

"You *what?*" Setting her cup upon the small table before her, she arose to face him, "Arran, I had meant this to wait upon a time of less difficulty than this, but since you have brought it up yourself, why do you wish me to be cooped up here, when I have helped you before with many a more dangerous task? What ever have I done to make you less confident in my abilities than you were before?"

Arran opened his mouth to speak, thought better of it, looked down at the decking, then looked at her again. "I will *not* lose you, Loreanna, the way I—"

She placed her fists upon her hips. "The way you what, Arran—the way you lost Bretta? We have no *idea* what happened to Bretta, more is the pity, let alone who may have been responsible for it. I will not *permit* you to assume the moral weight of the entire galaxy each time something happens that is beyond anyone else's control. It is . . . it is arrogant and presumptuous of you! And I will not permit you to treat me like a child, which is even more presumptuous!"

He narrowed his eyes. "What do you mean, 'assume the moral weight of the world'?"

Emphatically, she crossed her arms. "Arran Islay, you know *just* what I mean."

And indeed he did, surpassing well. Despite what he had always believed to be an overwhelming weight of evidence condemning him, Loreanna had always believed—without a shred of evidence of any kind at all—that he was not to blame for what had befallen the Jendyne cadets. Believing that most of the time Loreanna thought "like a man," Arran held this to be her single "womanly" lapse of logic. They had talked it all out many years before without reaching any particular accord, and this was the first time it had come back in a long while.

"Loreanna," he told her, "I am the *captain* of this vessel, and your husband—"

It was not quite a pout: "Yes, apparently in that order!"

He threw up his hands. "Now what in Ceo's name does *that* mean?"

"It means, Captain," Woulf replied for her, entering the room, "that Loreanna has been lacking those comforts only a man can provide—but for no longer."

"WHAT?"

Both Arran and Loreanna spoke at once, dumbfounded by what they heard and saw. Woulf, naked from the waist up and barefooted as well, had come into the sitting room still fastening his trousers. His long dark hair was rumpled and the glazed expression upon his face spoke of secrets between him and his half sister.

"Arran, I—" Loreanna began, feeling her life begin to slip out of her control.

"You filthy *rapespawn*—" In a perversely detached compartment of his mind, Arran realized that it was the first occasion he had ever said this to anyone he knew it to be literally true of. He raised one of his thrustibles and pointed it

at Woulf, as Woulf's right hand slithered down to the handle
of the scabbarded knife upon his belt. The scarlet blossom
of Arran's designator centered upon the younger man's
chest. There was a strange hunger in Woulf's eyes.

"Captain!" The door slammed open again as Tompkins
of the combat watch slammed to a halt. "We've got unpleasant company—a sixteen-gunner by the look of her, sniffing
about for a trace of us and big enough to finish us in our condition!" Arran glanced back at Woulf, then at Loreanna, as a
tortured look flitted across his features. Then he whirled and
followed Tompkins out of the door.

"Why—!" Loreanna barely had time to get the syllable
out. The last thing she recalled was Woulf's street-scarred
knuckles coming straight at her face.

"Your surmise is entirely correct, my dear half sister,"
Woulf informed Loreanna an indeterminate amount of time
later. With heroic effort, she swam upward into consciousness as if from the bottom of a murky body of water. The
fact was that she had said nothing at all to elicit Woulf's
mocking response. Between the agony in her jaw, the
appalling confusion of her slowly returning awareness, and
a moldy-smelling kefflar gag he had forced into her mouth
before beginning to tie her to the copilot's chair, she was
unable to speak.

She had a distant memory, almost as if in a dream she had
had a year ago, of his having half carried and half walked
her down the outboard ladderwell from her quarters to the
boatdeck— although she could remember little else. Certainly she did not recall his lifting her into this launch.
Before she knew it, he had twisted her arms painfully behind
the back of the seat and tied her wrists together so tightly she
felt her fingers begin to go numb almost at once.

Since *Osprey*'s auxiliaries were racked upon their stern
reaction tubes, Loreanna found herself, in effect, lying
upon her back, with her legs up in the air, and would
remain so until she was taken from the boat, or the vessel,
she was being tied into was cast off from its moorings and

launched into the Deep. It had been interesting earlier this morning. Now it felt to her as if she were being stood upon end inside an oddly appointed coffin, but a coffin nonetheless.

"My assumption is that you surmised that I spotted your overly zealous husband barreling across the maindeck with blood in his eye—dear me, what an appropriately mixed metaphor: 'barrels of blood.' I guessed what it was all about—wholly correctly, as it happened—and decided to take whatever advantage I might of the tactics of the moment. And if I do say so myself, as I shouldn't, I've always been rather adept at that sort of spur-of-the-moment improvisation."

Loreanna said nothing because she could not. She had noticed that his accent and demeanor had begun to change. Now, more than anyone, he sounded like Lia's foppish messenger. *"Buckets of blood," indeed!* If only she had listened to her own misgivings about him. How could Arran ever forgive her—how could she forgive herself—for falling into the hands of a lunatic like this?

Having apparently made himself satisfied with her bonds, Woulf swung up and safety-strapped himself into the left-hand command seat. He then began working his way through the boat's lengthy preflight checklist. They were in the same steam launch they had examined earlier this morning—she recognized a desiccated insectoid lying, with its legs straight up, against an upraised edge of the control panel. Woulf was preparing to make his escape into the Deep.

She was being kidnapped! The image of Lia came into her mind again, along with thoughts of her captivity upon Skye during the Black Usurpation, and what the former Islay tutor had endured at the hands of Arran's corrupted brother, Donol. She promised herself now that her revenge upon Woulf would be no less savage.

"The truly humorous part is that our mighty captain is going to lose you, my dear, because just now he's busy preparing himself and his crew for fight or flight with regard to a vessel that hasn't the least intention of bothering with him."

Woulf held up a small black object in one hand. "A communicator. Just one of the many benefits of stealing one's science and technology from ten thousand cultures. That ship out there has come at my command, simply to take me home, Loreanna! And unless your husband is more sanguine in his jealousy than I guess him to be, your presence beside me (although it should also have later, more pleasurable consequences) will assure that for a critical moment he won't blast us into particles as we take our leave of his regrettably bedraggled ship. Of course, I could be wrong. Is he a jealous enough fellow to kill you, too?"

At this point, Loreanna did not care, one way or the other. She gave her captor a sideways glance—all she could manage—that would have killed him had she been able. She would still kill him, when the opportunity arose—or, Ceo help her, make the opportunity, herself, if that seemed to be the only way.

Bad enough that he was doing this to her, whatever *this* turned out to be, but to leave Arran with an idea they had been . . . had been *with* each other as a final impression of a wife of fifteen loyal years was beyond her ability to bear it. She had no illusion that she was intended to survive this, but she was sickest at the thought of her husband believing she had let this dirty barbarian bed her, even sicker at the enormity of what he had managed to do in a single consummately evil stroke, to her, to her husband, and by extension, to her five surviving children, who would grow up believing she had betrayed them.

"I suppose . . ." Reading the complex instructions, and flipping switches in response, he kept both eyes upon what he was doing, but continued speaking to his prisoner. "Before we go any further with what I hope and trust will be one of my longer, more interesting, and more *intense* relationships (I should be able to make you last as long as a week, if I restrain myself sufficiently), I ought to let you know—for the sake of honesty if for nothing else—that you aren't my sister, Loreanna dear. Although that would hardly stop me from what I'm planning to do with you in any case. I'm not your brother. And that drooling old ruin up there below the quarterdeck certainly is *not* my sainted mother."

She looked all of the obvious questions at him.

He shrugged. "As a matter of fact, I happen to be just about eight hundred and fifty years older than Jennivere is. I can explain all of that later, if you like, during—what is the quote, 'a pause in the day's recreation'? I don't think that's right. It will be such a pleasure to get a deep epidermal lavage and a decent haircut!"

He contemplated the luxury in silence for a moment.

"Although she's almost certainly *your* mother. I had her upon the list to be searched for, acquired, and reassembled, you see, more or less to order, naturally wishing every moment of the time that it was Lia Woodgate's old mum we'd finally stumbled across. Nobody has the faintest idea of *who* she is, were you aware of that? It made for a rather more oblique approach than I prefer."

Suddenly Loreanna knew, for no logical reason she would ever be able to put a finger on, if not what had become of her daughter, then at least who was responsible. The necessity of killing him increased geometrically in a mere heartbeat.

"Quite a kick in the old morale for poor dear Arran, don't you think, the appearance of impropriety that I so quickly and adroitly improvised for you and me, eh? And it almost became a plausible excuse to kill him, too, had my friends not arrived a trifle earlier than I anticipated and interfered with it."

She wished she could tell him that Arran would have killed him, instead. She had every confidence this was true, having seen him do it, at need, upon occasion.

"Oh, I realize that it's bad form to gloat," Woulf went on, "but I *beg* you to understand, my sweet, that the creatures I labor for, however long they and their predecessors have kept me alive to suit their own peculiar purposes, are scarcely any more human or competent than your poor gibbering old mother, and not good company at all, let me

assure you. If anything, they seem to be deteriorating. I
haven't had a decent companion for, oh, a *very* long time. I
desperately need somebody to talk to, and in your case,
there's so much to *tell . . .*"

He sighed. "Unfortunately, the first order of business is to
take you to meet them. I confess I'm not altogether certain
of why, although I know they would have preferred the new
Monopolitan Ceo. I'm told they have a unique use for you
that will not interfere with any pleasures I plan extracting
from you, myself."

Woulf flipped a colorfully striped arming cover and tog-
gled the switch. Beneath them—with respect to the present
orientation of the steam launch—a hatch hinged open. The
transparent-paned bow of the little auxiliary craft tipped outward until they could just see the §-field before them
sparkling faintly. He squeezed the grips of the steering yoke,
they were pressed back sharply in their seats, and then they
were out and through the field, headed around the asteroid
Arran had moored the *Osprey* to, and toward the awaiting
sixteen-gunner.

Woulf laughed and laughed, obscenely.

Loreanna would not cry. No matter what happened to her
now, she promised herself that she would not cry. No, not
until this rapespawn of a slaver was dead!

He stood upon the quarterdeck, at the newly repaired
taffrail, his mouth open.

No one could have been more amazed than Arran when
the sixteen-gunner—which he had assumed to be an Oplyte
Slaver scout or patrol vessel failed, either to attack the
Osprey where she lay hove to for repairs beside her asteroid,
or to sprint away as quickly as could be managed, in a panic-
inspired search for a more effective sister vessel. Those
seemed to him the only likely options; the thought that she
might belong to some third party, Arran dismissed almost
without thought. Timing alone—just sufficient for the warships that had escaped from him to reach some outpost—
was enough to convince him of her identity.

In her primest condition, Arran's heavily armed, heavily sparred corsair would have vastly overmatched the little single-tiered scout, either in combat or turn of speed. Yet it would be clear to any experienced starship handler—with decent eyes or effective instruments—within a hundred klommes of this place that the *Osprey* was damaged and virtually helpless, either to fight or run. That other captain out there, without a doubt upon strict and highly unwelcome orders of some kind, had been forced to miss an easy kill—and in ordinary circumstances, commendation and promotion—and was more than likely hopping mad.

And that is precisely *what the idiot deserves,* Arran thought to himself with a most self-satisfied expression upon his freebooter's face, for becoming a member of a military hierarchy—and a lower-echelon one at that—instead of simply remaining his own man. Nonetheless, it would be necessary, now that the enemy knew she was here, to move the *Osprey* just as quickly as could be contrived. If she could achieve any headway at all, one asteroid looking much like another, she could be a million klommes off and well hidden before anyone arrived.

Arran felt the adrenaline—not all of it generated at the giddy prospect of fighting another ship-to-ship battle—begin to ebb from his bloodstream. Dreading the unfinished personal business that awaited him in his own quarters below, he watched the colors that the other vessel created within the §-field. Gradually, they dwindled with the increasing distance she was almost casually putting between them. Perhaps he was giving the other side too much credit. Perhaps that other captain out there was simply another fool or a coward—like the astonishing eleven, altogether, whom he had been easily able to fight off earlier.

Without entirely being aware of it, Arran initiated the endless series of calculations he deemed necessary to move *Osprey* in her present disarray. He became aware, abruptly, that Phoebus was soliciting his attention from across the maindeck with a number of broad and ridiculous gestures. Whatever it was disturbing the giant, apparently it was something he felt that he could not yell. Arran nodded back at Phoebus, turned from the taffrail, and glancing round the quarterdeck one final time, stepped down onto the main-deck. The two men met beside the mast, the captain keeping an eye upon the §-field, puzzling out some minor peculiar-ity he thought that he had seen just before the vessel disap-peared.

"Meboy, there's somethin' that weird goin' on." As if to illustrate the point, Phoebus scratched his head. From ancient acquaintance, Arran knew that the man was seldom confused about anything, and even less inclined to admit it when he was. He forgot everything else he had been think-ing about and paid his first mate strict attention. "We seem t'be missin' one of our boatdeck launches."

Immediately, a sick thrill of almost mortal terror surged through Arran's body. Somehow he suddenly knew *exactly* what was going on. Without so much as a word to his first officer, he pelted across the maindeck toward his own quarters, followed closely by Phoebus, who was rather faster upon his feet than he appeared, only to find the suite of rooms he shared with Loreanna otherwise undisturbed, but devoid of occupants, and wide-open outboard ladder-well hatch leading below—including down to the boat-deck—where the nearest berth lay empty. The deck at the foot of the berthing rack was still warm and damp from steam.

By now, Phoebus had finally caught up with his captain and begun to ask him questions, all of which Arran ignored as he raced back up the ladderwell again to his quarters, where there remained not a trace of Loreanna to be discov-ered. He had broken out in a prickly sweat; the sensation he felt in his body, especially in his arms and legs, was akin to that of electric shock or a quickly acting poison. His entire universe seemed to be collapsing about him.

Or perhaps, he thought, it was exploding.

He whirled to face his now thoroughly confused first offi-cer. "Find me Woulf! Tear this ship apart, if you have to, but find me Woulf! I thought I saw some indication in the §-field that our visitor had retrieved something smaller than she was, but the signs were vague and fleeting. I assumed it was some pretty rock they had chanced to discover, or even one of their own steam launches. Now I wonder—and I shall continue to wonder until you *find me Woulf!*"

"And Loreanna?" Phoebus inquired. "Or oughtn't I even t'be askin' such a thing?" Arran looked down at his feet and slowly shook his head. This was the worst day of his life—including the day his father had been murdered—yet he would have given his whole life just to live it over again and make it right.

"If anyone is privileged thus, it is you. Because of Bretta, things have been ill between us. We quarreled. I nearly killed Woulf, and now I wish I had!" Arran cast an eye about the room until it lit upon the dull sheen of some object lying underneath the settee at its front edge. He stooped and scooped it up. Phoebus looked a question at him with his great bushy eyebrows, and almost stood upon tiptoe to see what he held in his hand, but Arran shook him off.

"I beg you, old friend, ask me no more. I require your report of the condition of the vessel, for we must not lose track of the ship that was just here!"

CHAPTER XXXV:
OVERMOMS IN CANDYLAND

He sat upon an outsized mushroom—a cheerful scarlet with huge yellow polka dots the size of his hand—and peeled back the Velcroed flap of the black ballistic nylon case he always carried among his effects. Carefully preserved with him every time he took what he thought of as "the Long Sleep," its collector's value as a nine-hundred-year-old antique must be something fabulous by now.

Unlike anybody else he had ever known, Woulf loved the noise that Velcro made.

Beside him flowed a meandering stream of some sweet, sticky, carbonated fluid he knew was fed by a bubbly spring somewhere upon the other side of the stadium-sized chamber. He had no idea what it was and—for obvious reasons—had never felt any urge to taste it. The original formula for this sort of beverage had been lost almost a millennium ago, and was precisely as dead as ancient Earth. He thought he might have recognized the smell even so, except that the air in here, as always, was laden with the harsh odor of disinfectant chemicals.

He shrugged.

Extracting a pair of brown, gritty-surfaced silica rods, each of them triangular in cross section with a groove down one face, he inserted them at the proper angle to each other in the black plastic base with which they had been provided all those centuries ago, and then added a slenderer section of brass, set in its own position, to protect his left hand from a slip of the blade.

He drew his big fighting knife from the scabbard upon his hip and admired it a moment, as he invariably did at times like this. Its blade was broad, perhaps five and a half siemmes at the widest (it had been manufactured to a different standard of measurement) and some twenty-three siemmes in length. When new, it had been a uniform matted dull gray, but ninety decades of contact with the sheath had polished its high spots, bestowing upon it the appearance of a beautiful patina.

All round the open clearing where Woulf sat and waited, stood a forest of orchard-sized trees. He knew that just beyond them the place was circled by a grim cadre of Oplytes at no greater than an arm's length from one another. They were one reason for the disinfectant. At close quarters like this they tended to reek, the older ones in particular, of two or three years' age, that had begun deteriorating. The peppermint trees that concealed them tastefully were remarkable, if only for the red-and-white stripes spiraling round their trunks, as well as for the brittle green leaves covered with fine sugary crystals, interspersed with clumps of soft, white, powder-covered marshmallow "fruit."

One of the obese, softball-sized mice that had developed in this place—"devolved" was a better word, he thought disgustedly—pushed itself past his feet, sliding upon a distended belly in lieu of front legs that had long since atrophied and vanished in this grotesquely overfed species. Woulf considered flipping his knife at the thing to kill it for practice, but relented. Blood being among the most corrosive of common substances, he was always careful to clean his knife and touch the edge up, whenever it had completed its gruesome work.

Today, the sharpening process served him only as a form of meditation, helping him to focus his thoughts and concentrate upon the next stage of his plans.

It might be vital: there was a feeling of change in the evil-smelling air down here, and given the way this mission had gone so far, nine hundred years of loyal and efficient service or not, he was one of the things most likely to be changed.

The knife, then. Its knurled cylindrical grip and minimal guard were of a piece with the razor-sharp swordlike blade, integral to it and of the same material, an alloy of steel which had once been thought of as technologically sophisticated, and was still superior to many another material put to the same purpose. The handle was hollow, capped with a fine-threaded O-ringed aluminum pommel piece, intended to contain a small assortment of survival items. Woulf had long since filled the cavity in with a small electric torch, bringing the balance point to the rear of the guard, making even the big blade quick and maneuverable in a fight, a feature that had saved his life upon more than one occasion.

Overhead, blind, genetically impoverished hummingbirds—the last in the universe since the destruction of their homeworld—plucked at cotton-candy clouds, spun freshly every day by spreighformers concealed within the arched ceiling.

Holding the blade straight and level, edge down, he drew

it past the left stone first, and then past the right, backward
toward himself and downward, as if removing the thinnest
possible layer from the surface of the stone, bending his
wrist at the final moment of each stroke so as to properly
sharpen the upwardly curved edge.

One and, two, and, three and . . .

He gave each side of the blade ten stroppings against the
corners of the stones, wiped the blade, then replaced the
brown rods with a pair of harder, smooth-surfaced white
ones. These he gave a full twenty strokes apiece, as lightly
as he could, and when he was finished, the wire edge of his
knife gleamed like a filament of fire in the subdued skylight
of the chamber of the *Uebermutti*.

As a fly buzzed past his face, he wondered, as he always
did, why there were no spiders in this place. As always, he
concluded that they had died of diabetes.

Woulf preferred this simple weapon above all others, for
it never ran out of energy or ammunition, it operated silently,
and it was virtually impossible for an unskilled enemy—that
amounted to practically everyone, these days—to seize and
turn against its owner. He had long since ceased to keep a
count—perhaps as long as five hundred years ago—how
many individuals he had killed with it.

He yawned. It was important to have something like privacy and quiet in which to consider the possibilities open to
him. The moments were rare, in this place, when he could
achieve that. He contemplated having callously used the
Islay girl. That had been rather enjoyable. Sex without violence, he had discovered early in life, was hardly sex at all.
And sex without *death* was scarcely worth the effort. Even
so, look at the disappointing way his moment with her
mother had turned out. These damned things never lasted
nearly long enough.

Or their artificiality palled. He had slept in stasis most of
the past nine hundred years. From time to time, whenever
there was a perceived need for his services, he would be
revived by his keepers and begin to live again. The tasks he
performed for them were hardly unique in a perpetually

bloodthirsty universe, but he strove to carry them out with what he pridefully trusted was a competence and determination absolutely unique in this slatternly, slovenly era.

For a time, as he regained his strength, received briefings upon whatever assignment he was to be given, made detailed plans of his own, and perfected his persona, he was free to do as he liked in his off hours. Luxurious rooms, the most sumptuous food, any kind or amount of companionship he desired—the Oplyte conversion process had no other use for female captives—was provided him. For a while afterward, as well, while he was debriefed for the archives and healed from whatever wounds he might have received, he lived in the same luxury.

And then to sleep again.

The next time he was awakened it might be a decade later, or a century. Usually it was more like the latter than the former, since he represented a precious and irreplaceable asset to those who naively believed they were his owners. And besides, they feared him, and dreaded the necessity of waking him up.

Of a sudden, figures could be seen moving along a winding garden pathway paved with high-temperature structural chocolate and bordered by half-buried disks of a brightly colored transparent sweet, standing upon their edges, with holes through their middles. Long ago, he had known the name of the substance represented—something about breaking them in the dark—but had forgotten it.

The ordeal was about to begin.

"How wonderfully appropriate it is, my dear. The Monopolity of Hanover, which gave you birth, happens to be the *first* civilization to be planted in this Cluster of stars, away from the home galaxy. And now—how perfectly delightful!—you have retraced our historic steps and reached the end of the Great Moonship's journey, to find the *last* human colony established in the Cluster!"

There were four of them, Loreanna observed, attempting to remain calm in spite of the circumstances she found herself in. Four unutterably repulsive creatures reclined in some variety of complicated mechanical lounge chairs, wheeled from one point to another wherever they wished by domesticated Oplyte slaves. They had been waiting for her in this bizarre place when she was led in.

Looking from right to left, she could not determine, at first, which of them was speaking, for none had moved her mouth—in fact, two of them had only tiny, puckered, vestigial orifices, surgically or genetically closed off. Now that she observed carefully, she could also see transparent tubes attached to mechanisms behind their chairs, leading beneath their draperies, where they were no doubt nourished automatically through insertions in their umbilical scars.

Thanks, she was willing to wager, to centuries of dependence upon this sort of technologized slavery, the monsters seated before her had degenerated physically, mentally, and no doubt morally, almost to the point that they were no longer human. She refused to speculate, even to herself, about what else went on beneath the draperies that covered their legs. Despite herself, there arose unbidden in her imagination, horrifying images of formless lower legs and shrunken feet, seamed together like the single lower extremity of a marine mammal.

Loreanna failed to suppress a shudder. Yet, despite the stultifyingly hideous sights that greeted her arrival here—and the countless humiliations already visited upon her before that—she could still thrust her chin up defiantly.

"The Monopolity did not give me birth," she insisted to them, "my mother did!"

A small amber light appeared at the base of the leftmost entity's throat. It had probably happened before but Loreanna had failed to notice it at first. The apparent leader simpered, "But have you never heard, that these things take a village?"

The light went out.

Probably the most horrible thing about the four was that they appeared to have no eyes. Like blind cave fish, Loreanna realized, they had somehow lost the ability to see. Instead, devices of some kind had been implanted in their shallow, vestigial eye sockets, with wires trailing into the hidden recesses of their chairs. Apparently they had busied themselves playing with the genes of others over the past ninety decades, but had been a trifle careless with their own.

Loreanna realized the irony of her position. As a prisoner, rather than an invader, she had reached the center of this malignant culture before her husband and his warship the *Osprey*. She was now at the necrotic heart of Oplyte Slaver civilization, facing its supremely depraved leaders in the kind of ultimate confrontation between good and evil that most cynics believe never really happen—although in many small ways, of course, they happen every day.

"I am Hillik," the leader informed her, her amber indicator lamp lighting again, "presently foremost of what we've come to call, over the centuries, the 'Overmoms.' "

Hillik was a female of broad face and forehead, wide cheekbones, sallow, oily features with just the faintest trace of an incipient mustache, and a single thick black eyebrow traversing the area over what should have been her eyes. Her bleached hair hung down to her shoulders in uneven, greasy-looking strings.

"Upon my right are my dear lifelong colleagues and associates Patteesh, Saraber, and Janareen. As you can see—she *can* see, can she not, Woulfie?—there is no one at my *left*, which is what we all wished to discuss with you."

Standing before them, stripped naked, and in the grip of restraints more onerous than any chains, Loreanna had no desire to discuss anything with these living horrors. All she wanted was to destroy them in some highly satisfying and extremely messy fashion. Perhaps wisely, she forebore to tell them, but stood before them in a silent dignity which had nothing to do with clothing.

Woulf had kept her tied up until he had reached the sixteen-gunner he had sent for. Then he had kept her drugged. She had wakened in an antechamber of this place where minions of Woulf's keepers had taken her clothing and pierced her body through several personal and tender places with enormous needles, both ends connected to cords they had handed to a little girl as leashes to restrain and guide her movements.

As Loreanna stood now, helpless for the moment and rigid in her outrage, she could feel an occasional droplet of her own blood fall upon the tops of her feet.

The child—doubtless an otherwise useless leftover from a slave raid—could have been no more than days older than her own five-year-old Glynna. Her mouth had been crudely sewn shut with coarse black suture. (Loreanna wondered how she ate and drank—then decided not to ask.) She sat upon a brightly striped artificial toadstool, leaving Loreanna no choice but to stand beside her.

"You see, my dear, there are supposed to be five of us." Judging by the red light at the wrinkled base of her throat, it was Patteesh who had spoken, a hideous apparition with a sharp-pointed face like a rodent, long, protruding chisel-teeth to go with it, a permanent molelike squint, and a simpering leer Loreanna somehow realized was the result of spending her life being "cute," in order to conceal the underlying poisonous nature of her personality. "There have always been five, but Elnerose passed away last year, which left four of us. We sorely need a fifth Overmom, do you not see, and we have chosen you for the honor."

Loreanna threw her head back, laughed aloud, and then ordered them to do something with themselves that she had never even *thought* before, let alone uttered. She suddenly understood, despite her dire circumstances, how a life of adventure (if that was what she was living, now) tended to enrich one's vocabulary.

"Well, I am greatly afraid it is much too late for that," Saraber replied evenly, and, looking at her skeletally gaunt, hatchetlike profile, dominated by a permanently power-drunk grimace, Loreanna believed her. "Nor have you a choice in the matter, my dear. In fact, however inadvertently, you are the reason we have distracted ourselves from our Thousand Years' War against the Coordinated Arm. So in that sense, if no other, you are one of us, already taking your own part in our decisions, and the rest will be the merest of formalities."

The remainder of the Overmoms, Hillik, Patteesh, and Janareen—a thick-featured ox of a woman with a keglike head topped in dirty thatching, who blinked stupidly and swiveled her head as if two steps behind everybody else—nodded agreement. Somehow the sight was so disgusting, altogether in its repulsive enormity, that Loreanna's knees grew shaky and she was nearly ill upon the spot.

" 'Formalities'?" she replied, striving to regain her aplomb. "What you mean is, doing to me whatever you have done to yourselves! I do not know what it is—I do not *care* to know—but it is almost as terrible as what you have always done to your victims." Mercilessly, she added, "In my girlhood science studies I have seen species of slave-keeping ants in exactly the same fix!"

It was Hillik who answered her. "What you may perceive, my dear, in your temporarily unenlightened state, as our various deformities, represent nothing more than a motherly sacrifice, made, in part, as a symbol of our renunciation of the physical world and its many temptations to selfishness. We have made our sacrifice purely for the sake of others, whose lives we have immeasurably improved simply by giving them a purpose. To refer to the beneficiaries of our sacrifice as 'victims' is therefore unsophisticated, unappreciative, and impolite."

The creature lifted a feeble hand to the wires extending from her face. Even her fingers were short, useless stubs. "These *bobshaws* we have adopted enable us to see whatever is actually seen by certain of our servants. They are, upon that account, greatly superior—both pragmatically and in a higher moral sense—to your merely organic eyes, which offer to you only your own, self-centered point of view. Two of our number are similarly and unselfishly equipped for hearing only what is heard and feeling only what is felt by others."

"As we communicate through our *vulnavias.*" It was

Janareen who had finally spoken, in a voice Loreanna could not help thinking of as hulking and brutish.

Loreanna looked at the wires plugged into the sides of their wattled necks. "Tell me, do you disgusting slavemongers no longer even *breathe* for yourselves?"

"I'll have you *burned* for that!" The hideous female whitened, and her atrophied arms began to jitter with rage. "I'll have you gassed, thrusted, and then *burned!*"

"Ah, Janareen," sighed Hillik, "do not be angry with the girl. She fails to comprehend why we have selflessly given away so many of our own senses and other faculties, simply because she is not yet one of us. As you know, all of that is about to be changed." The leader abruptly redirected her attention to Loreanna. "It is simply so that we may see with the eyes of others, hear with the ears of others, and, well, 'walk a mile in their shoes,' as the old saying goes."

"These others," Pateesh went on, smiling so sweetly at Loreanna that she felt the urge to vomit once again, "we send out into the endless Deep in order to survey our vast interstellar empire—for everything we touch belongs to us—and to discover new worlds to conquer. Woulf, here, for example, never told you—because he never knew until this moment—that *he* is one of our observers."

"What?"

"Although we stay here, deep in our cavern, we see the universe *through* him."

Loreanna had tried to turn at the sound of his voice, but was forced to stop as the needles impaling her threatened to rip themselves from her flesh. She had not realized he was here. At Pateesh's humiliating revelation, he had leapt from the object he was sitting upon—another mushroom, it appeared to be—and now stood, knife in one hand, sharpener in the other, trembling with fury.

"He is our . . . instrument," Janareen began adding tentatively. "He is our—"

"He is our *dick,*" Saraber substituted a franker term. "When Woulf took your drugged and helpless body, we four took it with him. How very enjoyable it was, too. I am surprised you aren't aching and bruised all over. By our reckoning, this means you now *belong* to us." The creature's tone changed as she added, tauntingly, "Just as when he took your *daughter, we* took your daughter!"

"Regrettably," Hillik observed soulfully, "the vessel proved inadequate to what was required of it in the end. But you will come to understand all of these complicated matters much better, I assure you, dear." Her tone was one of exaggerated patience. "And we shall assist you to understand, by having you converted to one of our own number, through a process very similar to Oplyte conversion."

"What?" A horrible chill went through her body.

"Perhaps you have wondered, as many have, why no female Oplytes are ever produced," Saraber chuckled. "For a very simple reason, really. You see, the Aggregate requires only five Overmoms. Did your girlhood biological studies not also tell you about queen bees? What would we do with a billion or two more?"

Pateesh shook her head. "And yet our metaphorical blood grows thin, and we feel a need, for the first time in our long and glorious history, to bring outside knowledge and insights into our circle. We had wished to convert your Ceo Lia in this manner, but she proved too old, too stubborn, too set in her ways. The device we had implanted in her by an agent died, rather than altered her. In fact, we doubt the woman was ever even aware that the attempt was made."

"You, upon the other hand," observed Hillik, "are young, malleable, and *here,* where your conversion can be repeated until it is successful. As an historical and societal analyst, you will make a most welcome contribution. Too long have we been limited to just this single, miserable handful of stars. Now it is time to go back where we belong, to deal once and for all with the Coordinated Arm and extend the benefit of our tender, loving care to an entire galaxy."

That was twice these creatures had mentioned this Coordinated Arm thing. Perhaps they were enemies with whom Loreanna's side in this struggle could ally themselves. For the sake of this vital new information alone, she must escape.

"A place for everyone," Janareen piped up cheerily, "and everyone in his place!"

"Take her away, now, Natalie," Hillik ordered the girl holding Loreanna's leads. "We have plans to make before her conversion, which I will personally supervise."

Under the disminded gaze of an Oplyte warrior that went with them, she was led away. No sooner had she been removed, when Woulf spoke out in protest.

"You *lied* to her about my having taken her aboard that sixteen-gunner! At your specific instruction, I never touched her that way! But I was promised the use of her once she was here! And now you say you'll make her one of you?"

Hillik smiled sweetly. "Would that be so terrible, Woulfie? Never mind, dear, you needn't answer. We know what we look like. All excepting for poor Janareen, I suspect, who cherishes her illusions. I will simply warn you to regard Loreanna's loss as a punishment, for your cretinous fumbling with the daughter."

Woulf was stunned. He resheathed his knife and began disassembling his sharpener for storage. "You mean for letting her die? You wanted to convert *her?*"

"What an intriguing thought. What sort of Overmom would Henry Martyn's daughter have made? No, for letting her *live,* you fool, for letting her *live!*"

PART SIX:
HENRY MARTYN'S DAUGHTER
YEARDAY 131, 3027 A.D.
JULLE 50, 519 HANOVERIAN
DECIMUS 10, 1596 OLDSKYAN

A TRISKEL IN THE TOWER SO HIGH
UNTO THE BEAUTY DID SAY,
"NOW WHAT IS THE MATTER, MY PRETTY MISTRESS,
THAT YOU'RE TRAVELING BEFORE IT IS DAY?"

"NO TALES, NO TALES, LITTLE TRISKEL," SHE SAID,
"NO TALES, NO TALES," SAID SHE,
"YOUR CAGE WILL BE MADE OF GLITTERING GOLD,
AND YOUR PERCH OF IVORY."

"NO TALES, NO TALES," VOWED THE LITTLE TRISKEL,
"NO TALES, NO TALES," VOWED HE,
"MY CAGE WILL BE MADE OF GLITTERING GOLD,
AND BE HUNG ON A MARSHBERRY TREE."

Chapter XXXVI:
The *Lamina*

Out of the silent depths of the Abyss they came, the raiders the Alliance had been warned of, spreading terror, destruction, and death in their gory wake.

Their first hint was a change in the colors of the §-field that protected the asteroid's surface, retaining atmosphere, moisture, and warmth in order to grow the staple crops required by the Aggregate as a whole for food, fuel, and industrial applications. The contrasting blush they normally associated with a visit from one of the regular steam-propelled freight shuttles did not come according to schedule. And as it swelled, deepening in hue, his people became afraid.

Alliance Leader Shoomer Zero Nine had been apprehensive for many weeks, himself, fearful that his own time would come, as it had recently to so many others he knew, and that, like them, he would be utterly helpless to prevent it. Neither the Fifteenth Locality to which he was required to report daily, nor the Aggregate above it, would grant him any additional Oplyte troops with which to defend the asteroid he administered. All he could do in advance was order his Burrow Mayors to hurl the unarmed bodies of their underlings against the savage horde, as if drowning them in a torrent of blood were an effective tactic.

Now the dreaded day had arrived; people in the street below were already screaming. Through the window of his office, located considerably nearer the surface than he now felt prudent, he watched agape as the enemy vanguard broke through the useless §-field—why were they not killed by it?—and knew his doom. The marauders were exactly as the recent telebriefing had described: a young human female figure, astride a monster straight out of his most lavish nightmares, bearing a heavy and illegal assault force projector upon each arm, brandishing yet another weapon nobody recognized. Behind her rode a horde of similarly mounted individuals, each of them hideously alien, no two of them alike.

They all screamed insanely as they attacked, scattering his peasants this way and that in blind, incontinent panic. To add to their cacophony, they had brought with them horrifying sonic contrivances—consisting of an armful of tubes and a plaid cloth bag—which, judging from their output and the effect it had upon the fleeing populace, ought to have been classed as weaponry and outlawed.

Some of his own folk fought back, fearing worse punishment did they not. No fewer than a thousand of his farmers died in the first five minutes as they raised their tilling implements in a hopeless defense against the murderous onslaught. The dozen Oplytes assigned to him died, too, half of them without getting in a solitary thrust. Under the protection of their fellow pillagers, the intruders stripped his soldiers of their weapons before moving on, arming another dozen of themselves. Wherever his people surrendered and threw their empty hands into the air, they were spared and ignored. Wherever they offered the least resistance, the bandits reaped them like their own wheat at harvest time.

Alliance Leader Shoomer Zero Nine enjoyed thinking of himself as a smooth man, a sleek fellow, clean-shaven, impeccably groomed, with the short, glossy hair of a sea mammal. He felt his outward appearance to be a manifestation of his inner philosophy. As he watched the slaughter through his office window— fist-thick safety glass installed against the chance of a decompression due to §-field failure—he had the beginnings of an idea. He had already sent a distress call to the Locality. He also knew from the experience of others—his dead friend Bonyor Ten came to mind—that help invariably arrived too late.

He would venture outside—once the sound and fury had

abated a trifle—under a white flag of armistice, and treat with these savages, himself. He would promise them anything, until help arrived and they were wiped out to the last man and monster. The young girl he would claim for himself—willing or not, she would bear him many offspring, as no peasant female of the Aggregate had so far proven capable of doing—as a reward for his most conspicuous and exemplary courage. After all, he might easily have stayed here in his heavily fortified office until they found whatever they were looking for, took it, and departed.

Alliance Leader Shoomer Zero Nine had just turned to depress the one and only button upon his otherwise extremely tidy and uncluttered desk, summoning his body servant of the day for a change of habiliment that would be suitable to this very historic—and potentially career-advancing—occasion, when his office door suddenly exploded inward. He was thrown to the carpeted floor and showered with reams of paper from the ruptured filing cabinets beside the door.

Picking himself up from behind the desk, he spat blood from a deeply cut lip. It streamed off his chin, ruining his suit. Despite the ringing in his ears, he heard the clatter of one of his teeth hitting the floor, and cursed. Through flames and billowing smoke strode the very girl he had been thinking of.

"Who *are* you?" he demanded imperiously.

"Bretta Martyn," she replied, her tone disarmingly pleasant.

"What is the meaning—" he began, but was curtly interrupted.

"None but what we make ourselves," she answered, elevating her odd weapon and pointing it at him. In spite of the desperate pitched battle she had been fighting, she had long, clean legs, exposed by ravel-edged shorts of a coarse workman's fabric, and a slender waist. The vest, which was all she wore above it, seemed to be made of animal skin, molding itself to her ripened contours as she breathed. "It's too late for you, bureaucrat—try again in your next life!"

The last thing Alliance Leader Shoomer Zero Nine saw—without knowing what it was—was the stainless quarrel she released from her crossbow. It penetrated his left eye, then his brain, and pinned him to the wall behind his desk, where he danced for just a moment like a marionette, and then dangled, motionless.

Outside upon the surface once again, having withdrawn her shaft and wiped the blood off upon the dead administrator's fancy clothing, Bretta blew the nickel-plated whistle hanging upon a thong about her neck, three shorts and a long, indicating to Tarrant and his people—her people as well, now—that this location had been sufficiently "pacified" that they could pull back to a preselected spot for a breather before gathering up their booty and returning home. There was a most specific list of items they wanted that they knew were here. In most instances, thanks to the continuous monitoring of all Aggregate communications Bretta had initiated, they even knew in what shed or burrow to look.

Her sentries were already where they were supposed to be, here upon the asteroid, patrolling in the nearby Deep, alert for any contingency. But with a dozen raids like this under her belt now, she knew from experience—without succumbing to any deadly complacency—that reinforcements from the Locality could not arrive for a considerable interval, and when they did, they would take the form of a solitary sloop, hopelessly undergunned for what it faced in her. Not that she had any use for a ship, yet. That might come later, and it might not. But would her father not be surprised—and pleased beyond words, she thought—if she returned to him commanding a captured vessel of her very own?

As far as her victims were concerned, that was the trouble with being a part of a collective, was it not? It certainly put the lie to the concept of strength in numbers. Nobody in a hierarchy cared about individuals—leaders always reckoned there were plenty more of them to go around—nor even, it appeared after a dozen raids, about individual aster-oid cities such as this one.

"Well, there's the final specimen, Princess!" Tarrant tossed a military thrustible at Bretta's feet, where she squat-ted in the cool shade of a self-conscious replica of a peasant village fountain. "There's nobody left among our party siz-able enough to strap this fellow on without the usual 'smithing job.' " With his free hand he pointed toward the similar weapon attached to his own tiny forearm. Still clad in its official gray-green Oplyte coloration, it looked absurdly short, but it was no less deadly than those that had remained unaltered.

Not many measures away, her people, understandably eager to get away from this asteroid and unwilling—or too keyed up— to rest, began hauling their loot out of the build-ings and tunnels, to be packed carefully in the central square. The little man sat down beside her in the dust, cross-ing his spindly legs and squinting up at her. Flies buzzed about his face, and the sun was in his eyes. "You know, Princess, there are some even upon our own side as might say that you were a trifle harsh with the mayor, here, or whatever he was." He laid a hand over his left eye. "Whoo—gives me chills just thinking about it!"

"Alliance Leader, Hanebuth, as you know perfectly well. Pray do not try cajoling me, my friend. The truth is that we are at war. That slug in there was a working part of a 'civi-lization' that has captured and enslaved billions over the centuries, and murdered billions more. By his own choice—did you see his clothes?—he was a beneficiary of the system that raped me, beat me half to death, and left me for a corpse. See what he and his did to you and your friends! And yet I let him die quickly. Perhaps I should not have done."

Looking at the ground, Tarrant slowly shook his head and toyed idly with the spare thrustible. "So we're at war now, is it? I had believed we were preparing to escape. You can't kill them all, Princess darling, more's the pity."

"I can if that is what it takes." She grinned at him and hoped (in vain, as it happened) that it was not a pretty sight.

"I can do *anything,* I know now, if that is what it takes."
Bretta thought back to all the endless, often painful, always
uncomfortable weeks she had spent sweating helplessly in
her body cast, healing, remembering. And more weeks,
learning to walk all over again.

The asteroids that had provided Bretta with a badly
needed refuge at the same time concealed the ultimate
stronghold of the Aggregate—known to the Coordinated
Arm as the "Clusterian Powers"—the seat of all of their
obscene machinations, the very wellspring of the Oplyte
Slavers' ill-gotten wealth and power. More than once, Tarrant had observed to her that these were all data that the
beleaguered Anastasia Wheeler would have given almost
anything to possess.

Bretta wanted nothing more desperately than to get back
to her family, to her mother, her father, her sisters, and her
little brother. Yet to survive, perhaps even to pass on this
vital information someday, she would now have to stop
waiting (to any extent she ever had) for help to arrive (for
what if it never came?) and strike out upon her own, as inde-
pendently as ever her father had.

Naturally, above all she had wanted to revenge herself
upon the murderous and brutal Woulf. Her dreams, both day
and night, were brimming with fantasies of extravagant torture and bloodletting. Bretta had also dreamed of fighting
against the Oplyte Traders, raiding slaver outposts as the
self-styled "Bretta Martyn," astride her trusty vacuum-
breathing whatever-it-was, leading her band of fugitive
grotesques exactly like Earth's ancient, legendary Robin-
hood and Merriman.

She had realized—thanks to everything her parents had
ever taught her—that she needed a plan, a requirement it
took the bright, energetic young woman less than a day to
fulfill. She would begin with a detailed analysis of all that
she could learn about her enemies. But first, she soon discovered, she would have to deal with her newfound allies,
overcome their timidity and passivity (something her father
had warned her of almost from the time she was an infant),

and this, to her great frustration, took her rather longer than a day.

Bretta feared she had become infatuated with Captain Nathaniel Blackburn, or at least the hologram of him Tarrant had shown her. But as her health and strength continued to improve, the little man had gone on telling her of his adventures in the stellar vicinity of Lost Earth and of the civilization—and more importantly, the extraordinary people—that had arisen out of its ashes . . .

Understand me, now, Princess, that the nonauthoritarian remainder of our species were still nominally headquartered on the Moon. Dwarfing all previous human achievements in its audacity and sheer expenditure of will, Earth's once-barren and -worthless satellite had now been equipped with an atmosphere of its own.

It boasted of fantastically beautiful cities scattered and gleaming like bits of jewelry over the once-lifeless surface, comprised of surrealistically tall buildings made possible by the low lunar gravity. Between them stretched long, broad, graceful, elaborate multilevel roadways. Everywhere they had provided abundant water, lush open space, luxuriant vegetation. Brilliant snow capped the impossibly prodigious Mountains of the Moon. And the often-violent Lunar weather seemed anything but artificial to any newly fledged immigrants such as ourselves.

But the important news was that humanity were now more numerous than they had ever been before their ultimately devastating war. Also, they had spread themselves, and their civilization, throughout the entire arm of the galaxy of which poor murdered Earth and her now-vibrant satellite happened to be a part. Anywhere anyone cared to look, human beings had colonized wherever conditions were right for it. And—unstoppable in their courage and ambition—they had matter-of-factly "terraformed" wherever conditions were not so favorable. (Although I always thought, myself, that they should have called the process "mooniforming.")

Along their way, they discovered many planets that were already occupied. Unafraid to "interfere" wherever "interference" was called for, they had never failed to establish cordial—and very mutually profitable—relationships with non-human species. It was said they even found a way to stop a centuries-long and highly destructive atomic war between the starfishlike Ewon and the Ogat "umbrella people." These two alien people had waged seven previous such wars and were upon the brink of mutual extinction. I myself have seen the column, two klommes tall and four hundred years old, that supports the titanic statue of Rene Aurelius, who negotiated an end to the Eighth Ewonese-Ogatik War. Now they had become valued friends to humanity—and would, all too soon, become our allies.

For it was with other human beings that Lunar humanity were to experience their worst disasters. Over the span of nine hundred years, they had experienced, and grown accustomed to, some forty-five generations of peace. And now, the descendants of the authoritarian evictees were heard from again in the neighborhood of the ancient home planet at a time when the Moon people were all too vulnerable to them, and the offspring of the former outcasts began to wreak their long-sought revenge.

Luna's chickens had finally come home to roost. When we arrived there with Anastasia Wheeler, the Coordinated Arm's War with the Clusterian Powers had already been raging across the galaxy for much the better part of half a century.

" 'Tis called *'lamina,'* Miss." The deformed old man tugged at a forelock in a manner Bretta detested and her father had put an end to upon moonringed Skye. Over the centuries, Bretta knew already from her many long convalescent discussions with Tarrant and his friends, the fugitives had domesticated these creatures, training them to perform tasks such as salvaging potentially useful refuse—like herself—from passing spacecraft or those the Aggregate had destroyed.

"All of them," she asked him, "or just this individual?"

"All of 'em, Miss. They're all called *lamina,* 'animal' spelt backwise. Don't ask me why—I didn't think of it—we've called 'em that for a thousand years."

Bretta nodded, her fatigue suddenly washed away by her excitement. Here she was, at long last, just where she had wanted to be for what now felt like most of her life. She leaned heavily upon both of her canes, necessary even within this microgravitic environment, if only to keep her in one place when she desired, or help push her from one place to another when it was required. Tarrant had demanded that she remain in bed for another week, but Bretta would have none of it. In the end, he had thrown up his hands and given in to her. It had been the beginning—and they both realized it well—of a serious habit.

Kombi, the old *lamina* keeper and trainer she was speaking with was one of the oddest beings she had met so far in a remarkably odd population. To begin with, like many another here, he possessed more than two arms—that sort of experiment appeared to represent a kind of research priority to the Aggregate, although she had yet to see one of their standard Oplyte models equipped in such a fashion. This fellow had three, positioned radially about a collection of collarbones that must have looked like an extraordinarily complex child's hoop.

Where her friend Kanvor the cyclops seemed to have been deprived of half his bilateral symmetry, Kombi, here, seemed to have acquired an *extra* half. He had three eyes, spaced evenly about his head, no nose of any kind she could discern, and a mouth that wrapped hideously round the lower half of his face like a terrible red wound. Even the poor man's lower body had not been spared, for he had three legs with feet pointing away in all directions. Bretta would have been more shocked at his appearance had she not been born upon a world where all life-forms native to that planet were trilaterally symmetrical, like Kombi.

But even had she not been prepared for his appearance, all her attention would have been riveted, precisely as it was now, not upon him, but upon the remarkable creatures he loved and had been placed in charge of by his fellow refugees.

They stood together deep inside the largest cavern within the asteroid—almost perfectly spherical and perhaps a hundred measures in diameter—upon a jutting platform that resembled a railed diving board. Clustered about them were three of the animals in question, apparently hoping for an extra treat of some variety from their old keeper since, he explained, he had brought them a guest. It was almost impossible to tell, in the almost negligible gravity of the asteroid, whether the three creatures were hovering, somehow, or merely standing upon some portion—difficult to see owing to their bulk—of their underquarters.

"Hold breath, now, Miss, whilst I give 'em summat." With no more warning than that, he lifted what she had presumed to be a fire extinguisher from its bracket upon the rail and sprayed in their general direction. "Formaldehyde," Kombi told her, coughing a trifle from the fumes. "One of the chemicals they graze upon in the open Deep, but never purer or more concentrated than what I give 'em. Can't let 'em have too much—too rich, y'know. But they do love it!"

The creatures bobbed and jostled to get at the rapidly dispersing cloud of noxious vapors. Despite the overpowering odor, Bretta watched, perfectly entranced.

All three of the *lamina* were perhaps ten measures long and half as wide, a little like a teardrop in shape, with the larger end at the front. A rounded dorsal ridge a measure high and half as wide ran tapering from the very front of the creature to the very back, serving as eyes, ears, and nose. The underside of the *lamina,* Bretta would learn, was rather more concave than the upper side. Nowhere could she see anything like a corner or an edge to the animals, who were as smooth, both in their contours and their texture, as a well-washed river rock, or a half-used bar of soap. Even as early as that, Bretta found herself wondering why a creature that had evolved in the Deep needed to be so streamlined.

At the time, what struck her most profoundly were the

colors the *lamina* displayed—or *failed* to display might have been a choicer expression. It was difficult to say precisely what color they were. They were glossy, that much was definite. They were dark—a rich, depthy black or blue—the same as the Deep itself. And yet if one looked away for just an instant, from the corner of one's eye they also seemed to be transparent, as if made of living glass.

She had expected the *lamina* to be cold to the touch, wet and slimy. But they were just the same temperature as her fingers, outstretched at the urging of old Kombi, as dry beneath them as the curved transparency in the room she had been given, and as rigidly resilient as a child's balloon. Kombi flicked one of them in a friendly, familiar manner with the nail of his middle finger. The sound was that which had once been rendered, in a different century, as "blimp"!

"Are they hollow, then?" She did not think such a thing possible.

The old keeper shook his head, one of the eeriest sights Bretta had ever witnessed. "Not so you could tell, Miss. They appear t'be filled with what they're made of on the outside, the same stuff through and through. Mind you, I've never cut one up to look. I've found one of 'em dead now and again, is all."

By now, one of them began nuzzling her hand. She caressed the surface it presented, and it pushed even closer, until the platform creaked and it backed away. "They seem rather intelligent," Bretta observed. "Have you given them names?"

Old Kombi puffed up for a moment with a proprietary pride. "That I have, Miss, that I have, indeed. These three lovelies here are Wynken, Blynken, an' Nod!"

CHAPTER XXXVII:
SHAH NAMAH

"Do you have even the faintest idea, Princess," Tarrant demanded, knowing before he began that it was useless—and also several weeks too late—to argue with the girl, "how dangerous what you are proposing to do happens to be?"

They both stood upon the narrow, railed platform extending out into the center of the *lamina* cavern. A single animal stood near. Dressed from head to toe in sturdy leather, plastic, and kefflar—her knife was upon her hip; she would never again go anywhere without it—Bretta had just handed him her canes. She took the rail in her hands, lifted herself, swung her legs over, and stood upon tiptoe at the outermost edge of the platform, holding on to the rail.

"*Pur*posing, Hanebuth, not *pro*posing. It is what I intend, without asking anybody's permission first. Either I am the owner of my life, or I am not."

His answer consisted of no more than a shrug, for what else could he say, agreeing with her as he did? Nonetheless, he was sorely afraid for her safety and must convey that much to her, at the least. Nobody had ever done what she was about to attempt—nor even thought of it before. And the idea of living out the remainder of his life inside this hope-forsaken rock, deprived of the brightly colored magic she had already brought to it, was more than he liked contemplating.

"I have watched carefully over the past weeks as I was getting the legs under me again. The airlocks are a long series of twisted tunnels—volcanic bubble-chains, I would guess—with viewports set in the wall of each chamber against any chance of intruders. They are connected by gates the *lamina* can nudge aside." She held up a §-speculum, an old-fashioned §-field detector she had found rummaging about the storage caves. Resembling a hand mirror set with clear glass, it now hung from a lanyard attached to her belt. "They must do it a dozen times before they are out in the open Deep; as soon as they experience a noticeable drop in the air pressure or temperature, up come their §-fields."

He nodded, reluctantly. "I know, Princess, I have watched you watching. Still . . ."

She shook her head, "I understand." She squatted down to look upon him between the horizontal bars of the rail. Abruptly, she reached out with one hand as she held on to the rail by the other, seized him by one spindly arm, dragged him closer, and kissed him upon the cheek. "And I do love you for it, my dear friend. Please have something hot for me to drink when I return, will you?"

An astonished Tarrant had to clear his throat. "You may rely upon me, Princess."

"Have I always not, Hanebuth?" And with those five words, she sprang free of the platform, dropping three measures to the back of the *lamina* below her.

She gave out a *"Whoop!"* that was almost involuntary. This was not the first time she had sat astride one of the Deep-going creatures. She had been doing it—as well as studying them from a distance—for weeks, until she felt ready to take it a step further. From the first, Bretta had noticed that the *lamina* were extraordinarily streamlined, which had struck her as puzzling. According to Tarrant, in their own way they closely resembled a long-extinct ocean animal of ancient Earth called a *manta* ray. She had wondered: if the *lamina* had evolved, were born, dwelt, and bred, in hard vacuum—rather than in the water—then why should their shape confer any particular survival advantage?

"I shall be back within the hour!" Bretta shouted, waving at him as the *lamina* began to pivot in response to pressure from her knee. "Now, my sweet Rakush," she spoke to the creature, uncertain whether it could hear her, but aware that the words soothed her, if nobody else. Kombi had told her it was a reproductive male—there were male *lamina* that never bred, but associated themselves with a breeding pair and helped protect them—named for the war-steed of an ancient hero his mother had told him stories about. "Now we shall see!"

As Rakush surged forward beneath her, she felt an effect she had awaited, the texture of the *lamina*'s surface, where she touched it, altering radically, adhering to her skin as well as to the fabric of her clothing. It was neither painful nor uncomfortable, not even in the slightest. Nor was it the strongest of attachments—Bretta could pull away whenever she desired to—but it kept her seated securely atop the *lamina*'s great dorsal ridge, exactly as if she were one of the creature's offspring, clinging to its powerful, protective parent.

Momentarily, Bretta thought back over the past few, increasingly exciting weeks. As she had continued to heal, she had made a point of becoming friends with handlers like Kombi—only too eager to talk about their charges—and with the marvelous animals themselves. She had found that they could somehow envelope themselves in a low-intensity, natural §-field, somewhat akin to the electrical field surrounding eel- and fishlike species native to many worlds. Apparently it insulated them from cold, heat, airlessness, micrometeorites, and radiation. It was by this means as well— exactly like many another of those eel- and fishlike species—that *lamina* managed to navigate and propel themselves.

Bretta had ultimately deduced that the *lamina* were streamlined in order to minimize the volume of their §-fields and, therefore, the energy required to generate them. Despite this, having observed them using the dorsal ridges of their broad backs to hold and carry their young—who appeared to be unable to generate a §-field for themselves—she had come to believe that they could be trained to generate a §-field big enough to protect a human rider, as well.

At the same time, Bretta had also discovered that she pos-

sessed a natural aptitude for handling the wonderful creatures, herself. But now the real test had begun, as Rakush
nudged open the first airlock upon its way into the open
Deep.

By the time the ninth of a dozen airlocks had sprung
closed behind them, Bretta was bitterly cold, out of breath,
and mortally afraid. The *lamina* she had observed had varied, from one individual to another, and from one day to the
next, with regard to when they chose to raise their personal
§-fields upon leaving the asteroid. She had never seen one
wait this long (although she had also never been in one of
these bubble-tunnels before, at least as a conscious passenger) and she worried that there might be something wrong
with Rakush, or that her presence interfered with some
important step vital to the process in question.

Of a sudden, Bretta's heart froze as she watched an
impossibly huge drop of bright red blood splash upon her
hand, and then another, and another. Her nose had begun
bleeding from decompression, and for all the practicing she
had done, she had no idea how to get Rakush to go backward, or even whether he could. And there was no longer
room enough for him in the cave to turn around in.

Bretta began to feel dizzy, to see things with difficulty,
through a pink gauze, and to lose consciousness. While her
life failed to flash before her eyes, she discovered what she
regretted most was missing the opportunity to watch Woulf
die slowly and in pain. She would have enjoyed seeing her
mother and father, as well. And she would *never* meet the
handsome Captain Nathaniel Blackburn!

At once, she felt a kind of tingling wave pass through her
body, and she was warm again. She was also able to
breathe—she *had* ascertained that *lamina* required oxygen,
just as she did, and manufactured it in much the same way
that a sailing vessel did, from the Deep's endless supply of
elementary particles. Now she was experiencing the process
firsthand, and enjoying it thoroughly. Perhaps her distress
was what had triggered this response in the animal. She

hoped she would not have to get a nosebleed each time they took a ride.

She unstuck her right hand—no residue of any kind came away with it, that was not how the adhesion worked—and slapped the great beast upon the ridge before her as Kombi had taught her to do. "Good Rakush," she told it, "gentle Rakush. You had me badly frightened there for a moment, but I believe now that this will work. Onward to the next lock, then, and away into the Deep!"

Which was exactly where they rode.

The risk had been worth it just for the view, she decided. As Bretta and Rakush slipped through the final gate, she discovered that the transparency in the chamber she had been given was not nearly as transparent as everyone had believed. Out here, separated from them only by the subtlest of §-fields—and billions of kiloklommes—the stars were pinpoints of multicolored glory and the immediate celestial neighborhood she found herself in, a whirlpool of diamonds.

She urged the *lamina* round for a look at the asteroid that had been her home and refuge over the past weeks, although it felt like a lifetime. In a sense, Bretta had been reborn here, or at least resurrected from the dead. A trifle less than three klommes in diameter, from the outside it looked like a root vegetable native to Skye called *nadlyaque* and considered edible only by livestock. Bretta began searching for her domed bedroom window but was soon distracted.

The Vouhat-Letsomo System, she reminded herself, had nothing that could be called a planet. More than anything, it resembled the ringed world where she had been born and raised—"reared," her mother always insisted—albeit upon a vaster scale. Tarrant had said that it was as if the rings of Saturn had been enlarged to fill the empty reaches between the orbits of Mercury and Pluto. Having never heard of them before, Bretta needed to be told of their significance. These were other planets in the Earthian system—it had not occurred to her that there might be other planets—named after the gods of prehistory.

Before Bretta knew it, she and Rakush had completed their circuit of the planetoid. She had never found her bedroom window; she had been far too busy looking outward to where she meant to go, rather than inward to where she had already been. Now she guided the *lamina* away from the asteroid to get an idea of his best speed, urging him outward, faster and faster with both her knees. Before she curbed him, their home had dwindled in the distance until it was another dot, indistinguishable among a thousand others, and she was utterly lost.

Panic filled her again until she gained control of it. Never mind: old Palfrey, the gentle female who had found her in the waste canister had been farther from home than this— almost outside the system in the interstellar Deep—and she had experienced no difficulty finding her way home. Bretta would trust Rakush to know where his next formaldehyde was coming from. She would enjoy the ride, meantime, learn to communicate with him better, and think, something she had less and less time for in these increasingly busy days.

Bretta had been surprised to learn, from Tarrant and the others, that for trade, or even purely social purposes, travel within the Vouhat-Letsomo System between the "particles" of its "rings"—some of them the size of planetary nation-states—was achieved upon an everyday basis by her Oply-toid rescuers with a relative ease, usually in makeshift *lamina*-propelled containers she had realized at once would never withstand the rigors of a voyage into the great Deep.

It had never occurred to anyone, before Bretta, that *lamina* might also be ridden. Given the animals' widespread use, in this system, as retrievers of a sort as well as beasts of burden, she thought that it represented a peculiar cultural blindness. Perhaps, she had reasoned, it was because so many of the fugitives had made their initial escape from the Aggregate in small auxiliary spacecraft—the Deep-going equivalent of life rafts and rowboats—piled up endlessly for eventual destruction by their captors and more or less forgotten for prolonged periods until some bureaucrat remem-

bered them, and ordered the current accumulation destroyed. And at the same time, the refugees appeared to have
few Deep-suits among them—even Bretta had believed, initially, that such protection would be necessary if *lamina*
were to be used in the manner she contemplated—not many
Deep-going civilizations, her own included, finding a sufficient everyday necessity for the technology to justify such a
lavish expense.

In any event, there was little to give her new friends such
an idea, and much to discourage it, whereas she had grown
up haunted by the images of war-steeds.

It was hard to say, but she believed Rakush had come to
a halt, relative to the many objects tumbling through the
Deep about them. Peering through her §-speculum, she
watched the outer margin of his §-field—it was the first time
she had observed it from within—as he ingested an otherwise invisible cloud of vapor that local gravity had temporarily gathered together at this spot. Kombi had spoken
with her about this very thing. It was ill discipline to let him
graze at will like this. He—and all his fellow *lamina*—would
take advantage of a novice handler if they believed they
could get away with it. With her knees, she urged Rakush
back around in the direction she guessed (for it was only
that) that their home asteroid lay in, relying upon him—and
upon the healthy appetite he had just manifested—to perform the detailed navigation.

Bretta's basic plan—provided she survived this first
excursion—was to create a kind of Deep-going "light cav-
alry" to gather equipment and supplies necessary to cobble
thousands of derelict spacecraft the fugitives had stolen into
a gigantic sailing raft. Having assembled it, they would use
the *lamina* to tow it far beyond the limits of the Aggregate's
instrumentation. Then, in the comparative safety of the
Great Deep, they would raise its §-fields and unfurl its
sails—which were the real detection problem—and make
for the Monopolity.

By "gather equipment and supplies," Bretta meant to take
what she wanted by force from thousands of slaver outposts

scattered throughout this system, although before this, understandably, the escapees had tended to avoid them. When her hosts had objected to this aspect of her idea, she had conceded that it established a definite "window." The Aggregate would no longer leave them alone once they had begun to make a nuisance of themselves. But this was all the more reason, she had argued, to start implementing her plan as quickly as possible.

Bretta privately believed she could ultimately bring an end to the Oplyte Trade. She was certain the Ceo Lia would dispatch an overwhelming punitive fleet to the Vouhat-Letsomo System the very instant she learned what was going on here—*had* been going on the better part of a millennium—perhaps even enlisting the military assistance of the other imperia-conglomerate. Upon the clean face of the open Deep, the Aggregate would lose any military advantage heretofore afforded by their mindless warrior-slave hordes. The horror and misery that her new friends had endured would never happen again, to anybody else. That might be small comfort to them, but it was all she had to offer at present.

Privately again, she understood that this established a second window: how long before the weakest spirit among these pitiable creatures persuaded himself, for the "good" of his fellows, to betray her to the Oplyte Traders? One legend that had survived a millennium of isolation from human-kind's native planet was that of Joanov Ark, a famous martyr whom Bretta had no intention of emulating.

It was then that she discovered another, more fundamental objection among her friends, to which she had lacked as easy an answer as she had had to the first. Bretta had already grown accustomed to the grotesquely distorted folk around her. Some were tiny—Tarrant was one of these—although they all had normal-sized heads, hands, and feet. A few among them were giants, three measures tall or greater. Most possessed the gray-green skin tone of "normal" Oplytes, and a number had scales or armor-covered hides. There were specimens with too many arms or eyes like

Kombi, and even a genuine cyclops, her friend Kanvor. Given the rigors of a precarious existence which tended to weed the dullards out, their minds, however, were little affected by what they had suffered.

Yet most of them, she found—and was ashamed for having failed to think of it herself—had no desire whatever to return to families and friends who doubtless believed them long dead and would only be horrified at what they had become. In the end, all she could promise was that no one would be forced to leave.

Before she altogether realized it—this kind of downgathering certainly would never do in combat, she realized, although it tended to demonstrate the ease and safety of her personal choice of transportation—the asteroid where they both lived loomed large before her eyes and whatever it was that Rakush used for the same purpose. Bretta did see her bedroom window this time—was that somebody standing in it, watching for her?—before they "headed for the barn."

Entering the central cavern, the girl was shocked to see Tarrant, Kombi, Kanvor, the kindly one-eyed giant, Nibwelt, the albino stilt-man, the cheerful Hornyak, armored and powerful, Shong, with his extra pair of arms, Stengaard the limbless, with his long, flexible nose, and even sleepy Pwee Nguyen, the "idiot savant" who looked like a fowl's embryo, all waiting for her in an apparently frantic state upon a platform which, had this been the gravity of a normal planet, their weight would have long since caused to collapse beneath them.

Giving Rakush a final, loving slap upon his dorsal ridge, Bretta alighted upon the platform herself, as all of her friends moved back to make room for her.

"To what do I owe this signal honor, gentlebeings?" she asked.

"Where have you been?" Tarrant almost shrieked. "You've been gone three hours!"

Squatting beside the late Alliance Leader Shoomer Zero Nine's decorative fountain now, a dozen violent and profitable raids later, Bretta laughed out loud at the memory, earning her an odd look from Tarrant, who still sat beside her.

But it had not been humorous then. Not when she had felt she was about to die from cold or decompression. (Rakush and his stablemates had eventually learned to put their §-fields up a trifle sooner than they had been accustomed to doing.) Not when she had believed herself lost among the floating boulders of the Vouhat-Letsomo System. And certainly not to Tarrant and her other poor friends when she proved to have been missing three times as long as she had promised. She would discover that what she called "Deep-riding" always had that effect, and always to carry a time-piece so as not to lose count of the hours.

She sighed. Of such trivial bits and pieces was progress fashioned. She arose from where she squatted, despite her age, feeling a residual stiffness in her muscles from injuries still in the process of healing—exactly as she experienced pain, and would for years, where her bones had been broken, when the atmospheric humidity or pressure changed about her, which was often. She dusted off her hands, took up her crossbow and the thrustible that Tarrant had taken: spoils of war, not the first for Bretta Martyn, and certainly not the last.

"Let us saddle up, then, old friend; it is time to go home."

"Not a moment too soon. I fear me I am not a good thief, which is why I never went into politics. I have endured trips to the dentist that I enjoyed more than this." Tarrant blew a whistle of his own, then began a long and complicated series of hand gestures, issuing orders to their forces to finish packing and begin to withdraw. At last he nodded. "By your command, imperious Princess."

She made a rude noise at him, then whistled for Rakush to come fetch her.

CHAPTER XXXVIII:
THE SEVEN-GUNNER

"Mr. Krumm!"

"Aye aye, sir!" Upon the quarterdeck beside Arran, Phoebus, bringing himself to his full imposing height, snapped an uncharacteristic salute at his captain.

Hands together behind his back in a tradition as old as sailing itself, Arran gave his vessel a final glance. "Kindly pass the word to cast off all lines!"

"Aye aye, sir!" Phoebus passed it at the tops of his not inconsiderable lungs. In no lesser hurry to be away from here than he, crewbeings scrambled, fore and aft—meaning aloft and belowdecks—to obey the *Osprey*'s first officer.

Through a violent storm of conflicting emotions, Arran found that he had been looking forward to this happening for longer than he could remember. For him and for his crew, life over the past several weeks had become a matter of restoring the *Osprey* to Deepworthiness, so that he might pursue the course taken by the smaller vessel that appeared to have carried Loreanna away from him. It had demanded a will of cast titanium upon his part to remain in this place, to complete the repairs, and not to go triskelling off after the sixteen-gunner while trying to complete them upon the fly at the risk of encountering the sixteen-gunner's vastly larger and more numerous fleetmates in an unready condition.

He had vowed he would not leave this forsaken system alive without seeing Loreanna. There were those at home upon Skye, friends so close they might as well be family, who could see to the raising of their remaining five children. (Loreanna invariably insisted that he use the word "rear," which he had always found ridiculous.) To judge from results thus far, he was not doing that good a job of it, himself. To undertake that job without the children's mother was unthinkable to him. He only wished, at present, that it was *unfeelable,* as well. His feelings just now were blacker than the shadow this asteroid cast across his vessel, concealing her from the hostile eyes of the owners of this system.

"And now if it pleases you, Mr. Krumm, instruct our crew to set all plain sail."

"Aye aye, sir!" Slowly they started separating themselves from the rock to which they had been moored for what seemed a lifetime. His *Osprey,* Arran found himself reflecting, had come to this place a broken, crippled bird. She departed it as competent as she had ever been for travel— and for combat—upon the Deep. Quite the opposite of his family, which, momentarily, excepting the awful loss of his daughter, Bretta, had arrived quite intact and departed separately.

"Tr'gallants and stun'sails, as well, I think me, Mr. Krumm."

"Aye aye, an' gladly, sir!" One order he need not give was to being the projectibles. Upon what was likeliest his enemy's home ground (he had begun assuming that from the first, which he now realized was quite uncharacteristic of him), even the most extreme precautionary measures seemed called for. He, himself, wore both outsized thrustibles upon his arms—many of his crew had weapons, as well—and he carried a little something extra, tucked into his waistband.

A little something extra that also happened to be his single particle of hope. And, at that very moment, *Osprey* broke out of the cold, black shadow of the asteroid, into the brilliant sunlight—and the promise—of a better day.

"Our course is sunward, Phoebus," Arran informed him, suddenly relaxing and setting fingers upon the tiller ball, "sunward toward the center of this system!"

" 'Twould be me own choice as well," Phoebus answered, eyeing the artifact pushed into Arran's waistband. This was the first he seemed to have noticed it.

*   *   *

BOWMM!! Arran ran a hasty hand through his hair, then used it to wipe dirt out of his eyes. Every time he triggered that enormous projectile—a small ship's chaser, to be accurate—occupying most of the available volume inside the fusion-powered attack launch he piloted, that vauntedly recoilless weapon rattled dust out of every crevice of the vessel, sifting into his face, into the controls before him, or simply set it dancing in the air before his eyes.

BOWMM!! This time he watched huge fragments of the enemy's two-decker, a ship of perhaps sixteen projectibles' strength, breaking off, floating away from the spot he was thrusting at. There was satisfaction in that, he thought, and in watching her mast crumple and collapse under the combined onslaught of the eleven launches he commanded at the moment. Over Phoebus's strenuous objection, he had made a point of taking a regular turn at piloting one, as well. As a kind of flanking vanguard, he used them alternately as harriers in aid of *Osprey,* and as hunters in their own right—it was important constantly to change his tactics so as to prevent his being predictable to the enemy—toward whom the larger and more conspicuous *Osprey* drove her victims, as if into a waiting fishnet.

BOWMM!! Once again, he thought, and to an enemy's dismay, the infamous Henry Martyn—Arran often felt the need to disassociate himself, personally, from the legendary character he had become, if merely to maintain an accurate notion of his capabilities' limitations—had brought technological innovation to an area of endeavor in which it had been altogether absent for hundreds of years.

Like a ship's garbage canisters, steam launches employed minor, passive crystalline §-field generators that fed off of the mother vessel's §-fields as they passed through it—by a §-process analogous to electrical induction—simply to permit them to leave the ship intact. Now, driven by a need he had always felt, to provide more power for the projectiles he had ordered fitted into them, Arran had equipped them with larger, *active* generators, salvaged from those vessels he had lately destroyed, which had the happy side effect of

increasing speed and maneuverability—that latter, principally, by reducing gravitic stresses upon their pilots—while
minimizing the need for reaction mass.

BOWMM!! The boat in which Woulf and Loreanna had
left him had not been modified; a projectile's bulk would
have precluded its use by two passengers, and Arran had
only recently thought of equipping his auxiliaries with §-
field generators.

Because the launches had no sails, their onboard fusion
reactors supplied the particles required by the §-field generators, there being no way to employ the reactor's output
directly, since the operation of a §-field prohibited the flow
of currents within a conductile. It was this phenomenon, of
course, that made the working of any starship, even in the
thirty-first century, a labor-intensive undertaking. Arran's
innovation brought *Osprey*'s auxiliaries uncomfortably
close, it would eventually occur to him, to the *nacyl* technology he believed had killed those four hundred Jendyne
naval cadets whose faces haunted his dreams every night.
Just now, lacking the time, he could not permit himself to
think about that.

Arran felt a need to be cautious in another respect, however, although it was the caution of a man running downhill,
faster than he was actually capable of running, striving desperately just to keep his feet beneath him. Not only were he
and his gallant *Osprey* in-system now, where sheer distances
did not prohibit rapid electromagnetic distress calls, but for
some considerable time, he had nursed a sneaking suspicion
that the slavers—like the *nacyl*, and unlike the imperia-
conglomerate—possessed some method of faster-than-light
communication.

BOWMM!! The sanguine trade he plied as Henry Martyn
was only possible—had only been possible through the
whole history of his species—when the quickest means of
sending a message was to place it onboard the quickest ship.
Arran took elaborate pains to attack his victims only by surprise, to strike first at what he believed their greatest possibility of calling for help, and to leave nothing behind,

afterward, to give the enemy a clue about him or his companions.

Arran eased back on the throttle to avoid colliding with another of the launches. They were, all of them, in the process of buzzing about their enemy like stinging insects, making broad loops that allowed them to discharge their projectibles without doing damage to their fleetmates, and to recharge their weapons (it only took a moment, these days) while their fleetmates discharged theirs.

The pilot he had passed so closely grinned broadly at him and gave him a cheerful gesture, although Arran knew it for the cheer of comradeship-in-arms. He and his people took little delight in battles such as this. The ship they had run across today had merely made the mistake of standing between Arran and where he wanted to go. Although *Osprey* would make use of whatever remained of her victim. Arran waved back, then shook his head in something resembling disappointment.

These people he had been fighting were hopelessly easy to vanquish. They had not a starsailor among them, nor a projecteur. They possessed no tactics and less strategy. They were commanded by no officers worthy of the name. He had expected something better—by which, of course, he meant something worse—of the fabled slavers. These sorry creatures represented no more than the corrupted, necrotic heart of a great dying beast waiting to be put out of its misery by the first living, breathing, thinking adversary who happened along. That did not imply, of course, it did not *need* to be done or that he would balk at doing it. It only meant there was less satisfaction in it than he had anticipated.

It was his turn again, already. He pivoted his steam launch (they needed another name for these things, he thought, incongruously) into a steep, diving turn, blasted as close to the enemy as he dared—he could see officers upon her quarterdeck, cowering under broken spars and fallen sails, covering their heads—and unleashed the projectible which he steered by aiming his . . . his *fighter,* that was it! By steering his fighter at the base of the truncated mast. At this range the result was more than gratifying. The vessel lurched, its entire §-field collapsed, and hundreds of officers and crew-beings, many of them with their arms and legs still flailing wildly, came floating helplessly away from their ruined and dying ship, to die horribly themselves of explosive decompression.

Arran felt not the slightest qualm. These were his mortal enemies, taken where they dwelt, almost in their sleep. They would not merely have delighted in doing the same thing to him, but would have taken even greater pleasure doing it to his wife and children and forcing him to watch. He knew these creatures by their nature; he had *always* known them. These heartless animals had, in one manner or another, twice stolen away from him virtually everything he loved in life. Let them die, then, he resolved, let them die and everything they stood for die with them, just as slowly and as painfully as his dire need for haste permitted.

Out of the silent depths of the Abyss they had come, raiders the Alliance had *not* been warned of, this time, prepared to spread more terror, death, and destruction. From the first moment Arran's steam fighters had broken through this asteroid's not very protective §-field, something had appeared very, very disturbing.

Their first hint was the color of the plaza flagging outside the entrance into the administration burrow: a rusty maroon, the color of soaked-in, dried blood. Estimating from splashes of it here and there, no fewer than a hundred victims—at least a dozen of them Oplytes, from the aroma alone—had been killed in disorganized fighting, and recently, by all the signs Arran knew so well.

Squatting down by some decorative fountainry, out of the full heat of the sun, Arran shook his head in mild amazement and confusion. What in the Ceo's name was going on here? Here he had believed that *he* was the only murderous criminal at large in this system. This asteroid beneath his feet was nothing but one enormous, glorified farm. Who other than he—requiring food, water, and other supplies for his ship and crew—would wish to raid such a meager larder?

It was astonishing to someone with as much experience at this business as Arran had. People in the streets when they had arrived could not even bother to scream insanely or run about in blind, incontinent panic, leave alone hurl their unarmed bodies at their attackers as he had seen them do upon more than one occasion. Shorthanded as he was at the present—a starship captain was *always* shorthanded, and Arran more than most, ever since he had thought of confiscating the other fellow's steam launches, fitting them up as fighters, and letting them escort the *Osprey* wherever she went—he would have been utterly helpless to prevent it. They had simply sat wherever they happened to find themselves and watched with idiotic, gaping mouths as their enemy broke through.

At least, he thought, he was beginning to get his bearings. According to the enthilled records he had recovered from the last vessel he had taken—a freighter with a regrettably empty hold, bound in this direction to take on cargo—this was one of 2078 "wheat alliances" operated within a jumble of boulders between two Cassini divisions that called itself the Fifteenth Locality. The local authority here was an "Alliance Leader Shoomer Zero Nine" presiding over some unspecified number of Burrow Mayors. Phoebus was down looking for that worthy now, under whatever rock the poor fellow had likely chosen to conceal himself. For his part, Arran had always been more than happy to let somebody else deal with these politicians. As long as it happened to be somebody like Phoebus.

Think of the devil, here he came, a bundle of some variety under one arm, and somebody of some variety, under the other. Arran demanded no explanation of his sturdy first officer. He knew Phoebus would get round to it in his own time. Krumm dropped both burdens at his captain's feet. "Well, sir, I found yer Alliance Leader Shoomer Zero Nine for ye—this ain't himself, more's the pity—an' I believe yer goin' t'be a trifle disappointed at what he can tell ye."

The infamous Baker was cooking up a show. "And what is that, Phoebus?"

"Absolutely nothin', because he's dead as dead, an' maybe a mite deader'n that. Over in his office—y'see that there window? About twenty-four hours, I make it, more or less, thrust through the eye somethin' horrible-like, an' smellin' to the Core. Don't know what happened in there, but the people hereabouts are mortally afraid t'go in there an' get his body. The flies're somethin' awful, too."

"It sounds like something I would have done. Which eye was it, right or left?" Phoebus had something definite in mind, and Arran had decided to help him.

"Right eye, sir. Straight through whatever brains he owned an' into the stucco behind him. But there I go again, fergettin' the manners: this here's Praffinman Twenty-nine, Chairthingy of the Council of Burrow Mayors, somethin' like that. When Shoomer turned up so willfully dead, I brought ye Praffinman, instead!"

Burrow Mayor Praffinman Twenty-nine was one of the homeliest human beings Arran had ever seen, with greasy locks, a comical mustache, and a nose almost the size of Phoebus's fist, with nostrils they could have docked a steam launch in. Just now the fellow was upon his knees, fingers entwined together, hands uplifted. "Don't hurt me! Please don't kill me! I'm harmless! I can assist you! I'll give you *anything!* I'll *do* anything! We have no money! These others took our crops and our machinery! Do you like our females? Take them! Take them! I'll help you find where they hid all the pretty ones! I beg you! *Please!*"

"Do shut up." Arran took Loreanna's pistol out of his waistband and shot him in the knee with it. The Burrow Mayor screamed and pitched over backward as the echoes of the deafening pistol shot rang unfamiliar through the plaza's atmosphere.

"Quiet him down, Phoebus, and stop that bleeding. There are questions I want answered, or I'll ruin his other knee and go upward from there. Tell him, Phoebus."

The first officer whistled slowly and shook his head,

stooping over the wounded bureaucrat to help him. The game was over for Phoebus. He had never seen Arran do anything like this before, nor seen his captain altogether this thirsty for revenge. Upon the other hand, he had never seen Arran's daughter disappear or his wife abandon him for a younger man. Being Krumm, he said as much.

"You are courageous, old friend." Arran lowered the hammer of the little pistol before jamming it into his waistband. "And with a high regard for the truth."

Tending the sobbing man's knee, he nodded cautiously. "That I do, sir."

"Then be aware of this truth, old friend. Loreanna did not leave me for any younger man. Loreanna did not leave me at all, not of her own free will, nor, I wager, under her own power. I do not believe that now, and I *refused* to believe it, even *before* I had the evidence against it. The only revenge I hope for—and I do hope for it, Phoebus, with every fiber of my being—is against the bastard Woulf, only after I know my Loreanna is safe and sound, or dead."

He looked down at the mayor and laid his hand upon the grip-frame of the pistol. "As I told you that day," Arran went on, "we quarreled, something we almost never do. For some reason, Woulf concealed himself inside the conrad and attempted to give an appearance that they had been up to no good. But this is *Loreanna,* Phoebus. No one was ever better loved than her by me—unless it was me by her! Something evil has been done to her, and I mean to find out what!"

Now he drew the pistol out again. Hastily, Phoebus backed away from the mayor. "Look: this is her *waltherweapon.* If Loreanna had abandoned me of her own volition, she would have taken this with her or left it upon the table or bed with its extra magazine, because I gave it to her. Instead, I found it beneath the settee. This fell from her dress pocket during a struggle of some sort."

Phoebus broke into a grin and nodded. "I thought better of her meself, I did. We'll find her, me boy—an' right as rain. Now what would ye have of me?"

Arran pulled the hammer of the *waltherweapon* back.
"Hold this idiot so that I can shoot him in his other knee—
unless he begins telling me what I wish to know. Somebody
has been here before us, and I *will* discover who it was!"

CHAPTER XXXIX:
A TOUCH OF THE *ULSIC*

High upon an upper deck, they heard a bell.

Down here below, all they could hear was their own
breathing.

And all they could see was nothing at all.

In some civilizations it had been torturers and execution-
ers. In some it had been those who collected human wastes
for a living and disposed of them. In some it had been those
who prepared the dead for burial or cremation. In some it
had been businessmen. In every civilization it should have
been those who accumulated and wielded power—but that
had never happened, and likely never would. These were the
"untouchables," whose livelihood was perceived as so invid-
ious that it contaminated anybody who practiced it, unto the
seventh generation.

In this civilization—which had no science, and almost no
engineering, just technology "borrowed" from a thousand
other civilizations over the course of a thousand years—it
was the ignoble souls who struggled without thanks, simply
to maintain the physical structure upon which everybody
depended for survival.

Andboard Twenty-five and his lifemate Yiingboard
Twenty-five were a pair of lowly §-field mechanics who, for
all they knew about the subject, passed on to them by their
families or discovered secretly and illegally by themselves,
would have been wealthy and famous in the Monopolity—

although they had no means of knowing it—and respectable and prosperous, even in the Coordinated Arm.

At this particular moment, however, it appeared that they were expected to perform as plumbers, or perhaps as electricians. In any case, by official order emanating from the highest authority, they were being transported some five million klommes—manacled and blindfolded—in order to effect repairs upon the various life-support devices of no less a personage than one of the Overmoms.

The air was very stale in the cabin. Small, hard-bodied things with many legs scurried across its floor. From time to time, somebody came to give them water, stuff an emergency ration into their mouths, and leave them again. No thought whatever had been given to their sanitary requirements, and now they wondered whether they would even be given time, at the end of their journey, for the circulation in their hands to restore itself. If not, then they were doomed.

Andboard Twenty-five and Yiingboard Twenty-five were afraid. At the start, they had spoken with one another of their fears—and greatly magnified them in the process. Now they simply suffered together in silence. Their friends Charjack Forty-two and Lenjack Forty-two, the previous technicians assigned such a task—literally their predecessors—had returned to the mechanics' Alliance that they all called home, had regaled Andboard Twenty-five and Yiingboard Twenty-five with their adventure, and had promptly been arrested and hauled away, never to be seen again. At first, their successors had worried that it was merely because the two had spoken, and they, themselves, had feared being arrested.

Some little while later, Andboard Twenty-five and Yiingboard Twenty-five had heard, from illegal but reliable sources, that Overmom Elnerose—whose life-support contrivances Charjack Forty-six and Lenjack Forty-six had labored upon—had died, following their attempted repairs, at the age of 104. Now Andboard Twenty-five and Yiingboard Twenty-five wondered what sort of task, for what sort of "client" awaited them, and with what "reward" for their toils, afterward.

Something tiny, hanging from the bulkhead upon a silken thread, brushed the face of Yiingboard Twenty-five. She jumped, startling Andboard Twenty-five. Of a sudden, they felt the starship give a tremendous lurch, and heard an explosion, then shouting, then sounds of running feet, and thrustibles being used.

For an instant the ship skewed wildly, then settled, apparently taken aback.

The door to their cabin—scarcely more than a locker—burst open, showering them with splinters, and they were handled roughly, but only for a moment, as someone pulled them into the companionway where they lay upon the decking.

A young girl's voice said, "Yes, Hanebuth, these are indeed the ones we were told about. Get those things off them, please. I would have a word with them. After I find them someplace to wash up, I will meet you again upon the quarterdeck."

Arran leaned into the man's face and folded his hands together before his own.

"Now let us confirm that I have understood you, good Praffinman: a young human female, bearing some variety of silent, deadly, technologically advanced weapon nobody recognized, riding a nightmare monster straight into an active §-field, leading thousands of ugly aliens, similarly mounted and similarly armed."

"This is that what you claim raided your little world," Phoebus added, "killed your leader, and stole everything you had not the foresight to nail down?"

Praffinman nodded, very eager to, please, encouraged by his fear, by the medicine (a shroom tincture, harvested upon Skye) he had been given for the pain in his knee, as well as an understandable desire to keep his other knee intact. "Indeed, Captain Islay, you are entirely correct. Er, you, too, Mr. Krumm."

Not wishing to be delayed upon this asteroid any longer, and unwilling to give away the secret of his fighters just yet—even to an unperceptive moron such as this—Arran had called for the new lubberlift to be lowered from the *Osprey*. He, Phoebus, and their "guest" were presently using it to return to Arran's warship. It was an elaborate, old-fashioned model, once intended for the comfort of wealthy passengers, although the sparser level they occupied now had apparently been reserved for common starsailors. Through decoratively beveled panes, Arran watched the remainder of his forces withdraw from the asteroid.

Praffinman Twenty-nine, Chairperson of the Burrow Mayors' Council, bobbed his ugly head up and down enthusiastically. "I tell you, Captain, they were everywhere, slaughtering simple farmers whose only offense was to attempt to defend themselves with their tilling implements, stripping our Oplyte soldiers of their weapons with which to arm themselves illegally, taking whatever they desired without so much as a by-your-leave. The assistance Alliance Leader Shoomer Zero Nine begged for from the Fifteenth Locality has even *still* not arrived!"

Arran shook his head. There was a pattern, here.

"Is this here negligence a usual sort of occurrence?" Phoebus asked him, interested. He lounged back upon the same circular sailor's bench they all shared, filling the atmosphere within the lubberlift with smoke from a reeking pipe.

"No," the Burrow Mayor responded, "it was *not* usual."

This was far from the first intimation they had had that something out of the ordinary was happening in this system. Judging from the number of ships they had seen leaving it—Arran no longer believed it was coincidence *or* good management that he had run across eleven warships upon the straightest line from here to the imperia-conglomerate—how few they had encountered since, and various signs he had seen upon this asteroid and others, the entire civil structure of the civilization was in the process of being plundered by its own leaders to provide troops and other resources for some reason he could not yet fathom.

He was not altogether certain that he wanted to.

"Nothing in the past nine months has been usual!" Praffinman complained bitterly. "I don't know why the Fifteenth Locality or the Aggregate won't help us! There have been rumors about their needing troops and vessels for the war."

"Against the 'Coordinated Arm,' whatever it proves to be," Arran nodded. "We began hearing about that with the first place like yours that we raided, and I discover that I grow more curious about it with every day that passes. One always hopes that the enemy of one's enemy will prove to be one's friend. We shall return to that. But just now, tell me, what kinds of things did they take?"

"The bandits, you mean?" Praffinman blinked. "Food, weapons, anything at all technological. Anything to do with light structural materials or Deep-going life support. Above all, anything with a touch of the *ulsic* about it."

"A touch of the *ulsic,* you say?" He turned to Krumm. "A touch of the *ulsic.*"

Over the fifteen years that they had been together, Arran had been taught many useful things by Loreanna, a perceptive historian, anthropologist, and social observer who might have had a remarkable career in academia, had that been her desire.

One of those things was that the word *ulsic,* applied to such everyday artifacts as spreighformers, a flagon that kept drinks at whatever temperature they had been when poured in, rooms that turned lights out whenever everybody left them, had been an acronym, hundreds of years ago, for "ultra large-scale integrated circuitry." Those, in the human civilizations he knew, who could manipulate or repair such things were rare; those who could create them were almost nonexistent. In this day and age, the word might as well have been "magic."

How many mindlessly murderous looters, Arran pondered, would refuse the offer of women he was certain Praffinman's predecessor must have made with the same alacrity that Praffinman had himself—provided that whoever killed him had allowed him the time—while searching for the highest bits of technology available?

I might have, Arran thought to himself, *but who else?*

Just then, the new lubberlift arrived at the stern of the *Osprey* with a *bump!* and was immediately drawn into her new liftdeck. The clash of closing hatches afterward, and the accompanying hiss of freshly admitted atmosphere were welcome sounds to both the captain and his first officer. They and their good crewbeings had worked hard, and for a long time, just to be able to hear them now.

Mr. Tompkins, looking freshly scrubbed and fit after such a discouraging martial exercise, was waiting to speak with Arran as he stepped out of the lubberlift.

"Welcome back aboard, sir. Mr. Krumm. Compliments of Mr. Suprynowicz, as well, who would have you informed that several of the long-range scouts you dispatched when this objective was secured have returned earlier than awaited, with news of a heavily laden transport vessel *inbound,* for a change, half a day's sail from this place. We believe, Mr. Suprynowicz and I, that there's more than a chance that this ship may take us closer to enemy headquarters, sir."

Arran nodded. "Whatever else may be going on, the bosses still have to eat?"

"Something like that, sir." Mr. Tompkins gave his captain a young man's grin, incongruously through his snow-white beard, and his blue eyes twinkled merrily.

"I agree. Mr. Krumm and I shall be on deck directly. Meanwhile, if it pleases you, kindly take this gentlebeing and lock him up somewhere that the killer-moss will not get him immediately. Get him something to eat and ship's clothes to wear. Look to his wound. If he lives, we'll have him refinishing shipmesh."

"Aye aye, sir!" And Tompkins and Praffinman were gone.

He turned to his first officer. "Phoebus, I would have you gather up the rest of the auxiliaries, then bid the sailing master take our *Osprey* at her best speed *gently* to intercept that inbound transport! Emphasize, to all hands, that there will be no visible battle damage done, for I have a use for her!"

"Aye aye, sir!" And Phoebus disappeared, as well.

Arran, for his part, retired to his lonely quarters to clean Loreanna's pistol.

The slaver transport captain was in his cabin when Arran discovered him, weeping copiously into his beard. "I shall be held responsible," he sobbed, "even though it is not my fault! The regular patrol was suspended months ago! I had no escort! All of our military ships and our Oplyte soldiers with them, are being sent out of the system for some reason. And now, because there will be no one else to take the blame, I will be court-martialed and executed, and my male relatives converted into Oplytes, and all my female relatives sold into prostitution!"

The man poured a cup from an enormous bottle that was more than just half-empty.

Arran found that he was mortally exhausted from the effort of restraining his high-spirited crew and overtaking and seizing this vessel without damaging her. He had surrounded her with two dozen of his fighters, which pushed their §-field-protected bows through the transport's §-field, nudged them up against the enemy quarterdeck, then brought her to a standstill until *Osprey* came alongside.

He wondered whether he would feel like this if Loreanna were beside him now, or his Bretta were alive. He sat down at the table opposite the weeping captain and poured himself a glass of whatever the man was having. "Because you were helpless to keep this unarmed, underbeinged ship of yours from being boarded?"

The transport captain shook his head, looked up, smeared snot out of his whiskers, and grinned. "No, because I was helpless to keep it from happening *twice*. You've fallen into a trap, sir, and let me say that it is of some considerable comfort to look upon the face of an even greater idiot than I am!"

Phoebus chose that moment to stumble into the officer's quarters. As the door swung open, the *Osprey*'s first mate brought in with him the noise of a hand-to-hand battle raging out upon the maindeck, where Arran had believed he had just avoided a battle. Phoebus lifted his thrustible and discharged it at somebody outside. *"Missed 'im! They were waitin' fer us, sir, layin' low, like!"*

The collimated energy from an enemy thrustible sang in through the door, just missing Phoebus, and smashing a lamp swinging from the ceiling beside his head as the transport captain cackled insanely. The giant officer roared out a curse, returned thrust, thrust again, and brushed lamp fragments from his hair.

By now, Arran had leapt to his feet and almost into the outstretched arms of Mr. Suprynowicz, who had dashed straight through the cabin door behind Phoebus.

". . . and now they are boarding *us*, Captain, they are boarding *us,* I say!"

Arran opened his mouth to reply, as something that was not a thrustible beam zipped by within a siemme of his face to bury itself in the wall behind Phoebus.

"What in the Ceo's name is *this?*" From the wall, with a great effort, Phoebus drew the hollow stainless-steel trajectile that had suddenly seemed to sprout there. The thing boasted no fletching of any kind, simply being heavy in its front half and lightweight in its back. Heedless of the mad thrusting all about him, and the awful danger of this strange new weapon, Arran surged forward. "Let me see that, at once!" He peered at it closely, then looked up.

"We surrender! Pass the word—we surrender!"

Just then, a long-legged she-warrior strode into the cabin, making it a very crowded place, indeed. Setting both fists upon her kefflar-clad hips, and taking a deeply relieved breath beneath the suede vest which was the only other thing—besides the pair of outsize thrustibles—that she wore, she laughed.

"No need to surrender, Daddy. Upon being boarded by a ship of a superior weight of projectiles, we did not resist, but simply waited and exchanged boarders, gaining ourselves the better ship. Did you not teach me that trick, yourself?"

"My Little!"

With that—and utterly mindless of the clash of deadly thrustibles it engendered—Bretta collapsed sobbing, into the arms of her equally tearful father.

Chapter XL:
Bobshaws and Vulnavias

"Give me that, you cretin!"

Woulf seized the hypodermic syringe from the servitor nominally in charge of the process and laid it against Loreanna's lovely exposed throat. At the same time, blocking the servitor's view with his body—the only light in the electronically shielded volcanic bubble from which this neglected dungeon had been fashioned came from the electric torch the servitor brought with her—he whispered to Loreanna.

"Now this *will* hurt considerably. As you know, it's a big, fat needle. There's just no way to avoid it. But I fear that, due in general to a rapidly decaying civilization, and a more specific fact that they've recently sent so many precious resources and key personnel out-system (I confess it annoys me that I can't discover why and I'm supposed to be good at these things), our dear Overmoms are about to experience their twenty-third exasperating failure in a row, where your conversion is concerned. Loreanna isn't going to get to be an Overmom—in effect, a female Oplyte—this time either. Isn't it simply fortuitous that I'm expected to help out because they're so shorthanded just now?"

With that, Woulf plunged the needle into Loreanna's jugular, refrained from pushing its plunger, withdrew it instead, and injected its full contents, mostly a saline-

based nutrient solution containing a single nanotechnological device, deep into the upholstery of the wheelchair
into which she had been tied. There it would die within the
next few minutes, exactly like its twenty-two predecessors.

Through the painful ordeal, Loreanna had maintained an
absolute, stoic silence. From both his words and his tone of
voice, she believed he was going mad.

"I was promised I would have you, my dear," Woulf went
on as he wiped a drop of blood from her neck with a white
fiber ball—then, as a humorous afterthought, paid the same
medical courtesy to the chair. "And I *will* have you. People
always keep their promises to Woulf, whether they intend to
initially, or not. When our benefactors find I've sabotaged
their . . . their aspirations, no doubt they'll decide it's time
to dispense with my services—nine-hundred-year tenure or
not—and probably have me converted into an Oplyte into
the bargain. So, before they can do that, we must make good
our plans to escape!"

"*What* plans to escape?" she whispered, despising him
and hardly daring to hope. If they succeeded getting away
from here, what sort of life could she expect?

"Indeed, Woulf," Hillik's voice came from behind them.
"*What* plans to escape?"

" 'Ret'nal'—it is trying to say '*retinal.*' These voice syn-
thesizers sorely need work. For a moment, I feared it was
asking us to pull our pants down!"

Pulling an autothille from her pocket for the dozenth time
since they had landed upon this asteroid, Bretta referred to
notes she had made during long conversations with Andboard and Yiingboard Twenty-five, whose gray mechanics'
clothing they were wearing at the moment, whose places
they were taking, and who had tutored them in defeating the
aging security machinery deep within the lair of the supreme
leaders of the Oplyte Slavers, whom Bretta had learned to
call the Aggregate, and whom the two technicians' insisted
upon calling by the absurd name—the absurd name they

called themselves, apparently—the "Overmoms."

"Well, as Hanebuth would put it, 'we don' *need* no stinkin' eyeballs.' Authorized maintenance override Alpha Zero Zero One Seven Two Nine Six. Code authorization Hillik Four," Bretta told the machinery, compelled to repeat herself—her heart hammering—when it failed to understand her the first time.

"Small wonder," her father replied to her earlier remark. He was letting both his thrustibles' designator beams sweep the corridor behind them, while keeping an eye out for their own forces—starsailors from the *Osprey* and Tarrant's (more correctly, his daughter's) strange people—following at what he hoped was a discreet distance, along a chain of what amounted to broken locks.

Uncle Sedgeley had violently refused to be left behind. After all, he had argued, Loreanna was his niece by blood, and for all intents and purposes had always been his daughter. Arran believed that the old man wanted to wreak vengeance against those who had destroyed his brother Clive, as well, not to mention poor Jennivere, who seemed to be deteriorating rapidly since Woulf had abandoned her—and upon either of those two accounts, Arran would not deny him.

Demondion-Echeverria and Brother Leo had come along as well, the former having been a duelist within his own imperium-conglomerate, and the latter having demonstrated his proficiency with a thrustible—something Arran had been unaware of until lately—in the several ship-battles they had recently fought.

In theory, they were all waiting for Arran's signal that the last barrier had been breached, to rush in and take over the place—whatever it happened to be. The map they had, passed on by Andboard and Yiingboard's predecessors, simply said "audience hall" with an enigmatic marginal notation, "diabetics beware." In theory: from his many years of practical experience, Arran knew too well how theory was likely to fare where military matters happened to be involved.

"What was that, Daddy?" He wondered whether she realized how incongruous the title sounded now, coming from someone who had proven herself so well. But perhaps, given everything she had survived, perhaps it was more needful than ever.

"Sorry, My Little, I was not aware that I had spoken aloud. I had meant to say, small wonder that everything in here so badly wants repairing. I had only just realized that, although I do not know when we made the transition, precisely, I believe that we have now entered the nine-hundred-year-old hull of the old starship from Earth's moon, the vessel the authoritarians were all sent away in."

Bretta nodded. "Which means that they *constructed* this asteroid by hand, piling small rocks all around the outside of the ship. I had noticed a while back that the corridors had suddenly become straighter, and wondered about it. We are through, now—quiet as the door opens—on to our next objective!"

"Well," Hillik chirped, "here we all are, together once again." Like all those of their ilk, Loreanna observed—and there were plenty upon Hanover—the Overmoms seemed willing to settle for appearances when they were denied the substance.

Having made a dramatic flourish of arresting Woulf (even now an enormous, rank-smelling Oplyte held on to each of his arms, although she had noticed that nobody excepting she, herself, seemed aware of the great knife that he still carried upon his hip) and brought him and Loreanna to their repulsive audience chamber, they had left her tied up in the chair they had employed to wheel her in.

At that, even with the softdrink stream below and the cotton-candy clouds above—not to mention the evolutionarily overspecialized vermin—it was vastly better than the last time, with all of those humiliating needles in her flesh. Loreanna wondered whether she would ever know what that had been all about.

"As you have already been told," a contented Hillik continued, "it is our intention and fondest hope that, fully converted into one of us, you will take the place of our dear, departed Elnerose. And despite the evil self-serving work of this hormone-soaked male obstructionist, here, that is *precisely* what you will do. I promise that it's simply a matter of time—the merest formality—and meanwhile, we have decided that you should participate in all of our deliberations."

The rest of the Overmoms, simpering Patteesh, skeletal Saraber, oxlike Janareen, always a heartbeat or two behind, nodded in that hideous manner of theirs.

"The first thing we believe you should know," Saraber told her as they wheeled Loreanna into line to the right of Janareen, "is that six weeks ago we dispatched an armada of a billion Oplyte warriors halfway across the galaxy to the Coordinated Arm, to finish our Thousand Years' War in one final, decisive blow."

"You mean a million, surely," Loreanna replied, immediately regretting it.

"No," Patteesh corrected her, "our sister meant a billion— a *thousand* million. Breathtaking, isn't it? It will take them three years to get there, and the estimated attrition rate from the voyage is twenty-five to fifty percent, but they will do more than finish the war, they will finish off the Loonie civilization *forever!*"

Hillik smiled. Save for Patteesh, she was perhaps the only one among the Overmoms still physically capable of doing it, and to Loreanna, the result was overwhelmingly repellent. "Elnerose, whom you will replace, was the last of the previous generation of Overmoms. Like all of them, she opposed this brilliant and daring policy of ours, warning, in her exaggerating manner, that it would strip the Aggregate of its defenses, and possibly destroy it altogether. She was one-oh-four when she finally left us— personally, I thought she would *never* die."

I could say the same for you, thought Loreanna.

"The second thing that she ought to know," Saraber could not smile, but there was an evil gloating in her voice which was probably as close as she could get to it, "is that Woulf's silly notion of taking her away from us is futile."

"That's right," Janareen put in dully. "There will be no place left to go!"

Hillik nodded. "At the same time that we have struck such a telling blow to the congenital rebels of the Coordinated Arm, we have dispatched *another* billion Oplytes to your vaunted Monopolity, to stem the evil selfishness that is festering there. In fact, they should be arriving just about now. And, my dear Loreanna, *their* estimated attrition rate is slightly less than *one* percent."

"It's too late for anyone or anything to stop them!" Janareen crowed exultantly.

"Is there a need to remind you, Loreanna, what Oplytes *do* to a world?" Hillik was quivering at the prospect of so much bloodshed and destruction. "Systematically deprived of any rations they cannot provide for themselves, as spoils of war, our troops will rape, kill, and eat virtually any living thing in their path until, in ancient, classical terms, every structure will have been razed to the ground, so that not a single stone will be left standing on another."

"Even the soil," Saraber intoned, "will not support growth for a million years."

Patteesh apparently thought of herself as the practical one. "In a single ingenious stroke, we shall have ended our war with the Coordinated Arm, put an end to the growing nuisance of the Monopolity of Hanover, and made of it a shiningly intimidating example for the edification of all the other imperia-conglomerate."

Saraber concurred. "At last the full fury of our Thousand Years' War against vile, recalcitrant individualism is about to be felt as far away as Hanover!"

Loreanna found that she must fight, now, to keep all of this real in her mind. These creatures were delighted to send billions to slaughter other billions. They reveled in it, all in the name of some collective, altruistic good.

"But first things first is the order of the day," Hillik

reminded them sweetly. "There is the matter of our once-loyal servant Woulf. For my part, I think the sentence he anticipated we might decree against him is precisely the punishment to suit his crime—he expressed a fear that, even after nine hundred years of 'faithful' service, we would have him converted into an Oplyte—and I believe that, for once, I should like to see it carried out here. We'll put his cage right over there, next to the lemonade waterfall. Guards, send for a servitor!"

At that moment, the door burst open and the Oplyte who had turned to obey Hillik was torn to shreds by the collimated beams of four thrustibles. Arran and Bretta stepped into the room, followed by Tarrant and Brother Leo. Others of both groups, sailors and refugees, were all crowded into the doorway behind them.

Hillik's eyes widened as she watched a crimson designator beam splash her chest, rise quickly, then flash blindingly in her eyes. She could not scream. Before anyone could react, her head exploded from a single, well-delivered thrust. In an enormous, scarlet cloud, everything behind her in the room, mushrooms and outsized candy canes, suddenly dripped with blood and liquefied brains.

A dozen Oplytes raised their thrustibles in response, but were cut down in deadly cross-thrusting from half a hundred different sources. As the battle raged, for the few seconds it lasted, the Overmoms died, one by one, as Hillik had.

"That," asserted Leupould, "was for what they did to me fifteen years ago!" The former ruler looked about him, remembering. "I know this place! By all the Ceos who ever lived, I know this place! I do not know how they got me here—"

"You feckless moron!"

Leupould was interrupted by somebody laughing in a voice that bordered upon madness. Somehow, Woulf had discarded his pair of Oplytes—both of whom were now lying broken and dead upon the floor with all the rest—and stepped in front of Loreanna, perhaps to protect her from all the thrusting. However, he now stooped directly behind her, with his big black knife at her throat.

"What you experienced happened upon *Hanover*, not here, and was merely an hallucination, induced by the injection of a nanothille. Another one of my missions!"

At once, Woulf found that Bretta had materialized beside him, slapped the knife away from her mother's throat, and wrapped her hands about his upon the handle.

He swiveled to face her, and the weapon disappeared low, between their bodies.

"Don't be a complete jackass, girl," he warned her as they struggled over control of his knife. "I'll kill you again! I'm a well-trained, powerful man—you're not even a full-grown woman yet! I've got *twice* your upper body strength!"

"So you do," she agreed. With a knee, she rammed the pommel up, into his belly.

He collapsed upon the floor with an unbelieving look frozen in his eyes, eviscerated.

Chapter XLI:
Large, Irrevocable Steps

Before the day was over, Jennivere had died in her daughter's arms. It was Loreanna's decision to consign her body to the Deep, but not until the *Osprey* had sailed far from the Vouhat-Letsomo System where her life had been destroyed.

Loreanna wept but little, for her mother's life had brought her little but pain.

She and her family—her husband Arran, her daughter Bretta—had much to say to one another privately, and little privacy in which to do it, with a reunion of the original traveling company—less both Woulf and Jennivere—and the addition of new friends, Andboard, Yiingboard, Tarrant, and the others. She found that she was particularly fond of Kanvor, the kindly one-eyed giant. They had little time, as well, for the *Osprey* would soon race to Hanover to see if anything remained of it after the Oplytes were through and if Lia still lived.

Loreanna could watch Leupould trying very hard not to think about the alternatives.

"However," Arran was explaining for the benefit of Phoebus and his wives, "the Oplyte Slaver culture was vastly rottener and more fragile than any among us quite appreciated. Apparently it was upon the verge of collapsing when we arrived—a direct result, in itself, of their decadent bad judgment—and Bretta Martyn's depredations managed to disrupt it far worse than even she anticipated."

"I do thank you, Father," Bretta put a hand up, "but, as you say, it was their incredible stupidity of sending all of their effective forces out-system that was responsible for their destruction, certainly nothing I managed to accomplish."

" 'Father,' is it, now?" Arran asked her with raised eyebrows. "What of 'Daddy'?"

" 'Daddy,' then." She pretended to pout, looking up at him through her lashes.

"Compliant *and* modest," Phoebus observed suspiciously. "Are you sure that this is *your* daughter and none other who has returned to you from the dead?"

Bretta punched him in one massive arm, while Tillie and Tula clucked at him.

"Well," answered Tarrant, "she'll have something truly to be modest about if we manage to warn Anastasia in time. The Oplyte invaders will be thwarted in their desire to consume the Coordinated Arm like the dire-locusts they are, because it will take them three whole years to get there, whereas it will take Bretta and me only three weeks, once I build us a new starship out of what my colleagues and I can salvage—uninhibited by the Aggregate—in this cursed system."

"Make that, *we*, Hanebuth." Bretta leaned toward the little man, her eyes shining and full of ideas. "I do love sailing, but I want to learn new technology!"

"Nor are you the only one, medear, surprise you though it may." Phoebus nodded at Tarrant. "Then the armada can be destroyed, thanks to the Moon's superior ship-technology, in the interstellar Deep, far from the Coordinated Arm."

"I do not know about this, myself," Arran shook his head, "sending my own daughter Bretta off with a virtual stranger to treat with this Anastasia person—"

"My *sister*, I will remind you, the Galactic Coordinator!" Anastasia, and what she had made of herself, was becoming the brightest spot in Leupould's life.

"Your darling sister, Brother Leo—and warn her that a billion Oplytes happen to be on the way to visit her—when I have only just gotten Bretta back."

"I resent that, Autonomous Drector-Hereditary," Tarrant protested. "I am no mere virtual stranger; my strangeness is completely *real*, I assure you! And besides, all the girl really wants is to meet her heartthrob, Nate Blackburn."

"Hanebuth!"

Arran was the first to laugh, for the reservations he had expressed had been at least partly feigned. He loved his daughter and would miss her while she was gone, but he was proud of her, as well, and would be happy to welcome her back, a diplomat, as well as his political heir, better prepared for her future.

"And beside that," Loreanna spoke, blushing at her own forwardness, but eager to make a certain point with a certain uncle of hers, "Arran will be occupied in his daughter's absence, preparing for the arrival of his *seventh* child—"

"Ceo's *name!*" The old man's reaction was as expected. "Can you not control your—"

"Whom Loreanna and I had thought," Arran grinned, adding his part to the conspiracy, "always provided, of course, he turns out to be a boy, to name 'Sedgeley.'"

"You prefer 'Frantisek'?" asked Demondion-Echeverria, raising his own eyebrows.

"Or 'Leupould'?" the former Ceo demanded.

Arran addressed Tarrant. "Hanebuth, I would be the last to deprive you and Bretta of the pleasure of constructing your own starship. I have seen the hologram of your late lamented *Windhover,* and she was unmistakably quite um, *yar.*"

Bretta grinned at her father.

"However, having learned a few things recently concerning the technology of sailless vessels—not to mention the murderous treachery of nine-hundred-year-old assassins—I believe that I should summon my good old friends and allies the *nacyl,* instead, whom, I believe, I can persuade to lend you one of *their* ships!"

From orbit, it appeared that Hanover had been *blackened* from pole to pole.

When they had come within proper range of the Monopolitan capital world, Arran had not been able to resist taking one of his speedy "new" auxiliaries out ahead of *Osprey* for a look at the planet, satisfied, if not precisely happy, to leave his starship in the large, capable hands of his trusty first officer, cheerfully breaking in many new hands fresh from the Vouhat-Letsomo System.

Nor had Arran been able to resist the demand of his beloved wife that she accompany him, worried as she was for Lia's sake. Having come close to losing her, he did not believe he could ever refuse her anything, ever again. Since the high-speed fighter-launches were comfortable only for a single individual, they had spent several hours in intimate contact, but unable to do anything enjoyable about it, since it was imperative that they remain watchful for the enemy.

At the sight of Hanover, baked like a marshberry over a campfire, Arran was grateful—and did not feel guilty for a moment about it—that his home and the remainder of his family were safe upon moonringed Skye, far away. He was certain that Phoebus would be equally grateful that Fiona-leigh had taken his ship the *Tease* out of Hanoverian orbit, into the Sisao-Somon System.

The planet below was empty. There was not even a hint of life upon its surface.

Arran watched carefully, and employed what instruments he had, but there were no other ships in orbit, only wreckage. The Ceo's Eye, the asteroid used to anchor a permanent lift cabelle down to the surface, had vanished without a trace. Nothing, not even Oplyte armies, moved across the war-scorched face of Hanover.

Loreanna sat, half in her husband's lap, doing her best to hold back her tears.

"I recall the coordinates," he told her, "of the Daimler-Wilkinson house. Phoebus wanted to play pilot that day, but I pulled rank with him, and now I am glad. They will have to do, I fear, as I have no other reference to land by."

"I do not care about the house, Arran—oh, of course I do, it is where I grew up. I care more for what may have become of Brougham and his people. But mostly, I wish to know what has become of Lia, and so, I believe, will her father."

"The Residence, then, estimating from the coordinates of your uncle's house."

Protected from atmospheric heating by her §-field, the launch made quick work of the landing, and Arran's estimate of the coordinates proved accurate. Although everything they saw had been utterly flattened and covered deeply in ashes, as if some monstrous volcano had erupted, shaken every building to the ground, and buried an entire world alive, from lower altitude, he and Loreanna could just make out the city street plan they remembered. Within minutes, he had set the launch down in what they both believed to be the Ceo's private garden.

"A billion Oplytes, you say? I can believe it. They fell upon our world and razed it to the charred ground you see all about you. We were not quite helpless. Our fleets in orbit annihilated one another and the Oplytes themselves were totally wiped out in the process of attempting to eradicate us."

Lia smeared the ashes round upon her battle-soiled face, found a cast-metal lawn chair that had survived somehow, righted it, and sat down, setting her weapon butt first upon the ground and letting it lean against the arm of the chair. She had found it, she explained, in one of several museums within the Residence. Loreanna realized that it was an automatic battle rifle, very roughly contemporary with the weapon her husband had so gladly returned to her pocket.

Behind Lia, three thrustible-armed survivors from her personal guard cast their eyes about warily, unable to believe their terrible struggle might be over. But the capital planet of the great Monopolity of Hanover itself, they knew, had been utterly destroyed by the next-to-last army of Oplytes in history. And in a very real sense their struggle—to survive—had only begun.

Brougham, who had arisen out of the ashes in much the same way Lia had, when Arran had hopped over briefly to inspect what was left of the family mansion, had brought bottles of wine from the Daimler-Wilkinson cellars, where he and his family had hidden themselves. There were no glasses, and nobody cared.

The first thing that Arran and Loreanna had seen, upon landing, had been an angry and tearful Lia Woodgate, emerging from below, into the nightmarish landscape. Deep within her underground command post and blast shelter, she had told them, she and her household had barely survived the hand-to-hand fighting. There were entire corridors choked with the dead bodies of Oplyte soldiers.

Just now, she shook her fist at what somebody had once called the enemy stars.

"But I know—I suppose that I always knew, but I have finally been made *aware*—that what made this possible had little to do with this Aggregate you speak of. They were merely the handiest instrument. The real cause was simply our accumulation of power and the illegitimate steps we took to retain it."

"What do you mean?" It would be amusing to hear her father's reaction to this.

"You know *exactly* what I mean, Arran Islay—or rather, Henry Martyn. The Hanoverian civil populace, just to iden-

tify our single most egregiously self-destructive stupidity—
have been forbidden to own or carry personal weapons for
almost as long as there has been a Hanover. I suppose that is
one of the reasons that our ancestors were expelled from
Earth's moon, as you have told me, in the first place,
because they advocated policies like that. But, if we had all
been armed, we might still have a planet. We might still have
a civilization."

"You still might, yet, Lia," Loreanna told her. "Skye will
be willing to help, and the Coordinated Arm has experience
in transforming uninhabitable planets."

Lia nodded grimly. "Then with help, we shall try. And I
believe that my aunt Anastasia will be able to instruct me in
something more fundamental than 'terraforming.' "

"That could well be," Arran agreed.

"Arran, Loreanna, I swear to you now upon my life that,
do we succeed, we shall take steps—large, irrevocable steps,
in the direction of unfettered individual liberty—to assure
that a disaster like this will never happen again!"

EPILOGUE:
THE GALACTIC COORDINATOR
YEARDAY 162, 3027 A.D.
AUGGE 30, 519 HANOVERIAN
PRIMUS 19, 1597

A YOUTH THERE WAS, LATE OF HANOVER,
WHO COURTED A BEAUTY SO GAY.
AND ALL THAT HE COURTED THIS BEAUTY FOR
WAS TO STEAL HER VIRTUE AWAY.

"COME GIVE TO ME OF YOUR FATHER'S GOLD,
LIKEWISE OF YOUR MOTHER'S DOWRY,
AND THE BEST SHIP THAT CIRCLES YOUR FATHER'S WORLD,
WHEREABOUT STAND TWENTY, AND THREE."

AND ALL THAT HE COURTED THIS BEAUTY FOR
WAS TO STEAL HER VIRTUE AWAY.
A YOUTH THERE WAS, LATE OF HANOVER,
WHO COURTED A BEAUTY SO GAY.

EPILOGUE:
THE GALACTIC COORDINATOR

"Hanebuth?"

"Well, Princess," Tarrant told her as he let the door slide closed behind him, "I've told them all about you, that you've been commissioned, indirectly but officially, by the Ceo of the Monopolity of Hanover, Lia Woodgate Wheeler—Anastasia's own niece, ain't it a small galaxy—to establish diplomatic and trade relations, and a military alliance against what's left of a common enemy, with the Coordinated Arm. They're both in there now, waiting to meet you."

"Oh, dear."

Bretta put down a magazine reader she had not been looking at anyway and, before she could control the reflex of a nervous warrior, checked the lavishly embellished thrustible she wore upon her right arm, a parting gift from her mother and father, spreighformed within the Overmoms' asteroid using a program written by Arran and machinery just repaired by their new friends Andboard and Yiingboard.

Tarrant clambered up onto the plastic-covered couch to sit beside her. "They can kill you, but they can't eat you, Princess, it's against the Geneva Convention."

"What in the Ceo's name are you talking about, Tarrant?" She shook her head.

"Nothing, Princess, nothing at all. An old joke, and I can see now that you're not in the mood. It's just that there's no reason to be frightened of these folks. Don't think of her as the Galactic Coordinator. Think of her as a little old lady impatient to see her grandchildren later on this afternoon. It might also help you to understand that she sees winning the

War against the Clusterian Powers—our old friends the Aggregate—as only her *second* priority."

This interested a future Autonomous Drector-Hereditary of Skye. "And her first?"

"Acting as a kind of 'political place-holder,' preventing her own people from using the war as an excuse to do what wars have almost always done to civilizations, obliterate each one of the individual liberties that make the war worth fighting. She's been doing just that for thirty years, and she's almost done."

"And what of Captain Blackburn?" Here was the real reason for all of her nervousness. Blackburn had been her hero since the moment she had seen his hologram.

"Well, time is a funny thing, Princess. He's older than I remember—I guess I don't get the same cues with regard to the passage of time whenever I look in the mirror that other people do. I think my personal clock stopped when they gave me that big hypo in the neck out in the Vouhat-Letsomo System. Nate's some older than I remembered, and you might as well hear this from me: he's got a wife and three daughters of his own, each of them older than you are. There now: the sonofabitch owes me a big favor; he'd dreaded telling you, himself."

Bretta nodded. "I had done a little bit of adding and subtracting upon my own. Captain-Inspector Nathaniel Blackburn would be forty-nine years old by now and—"

"And Anastasia's likeliest successor." The little man was now certain of what he had long suspected anyway, that nothing could ever destroy—or even seriously damage— Henry Martyn's daughter. "What the news we bring Blackburn chiefly means is that the Galactic Arm *he* coordinates will be one that's at peace. Everybody wants to see Rakush and Marengo when we bring them from El Six—it's happy I am we held out for a *nacyl* ship big enough to transport them. Give these folks a year, they'll be racing *lamina* from here to the Centauris!"

They sat together a while, quietly, just as they had done when she was recovering.

"Well," she answered at last, "in a way I guess it is better that Captain Blackburn is spoken for. I would not care to be disillusioned. I have always maintained that any man I give myself to had better be a better man than I am, and—"

"And at least half the man your father is, I know." There came a long pause as Tarrant scratched his chin. "About how tall would you say Arran is, anyway?"

"What?" She shook her head. She seemed to be understanding her old friend less and less well with every day that passed here upon the homeworld's Moon.

"Nothing. While I was in there, the Coordinator made some calls. She's offered me an experimental course of gene therapy which not only may undo the damage done me by the vile Oplyte Traders, but restore my youthful vigor, as well!"

Bretta laughed and clapped. "Wonderful, Hanebuth! And what will you do then?"

"Oh, I have an idea or two in the back of my mind." Turning it this way and that, he pretended to examine the back of his hand, startlingly green in the sunlight streaming through the office windows. "Beware, Princess, I was once considered quite a handsome fellow; you may discover that you've kissed a frog!"

TOR
BOOKS The Best in Science Fiction